A Carriage for the Midwife

Also by Maggie Bennett

A Child's Voice Calling
A Child at the Door

A Carriage for
the Midwife

MAGGIE BENNETT

Century · London

Published by Century in 2003

1 3 5 7 9 10 8 6 4 2

Copyright © Maggie Bennett 2003

First published in the United Kingdom in 2003 by Century

The Random House Group Limited
20 Vauxhall Bridge Road, London SW1V 2SA

Random House Australia (Pty) Limited
20 Alfred Street, Milsons Point, Sydney,
New South Wales 2061, Australia

Random House New Zealand Limited
18 Poland Road, Glenfield,
Auckland 10, New Zealand

Random House (Pty) Limited
Endulini, 5A Jubilee Road, Parktown 2193, South Africa

The Random House Group Limited Reg. No. 954009

www.randomhouse.co.uk

A CIP catalogue record for this book
is available from the British Library

Papers used by Random House
are natural, recyclable products made from wood grown in
sustainable forests. The manufacturing processes conform
to the environmental regulations of the country of origin.

Typeset by SX Composing DTP, Rayleigh, Essex
Printed and bound in Great Britain by
Mackays of Chatham plc, Chatham, Kent

ISBN 1 844 13017 7

Dedicated to the Staff of the Maternity Department at

Trafford General Hospital, Manchester,

And including Midwives and Nursing Auxiliaries,

Past and present, living and dead.

With affection and profound admiration.

'And when I was born, I drew in the common air . . . and the first voice which I uttered was crying, as all others do.'

'For all men have one entrance into life, and the like going out.'

From the Apocrypha, The Wisdom Of Solomon, chapter 7, verses 3 and 6

Part I: 1767–1774

The Growing Years

Chapter 1

'Don't 'ee run on too far ahead, Poll!' Susan warned her younger sister. 'Oi ha' to keep hold o' Bartle's hand, an' his little legs won't go as fast as yourn!'

Polly turned round and made a saucy face.

'Watch yerself, Sukey. There be two fine young men comin' up behind 'ee!' she called.

'Aye, keep yer skirt down, little maid!' grinned old Goody Firkin, the beggar woman who had tagged herself on to the trio of ragged children making their way up through the beech grove to Bever House.

Susan smartly pulled her young brother to the side of the path as a well-built boy of about eleven shot past, completely ignoring them. He called over his shoulder to another boy further down the wooded track.

'Make haste, Ned, or they'll have slit the beast's throat and strung him up before we get there!'

'You go on ahead, Osmond, and I'll follow,' panted his younger brother, who was not as eager to witness the pig-killing in their father's stable-yard, though the rector had let them off the last half-hour of their morning lesson for the purpose. Young Edward Calthorpe's face was flushed and his wavy light brown hair dishevelled; his shirt had come untucked from his nankeen breeches, and his stockings were dirtied and torn from falling headlong over a beech root. When he caught up with the little group he eyed them warily, being half-afraid of Goody Firkin; she lived down at Ash-Pit End where the turds from the midden buckets were thrown. She had a trick of lifting her skirts up above her skinny knees – sometimes even higher, so the blacksmith's son had said. The village children teased her from a safe distance, yet here was this bright-faced little girl of about seven, chattering away to Goody as if to a grandmother, making the old woman cackle with mirth. Now she was smiling at him with friendly curiosity in her grey eyes, and he felt drawn to her, enough to overcome his awe of Goody Firkin.

'Are these your brother and sister?' he asked politely.

She bobbed a curtsy as the other two stared round-eyed.

'Aye, master, Oi be Susan Lucket, only folks calls me Sukey, and this be my sister Polly and our little brother Bartle – he's only four. We be come up from the Ash-Pits fur the pig-killin'. 'Twill be fine sport!'

She had a high, wide forehead that gave her face a heart shape. Her straight brown hair was pulled back and tied with a strip of calico, and her shapeless frock was of the same material, coarse and hard-wearing, woven by the inmates of the House of Industry at Belhampton, that dreaded place also called the workhouse.

Edward Calthorpe felt half ashamed of his own well-stitched clothes and leather shoes. On Susan's part she saw a son of the gentry, a healthy, fair-complexioned boy with dark blue eyes, as distant from her as his father's carriage horses were from the carrier's poor hack.

'Turn round, Bartle, the young master don't want to see yer bare arse,' she said quickly.

Hearing an outburst of shouts from the direction of

4

Bever House, they all hurried on up the track and into the stable-yard where the huge boar had arrived from Squire Hansford's piggeries, led by young Henry Hansford, a tall lad of thirteen or so. An excited crowd of outdoor servants jostled with spectators from the village, and Mr Calthorpe adjusted his hat and his expression as befitted a landowner and Justice of the Peace. He frowned at the sight of the notorious old beggar woman and the rough, bare-footed children trooping in. The poor of Beversley were a constant thorn in his side.

The children gazed round the yard open-mouthed, especially at the two little Calthorpe sisters in their neat, clean frocks, standing beside the most beautiful young lady that Susan had ever seen; she wore a grey gown and a wide straw hat, and her blue eyes were just like Edward's. Susan wondered if she were their mother.

All attention was now focused on the great pig whose eyes glinted suspiciously on each side of its massive head, as if it knew that the babble of voices boded no good. A roar went up as the pig man grabbed its back legs, deftly tying them together with a rope while two farm hands seized the front quarters. The beast toppled over on to its side, to the cheers of the onlookers, and four men then heaved the great pink and black body over a slaughtering-stool cut from an ancient tree trunk. While Osmond Calthorpe and Henry Hansford shouted and jeered at its furious grunts and struggles, the pig-sticker approached it head-on with a long, sharp knife. The Calthorpe sisters clung to the young woman's skirts, and Edward found himself shielding the three Lucket children, who shrank within his encircling arms; forgetting his own nervousness, he suddenly felt much older. They pressed closely, burying their faces in the soft cotton of his shirt when the hideous death-howl went up; it quickly turned to a bubbling, gurgling suffocation as blood choked the air passages.

When the children peeped again, the men were heaving the body up with ropes, to hang upside down from an iron hook set into a crossbeam. A red torrent poured from the veins on each side of the bulky neck into a stoneware bowl. They all gazed up at the object dangling from the hook, like a man's body swinging from a gibbet.

'Oh, the poor ol' pig, he be dead!' wailed Polly.

'Hush, Poll, ye'll stuff yer little belly when 'tis cooked,' said Susan, glancing up at Edward, who smiled and nodded.

'Yes, we shall all eat pig-meat at the harvest supper!'

The first excitement over, the two Calthorpe sisters turned their attention to the strange children clustering round Edward and the queer-looking old woman.

'Is not your mama with you?' asked the elder girl.

'Oh, no, miss, she ha' the babby to look arter, an' we got two other boys, Will an' Georgie,' replied Susan. 'They be too little to walk wi' us.'

'Aye, we ha' walked a long, long way, 'cross the Beck!' added Polly proudly, while Bartle gawped at the two rosy-cheeked girls, who stared back at their thin, sunburned faces.

Osmond now appeared, his light blue eyes flickering coldly at the strangers. Susan quickly curtsied, nudging Polly to do the same, and turned Bartle round to face the older boy so that his bare backside was hidden.

'Who let these brats into the yard, Edward? And the old hag?'

Susan spoke up quickly, with a darting glance at Edward. 'We be come up to see the pig-killin', master.'

''Tis all right, Susan, there's no harm in seeing the pig,' said Edward, giving his brother a pleading look. 'Father said that the villagers could come up to watch.'

'But not dirty, lice-ridden beggars like these,' retorted Osmond. 'Our sisters will catch some infection! Go along with you, Selina, and you too, Caroline – go and find your skipping-ropes and play.'

Raising his voice he dismissed the Luckets. 'All right, you've seen the pig, now be off – and you, too, old woman. Pooh, that boy stinks like a midden!'

He wrinkled his nose and turned to rejoin Henry Hansford. Susan guided her charges away, but Edward saw Bartle's round eyes turn longingly in the direction of the kitchen door, from which an aroma of baking drifted across the yard.

'Wait outside the yard for a minute,' he whispered. 'I'll see if I can find you some titbits.'

Checking that his brother's back was turned, the boy approached the young woman in grey, who nodded and went into the kitchen to speak to the cook.

When Edward returned with a paper bag filled with gingerbread and a handful of freshly baked biscuits, Susan gave a gasp of delight, curtsied gratefully and ran off to catch up with her brother and sister.

But Goody Firkin stood her ground and, to Edward's horror, raised a gnarled fist in Osmond's direction.

7

'Upstart puppy! Ye be no de Bever but an upstart lawyer's son!' she cried, loud enough for everybody to hear. 'An' ye'll answer for't, as'll all fine folks who lets the poor go hungry!'

There was a moment of dead silence, and then Osmond reacted with fury.

'Get after her and give her a good beating!' he ordered the men in the yard, but they only shuffled and mumbled, and turning round, Osmond saw that the young woman in grey had come up close behind him and was gravely shaking her head. He opened his mouth to defy her, but closed it again, turning away contemptuously. Nobody made a move, and the beggar woman disappeared into the beech wood, leaving the echo of her parting shot in their ears.

Edward gave a silent sigh of relief, and sent a grateful look in the direction of his cousin for her intervention.

Sophia Glover reached the top of the track, and turned to look back at the village nestling in the valley, divided by the wide stream of the Beck flowing from east to west, and dominated by the steeple of Great St Giles. She was in no hurry to go indoors, where the talk would all be of tomorrow's harvest supper, but paused and breathed in the peace of the September twilight. The last of the corn had been cut, the orchard fruit was gathered, and as the sun sank down towards Wychell Forest, deep shadows stole across the empty fields; the call of a nightjar only emphasised the silence. It was an idyllic rural scene, and yet Sophia's thoughts were troubled, and she clasped her hands tightly round the handle of the empty basket she carried. More and more these days she wondered what the future held for her; her four young cousins would soon have no further need of her supervision, and Osmond was already almost beyond her control. She longed to befriend the poor of Beversley – like that little girl with her brother and sister, and the poor old woman with them.

A pheasant flew up with a sudden loud flapping, breaking in on her thoughts and heralding the approach of a man with two dogs.

'Why, Sophy, I thought you would be indoors at this hour,' said Mr Calthorpe with some surprise.

'Good evening, Cousin,' she answered quickly. 'I've been visiting a young couple at Crabb's cottages. The wife was brought to bed last night with a first child, and Mrs Coulter found it a hard birthing.'

Calthorpe made a noncommittal sound. 'You are a good friend to the village, Sophia, but could it not have waited till tomorrow?'

'I am going to visit my grandfather in London tomorrow.'

'Oh, yes, of course, I had forgotten. You will miss the harvest supper, then?'

'I doubt if it will miss *me*, Cousin.'

'Hm. You know, Sophy, Gertrude and I truly appreciate you, especially all that you have done for the children. But there really isn't any need for you to trouble yourself with the cottagers.'

'It's those who live south of the Beck that trouble me, Cousin,' she replied, looking straight at him.

His brow darkened. 'Does Mrs Coulter attend the women of that place? I would prefer the midwife to stay away from their dirt and disease.'

'She doesn't often attend in Lower Beversley, Cousin. There is a handywoman who does what's necessary – she and Parson Smart between them do the physicking, and treat a few animals as well. It helps to eke out his shameful pittance from the rector.'

Calthorpe made no reply, and she went on eagerly, 'Cousin Osmond, I wish to visit some poor children who were up here for the pig-killing. Edward says their name is Lucket, and—'

'I have to forbid you to go near the Ash-Pits, Sophia. The Lucket man is a notorious drunkard, and I'd be obliged if you do not encourage Edward to associate with such as they. He is but a child, and need not concern himself with beggars. Mrs Calthorpe was displeased when she heard about it.'

'In that case I will bid you good night, Cousin,' Sophia answered coolly. 'I have to rise early tomorrow to board the London stage at Belhampton.'

'I will drive you over to meet it, Sophy.'

'Thank you, but I've already arranged with Berry to take me in the gig. Goodnight, Cousin.'

She began walking towards the house, but he called after her. 'Give my kind remembrances to my uncle – and enjoy your visit.'

She stopped and turned. 'Thank you, Cousin. I'll give my grandfather your regards.' Her blue eyes gleamed as she added, 'And a good account of your stewardship, Osmond.'

And away she went, a light-stepping figure disappearing into the dusk, leaving Calthorpe to sigh and shake his head. He well knew his cousin's worth, but she was also an embarrassment, irritating Mrs Calthorpe with her grave observations on the plight of the poor of Beversley, and constantly pricking his own conscience; heaven knew that the poor troubled him also, but a man in his position could not easily overturn the established order. Even Christ had declared that the poor are always with us.

He sighed. He had come out with his two setters to take the air, and to escape from Gertrude's endless talk about the harvest supper. For his part he wished for all the junketing to be over.

He called the dogs and continued on his solitary way.

'Ol' Goody Firkin be wrong, Poll, the Calthorpes don't let poor folks starve! Look at all them tables, full o' meat an' pies an' tarts fur everybody to eat!'

Susan's eyes sparkled, searching the crowded Bever stable-yard for a sight of Master Edward. All the Luckets had come up for the harvest supper – her father, mother, Polly, Bartle, Will, Georgie and little cross-eyed Jack, who still suckled at the breast. As voices and laughter rose on the fine, warm air, Susan felt that she had wandered into a different world, a place where everybody was happy and could feast on as much delicious food as they wanted. Surely Heaven must be like this!

She saw Mr Calthorpe at the far end of the yard by the closed gate, standing with his wife beside him; on a nearby wagon sat the musicians, the shepherd with his flute, two fiddlers and a little Irish tinker with handbells. At a signal from Calthorpe to his bailiff, they began to play, and at the same time a great shout went up from the company, for the gates swung open and a huge decorated haycart rolled in with the Harvest Queen enthroned on a bed of corn sheaves, surrounded by her attendant maidens. She was dressed in a single white linen sheet, drawn up on one shoulder, leaving the other invitingly bare. Her admirers roared and stamped in appreciation as she smiled and waved her arms, almost dropping the sheet that only just covered her breasts.

Susan thought that she had never seen such a wonderful sight; even the food was forgotten as the Queen on her flowery bed progressed round the yard, drawn by two massive shire horses handled by the Bever coachman, who reined them in expertly.

The church choristers led the company in the harvest song, repeated over and over again to a familiar hymn tune that everybody knew.

'We have ploughed and we have sowed,
We have reaped and we have mowed,
We have brought home every load,
Harvest Home! Harvest Home!'

The handbells rang out merrily above the melody, and although the rector muttered his disapproval of the use of church music for such pagan goings-on, nobody heard him but his elderly spinster sister, who nodded in agreement while privately enjoying the offending spectacle.

Susan caught sight of young Osmond Calthorpe swaggering around with Henry Hansford, gaping at the Harvest Queen with an appreciation he would not have shown to the plump dairymaid in her everyday kirtle and apron. And there on the far side of the yard she at last saw Edward, looking rather bewildered and surrounded by a rabble of grinning village children, who had formed a circle around some kind of entertainment.

Edward was indeed very uncomfortable. In searching for Susan he had ventured towards the noisy youngsters and saw to his dismay that they were laughing at the antics of Goody Firkin. She was capering to the music, throwing up her threadbare skirt and curtsying to the jeering onlookers.

'Dance, Goody, dance! Show off yer beauty!' they yelled as she skipped and twirled, a dangling kerchief tied round her almost bald pate, her rheumy eyes seeing a scene from long years ago when she had been young and a man had thought her beautiful.

Edward turned sharply when a little girl's voice shrilled above the others.

'Stop it, *stop it*, Oi tells 'ee, leave her alone, ye stinkin' varmints! Go an' gorge yeselves on roast pig, afore ye gets thrown out o' the yard!'

Susan Lucket's words were heeded. The mention of food, combined with the threat of losing the chance of eating it, did the trick, and with a few more derisive hoots the children made for the tables. Susan shook the old woman by the arm.

'Stop makin' a fool o' yeself, Goody, an' sit down, or they'll give 'ee the beatin' 'ee missed the other day. Wait here, and Oi'll bring 'ee a dish o' summat 'ee can eat.'

And turning round, Susan came face to face with Edward, who felt shamed by her spirited defence of Goody.

'Susan! Let me fetch food for you and – er – Dame Firkin,' he stammered, and was rewarded by her radiant smile.

'Edward! Oh, Master Edward, Oi be that pleased to see 'ee again,' she told him. 'Poor ol' Goody don't mean no harm, though she be crazed, but the young 'uns make sport o' her and drive her dafter still. Let's go an' get her a dish o' roast.'

Edward willingly led her to a table where he picked up two plates and piled them with slices of meat.

'Get some bread from that basket over there,

13

Susan, to dip in the fat – there, see – and take her a mug of ale. I'll keep this plate for you,' he added with an air of authority.

When Goody was settled in a corner of the yard, picking at the meat with her fingers and sucking it through her toothless gums, Susan sat down on a bench with Edward and chatted happily as they ate.

'Me dad be over there wi' the reapers, see,' she pointed with a crust of bread across the tables, 'an me ma be sat yonder wi' other mothers an' babbies.'

He followed the direction of her finger, and saw a black-browed, bristly chinned man with features thickened and reddened by drink, though he was not yet thirty; and at another table sat a dun-faced woman who had been a rosy country girl a few years ago, but was now worn down by hardship and annual childbearing. She clutched a cross-eyed baby of about six months, who clung to her breast, and ate while it sucked, licking her fingers and taking little part in the talk of her women companions, most of whom had young children with them.

'The babby's called Jack, an' me two little brothers Will an' Georgie be close by, see, along o' Bartle.'

'And where's Polly?' asked Edward, smiling.

'Standin' over there, gawpin' at the Harvest Queen!'

Edward looked long and hard at the Lucket family; it was his first real sight of poverty, and he was just beginning to realise how little he knew of the world beyond the Bever estate.

A pair of stout ladies were walking nearby, and they too were looking at the Harvest Queen.

'Nearin' three months, wouldn't 'ee say, Madam Coulter?'

The Beversley midwife pursed her lips as the

14

handywoman from Lower Beversley chuckled and continued, 'It be allus the same at summer's end, all that rompin' in the hayfields, an' her wi' no sense. The farm hands'll call each other out an' break skulls sooner'n wed a gal they've shared behind a haystack!'

Mrs Coulter frowned and shook her black-bonneted head. A sailor's widow, she was greatly respected in Beversley, and did not care to be treated as an equal by Widow Gibson from below the Beck. The handywoman tried a change of subject.

'By the way, madam, there be a little body Oi *don't* see here today – your friend Miss Sophia. Does *her ladyship* not like the bastard daughter o' the house to be seen?'

Edward stiffened as he overheard this remark, and strained his ear to catch the midwife's reply.

'You must be more careful o' your tongue, widow. Miss Glover is in London on a visit to Lord de Bever.'

'Be that so? Then Oi hopes she enjoys herself, poor thing! She be neither one thing nor t'other up at Bever House.'

A sudden commotion in the eaves of the stable loft broke into their exchange, and a small, dark, birdlike creature flew across the yard.

'Oh, look at the airy-mouse!' cried Susan, and called out:

'Airy-mouse, airy-mouse, fly over my head,
And ye shall have a crust o' bread!'

Edward was amused at this address to the bat, but in the next moment Goody Firkin quavered a warning.

'That be no bringer o' luck, poor little maid! Winter comes on cruel an' deep, wi' bitter hunger for the

15

poor. Eat yer fill, poor lamb – there'll be nought fur yer little belly soon!'

Heads turned towards the old woman who stood with upraised arm, her sunken eyes blazing like some messenger of doom. In a low tone Mr Calthorpe ordered his bailiff to have her removed, for fear that she would frighten the superstitious villagers and ruin the evening.

But Goody Firkin was not to be so easily dismissed. As men's hands were laid upon her bony frame she let out a shriek that froze the blood of her hearers.

'Turn me off the old lordship's land, will 'ee, upstart lawyer? Ye'll live to repent in grief an' shame by and by. *Grief an' shame*, Oi tells 'ee!'

Her wails rose as she was hustled out of the stable-yard, and Calthorpe ordered the musicians to play something merry; but before two bars had been played a whole series of bats flew out from under the stable loft. The players faltered as the creatures rose in a dark cloud, filling the air with the humming of their wings and their high, eerie squeaks. They whirled round in a circle, and then, as if at a given signal, they headed southwards, diving and dipping over the Beck until they were lost to view.

''Twas the ol' woman called 'em up,' muttered some low voices. ''Er'd been burned at the stake in times past.'

But Susan spoke up clearly in defence of Goody and the bats. ''Tis not so! Poor Goody never hurt a fly, nor do the little airy-mice. They be but goin' huntin', like on any other night.'

The musicians started up again, but a raucous element had now overtaken the company, borne in on a tide of strong ale. The rector took his stately leave, followed by the Hansfords, the apothecary and the more prosperous farmers, and Mr Calthorpe ordered the yard to be cleared.

'God pity the wives and little ones tonight,' muttered Mrs Coulter, tying her bonnet strings. 'Look at that great fool over there, he can't stand upright.'

'Ay, that be Bartlemy Lucket, an' see, he ha' pissed under the table,' replied the handywoman. 'An' there's his poor wife Dolly Potter that was, nursin' her sixth – an' there'll be another afore that squinter be weaned, Oi'll wager, lookin' at her from the back!'

'God help her,' shuddered Mrs Coulter.

'Ay, it be no uncommon sight fur Bartlemy to be led home by that poor child, to keep un out o' the ditch, an' pissin' all up the lane.'

'Hush, that's enough, Widow – he should be horsewhipped!'

'It be true, though. I seen little Sukey puttin' un's great spout away in un's breeches to save the shame on't.'

'For heaven's sake, woman, say no more. Come on, let's go home together for safety, and get within doors.'

The boy and girl were still sitting on the bench in the deepening dusk, and Edward felt her shiver. He put his arm around her, and they huddled closer together.

'Are your parents going home yet, Susan?'

'Ay, there's Ma leavin' with the little 'uns, and Oi'll ha' to carry Georgie,' said Susan reluctantly, for she wanted this wonderful evening to last as long as possible. She also hoped that her mother would not send her back to fetch her father, for she was tired, and the surfeit of food had made her sleepy.

17

A buxom woman in a blue cap and white apron bustled up to Edward, pointedly ignoring Susan.

'Y'r mother says ye're to come in at once, Master Edward. This be no place for a child!'

'Good night, Susan, and I hope—' But before he could say more Edward's arm was gripped and he was pulled away none too gently. He had never felt so humiliated in all his nine years. What would Susan think of such a milksop?

As it turned out Susan did not have to guide her father's steps that night. He tripped on a flagstone in the yard and managed to crawl into the box of Mr Calthorpe's best carriage horse, where he lay in a stupor, awash in his own vomit and kept warm by the horse. A startled stable-boy found him the next morning.

'Ay, the stink o' shit an' spue was wusser 'n horse dung. Him was that white, Oi thought un was dead!' the lad reported, laughing heartily every time he told the tale.

Mr Calthorpe had Lucket committed to Belhampton Gaol for ten days, and forbade him to work on the Bever estate again, while Mrs Calthorpe took Edward to task for deserting his sisters and spending all his time with the child from the Ash-Pits.

The boy mumbled some kind of apology, but the little girl's face haunted him, along with Goody Firkin's dire prediction. How would Susan and her young sister and brothers fare when winter stocks ran low? Edward had never thought about the lives of the poor before, but from now on he was never to forget them.

Chapter 2

Susan was desperately clinging to sleep and a beautiful dream of warmth and food and summer days where she and her sister and brothers ran through the fields beneath blue skies; she tried her best to clasp it and keep it, but it slipped treacherously away, fading into a thin memory of itself.

It was gone. She was awake and lying beside Polly, Bartle, Will and Georgie in the hay-loft that had been used as a chicken roost in better times; she was unable to go back to sleep for the gnawing pangs of her empty belly. It was still an hour before the winter sun rose, and she heard her mother moan and stir.

Quietly withdrawing herself from the tangle of arms and legs entwined under two stained blankets, Susan peered down to the one room where the family lived and where Dolly slept with baby Jack. Bartlemy lay on a heap of old clothes in a corner, his right leg propped up on a bag of straw, swollen and inflamed. The only point of light was the faint red glow of the remains of the fire, but Dolly had woken with the cold, and now proceeded to poke the embers with wood splinters, adding dry twigs from a nearby pile. In the resulting small blaze Susan clearly saw her mother's face. The innocent vanities of girlhood had long been left behind in a daily struggle for existence; Dolly's skin was grimy, her hair lank, there were gaps in her teeth and the sour smell of poverty clung to her flesh. The dark-eyed ploughboy who had pursued her through the summer fields now lay helpless in a fever, unable to escape to the alehouse while his wife and children starved, and Dolly carried their seventh child in her womb.

Susan watched as her mother pulled up the coarse woollen gown she wore night and day, and squatting over a pail, relieved herself.

Baby Jack awoke with a snuffling cry, and Dolly hushed him in her arms, whispering softly. 'Hush, my sweet Jack, my poor little boy. 'Twill be the poorhouse for us, or starve.'

Susan trembled, for she had heard stories about the dreaded place where families were separated and orphaned children slept in the same rooms as the deformed and the crazed. She tried to blot out such pictures by remembering that wonderful September evening in the stable-yard of Bever House, where they had filled their bellies with roast pig-meat and she had talked with Master Edward until dark. Would she ever see him again? Did he even remember her? She knew that she would never forget how happy she had been.

Everything was changed now. It was ten days into January, though Susan had lost count of time. The year had begun with continuous snow for a night and a day and another night, and it still lay frozen in great drifts. The familiar winter landscape of ploughed fields and leafless trees had turned into a silent white wasteland by day and a pathless darkness by night; the huddle of windowless cottages known as the Ash-Pits were pencilled outlines on a blank canvas as the dull red sun rose and fell, bringing scarcely seven hours of light to each day.

A hoarse grunt erupted from the bundle of rags and straw where Bartlemy lay, and Susan held her breath, hoping he would not wake yet. She was beginning to realise that Da was the source of the trouble that had overtaken them, as much as the hard winter. He had been laid up since Christmas with an injured leg, having fallen in Farmer Bennett's bottom field while returning from the alehouse; he had lain there until a farm hand, out early, had found him half-frozen and brought him home. Dolly had scarcely spoken to him since, but Susan had heard her saying to nobody in particular that she was worse off than a widowed mother of orphans, 'fur then Oi might ha' asked fur parish relief, an' folks might ha' bin more forthcomin'.'

But Bartlemy had made the name of Lucket a byword, and the shame fell upon them all. Susan felt it more keenly than her younger siblings, and asked herself why the Calthorpe boy should trouble himself with such riffraff as the Luckets.

Yet he had sought her out and talked with her, just as if she had been one of his pretty little sisters. Remembering again his kindness to her and Goody Firkin, she smiled and let her thoughts dwell on the better life she had glimpsed. One day, she told herself, one day she would find her way out of the Ash-Pits, and take Polly with her.

But meanwhile shouldn't she try to do something for them all – her mother and sisters and brothers? Shouldn't she go out and beg, as some other poor folks did? But where could she go?

The nearest farm belonged to Thomas Bennett, a dour-faced, taciturn man who had long ago ordered Bartlemy Lucket off his property. Mrs Bennett was a thrifty housewife with a son and three daughters; she kept a couple of maidservants and was known for her good, plain fare. Surely she would take pity on the starving family if Susan were to knock on her kitchen door and beg for the leftover rinds of bacon or crusts of bread? Vegetable peelings could be boiled up to make soup, and half a pound of oats would go a long way. And if Mrs Bennett could spare a little honey . . . Susan's mouth watered.

Yet the Bennett farmhouse was a good half-mile away up a steep track, now covered with snow, and Susan had neither cloak nor boots. In braving the wrath of the farmer, the danger of falling and freezing to death in the bitter cold was a real possibility: a nameless traveller had been found still and cold in Quarry Lane a few days ago.

Yet something had to be done, she knew, or at least tried. She *would* go, she decided, but not until the afternoon, when the air would be slightly less cold.

But before then they had a visitor, an angel of deliverance in the guise of poor Parson Smart in his ancient greatcoat and cracked leather boots that let in the snow.

Dolly's dull eyes widened hopefully at the sight of the black figure at the door, and she called over her shoulder to Susan as he stepped across the threshhold.

'Sukey! Make haste an' line up Polly an' yer brothers – the parson be come!'

Picking up little cross-eyed Jack in her arms, she stood waiting for Mr Smart to speak of parish relief; Susan and the other children stood staring dumbly at the glistening dewdrop on the end of their visitor's nose.

'Good, good,' he nodded uncertainly, giving them a vague smile. 'I hope that you are all good children, giving comfort to your mother and – er . . .' He glanced towards the dark corner where Bartlemy lay.

22

'You must bring them to church, goodwife, as soon as the weather improves.'

Absurd though he appeared, Susan sensed that here was a man struggling to do his Christian duty in the face of want and misery.

'Don't we get no parish relief then, Parson?' cried Dolly, and Susan saw his eyes fall before her desperate need. In his haste to see smiles in place of blank stares, he started gabbling his message.

'I have been to see Mrs Bennett, who in her charity has some victuals for you if – if young Susan will call at—' he began, but Dolly broke in with a shriek.

'What?' she cried, her pinched face alert. 'Has Sarah Bennett bread for us? Today? *Now*?'

'Yes, woman, this very hour, if you will send the child up to her.' He turned to Susan. 'Go to the scullery at the back, and keep out of the farmer's sight behind the hedge, for if he sees you – well, take care he does not. And have you a jug to take with you?'

'Take the crock jug, Sukey,' cut in Dolly, her sunken eyes glinting wildly. 'Go on, get 'ee gone up to her back door!'

'The *scullery* door,' Smart corrected her.

'What ha' she got fur us, Parson?' asked little Polly.

'I don't know, child. I heard her speak o' barley bread and a cut off a hind o' salt bacon – and she asked for a jug to be sent.'

The children's weak cheers were too much for the parson, who had wrestled long and hard with himself before going to beg from the Bennetts. His own wife was having to make a dinner from thin, meatless soup and baked potatoes to feed their hungry brood in the draughty parsonage; he would feel the lash of her tongue if she ever found out that

23

he had gone to Sarah Bennett on behalf of another family. Yet at this moment he knew that he had done right, and a constriction arose in his throat; he turned away from their grateful eyes to wipe his own with the back of his hand.

Dolly had no interest in his reflections. She picked up one of the rag rugs that had covered her and the baby as they slept, and threw it over Susan's shoulders.

'Get goin', Sukey. Put yer dad's boots over yer feet an' make sure 'ee don't spill nothin', nor fall down in the snow. Go on, go *on*!'

Susan went forth on her errand without mishap, and arrived at the Bennett farmhouse kitchen, a haven of warmth where a hearth fire supplied heat to an adjoining bake-oven and a large black pot hung over it on a triple chain. The flagstoned floor was warm to her feet, and the aroma from the pot indescribably delicious.

'These are thin times for us all, Sukey,' said Mrs Bennett briskly. 'This is for Dolly and you children, mind, not that idle drunken oaf. The farmer's temper do rise at the very name o' Lucket, so be sure ye don't let him see ye.'

The jug was filled from the stew pot, and bread and bacon wrapped in a knotted cloth. Mrs Bennett's sharp words were softened by her tone, and Susan sensed that the woman's heart was at variance with her head.

'Tom! Tom, where are ye? Come down and take this girl back to the Ash-Pits, will ye? Ye can help carry the – see she doesn't fall down.'

A blunt-featured boy of about nine clumped into the kitchen in response to his mother's call.

'And whatever ye do, don't let your father see.'

His duty done, Smart made his way back to the parsonage of Little St Giles, from which he served Lower Beversley. He was chilled to the marrow of his bones, but his heart was lighter, and he looked forward to a game of backgammon with his older children, to take their minds off the rigours of winter.

But his plans had to be set aside, for Dick the carrier was waiting for him with grim news. Goody Firkin's corpse was laid across his cart, staring up at the empty sky.

The day that was to change Sophia Glover's life began inauspiciously enough. A fire had been lit in the library, and she had set the boys to write an essay on the countryside in winter.

'May we not play beggar-my-neighbour, Sophy?' asked Osmond, restless with the long confinement indoors. 'I vow that I'll be thankful to see even the old rector's study again, for 'tis poor sport here with a woman for tutor,' he added in a lower tone but still loud enough for his cousin to hear. He got up and sauntered over to the window, his hands in his pockets. 'How merrily would we glide down the slope if we had Henry's sledge! Cannot a manservant be sent to Hansfords' for it?'

'Indeed not, Osmond. Come back to the table, you are disturbing your sisters,' replied Sophia, suppressing a strong desire to box his ears. The girls were fidgety and inattentive when their brothers were present, and no sooner had they settled to their tasks than Osmond jumped up again.

'Look there, out of the window, is not that the carrier's horse?' he cried.

They all ran to look, and sure enough, the old horse

25

usually seen drawing Dick the carrier's cart was now making his slow way along the white track that had been dug in the snow from the front gate round to the stable-yard. Dick and his son were on foot.

'Come on, let's go down and find out what news they bring!' said Osmond, glad of any diversion, and rushed from the room without a backward glance. The others followed, clattering down the backstairs to the servants' quarters, the domain of Martin the butler and his wife.

Sophia rested her elbows on the table and let her head fall between her hands. Keeping her young cousins occupied during this severe weather was weary work – but what would become of her when they no longer needed her? What was she, after all, but a nobody, a bastard offshoot beholden to the Calthorpes for a roof over her head? It was seven years since she and Bever House had been placed in the care of her cousin Calthorpe by her grandfather, old Lord de Bever, who had built the manor house forty years ago and brought his beautiful girl-bride Sophia Calthorpe over the threshhold; nobody could have foreseen at that time how soon the ancient name would die out. The death of Sophia in giving birth to their only son, Humphrey, who had himself died in agony with an inflammation of the bowel before he was twenty, had turned Lord de Bever into a bitter and disillusioned man, and at sixty he had quitted Beversley for London, to live out the rest of his life in St James's Square.

But first he had summoned his wife's nephew to assume ownership of the estate.

'No need to wait till I'm dead, Calthorpe,' he had said bluntly. 'You might as well learn to hold the reins now as later. And those boys of yours will need to be brought up as responsible landowners – they are but toddling yet, but they'll have to learn thrift, for ye'll not get my money till I've gone.'

Osmond Calthorpe bowed. 'I shall devote myself to the estate and to Beversley, Uncle,' he had replied, hoping that Gertrude would show equal discretion, and not rejoice too openly at their sudden advancement.

Lord de Bever gave a grunt. 'Hm. And there is one important condition.'

'You have only to name it, Uncle.'

'It concerns my granddaughter, Sophia Glover, sired by my son on a sempstress before he died, and the mother soon followed. I've kept the poor orphan at Bever House, and though I never gave her my name, I've settled an annuity on her, and you are to make a place for her here with your children. She's in her thirteenth year, a quiet, devout little thing, but no fool. She can read, write, sew and play the pianoforte. She'll be no trouble to you.'

Calthorpe had bowed again and promised that his cousin Sophia could count on a home with his family for as long as she needed a roof over her head.

'I shall send for Sophy betimes to visit me in London,' said de Bever. 'She is the only soul left in the world who truly loves me.'

Calthorpe was about to protest, but thought better of it; and so the Belhampton attorney and his wife had been elevated to county gentry. Sophia had grown to womanhood under their guardianship, and had more than repaid them by acting first as nurserymaid and later as governess to their children; but of late her situation had grown increasingly irksome, and she longed for a little place of her own where she could come and go as she pleased. Her grandfather's allowance was not sufficient to give her independence, but she was able to help a few needy families, recommended by her friend Mrs Coulter, though the midwife discouraged her from crossing the Beck into Lower Beversley.

'They're a rough lot with no respect for their betters, Miss Sophia. Best leave them to poor Parson Smart.'

A shout from below indicated that the carrier had arrived at the kitchen door, and Sophia too went down to find out what errand had brought him to Bever House under such difficult conditions.

The kitchen was buzzing with activity as Dick and his son made themselves at home, much to the irritation of Martin, who frowned when his wife set two steaming mugs of hot cordial in front of the arrivals. Sophia sat on a chair in the corner from where she could discreetly watch and listen, an outsider here as much as upstairs.

While the four children gathered round young Dick, who was warming himself on the hearthstone, old Dick stretched out his legs under the table.

'Here, Martin, a little summat fur the still room, from the rectory,' he grinned, tapping the side of his prominent nose and handing over a leather bag that clinked as the butler took it. Everybody knew that smuggled brandy made its way up to Beversley, but Martin was infuriated by Dick's over-familiarity and lack of discretion.

'A word in yer ear, Martin – Oi got a packet here fur Mr Calthorpe, to put into 'un's hand an' no other 'un's!'

'Ye may give it to me, then, for ye may go no further 'n this kitchen,' the butler told him loftily.

'Ah, that Oi will not! I got me orders.'

'Hand it over at once, d'ye hear? Or I'll send for Mr Calthorpe's agent.'

Dick drew the packet from the depths of an inside pocket. 'And moind 'ee takes it straight up to yer master! It be from Lord de Bever's Lunnon house by its mark, and ha' lain at the post house in Belhampton these two weeks past, 'cause o' the snow.'

Martin left the kitchen, leaving old Dick to harrow Mrs Martin and Sophia with gruesome tales of unburied coffins and an outbreak of the dreaded white throat at the House of Industry.

A scream from Caroline brought Sophia to her feet. 'What have you been telling her, young man?' she demanded of young Dick.

'Oi ain't said nothin', miss, only told 'em how poor ol' Goody Firkin froze to death in the snow.'

'Goody Firkin?' repeated Sophia in horror. 'Isn't she a poor, crazed old woman who lives at Ash-Pit End?'

'Not any more, her don't,' cut in old Dick, glaring at his son for ruining his best story. 'Sexton found her in the churchyard o' Little St Giles, stiff an' stark. Must ha' laid there all night. Her eyes were open an' staring as if—'

'Stop, stop, don't say any more,' begged Edward, deathly pale.

Osmond's lip curled. 'Stop, stop, Dick, boo-hoo, boo hoo!' he mocked, but Sophia turned on him.

'*Be quiet!*' she commanded with such cold fury that he shrugged and was silent.

'Good God, how can we live in luxury and idleness while the poor are dying outside the gates?' she went on, trembling with emotion. 'It is a disgrace, a scandal! I'll tell you what, Mrs Martin, I shall no

29

longer lead a useless life in this house. From now on I shall visit the poor of Beversley, whatever Mrs Calthorpe says!'

They all stared at the young woman as she stood in the middle of the kitchen, her eyes blazing. Edward spoke up.

'And I'll come with you, Cousin Sophy.'

At that moment the door from the passage opened and Martin marched in, bursting with importance.

'Master Osmond, Master Edward and ye two little girls are to go straight up to y'r parents – and yeself too, Miss Glover.'

He then briskly dismissed the indignant carrier and his son, who had brought the news of Lord de Bever's death three weeks previously in London, aged sixty-eight.

In the chill of her room Sophia studied the copy of her grandfather's Will and the letter written in his archaic hand. In her emotional state she found it hard to follow the legal complexities of the first, but through her tears she was able to decipher the message of the second.

I did not acknowledge thy Mother, but I now bestow upon thee, Child of my own Son, enough of this World's most desired Commodity as will make thee happy or wretched, according to Usage.

I do thy young Cousins equal good Service by bestowing upon them the need to earn their Livelihood, for which they will not thank me or thee.

I know thy habits are not of Idleness or Extravagance, but beware of mercenary Suitors and use well the Power that Gold will give thee.

My days diminish, and I bid thee farewell, my Child. On thy Father's and Mother's graves forgive thy sorrowing Grandfather,

Humphrey de Bever.

Turning back to the Will, Sophia gradually understood it to mean that while her grandfather had bequeathed Bever House to his nephew and descendants, she was to inherit a half-share of the old man's fortune, a sum in excess of thirty thousand pounds. The other half was to be divided among the Calthorpes.

She now recalled certain fond looks the old gentleman had given her during her last visit to London, at the time of the harvest supper. She remembered the tenderness of their farewell, more truly loving than at any time in her lonely childhood; and as she emerged from the shock and sorrow of his death, she began to realise what he had done for her. She was no longer dependent on her cousins; she could buy a house of her own in Beversley and live the life she desired, as a true friend and benefactress to the poor. Her prayers were answered!

She kneeled down beside her bed.

'Yes, dear grandfather,' she whispered. 'I *will* use it well, with God's help!'

Mr Calthorpe thought he understood the reasoning behind his uncle's Will. His son Osmond would have to earn the right to lord it over Beversley as a landowner. With an Oxford degree he might make a career in the law or politics, and Edward might look for a commission in the army or navy, or perhaps take holy orders, in which case there were several

31

comfortable livings to be had in the county. Selina and Caroline should be able to make satisfactory marriages to professional men, or even into the new rapidly rising mercantile class.

All in all, Calthorpe bore no resentment against Lord de Bever, for he believed that his sons would benefit from the apparent harshness of the will. And he was happy for Sophia's good fortune.

Not so Gertrude Calthorpe. To her it was a cruel parting shot from a spiteful old man who had given with one hand and taken away with the other. Of what use was property without the wherewithal to live as property owners? They would be a laughing stock with all their economies!

And as for that treacherous Glover girl, the sooner she was out of the house, the better. She must have used flattery on the old man, and carried lying tittle-tattle to him about life at Bever House. Why else should he have taken bread from the mouths of those he had planned to honour?

Chapter 3

Susan woke suddenly and sat up in alarm beside the still-sleeping Polly. It was pitch-dark. She peered down from the roost at the last fading embers of the fire.

There it was again, the sound that had wakened her. It came from her mother, moaning as she stirred and turned over. Susan had grown used to hearing Dolly's nightly groans and mutterings when sleep brought dreams of her lost boys.

Bartle, Will and Georgie. It did not seem possible to Susan that she would never see them again, and her uncomprehending grief made her constantly alert for Polly; her greatest terror was of losing the little sister on whom she now lavished all the love that Doll seemed not to want. Neither did their mother seem able to show her daughters any affection since the fearful toll taken by the white throat.

After the parson's visit, hope had returned to the Ash-Pits; the victuals that Susan carried from the Bennett kitchen two or three times a week had literally saved them from starvation, and the good Nathaniel Smart had rejoiced at his part in their rescue. He had meekly bowed his head before his wife's accusations, heartily thanking his Maker for using him to save the Lucket children.

He was not allowed this comfort for long. By the third week in January a thaw set in, and the milder air blew the dreaded infection into one damp dwelling after another. Children weakened by a winter diet were struck down by the swift and deadly malady that had begun in the House of Industry; they became feverish, with painfully sore throats, and within hours a greyish membrane spread across the back of the throat. Susan could still hear the sounds of her brothers gasping for air on the night when death had claimed all three between sunset and dawn. She and Polly had survived, and so had baby Jack, kept strictly apart from the sick children in the roost; in fact Doll's fanatical protection of her squint-eyed youngest son was part of the remembered horror. Even Bartlemy had prayed aloud for God to take pity on them, swearing to reform and never drink strong ale again if his children's lives were spared, but when the winter sun rose on the first day of February, the three small brothers lay still and silent. Their burial was charged on the parish, which was all that Parson Smart could do for them. He had been forced to promise his wife that he would not visit any dwelling while the white throat raged, for fear of bringing it home to their own family – and he never forgave himself for deserting those whom it seemed that God Himself had forsaken.

It could never be proved that the infection was carried up from the Ash-Pits to the farmhouse when the Bennett children caught it. Tom, Sally and Marianne recovered, but little Annie died two days after the losses at the Ash-Pits. The farmer's wrath was terrible, adding to his wife's grief, and all traffic between the two families ceased.

At Bever House Edward and Caroline fell sick with colds on their chests, and were visited daily by Mr Turnbull, the apothecary. He made them open their mouths while he peered down their throats with the aid of a mirror reflecting the light of a candle held by Mrs Ferris, the tall, black-haired woman who had replaced Miss Glover as nurse. Within a week they had recovered, none the worse for the scare.

But Susan's world had become full of shifting shadows in which Death lurked; she lived with uncertainty, for nothing could be relied upon. Bartlemy's leg healed slowly, though stayed shorter than the other, and he began to find casual labouring jobs, avoiding the alehouse on his way home; but Dolly scarcely looked at him, and seldom spoke to any of them. She withdrew herself behind an invisible barrier with Jack and the child almost ready to leave her womb.

Little Polly turned instinctively to Susan for comfort and reassurance, and gradually the elder daughter became the linchpin of the family. Bartlemy patted her shoulder, and said she was 'her dad's good gal, his kind little Sukey', words which Doll appeared not to hear, for her face remained blank.

There it was again: a sharp moan and a painful gasp as if Dolly was lifting a heavy pail, then silence for a few minutes, followed by another groan.

Bartlemy rose from his corner and lit a candle.

'Do 'ee want me ter go fur Widder Gibson, Doll?'

'No, Oi must be me own midwife, we can't pay fur no other,' groaned the woman, and Susan heard Bartlemy growl something about 'it'll come anyway,' which worried her still more. What would come? Was it Death yet again? Was her mother dying?

'What about Jack?' she heard Bartlemy ask.

'Sukey can mind un when the time comes – him'll be all right wi' me fur now – oh! Ah!' This time the cry of pain was louder and lasted longer.

Susan was frightened, and called down to her mother, 'Ma! Ha' ye got a pain in yer belly?'

'Hush, Sukey, ye'll wake Jack. Go to sleep,' gasped Doll.

But it was impossible to sleep with the noises getting louder and coming at shorter intervals, interspersed with Bartlemy's useless mumbling.

'Oi better go fur Widder Gibson, Doll.'

The only reply was another moan, and the next hour was a nightmare of worsening pain for Dolly and mounting terror for Susan. The woman's agonised yelps sounded like a stoat or a weasel caught in a gamekeeper's trap. Jack woke up, and his howls woke Polly.

'What be up wi' Ma, Sukey?' her little voice quavered.

But before Susan could answer, Bartlemy bellowed up urgently, 'Sukey! Sukey, gal, come and take Jack from yer ma!'

'You wait up here, Poll, while I go down,' whispered Susan, her foot on the rickety ladder.

'That's it, Sukey, take poor little Jack up to be wi' Polly,' groaned Doll, handing the bawling infant to Susan, who carried him up to the roost and laid him as far from the edge as possible.

'Ye'll ha' to look arter Jack while Oi stays along o' Ma, Poll. Don't 'ee let un fall!'

'Be she dyin?' asked the little girl tearfully.

'No, she jus' got a bad pain in the belly. Be a brave girl, Poll, an' say "Our Father" like in church,' said Susan, hiding her own dread of whatever awful fate was about to befall them.

'Oi fergits the words!' wailed Polly, clinging to her sister.

'Ssh, Poll, just hold on ter Jack, an' don't let un

36

tumble down below,' answered Susan, who was beginning to understand that everything now depended on her keeping her head.

'Help! Help me, fur the love o' God, help me!' shouted Dolly, and Susan disentwined herself from Polly and shinned down the ladder.

'Shall Oi go fur the handywoman, Sukey?' asked Bartlemy, hovering helplessly.

Susan heartily wished him out of the way. 'Ay, go on, Da,' she said, and he at once picked up his stick and stumbled out of the door, thankful to be out of earshot. It was still dark.

Dolly shrieked and writhed from side to side.

'Oh, God – oh, Lord, help me!'

'Ssh, Ma, take hold o' me hand.'

Lying back on her straw bed, Dolly clutched Susan's hand so tightly that the little fingers were cruelly squashed together, but Susan scarcely felt it because all her attention was now concentrated on what was happening. She watched round-eyed as her mother drew up her knees: all at once the sound of grunting and straining made Susan think of when she herself had to sit on a pail to do a turd.

'Oh, Ma, be it a great, hard turd 'ee got there? Won't un come out?' she asked as Doll's muscles tightened again to boardlike hardness. 'Go on, then, push un down and get un out!'

She took courage at her own words, for if it was only a matter of pushing out a great big turd, her mother would surely feel better afterwards. Dolly's face was contorted, her eyes closed, her mouth stretched in an agonised grimace; her legs were drawn up and apart, and her arms flailed helplessly.

'Take hold o' yer knees, Ma,' ordered Susan instinctively. 'Get yer hands under yer knees an' pull

37

on 'em – heave away! Oi be here beside 'ee, Ma – heave again, heave! Heave!'

It worked. The uncontrolled cries gave way to the steady, purposeful sounds of an immense effort. Susan pulled up Doll's woollen skirt, and by the light of the candle saw that the fleshy hole was filling up with something dark and round and damp: something that moved forward with each straining push.

And at the same time all Susan's fear melted away: she was here with her mother at a time of – what? She had seen Death at close quarters only a few weeks ago, and she now knew that this was *not* Death. Nor was it something as mundane as passing a great, stinking turd. No, this was an ancient miracle, this was Life, like the trees and fields and harvest of the earth, this was blood and breath: a huge elation seized Susan as she understood that this was *Birth*!

All at once the groans and cries were explained. Susan's mind went back to when Jack had been born, and Georgie before him. She had been sent to Goody Firkin with Polly and Bartle while Mrs Gibson had bustled around their cottage and the same kind of noises had been heard. They had eventually been called back to find a new baby boy lying beside their mother. Susan had not fully understood how it had arrived, but now she knew, for here, surely, was another baby – and she felt that she had known all along.

Without any sense of repugnance she put her little hand over the roundness that was advancing from Dolly's body, while from the woman's throat came deep grunts and indrawings of breath between each long effort. There was no sound from Polly or Jack, who had fallen asleep above them. The woman and her child-midwife were alone in the winter dawn.

The dark, hairy head now filled the circle of stretched flesh. Susan felt it push against her palm, and as it thrust forward she saw a forehead appear, then two round, staring eyes; a little nose came through, wrinkling on contact with the air; a mouth, dribbling thick spittle; finally a chin, and so the head of a child was born. Dolly gave a long, low moan.

Ancient wisdom prompted Susan to put her forefinger into the baby's mouth and clear away the spittle; the stimulation of this made it gasp and take its first breath. Air bubbled out through the moisture, and a second breath came out with a little mewing cry; there was a snuffle and another cry, louder than the first. The head rotated between Susan's hands, and the shoulders appeared, one arm was freed and then the other, followed by the rest of the body and a gush of cloudy fluid. The little legs began to kick, and the room was filled with the piercing cries of Doll Lucket's seventh child.

Susan was jubilant, and cried aloud in joyful wonder.

'Oh, Ma, it be a little boy! An' he got a rope thing on un's belly.'

'Ay, it needs tyin' off an' cuttin',' muttered Doll. 'There be a bit o' string in me pocket to tie round it in a knot, see – make sure it be tight, then cut below it. Fetch the knife from the table, an' be quick, un mustn't get cold. An' there be a length o' clean cloth to wrap un in, under the straw here, see. Cover un over, Sukey, him be but newborn.'

With fingers that trembled with excitement Susan tied and cut the slippery cord with its three inter-twined blood vessels, and wrapped the baby firmly in the cloth, winding it round and round his squirming body.

39

'Oh, look, Ma, he ha' shitten already!' she exclaimed with a smile of surprise.

'Wipe it off and give him to me. Oi'll feed un wi' what poor milk Oi can make.'

Susan watched in awe as the child began to suck. As long as she could remember there had always been a hungry baby latched on to her mother's soft and often empty breasts.

'What'll he be called, Ma?' she asked, putting her face close to the baby's.

'Job, out o' the Bible,' said Dolly promptly, looking fondly down on the child in her arms. 'Him was a man o' many troubles, but un never gave up. Neither will 'ee, my little Joby.'

Susan began to clear away the soiled straw, but Doll stopped her.

'No, wait, Sukey, while he sucks – 'twill bring the arter-burden. Ah! There it be!'

When she saw her mother pushing down again, Susan half expected another baby to emerge, but what flopped out between Dolly's legs was a piece of raw meat, bloody on one side and glistening reddish-purple skin on the other.

'Put that in the basin, Sukey. It ha' fed the child in the womb, an' now 'twill feed us all. It must be cut up small in the pot over the fire, and we'll ha' dinner off it today.'

Susan sighed for sheer relief and happiness, overwhelmed by all that she had seen and learned from this amazing happening, and even more by her own part in it. She had helped her mother to give birth, and had cared for her new brother from the moment he was born. She now gazed in satisfaction while he fed, marvelling that Dolly's agony was now so completely forgotten.

It was almost daylight, and as the candle flickered out, Widow Gibson hurried through the door. She had run all the way from her cottage in Quarry Lane, and when she saw the situation, she was full of praise for Susan.

'Her's done a woman's work fur 'ee, Doll Lucket, an' Oi hopes as 'ee be as proud o' her as 'ee ought,' she said as she bustled round the dingy room, getting the fire going and depositing a basket of clean rags she had brought, together with a block of hard yellow washing-soap. She poked Susan playfully in the ribs.

'Oi tells 'ee, little Missus Lucket, Dame Coulter an' me'll ha' ter look out fur oursel's, else us'll lose our women ter the new Beversley midwife – an' her hardly eight year old!'

Susan glowed, and dared to hope that her mother would also value what she had done, and maybe show it with grateful smiles, kind words and kisses.

Polly and Jack were brought down from the roost, and Polly stared and marvelled at the new little brother, only eleven months younger than Jack.

'His name be Job, out o' the Bible, but we'll call un Joby,' Susan told her proudly.

So Joby he was called and Job he was baptised by Parson Smart, just as the snowdrops were lifting their brave white heads in the churchyard around Little St Giles.

Susan had another good reason for remembering that day. Watching the ceremony was a serious-faced young woman who spoke to the parson afterwards and smiled at Susan, who recognised her as the lady she had seen at the pig-killing at Bever House all those long months ago, with Edward. She introduced herself as Miss Glover, and they then saw her from time to time in Lower Beversley. She now lived in a handsome stone cottage that faced the village school at the lower end of Beversley's main street. She even came to visit their home at Ash-Pit End, which thrilled Susan and Polly, though Doll Lucket received her with blank stares and no word of acknowledgement for the home-baked bread and pies she brought with her. Miss Glover told Susan that Edward had been sent away to school at Winchester with his elder brother.

There were to be no more Lucket children. Dolly was done with child-bearing and the coupling that preceded it. She tied Joby to her back and went out to find work in the fields, hoeing and hand-weeding, a solitary figure who kept apart from other female workers, and met good and bad times with the same stony silence. The only emotion she ever displayed was her doting fondness for her two pretty little boys, as she called them, though Jack was a whining child whose nose continually dripped and whose eyes never looked in the same direction.

But the winter of death was over, and young Susan Lucket greeted the spring of 1768 with new heart and renewed hope, all unaware of the foul shadow lying in wait for her.

Chapter 4

Susan ran up to her sister and slapped her face hard.

'What d'ye think ye're about, Poll, hangin' around outside the alehouse? Oi've a good mind to box yer ears fur 'ee.'

Her blazing anger was a measure of her fear and anxiety, for she had spent the past hour searching high and low for her naughty little sister. They had been toiling in the Bennett hayfield all day under a merciless July sun; from six in the morning the men's scythes slashed through the green stalks that fell in swathes for the women to gather, following the men as they circled round and round the field from the edge towards the centre. The women's backs were bent and their hands bleeding from the barbed thistles among the grass; Susan worked alongside them, a wiry girl of ten, while Polly and the two toddling boys chased the rabbits towards the middle of the field where they took refuge in the last remaining clump. As the scythes advanced towards them, the luckless creatures made a desperate bid for their lives, scampering in all directions, their white tails bobbing. A roar went up from the men as Farmer Bennett's gun was lifted and fired many times, sending lead shot into heads and bellies; the soft bodies flew up in the air, and blood stained the yellow stubble. All hands received rabbits for the pot that night, and when the haymakers at last trudged wearily to their homes, Doll Lucket held Jack's hand while Susan dragged a half-asleep Joby.

'Where be Polly, Ma? Ha' ye seen her?'

Doll shook her head and kept walking, but Susan began to be alarmed. She hoped against hope that Polly had gone on ahead of them, but when they reached the Ash-Pits there was no sign of her. Panic-stricken, Susan at once set out to search the fields and hedgerows, calling out to her sister and trying not to picture her caught in a trap or fallen into a ditch.

'Polly! Polly, where be ye? Oh, Poll, come out, come back, don't be lost, Polly!'

At last, exhausted and despairing, Susan began to make her way back to the Ash-Pits to see if Polly had turned up there, and went by way of Mill Lane where the Swan Inn stood near to the parsonage of Little St Giles. A crowd of men and a few women sat outside on benches, laughing at the antics of a saucy little girl who was dancing for them, holding up her skirts and stepping lightly to the strains of a fiddler, in return for sips of ale and morsels of bread and cheese.

'*Polly!*'

Susan's relief erupted in furious reproaches, and she slapped her sister in front of the company.

'Ye bad, bad gal! Oi bin seekin' 'ee this past hour, an' Oi be that fagged. 'Ee deserves a good whippin', an' 'ee'll get no rabbit stew tonight, ye little numbskull!'

Polly put her hand up to her reddened cheek, frightened at such an outburst from her usually easy-going sister.

'Oi didn't mean ter run away, Sukey,' she whimpered, cowering in a pathetic manner. 'Oi jus' be come to find Da.'

Her look of surprised innocence had its intended effect, and Susan rolled her eyes heavenwards.

'Oh, Poll, Poll, how Oi ha' feared fur 'ee! How Oi ha' prayed to find 'ee!'

44

The younger girl quickly seized her advantage, and stood with eyes downcast, her hands clasped behind her back.

'Oi never meant to frighten 'ee, Sukey. Oi be sorry.'

Bartlemy Lucket rose from a bench against the wall, and came towards them. He had taken enough ale to flush his features, but was not drunk. In recent years he had become more regular in his habits, and a somewhat better provider, so that Susan sometimes felt quite sorry that Dolly took so little notice of him; but at this moment she felt nothing but impatience.

'Why'd 'ee let Polly foller 'ee to the Swan, Da? Oi bin half crazy wi' worry, thinkin' she be drownded or summat!'

He looked suitably regretful. 'Ah, 'ee be a good gal, Sukey, an' her be a little baggage. Don't 'ee fret no more, then. Oi'll walk along o' ye, soon as Oi finished this'n.'

He uptilted his mug and drained the last quarter-pint of ale. 'Run along home now, Polly, an' tell yer ma we be comin'. Go on, gal – no, not 'ee, Sukey. Wait fur me. 'Tis a fine evenin' fur a stroll.'

Susan was by now exceedingly tired, and longed to be at home and up in the roost with Polly, yet she waited for her father, who was the only person to show any appreciation of her. She had dimly made the connection between Doll's complete indifference to him and the fact that Joby had been the last child. The strange sounds that at one time used to drift up to the roost had ceased ever since that terrible winter when three brothers had been taken and one had been born. Susan was a country child, and had seen the boar and the sow going about their natural business, the bull with the cow and the cock with the hen; it seemed to her a strange activity that the female

45

had to endure. Remembering the vague uneasiness that Doll's protesting moans and Bartlemy's thick grunts had given her, it was a relief that it no longer happened. Even so, she thought that Da deserved a few encouraging words for the effort he now made to keep off the drink and stay in work. Even Farmer Bennett now tolerated him at such busy times as the spring ploughing and sowing, or as now, at haymaking.

'Oi'll walk along o' ye, Da,' she agreed, having seen Polly running off down the lane in the direction of the Ash-Pits, making herself scarce after the trouble she had caused her sister. 'Only 'ee must come now, Oi shan't wait fur 'ee.'

So the father and daughter walked along Mill Lane together. On one side was the ditch and the hedge next to Bennett's paddock field, and on the other side a shallow bank rose up to a wooded area where foxes prowled in the undergrowth and rabbits burrowed deep into the soft soil of the bank. Under the trees a thick, luxuriant growth of bracken covered the ground, the tough fronds standing four or five feet high.

Bartlemy took Susan's arm. 'Here, this way, Sukey, into the wood.'

She stared up at him in surprise. 'That ain't no quick way, Da. 'Tis hard goin', it be that overgrown.'

He smiled oddly, his eyes glittering in a way she had not seen before. Was he drunk? No, she decided, just a little silly after a couple of pints.

'Come on, Sukey, over by here, gal,' he muttered, dragging her bodily off the lane and into the darkening woods.

'No, Dad, *no*, there be snakes an' all sorts. Let's jus' go home. *Da*! What be the matter?'

46

For he was panting as if he had been running, and held on to her with a grip she could not escape. For some reason she suddenly thought of the little rabbits in the hayfield that day, helpless to avoid their fate.

'Be a good gal, Sukey – a bit o' a game wi' yer dad, eh? Like this, see? Come on, be quick.'

And Susan found herself down on the ground, with her face pressed into the bracken. She lay prone, and felt her skirt being roughly pulled up, exposing her bare buttocks. Like other poor children she wore no underwear, and when she felt her skin being touched and her thighs separated, she began to howl and struggle instinctively. Then there was a sensation of weight upon her squirming body, which the man approached from behind, and her face was pressed even harder into the dense green ferns, muffling her horrified protests.

What happened next did not take long. There were gasps and grunts and 'Keep still, Sukey, good gal,' in a low growl, and something hot and fleshy thrust between her thighs. One last grunt and it was over.

He got up and she lay motionless on the ground. She felt her skirt being pulled down over her bare backside, but could not move. Her nostrils were full of the acrid smell of the bracken, and she heard his voice speaking as if through a mist of shame and nausea and incomprehension.

'Get up, Sukey, an' come on home. Yer Ma'll be lookin' out fur 'ee.'

He bent down and grabbed an arm; clumsily she staggered to her feet and let herself be dragged out of the wood and into the lane.

'Come on, Sukey, there be no harm done. Take hold o' yer Dad's hand, there's a good gal.'

47

Dazed and trembling like a leaf, she was pulled along the lane towards the Ash-Pits. As she walked she felt a stickiness running down the inside of her legs, and in time to come she would always connect its smell with the other smell of bracken crushed by the weight of a child and a man.

She ate nothing and spoke to no one when she stumbled through the door, but climbed straight up to the roost.

'What be up wi' ye, Sukey?' asked her sister, but Susan did not reply. That night she wet herself, and Polly complained loudly about the soaked blanket.

''Ee be a dirty ol' pig, Sukey, no better'n a babby!'

Susan made no answer, nor did she speak or raise her drooping head for the next three days. Bartlemy spoke jocularly to her, but she shrank from him; Doll gave no sign of noticing that anything was amiss. Polly became frightened.

'Say summat, Sukey – Oi don't like 'ee to be quiet!' she begged. 'Oi be sorry fur bein' a bad gal – sorry Oi called 'ee a pig – only speak to me, Sukey, please!' And she put her arms around the sister who had always shown her love, while tears trickled down her cheeks. ''Ee be a good'un, Sukey – an' Oi loves 'ee!' she sobbed.

And because of Polly's innocent plea for attention, Susan managed to rouse herself and whisper, 'Don't 'ee worry, Poll, Oi'll be better by an' by.'

On that first occasion Susan was utterly confused and did not understand what this new experience meant. She only knew that something *wrong* had taken place, something that should never happen, and that she was part of it, an unwilling accomplice. It was shameful and untellable, a hideous secret that

48

placed her apart from Polly and the boys, and over which she had no control.

At first she tried to send silent, imploring looks towards her mother, pleading with Doll to notice her, to ask what was the matter, to help her in some way; but the woman turned her head away and would not or dared not acknowledge the burden that her daughter was being forced to bear, first in fear and dread, then in helpless resignation, unable to escape for she had nowhere to go. As the months went by, Susan came to know that she was the third party in an unholy alliance; and love died without a word being spoken.

But Polly still needed her, perhaps more than ever now. It seemed important that Polly should never know or even remotely suspect that such a thing could happen. Susan's love for her heedless young sister became even more fiercely protective, and helped her to survive when the shadow fell across her life and the light went out of her eyes.

One day, vowed Susan, *one* day when I'm older and can work and earn money, I shall leave the Ash-Pits and take Polly with me. And we shall never see those two again.

Never.

Chapter 5

'Susan!' called Mrs Bennett, leaning over the gate. 'Come here, girl, I need you to go up to the school. Leave the harrow and come. No, not you, Polly – I want a girl o' sense. *Susan!*'

The prospect of a glimpse inside the village school brought a momentary brightness to the girl's grey eyes.

'Keep on follerin' them horses, Poll, and watch the boys while Oi be away,' she muttered, and ran up the barley field to where the farmer's wife stood holding her daughter Marianne's needlework bag.

'The silly, giddy girl left it behind on the settle,' she grumbled, 'but I don't want her shown up in front o' the Calthorpe girls. Hurry up, Susan, and get it to the little goose in time!'

The barefooted girl hurried down to the bridge over the Beck and across the green; skirting the pond she reached the main street, and straightway heard the clop of hoofs, the creaking of leather and the rattle of iron-rimmed wheels on cobblestones. She stared open-mouthed as the stately equipage passed quite close to her, its bodywork gleaming in the spring sunshine. Four high-necked horses were kept under control by the coachman perched aloft in front, his tricorn hat over his wig. Susan jumped back in alarm at his angry shout.

'Watch out, yer silly wench. D'ye want to be trampled down?'

She almost lost her footing as the back wheels swept by, retreating in a light cloud of dust. A woman's face glared from the window, and Susan's heart hammered. She had never been so close to the Bever carriage, and was astonished at its size and height, so much grander than Miss Glover's two-seater pony-trap that she drove when visiting in Beversley.

Recollecting her errand, Susan ran down the street, past the bakehouse and blacksmith's forge to the school, a tall house at the end, almost facing Miss Glover's cottage. She marched up to the front door and pulled on the bell rope, hoping to get a peep inside the place where Mrs Bryers taught her pupils those magic signs that could form themselves into messages for folk to send to each other without having to speak face to face. Susan's imagination had been fired by Miss Glover's ability to read the Bible and Prayer Book and the *Hampshire Chronicle*, and the way she wrote notes and lists on pieces of paper. Oh, happy children whose parents could afford the weekly shilling to send them to Mrs Bryers' school!

She smiled eagerly at the maidservant who opened the door a crack.

'Mrs Bryers don't want no beggars round here.'

'If 'ee pleases, Oi ha' – er – Miss Marianne's sewin' bag,' faltered Susan, holding it out and trying to look past the maid's shoulder.

'Then ye've no business wi' it,' came the reply as the bag was snatched from her hand. 'Be off wi' ye.'

And to Susan's utter dismay the door was shut in her face. She knew that she should return to the barley field, but such was her desire to see inside the temple of learning that she decided to try to peep in at a window. The front of the house opened on to the

51

street, and there were three tall windows, one with a convenient mounting-stone beneath it. Susan climbed on to this and stretched herself up until her head was above the windowsill.

And there it was, the big room with girls and boys seated on wooden forms, the smaller ones at the front. She recognised Selina and Caroline Calthorpe at the back with the Bennett girls, and Rosa and William Hansford somewhere in the middle with three of the Smart brood. She saw the Grimes children from the bakehouse and the Dummets from Crabb's cottages, most of them younger than the thirteen-year-old girl who gazed in with such longing. The formidable figure of Mrs Bryers stood by the blackboard on which there were groups of those magic signs written in chalk.

Suddenly Rosa Hansford jumped with a cry.

'Mrs Bryers, Mrs Bryers, there's a face looking in at us!'

By the time they had all turned their heads in her direction, Susan had already dropped down and was heading for the road – straight into the path of a high-stepping young stallion and his rider. A confused jumble of impressions followed in quick succession: rearing hoofs, her own scream of terror, a boy's shout – 'No, Juniper, *no*!' – then the hoofs plunging down on the cobbles, missing her by inches, and another shout as the young rider slithered down the horse's flank, clinging first to the mane and then the neck, reaching the ground feet first but overbalancing as the horse shied violently sideways.

A boy lay sprawled in the dust, his jacket and breeches dirtied, his hat lying several feet away. The horse circled nervously round him, empty stirrups dangling.

Susan's mouth went dry with fear, and she fell to her knees beside the young horseman, thrown from his seat because of her stupidity. To her indescribable relief he stared at her, blankly at first but then his eyes focused into recognition. He gave an uncertain smile and put his hand to his head.

He was Edward Calthorpe, alive and conscious.

'Susan,' he said. 'Little Susan!'

'Thank God,' she murmured. 'Can 'ee move, master? Be any bones broke?'

For answer he heaved himself up into an undignified position on hands and knees.

'I trust you are well, Susan?' he enquired politely.

'Oh, never mind about me, master – can 'ee stand up?'

He stretched experimentally and slowly hauled himself to his feet, straightening his back. A trickle of blood oozed from a cut above his right eye, but he smiled as he held out his hands to her, to pull her up beside him.

At that moment Mrs Bryers came running out of the school, her black skirts flying.

'You should be whipped, you idle creature! First you gape in at my window like a monkey, and now you've brought Master Calthorpe off his horse. He could have broken his neck!'

And then there was another voice, quietly stern.

'Thank you, Mrs Bryers, you may return to your pupils. I will take charge of my cousin and the girl.'

Miss Glover's cool authority had an instantly calming effect. She took hold of the horse's bridle and led him to her gatepost, where she tethered him. Mrs Bryers gave a last glare at Susan and went back into the school while the boy and girl followed Miss

Glover into the handsome stone cottage set back from the road in a pretty summer garden.

When Susan found herself sitting on a cane-bottomed chair in a neat parlour with Edward seated beside her, her spirits rose to a point that was almost happiness. It was more than relief for Edward's safety, it was a sense of lightness and freedom. She looked around at the curtained windows and the carpet on the floor, savouring a way of living immeasurably distant from the squalor of the Ash-Pits. She already thought Miss Glover the wisest and most beautiful grown-up lady she knew, and now she realised that in her presence she was safe, with no need for the wariness that had become habitual to her.

'I shall fetch water to bathe that cut, Edward, and my maidservant will brew tea for us,' said the lady. 'And then you must tell me exactly what happened outside.'

''Twas not because of this poor – 'twas not Susan's fault, Sophy,' said Edward quickly. ''Twas that mettlesome Juniper. My usual mare was – in use, so I had to take him.'

Miss Glover nodded, and as soon as she had left the room he turned eagerly to Susan.

'You know, I still remember that harvest supper when we met,' he said, 'and how you stood up for the bats!'

She smiled shyly. 'Oh-ah, master, that were a long time ago, just afore that bad winter when my three little brothers died o' the white throat an' my brother Joby were born.'

Her eyes darkened at the memory, and Edward bit his lip.

'I'm sorry, Susan, I'd forgotten that it was such a

54

bad time for the – for so many Beversley people. Yes, of course, poor old Dame Firkin – I recall it all now. I beg your pardon for bringing it to mind.'

She did not reply, and he experienced a strange awkwardness, almost a feeling of inadequacy. Had he but known it, it was the same unease that his father had long felt when reminded of the plight of the poor in Beversley.

His cousin Sophia returned with a basin of water and set about cleaning the cut above his eye; he tried not to wince as she dabbed the skin dry and put a folded white handkerchief over it, tying the ends together at the back of his head.

'I think that will suffice, Edward, for the bleeding has stopped,' she said, picking up the basin and turning to Susan.

'Now, young Susan, what brought you up to Beversley alone today?'

Blushing and stammering, Susan explained her errand for Mrs Bennett.

'And you were working in the barley field?' asked Edward.

'Oh, ay, master, me an' Polly was follerin' the horses pullin' the harrow, and Jack an' Joby was scarin' the birds off the spring barley. We get what outdoor work we can, soon as the days start gettin' longer.'

He shook his head wonderingly. 'Yet you are still but children, Susan, about the same age as my sisters – and *they* are back in school today.'

It now occurred to him how different she appeared from the saucy, bright-eyed child who had chatted and laughed with him – how long ago was it? He had been sent away to school soon after, and had largely lost touch with events in Beversley. He and Osmond

55

had been home for Easter, but had to return to Winchester in two days' time. Looking at this poor, barefoot girl who had almost run under his horses hoofs, he was obscurely ashamed of his privileges in the face of her poverty.

A tray arrived with a teapot, milk jug, cups and saucers, and Miss Sophia looked thoughtful as she poured out the fragrant brown brew that Susan had never tasted before. Edward handed her a cup balanced on a saucer, which she gingerly took with both hands.

'You deserve this more than I do, Susan. Here, let me put in a spoonful of sugar for you,' he said.

'Thank 'ee, Master Edward. Thank 'ee, Miss Glover.'

As far as Susan was concerned, this fourteen-year-old boy was like a being from another world, so finely dressed and clean. Yet he spoke to her as if she were one of his sisters, with kindness and courtesy. She had never known a man to be gentle like this, and her heart swelled. Miss Glover was smiling at her, so she was not going to be chastised again. She sipped her tea gratefully, and felt that life could hold no greater bliss.

A sudden loud ringing of the doorbell announced the arrival of Edward's elder brother, who strode into the parlour, nodding to Sophia and completely ignoring Susan.

'What the devil have you been up to, Neddy? Could you not keep your seat on young Juniper?'

'If you had not taken my Duchess, I wouldn't have needed to saddle him,' retorted Edward.

Osmond shrugged and went to the window. He looked bored and discontented as he accepted a cup of tea from Sophia.

'How dull it has been in Beversley these two weeks, with Henry away at sea! Even Winchester has more to offer a fellow.'

His light blue eyes roved round the room, and briefly lighted upon Susan. She felt his contempt for her poor gown, and was conscious for the first time of her bare feet in Miss Glover's parlour. She blushed crimson as she looked down at them, tough and leathery, with grime ingrained between the toes. In an instant her elation vanished; she was reminded of her low status and with it the unspeakable secret burden she carried. She felt unfit to be in this room among this company, and she hung her head in shame, unable to meet Edward's eyes again. Just suppose he knew about *that*: how horrified he would be – and Miss Glover! Her mind reeled away from the very thought, and she did not notice Sophia Glover eyeing her attentively.

Osmond laughed at his brother's bandaged head.

'Good God, Neddy, you'll frighten the populace out of their wits, looking like a corpse on horseback, pale and bloody! Come on, let's be going. We have to meet with the carriage at Pulhurst, and Father will be complaining as usual. I shall say I had to stay and tend you. Good day, Cousin Sophy. Come *on*, Ned!'

Susan still sat with lowered head, so did not see Edward's bow to her as he left.

As soon as Miss Glover had gone to see the brothers on their way, Susan rose to leave; but the lady came back and asked her to stay a few minutes longer.

'Sit down, Susan. I have something important to say to you.'

The girl braced herself for the scolding that Miss Glover must have saved until they were alone.

'Don't look so worried, Susan! I have been talking with Mrs Bennett and Mrs Gibson about you, and they both speak highly of your good sense.'

Susan was so surprised that she raised her head and blinked. What was coming now?

'And I think that you should be given the chance to learn the alphabet, Susan. Would you like to try?'

Susan was utterly bewildered. 'Beggin' yer pardon, Miss Glover, but what do that mean?' she faltered, though even as she spoke her heart leaped at the sound of the magic word, as if it could transform her life and begin her escape from the Ash-Pits. She waited, hardly daring to breathe.

'The *alphabet* is made up of the twenty-six letters that form the words of the English language,' replied Miss Glover, smiling. 'And I will send you to Mrs Bryers' school to learn how to make them into words to read and write. Would you like that, Susan?'

Chapter 6

The immemorial rhythm of the fields moved from sowing to growing, and with the passing of the summer solstice haymaking time came round once again, when all available labour was in demand.

The Bever carriage was sent to bring the Calthorpe brothers home from Winchester, and young Midshipman Hansford came home on leave from the navy's Royal Academy at Portsmouth. Osmond listened eagerly to Henry's stories of life at sea, and longed for manhood; the stirrings of his young body had become a craving for that mysterious coupling with a female body, about which his fellow scholars joked but for which Osmond had found no opportunity, either at school, or at Bever House, where some of the maidservants smiled slyly at him but were unable to escape Mrs Martin's vigilant eye. The only woman allowed to enter the brothers' bedchamber was the one-time nursemaid, black-browed Mrs Ferris, forty if she was a day, who glided silently in with clean linen and hot water in a china pitcher. Once or twice Osmond thought he sensed her dark eyes upon him, but when he turned to face her she always seemed busily occupied. The burgeoning of Nature all around him, and the animal kingdom's universal drive to procreate was a torment to the handsome, well-built boy, now seventeen; his virgin state grew more irksome daily.

*

''Ee be that dull, Sukey, since 'ee started goin' to that ol' school,' grumbled Polly, lying on the grass.

'Oi may be dull to 'ee, Poll, but Mrs Bryers do say that Oi be – that Oi *am* – the best in the class,' replied Susan with modest pride.

'Tha's 'cos 'ee be the oldest on 'em!' laughed Polly scornfully.

The sisters had been working in Farmer Bennett's hayfield, and were resting in the shade at midday. As soon as they sat down under the hedgerow, Susan had got out the well-worn reading primer that Miss Glover had given her. There was little time for studying, and she only attended school on two mornings a week during this busy season.

'Hush, Poll, Oi ha' to know this page afore Oi sees Mrs Bryers again.' She began to whisper the words to herself as she deciphered each one. ' "Tom sat on a fat nag." '

'Tibby Dummet do say 'ee might as well teach a cat her letters as a poor gal,' mocked Polly. 'For then Puss'll give herself fine airs an' catch no more mice – an' a gal won't work indoors or out if her nose be stuck in a book all the time, like yourn!'

Susan did not reply, but smiled in secret satisfaction. The word *cat* was special to her, for it recalled the actual moment when she had grasped the principle of building words from letters.

'Take the letter C,' Mrs Bryers had said. 'C says *c*! say it after me, Susan, c!'

'C!' repeated Susan, nodding. She had learned the sounds that each of the letters made.

'Now A,' went on the teacher. 'A says *a*!' She broadened her mouth to make the vowel sound, and Susan did the same.

'And now T,' said Mrs Bryers, tapping her tongue

against her front teeth. 'T says *t*!' She smiled as she led the eager girl towards the door of literacy. '*T*!'

'*T*!' tapped Susan breathlessly.

'Now put all three sounds together, *c* and *a* and *t*. What do they say?'

'*C* – *a* – *t*.' Susan rapped out the three separate sounds.

'Faster! Run them together, Susan.' Mrs Bryers smiled encouragingly, and Susan saw light dawning.

'C-a-t. *Cat! CAT!*' Susan almost shouted the word, an explorer discovering a new country. 'Cat, cat! So *that* be readin'. Oh, Mrs Bryers, now I can learn *all* the words!'

And sure enough, she progressed rapidly from then on, and now, after two months, could read and write simple sentences. She never forgot that moment of enlightenment that compensated for the painful humiliation she had undergone on her first day, when nervous but avid to learn she had been the first pupil to arrive on a bright morning in May, wearing a new smocked cotton gown that Miss Glover had given her, and a pair of wooden pattens on her feet.

Mrs Bryers had greeted her somewhat doubtfully, and sent her to sit by herself at the back. No child from the Ash-Pits had ever attended the school, and Mrs Bryers thought that Miss Glover had been unwise to bring such an awkward, uncouth girl to sit with her betters. When the others arrived, they looked askance at the new scholar and chattered among themselves.

Susan curtsied to Edward Calthorpe's sisters. 'Good day to ye,' she said carefully. 'If ye please, Oi be Susan Lucket an' startin' school today.'

The only response was a long, unfriendly stare

from several pairs of haughty female eyes. They then turned away and put their heads together, glancing in her direction as they whispered and tut-tutted. When Mrs Bryers rang the handbell that summoned them all to assemble and repeat the Lord's Prayer, Susan could see the Calthorpe sisters and Rosa Hansford, still shaking their heads and muttering behind their hands.

Mrs Bryers then read Psalm 19 aloud, and Susan listened intently to its majestic cadences about the vastness of Creation and the timelessness of Eternity; but she soon became aware of a rustling and tittering among the girls, a stifled laugh and heaving shoulders; then Selina exploded in a fit of giggling, and Susan saw that Rosa was holding her nose and glancing towards Susan in a meaningful way.

The awful truth was clear: *she* was the object of their mockery. Nobody wanted to sit near to her because she was from the Ash-Pits. And she smelled.

Other children saw Rosa holding her nose, and the laughter spread. It ceased when Mrs Bryers looked up with a frown, but Susan heard no more of the psalm; she flushed scarlet, and for one moment was tempted to run out of the school and never return.

Only for a moment, though, for she was here to learn all she could, whether welcomed or cold-shouldered. How else might she raise herself from the Ash-Pits and the dreadful thing she regularly had to endure? It was something these stupid, cosseted girls could not possibly imagine, and set her apart from them far more than any unfriendliness on their part.

She straightened her shoulders and set her mouth in a determined line: even as she smarted under their ridicule, she vowed that nothing, absolutely *nothing*, would prevent her from learning to read and write as well as the best of them.

So on that first miserable morning Susan learned and memorised the alphabet from A to Z, a fact that Mrs Bryers did not fail to notice. She made no further attempt to speak to her fellow scholars, but sat bowed over her slate until the midday break when the others went out to play at the back of the school and eat the bread and cheese they had brought with them.

'Don't you want to go outside too, Susan?'

'No, thank 'ee, Mrs Bryers.'

'Have you brought anything to eat?'

'No, thank 'ee, Mrs Bryers.'

The teacher retired to her own private parlour, leaving Susan alone in the classroom, but not for long. A tall, rather gawky girl with a chipped front tooth slipped in quietly.

'Have some o' this barley bread, Susan. It's too much f'r Sally and me.'

Susan looked up to see Marianne, the younger of the two Bennett girls and something of a scatterbrain. It was her forgotten needlework bag that had begun the chain of events that had brought Susan here today.

'Thank 'ee, Miss Marianne, that be good o' ye,' she said, but added quickly, ''Ee don't ha' to stay in here wi' me. Oi got a lot o' learnin' to do.'

For she had already discovered there was more to education than reading and writing; there were social differences that put her at the very bottom of the scale. And the one way of asserting herself would be to outstrip them all.

'Come, Poll, we ha' rested long enough,' sighed Susan, closing her book and tucking it inside her bodice. 'The others are startin' again.'

'No, Sukey, wait – see o'er there by the gate, three fine gen'lemen be lookin' our way.'

Susan's heart gave a sudden leap at the sight of Edward and his brother with another tall, fair-haired young man. She did not care to be seen toiling in a field, especially with that dark, menacing presence among the men working some way off.

'Don't look at 'em, Poll. We better get back,' she muttered.

But Polly had returned Edward's smile, encouraging him to approach them. He had been drawn to seek out Susan in Lower Beversley, much to Osmond's irritation and Midshipman Hansford's amusement.

''Tis a disgrace that these girls should labour in the fields all day while we play fools on horseback, Henry! We talk of abolishing the enslavement of negroes, yet turn a blind eye to the condition of the poor among our own people—'

'Oh, spare us your pious sermons, Neddy, on matters you know nothing about,' sneered Osmond. 'I'll wager the parents of these girls drink every penny they earn and then come whining for parish relief. You listen too much to Cousin Sophy's cant.'

'Whoa, Osmond, steady on. You are as cross as a bear since you returned from school,' chided Henry. 'Edward may surely talk with the girl if he pleases.'

The boy had already dismounted and was walking over to the Lucket sisters.

'Good day to you, Susan. I had hopes of seeing you,' he said artlessly. 'So is this your sister, Polly?'

Susan gave a half-smile, but her eyes looked towards the new-cut grass that the women were raking up into a line of haycocks; Farmer Bennett's eyes missed nothing.

'Aye, master, this be Polly.'

'And *this* be our brother Jack,' added the younger sister as a small sun-browned boy sidled up to them and gave Edward a cross-eyed grin. Edward was surprised at his own instinctive recoil; why should Susan's poor little brother send a shiver down his spine? After all, he couldn't *help* having a squint.

'And are your father and mother working in this field too?' he asked, shading his eyes as he looked towards the circling haymakers, the men cutting, the women raking and gathering.

'Oh, aye, Ma be o'er there wi' Joby, and Da be—' began Polly, but Susan cut in quite sharply.

'If 'ee please, master, we ha' to get on, or the farmer'll be arter us fur gossipin',' she told him, and he glimpsed the shadow in her downcast grey eyes. He supposed it was the effect of poverty and the deaths of her three brothers that had brought about this change, yet he sensed a wariness in her look and tone, as if she were on her guard. It troubled the boy in a way that he was too young to understand, and reluctantly he took his leave and returned to the gate where he had left his horse. Osmond had ridden off, disgusted by Henry's defence of Edward, but the young midshipman seemed inclined to talk as they rode at a leisurely pace back to the village centre.

'What did Osmond mean when he spoke of your cousin Sophia, Edward? He said you had been – er – influenced by her.'

'Cousin Sophy is a great friend to the poor, and she says that faith must be shown in good works or it is worth nothing,' replied the boy promptly, having spoken at length with Sophia the previous day.

'Is that what she says? And why didn't I see her in church on Sunday?' smiled Henry.

'Because she quite often goes to Little St Giles to hear Parson Smart preach. She prefers him to Dr Gravett, she says.'

Henry laughed. 'I don't suppose the rector cares for her praise of poor Smart. But tell me more, Edward. I hear that Miss Glover visits filthy hovels where nobody else ventures.'

'Yes, she stands up to drunken cottagers who mistreat their families – and when your mother threw out that fat dairymaid, Sophy took her in to save her from the workhouse.'

'Ah, yes, the girl who was with child,' nodded Henry, recalling his father's stern questions at the time. 'And didn't I hear that both our mothers were offended some time ago when Miss Glover introduced a ragged, verminous child into the village school? Did you ever hear the outcome of that?'

Edward gave him a coldly triumphant look. 'Yes, I did, Henry. Sophy took no notice of your mother or mine, and the child you speak of has far outstripped her so-called betters – in truth, she is the best pupil in the school!'

Too late Henry saw his blunter. 'Edward! Are we speaking of the girl in the hayfield – your little friend Susan? Oh, I beg your pardon for my foolish words, I had no idea – I did not know 'twas she.'

'Well, you know now, Henry. And our sisters have benefited, for they have to work that much harder to keep up with the charity child!'

That night Edward woke suddenly and sat up in bed, roused by the whine of a door hinge and a light patter of feet on the floorboards, followed by a creaking of Osmond's bed and a suppressed gasp. A painted Chinese screen separated the two beds, and some

66

instinct warned Edward not to call out.

Then the murmurings began.

'Ah, I knew you were there – and you have come to me!' Osmond sounded eager but also somewhat uncertain.

'Hush, don't wake y'r brother. Move over and make room f'r me.'

The voice was low and definitely female; Edward could hardly believe his ears. Sighs and murmurs followed, and Osmond made a sound that was almost like a groan.

'Here, let me show you. Put y'r hand here—' she whispered.

'Oh, this is what I have lain awake longing for, night after night! And now you are here, my—'

'Call me Jael, Osmond.'

'Jael! Oh, Jael, you are so beautiful. Mm-mm!'

'Kiss me, Osmond – ah, kiss me!'

Edward lay wide awake, tense in every muscle, holding his breath for fear of being heard; but the lovers were entirely absorbed in each other, and Edward had no choice but to listen as Mrs Ferris led his brother through the door from boyhood to man.

'Oh, Jael, Jael, I've never known – this is my – oh! Ah! Jael – *Jael*!'

She laughed softly, tenderly. 'Hush, hush, my sweet love. We mustn't wake the boy.'

But in fact Edward lay staring into the darkness long after she had glided away and Osmond had sunk into the deep sleep of satisfied desire.

At the same time Susan also lay awake beside the slumbering Polly. The day had ended dreadfully for her. Polly had been carted away by Doll, and although Susan had kept tight hold of Jack's hand, the boy had been forced from her side when she was dragged down into the hollow where the ditch had dried out. What happened next had followed the usual sequence, and Susan dealt with it as she had taught herself to do: her whole body stiffened into rigidity, her eyes were tightly closed, her hands clenched into fists and her mind blanked out as if a curtain was drawn across her consciousness, separating it from what was being done to her unripe body. It was her way of coping, her means of survival until the day when she could escape and take Polly with her.

Yet now, as she lay beside the sister who needed her, she thought of Edward, so kind, so *clean*, so far removed from her hateful knowledge; and she started to weep silently in her loneliness, for there was nobody in the world who knew how she had been betrayed. Except the two who above all others should have looked after her.

So Susan shed tears as she mourned for her lost childhood, but noiselessly, so as not to wake her sister.

Chapter 7

Susan was fourteen when her monthly flow began, and she never forgot the day. The bloodstain on her petticoat meant that her body was changing; there was already a burgeoning of her little breasts and a soft fuzz of hair in that secret place that was muddied with shame and pain. And she was taller; field labour had hardened the muscles of her arms and legs.

Susan stared at her own blood, the signs of womanhood, and some deep, primitive instinct sprung into life: this was her body, which belonged only to her. She was no longer a helpless victim, but a woman with rights over what was hers, and a duty to protect it. It was time to escape from the shadow.

What should she do? She could leave the Ash-Pits at any time and find work as a maidservant, in or out of doors, but there was Polly to be included in her plans. Susan decided to consult the lady who had helped her before and was known as a friend to poor women and children, so she called at the Glover cottage early one morning in August.

'If ye please, Miss Glover, Oi need to find work f'r Polly an' meself,' she said carefully. 'There be not enough to feed us all now the boys ha' got bigger, an' besides, Bartlemy be a drinker, an' . . .'

She hesitated. Unable to tell the untellable, she had planned to say that her father regularly beat them, though in fact he never had.

Miss Glover listened and nodded without pressing Susan to finish the sentence.

'I understand you, Susan. As a matter of fact, I've been thinking about this. Now that you have finished school, you need to start earning money for yourself rather than for your parents. Now, I hear that a laundrymaid is needed at Bever House. Would you like me to speak to Mrs Martin for you?'

'Oh, but ye see, Miss Glover, 'tis Polly as well,' said Susan anxiously. 'Be there work f'r two laundry-maids?'

Sophia smiled and shook her head. 'I really don't know about Polly, Susan. She's only twelve years old, isn't she?'

'Nearly thirteen. Oh, she can't be left at the Ash-Pits wi'out me, Miss Glover!'

'Why are you so worried about her, Susan? Do you mean that she would be in danger of being ill-treated?'

'Oh, aye, Miss Glover, ill-treated.' Susan grasped at the word. 'He'll – he'll ill-treat her when he be drunken. Please, Miss Glover, Oi couldn't leave her in that place!'

She clasped her hands together beseechingly, and Sophia was startled by the real terror in the wide grey eyes. This girl is hiding something, she thought, and the matter must be urgent.

'All right, Susan, don't worry, I will see what can be done. Go to your field work now, and leave this to me.'

Susan stared dumbly at her, as if wanting to say more but not knowing how. Sophia smiled reassuringly.

'I promise, Susan.'

'Thank ye, Miss Glover – oh, thank ye!'

70

Susan spoke from the heart, but the crisis came sooner than anticipated, for the very next evening the shadow pounced upon her in the bracken alongside Quarry Lane. Her brother Jack had been trotting along beside her, and quite suddenly disappeared.

'Now, Sukey, be quick. Another little game wi' yer dad, eh?' – the sickeningly familiar growl.

His hands were on her buttocks, pulling up her skirt. A wool pad and bandage were in place to absorb her flow, yet she could sense the great fleshy thing ready to thrust between her thighs; but this time she neither bent over in submission, nor let herself be thrown to the ground. Instead she straightened up and turned round to face him, eye to eye, for the first time.

'Stop it! Oi won't have 'ee, never again.'

After a moment's glaring hesitation he lunged at her, grabbing at her gown; that was when she began to scream and hit out with both fists, so that he had to duck and dodge.

'Hush up, Sukey, hush up, yer little fool,' he muttered, and, seizing her round the waist, he put a hand over her open mouth. She sunk her teeth hard into it, and he yelped.

'Damn 'ee, yer little cat, wha's up wi' ye? Shut yer mouth, can't 'ee, else folks'll hear!'

But now the rage and fury – and the bitter sorrow – pent up for four years burst forth in retribution, and Susan discovered a strength she had not known she possessed. She attacked him like a wild animal, kicking and punching, using her nails as claws and all the while spitting out a stream of defiance.

'No! No! Stop, Oi won't have 'ee, never! Stop, stop, Oi won't have 'ee – Oi hates 'ee!'

It took him completely unawares.

71

'Shut yer mouth, yer silly bitch – aaah! Keep yer noise down, will 'ee? Ouch! Damn 'ee!'

He put up his arms to shield himself, but she screamed and hit out all the more, raising her voice and planting a kick squarely into his hated male part. A howl of agony went up as he doubled over, clutching at himself and cursing while Susan turned and ran like the wind, away from the sight, the sound, the touch and the loathsome smell of him.

Never again, never again – and although she gasped and sobbed as she ran blindly on, she was conscious of a huge relief. For it had been an exhilarating experience, a striking back against what she had mutely endured for so long but had never in her heart accepted. It was over, finished, done! *She was free!*

Just for a split second she saw Jack's face above the bracken, his crossed eyes staring in two directions, his mouth agape. Then he disappeared. Susan could not guess what he might have seen, but knew he must have heard; only later did she realise that the boy had regularly stood guard as lookout.

When she reached Mill Lane, instead of following it towards Ash-Pit End, she turned up the steep track leading to the Bennetts' farm. Her pace slackened but she stumbled on until she reached the house and continued round to the back yard. The kitchen door was open, and Susan leaned against it, panting and dishevelled. Her new-found strength seemed to drain from her, and she raised imploring eyes to the farmer's wife, who stared at her in astonishment.

Sarah Bennett was having a trying time. In the middle of preparations for her daughter Sally's wedding to a young country attorney, two maidservants had left to better themselves in Belhampton, and

72

Bessie, her youngest, born after little Annie's death, was down with the measles. The men would be coming in for their supper, and Thomas would roar if it wasn't on the table. And now here was the Lucket girl with some dire message, by the look of it.

'What is it, Susan? What's happened?' she demanded sharply.

'Ha' ye got a place f'r a maid, Mrs Bennett?' begged Susan between gasps. 'Oi'll work f'r nothin' but a crust o' bread an' sleep on the floor, only don't send me away.'

In normal circumstances no Lucket would be allowed over the doorstep, but the girl looked ready to drop, and Sarah relented.

'Go wash your face in the pail by the scullery, and then come and stir this pot, Susan. And keep out o' the farmer's way, or he'll send you packing.'

Miss Marianne Bennett had appeared on Sophia's doorstep in the summer dusk, wrapped in a hooded cloak.

'I've got a note for you from poor Susan Lucket, Miss Glover,' she said importantly, handing over a torn piece of paper. 'My mother doesn't know I've come, but Susan begged me. She's in a bad way, Miss Glover,' she added, lowering her voice and clearly enjoying every moment of her secret errand.

'Merciful heaven, Marianne, what do you mean?' cried Sophia in alarm, forgetting to ask the girl to sit down as she studied the scrawled message.

Dear Mis Glover pleas for Love of God take Poly
who will be beat by Farther
I am at the Benets to be maid
Pleas safe her this night Susan Lucket

73

Sophia frowned and bit her lip. 'Has your mother taken Susan in as a maidservant, Marianne?' she asked.

'Yes, today, only an hour or two ago, and Susan asked me to come to you straightway, Miss Glover,' replied Marianne with a significant look. 'There are terrible stories told o' the Luckets, you know. They call the mother Mad Doll.'

She went on to give a fairly vivid account of Susan's sudden appearance at the farmhouse, and Sophia realised that whatever the reason for Susan's fear for her sister, there was no time to be lost.

'All right, Marianne. Go home and tell Susan that I'll go at once to Ash-Pit End and bring Polly back with me. Tell her that Polly will be safe under my roof tonight.'

Within twenty-four hours the news was all over Beversley that both the Lucket girls had left the Ash-Pits to work as maidservants, thanks to the intervention of Miss Glover following a family crisis. Susan was at the Bennetts' and Polly was in the laundry at Bever House, and they were thought to be very lucky to get such good places, considering where they came from. Bartlemy was a drunken sot and Doll Lucket had gone so wild and strange that neighbours avoided her and threatened their naughty children with a visit from Mad Doll.

Polly found herself the youngest maidservant at Bever House, with two blue stuff gowns, two aprons, two frilled caps and a pair of clogs. She slept on a straw pallet in a whitewashed room with three other girls, and hardly ever thought how this amazing change had come about, or why Miss Glover had so suddenly arrived at the Ash-Pits to remove her at the end of that day when Sukey had gone missing and Da was carried home dead drunk. That was all past, and Polly gave herself up to the happy present where her pretty, smiling face and coaxing ways made her the pet of the servants' hall.

Susan had to make sure that Mrs Bennett never regretted taking her on. She learned how to scrub the dairy, sweep and polish rooms, shake feather beds and empty chamber pots quickly and quietly, without stopping to chatter. What was drudgery to other servant girls was joyful freedom to Susan, and memories of her past life began to fade, returning only in terrifying dreams from which she awoke with sobbing relief. Her eyes brightened and lost their wary look; her complexion cleared, and even the dour farmer was heard to remark that 'Ye'd never know that wench was a Lucket.'

Miss Glover kneeled beside her bed and gave thanks for her part in rescuing the Lucket sisters from poverty and fear. She had put her pride in her pocket and begged Mrs Calthorpe to show her well-known benevolence by taking on a poor girl in the laundry, and Polly seemed to have settled well. And if there were some puzzling aspects about Susan's dramatic appeal on her sister's behalf, Sophia asked no questions but simply rejoiced at the great improvement in both their lives.

Widow Gibson sat at her cottage door in Quarry Lane and kept her own counsel. Poor Sukey Lucket had suffered for too long, but now she was safe, thank God, and so was that silly little creature Polly, though the old handywoman guessed that she would never know just how much she owed to her elder sister.

Part II: 1778

Maidservant

Chapter 8

The dawn chorus was already in full voice when Susan stole silently downstairs, avoiding the creaking stair fourth from the bottom. From the hallway she took the tiled passage to the dairy, cold and clean-smelling; gliding through, she lifted the latch and went out into the May morning. The sun was risen, but the air struck chill on her skin; a heavy dew lay on the grass, and she bent down to dabble her hands in it, rubbing her cheeks with the crystalline drops that would turn to vapour in the sun's rays.

She remembered how she and Polly had dabbled-in-the-dew as children, washing their faces as milkmaids did. Sadly she now saw little of her high-spirited sister, but knew that she was safe and happy at Bever House, quite a favourite of Mrs Martin, so Miss Glover assured her.

Susan breathed a long sigh of contentment as Great St Giles' clock struck five. It was her habit to rise before the rest of the household was stirring, to enjoy the beginning of the day in solitude. This was the hour when she could indulge her secret thoughts, and conjure up the face of Edward Calthorpe; she saw him smiling at her and heard his voice addressing her – as a child at the harvest supper, as a growing boy handing her tea in Miss Glover's parlour and seeking her out in Bennett's hayfield. There had been a few distant glimpses of him since, but when his schooldays at Winchester had ended he

79

had gone to Oxford, and she could hardly hope to meet him again. He was her ideal, as unattainable as a hero in a story, but Susan would never dream of sharing these memories with the other maidservants, who giggled and whispered about their sweethearts, especially when the outdoor hands came clumping into the kitchen. The farmer's son, Tom, was an awkward lad, who blushed when the saucy girls simpered at him, but Susan lowered her eyes and got on with serving. Her innocent daydreams set her firmly apart from the clumsy overtures of farm hands, the glances they gave her, sometimes shy, sometimes boldly direct; and she shrank from any actual contact as too close, too gross a reminder of the past.

Her modest demeanour endeared her to Mrs Bennett, who preferred her above any of the others to assist on baking days. It was during these times of working together that Sarah Bennett began to confide in the quiet girl about her worries over her eldest daughter.

''Tis four years since she was married to Percy Twydell, and miscarried after a year, poor girl. 'Twas a great grief to her, and then she went two years without conceiving, so feared she might have become barren,' sighed Sarah Bennett, mixing yeast with sugar to add to the earthenware bowl of flour. 'Now she expects to be confined some time in June, but I think she must be due sooner than she reckons, for she is such a great size. Poor Sally! I wish she could have Mrs Coulter as midwife, as I did, but they live at Pulhurst and that's too far for Mrs Coulter to go with her rheumaticks.'

'What's it about Mrs Twydell as worries ye, Mrs Bennett?' asked Susan. She was fascinated by the mysteries of childbearing, remembering how she had helped Doll at Joby's birth.

'Her ankles are swollen with the dropsy, and I fear she may have the mother's malady that some women get when with child,' replied the farmer's wife with a frown. 'I've heard Margaret Coulter tell o' women who started having fits when the child was due to be born, and one who died with her child. This swelling up is a first sign, and I wish that my Sally were here under my own roof. Percy's got no idea how to deal with her – you can't expect a man to know of women's matters.'

Susan hardly knew what to say to comfort her mistress, but it seemed that the Pulhurst midwife had recommended the young mother-to-be to rest as much as she could on a bed or couch, and to keep her swollen legs raised.

'She's told Sally to take rhubarb to keep her bowel open and reduce the fluid in her body,' said Mrs Bennett, shaking her head doubtfully. 'I declare I shall not have a full night's sleep until she be safely delivered.'

'Maybe ye worry overmuch, Mrs Bennett, bein' her mother,' said Susan gently. 'In a week or two 'twill all be over, an' the pains forgot, I dare say – an' ye'll have a baby to hold an' hush!'

'I pray that you be proved right, Susan. The trouble is that my Sally's always been one to worry about herself, and we all fussed over her when she miscarried. Perhaps she needed firmer handling, though it breaks my heart to see her crying.'

Mrs Bennett wiped her eyes on a corner of her apron, and Susan stopped kneading dough for a moment.

'Why don't ye go an' visit her this afternoon, Mrs

Bennett? Me an' Bet can see to the chickens an' get the men's supper in the pot. Ye could take Bessie with ye to cheer her sister!'

'You're a good girl, Susan,' replied the anxious mother gratefully. 'You're right, I'll get young Tom to drive me over to Pulhurst in the three-seater. But I'll leave Bessie here, for 'twill be women's talk, and not for little ears.'

Sophia Glover had been visiting at the parsonage of Little St Giles when she saw Mrs Bennett setting off for Pulhurst. It gave her an opportunity to call at the farmhouse in the hope of having a few words with Susan.

'I'm that glad to see ye, Miss Glover! Mrs Bennett be gone to visit her daughter at Pulhurst, Miss Marianne has walked out with another young lady, and Bessie is working on her sampler.'

After duly admiring Bessie's embroidery stitches, Sophia sat down with Susan in the kitchen, and was told of Mrs Bennett's fears for her daughter.

' 'Tis a pity that Mrs Coulter cannot attend her, but she has become sadly crippled by the hip-gout and cannot travel any distance to a confinement,' said Sophia, who was becoming increasingly concerned for Beversley's only midwife. 'Mr Turnbull has tried various remedies and poultices, but nothing gives her ease from the pain for more than an hour.'

'I'm sorry to hear on't, Miss Glover. And ha' ye seen Polly?' asked Susan eagerly.

Sophia smiled. 'It seems that your sister has a way of breaking the hearts of the menservants without losing the friendship of the maids at Bever House! Why, she has even won over that grim-faced old coachman Jude, who let her take the reins of the gig

82

and drive it round the stable-yard. Mrs Martin could hardly believe her eyes!'

Susan clasped her hands together. 'Oh, can't I just *see* her, my saucy little Poll! She'll be lookin' out to be Harvest Queen, I dare say.'

Sophia's smile vanished. 'I doubt there'll be any harvest celebration this year, Susan. This wretched war against our American colonies is taking its toll, and land taxes are going up to pay for it. My cousin Calthorpe is feeling the pinch.'

Susan had managed to keep up with the progress of the war through reading the *Hampshire Chronicle* when the farmer had finished with it. She read it aloud to the other house servants, and was under the impression that the war was going well.

''Tis said that the army and navy'll soon get the better o' the rebels, Miss Glover.'

'Yes, that's what Dr Gravett says, but Squire Hansford is not so certain, and maybe he has better knowledge, with his son in the navy,' replied Sophia, lowering her soft blue eyes. 'This war has already lasted three years, and caused great divisions in Parliament, especially now that France has declared its support for the Americans.'

'And does the squire fear for his son?' asked Susan, recalling the tall, fair young midshipman who was a close friend of the Calthorpe brothers.

'Henry's parents cannot help but fear for a son on active service in time of war,' answered Sophia gravely, and Susan was suddenly struck by an alarming thought.

'But the war'll be over afore Master Edward be done with . . .' she began, then hesitated, unable to find the right words.

'My cousin Edward has another year yet at

Oxford,' answered Sophia, not adding that Osmond had lately been sent down without obtaining a degree, to the dismay of his mother and anger of his father. 'It's likely that the war will be finished by then, one way or another. There are those in Parliament who would grant the colonies their independence. But, Susan, there is something else I must tell you, something much closer to home. This business of parish relief—'

Susan stiffened immediately. 'I've heard somethin' o' the matter, Miss Glover, but it don't concern me. If they – if the Luckets want parish relief, they must ask for't.'

'They – your parents have done so, Susan, and must attend Divine Service at Great St Giles in order to receive it from Dr Gravett. That will be on the first Sunday of next month, so I'll be glad to have your company at Little St Giles on that day.'

Susan knew that her friend wanted to save her from witnessing her family's humiliation.

'That's good o' you, Miss Glover, but it'll be up to Mrs Bennett. She likes all the house servants to go to church along o' her an' the farmer an' – oh, *heavens*!'

'Why, Susan, what is it? What's the matter?'

'The Calthorpes'll all be there at Great St Giles, an' their servants! Oh, poor Polly!'

Susan's sudden wail would have been almost comical except for her distress, and Sophia Glover was impressed yet again by this girl's care for her younger sister – and her complete indifference to her parents. Susan had never once visited Ash-Pit End, though she had seen her brother Joby, who worked at the blacksmith's forge, holding horses, fetching fuel and doing whatever jobs a sturdy ten-year-old boy could find in that place of flying sparks and kicking hoofs.

Sophia Glover personally doubted whether careless little Polly would be that much affected by seeing her parents held up as a public example of improvidence, but she refrained from saying this to Susan, and simply pointed out that the dreaded day would come and go like any other day, and be forgotten by Polly, who had so many happier distractions.

Now past his fiftieth year, Mr Calthorpe had been looking forward to handing over some of his duties to his elder son, and it seemed that the time had come with unexpected suddenness. He spoke earnestly to Osmond as they walked round the Bever estate, his heart responding as always to this land in his care: the trees shimmering in their tender new foliage, the meadows gleaming green and gold with cowslips. In the hedgerows bloomed wild irises and cascading honeysuckle, purple vetch and red campion, jewels of colour against the white froth of may blossom. Fields, woodland and water teemed with a new generation of wildlife – scampering, burrowing, flying and swimming.

'See that little red squirrel, Osmond, how he runs up the tree and looks so boldly at us? Is there anything fairer than our Hampshire countryside in spring?'

Osmond's attention was certainly engaged, but not with the landscape.

'You will need time to learn to hold the reins, Osmond, but you will have more leisure than when I was thrown headlong into landownership, already a married man with a family. I've been well served by an excellent bailiff and agent, but they're getting on in years, as I am. When this wasteful war is over, there must be some changes. We should look into the new methods of crop-growing, take on more staff – Osmond? Have I your attention?'

Calthorpe stopped in his tracks and looked hard at the handsome young man beside him.

'Father, is not that a most delightful picture, the little maid heading our way in her blue gown and cap? She seems to be bringing a message for us.'

Mr Calthorpe frowned. 'You had better watch your step, Osmond, and attend more to your duties than to the sort of distractions that earned you disgrace at your college.'

'Disgrace is a strong word, Father, considering how some of the Fellows carried on,' replied Osmond lightly. 'If you had seen the old chaplain, too drunk to take Divine Service, and the liberties taken by some of the tutors, you might suspect I'd been made a scapegoat for others more deserving of blame.'

Mr Calthorpe checked the rebuke on his lips as Polly Lucket approached them, her pretty face aglow and her dark hair escaping from under her frilled cap. She knew that she must not speak to the gentlemen unless they first spoke to her, but she dropped a curtsy.

'Have you a message for me, maid?' asked Calthorpe briskly.

'Good day to 'ee, sir – and sir. Oi be takin' a letter to Squire Hansford's, sir.'

'Indeed? Then be on your way, and do not loiter.'

Calthorpe dismissed her with a curt nod, but saw the smiles that passed between her and his son, and the way Osmond's hand darted out to pat her little bottom. Her cap askew, she skipped down the track, checking that Miss Caroline's letter to Miss Rosa was still safely tucked into her bodice. Her heart beat faster at the way Mr Osmond's bold blue eyes had looked upon her. Only that morning she had carried his newly pressed linen up from the laundry, though she had not got as far as his bedchamber because that queer-looking Mrs Ferris had taken it from her. Polly giggled to herself. He wouldn't get many smiles from that old black crow!

Mr Calthorpe noted his son's appraising look at the maid's retreating figure, and faced the fact that Osmond presented a problem. Something would have to be done without delay to instil some sense of responsibility into him.

But *what*? He was no longer a boy, but a strongly built man of almost twenty-two. He could not be thrashed and sent to his room on bread and water, nor could he be dispatched to the rectory for a homily from Dr Gravett. How in God's name was a father to discipline a self-willed son who had always been allowed to have his own way?

There was a possible answer, Calthorpe knew.

In Belhampton these days a number of military men were billeted on households and inns. They paraded round the town in their red coats and tall peak-brimmed hats, many of them new officers hastily trained to join Generals Carleton and Howe in a new, incisive drive against that upstart Washington.

Calthorpe knew that Gertrude would become hysterical at the very thought of Osmond in the army, perhaps leading a company of men against the colonial rebels on their own soil, so unimaginably far away. He could already hear her protests, but he would have to point out that it could be the making of their son, who might return as a hero with a completely changed attitude to life.

Or he might . . .

Calthorpe set his mouth in a determinedly straight line. He needed to be proud of his son, the heir to Bever House.

Edward returned from Oxford at the beginning of June, to be warmly embraced by his father. Two years of college life had brought about changes: his face was thinner, with a sharper look in his dark blue eyes that warned off triflers and mockers. He was not inclined to speak of his experiences in any detail, nor would he be sounded on his brother's escapades.

'If he is to be an army officer, Father, his college career will be quite forgotten in the dangers he must face.'

Mr Calthorpe could only nod in sombre agreement, and their talk turned to village matters.

'Those applying for parish relief are to attend Divine Service at Great St Giles on Sunday next,' said Calthorpe, turning down his mouth. 'No doubt Dr Gravett will pillory them in his sermon, and the church will be packed full for the entertainment.'

Edward frowned, having never forgotten his encounter with the family from the Ash-Pits, and he wondered if they – if *she* would be among those arraigned before the congregation.

Oxford had taught him a great deal, and not only about the classics. He had been quickly disillusioned about some aspects of undergraduate life, notably the sheer number of bottles consumed by the young bloods, and the resulting disorder. He had become known as Neddy Pokerface, the subject of many bawdy suggestions, loudly expressed. When one night he was set upon by a gang of drunken students who tried to strip off his clothes and force him into bed with a naked woman from the town, he had fought back with unexpected ferocity, landing punches in faces and kicks in groins that had given his assailants a new respect for Pokerface.

Nevertheless, the incident had sharpened Edward's awareness of his young body's needs and the ideal of womanhood that he secretly cherished. A persistent memory of two large grey eyes in a sweet, heart-shaped face had remained with him over the years, and he believed that only in Beversley would he find the girl of his dreams.

Chapter 9

Susan was in an agony of indecision.

The Bennetts had left for Great St Giles, accompanied by all the servants except herself and Bet, who had been told to stay behind and turn the roasting-spit to make sure that the joint was evenly cooked. Susan knew this to be Mrs Bennett's way of sparing her the sight of the applicants for parish relief, with Mad Doll as the main attraction, and she was grateful because she had been dreading this day.

But she was worried about Polly, who might be shamed and ridiculed because of her family. Their mother had become a byword in Beversley, and that was another thing: ought Susan to feel some concern, some pity even, towards the unhappy woman who had borne her? While she shrank from even a distant glimpse of Bartlemy, she could not dismiss her mother and brothers so completely. In short, she needed to know the outcome of today's business, and to be on hand if her sister needed her.

In twenty minutes Matins was due to begin. Susan made up her mind.

'Bide here an' watch the meat, Bet, while I go up to church,' she said, pulling off her apron and taking her bonnet down from its peg in the passage.

'But missus said we was to—'

'I know, but I ha' to be there,' muttered Susan, tying her bonnet strings. 'I'll slip in at the back where

I won't be seen, an' get out afore it ends. I got to be there, Bet.'

'Missus be sure to see ye!' warned the maid, aghast at such disobedience, but Susan was already hurrying down the track.

From Bennett's Lane she took the path beside the paddock field to the bridge; crossing it she turned up towards the churchyard and a small door that opened into the south transept. She entered with bowed head, her face hidden by the calico bonnet, and sat down in a pew at the very back.

At once her whole body tensed at the sight of her parents and brothers seated behind the ancient stone font. Further forward were the Bennetts, and further still were the raised stalls at right angles to the carved rood-screen that separated nave from chancel; here the Calthorpe and Hansford families sat facing each other.

Susan lowered her head and silently mouthed the Lord's Prayer.

Widow Gibson had deserted Little St Giles this morning. With Mad Doll Lucket in the congregation anything could happen, and you never knew, a body might be needed if there was any trouble. As well as the Luckets lined up in the dock of the undeserving poor, the handywoman's sharp eyes took in Susan kneeling in her back pew, and she clicked her tongue against her remaining teeth. What was Sarah Bennett thinking of? Anybody with a heart would have locked that poor girl up until Divine Service was over. She looked towards the north transept and picked out the younger sister trying to hide herself among the Bever House retinue, a pretty little thing but without Sukey's sense. And Lord save us, there was to be music, as if the service wouldn't be long enough! Two fiddles and the shepherd's flute, along with three braying men and two warbling ploughboys to lead the singing: any minute now the steeple clock would strike eleven, and they'd all blare forth.

Squire Hansford favourably compared his absent sailor son with the Calthorpe heir, whose handsome face had a bloated look this morning. Rosa's smiles clearly made less impression on Osmond than the row of coy maidservants seated on their bench like birds on a perch, and the squire privately hoped that his daughter's dreams would come to nothing.

Gertrude Calthorpe's eyes rested fondly on her elder son. Let the silly Hansford girl make sheep's eyes at him if she liked! Both families expected Henry and Selina to make an eventual match, for they showed every sign of being madly in love, but Osmond was destined for something better.

She turned to observe the strangers from Lower Beversley.

'Just look at that odd woman,' she whispered to her husband. 'And that boy's villainous squint. *What a row of wretches!*'

Mr Calthorpe did not answer at once. He had suddenly made a connection in his mind.

'Wasn't there a clever older girl in that family, that Sophia sent to Mrs Bryers' school?' he asked.

Gertrude shrugged in irritation at the mention of the girl from the Ash-Pits who had so outshone her own daughters at reading and writing.

'Possibly so, Osmond. In fact, I have another daughter of theirs as maidservant – see, over there? Now do not scold me, for I took pity on her.'

92

Calthorpe identified the curly-haired maid as the one who had taken his son's fancy, and nodded his approval.

'That was well done, my love, an act of Christian charity.'

She smiled coolly. 'Thank you, Osmond. One does not always trumpet one's charitable deeds to the world, as some do.'

Polly's pink cheeks and fluttering eyelashes assured Osmond of his disturbing effect on her. Little temptress! He looked forward to a leisurely pursuit of Polly, culminating in capture and ultimate possession. He'd show her! The very thought of her softness aroused his hardness. Life in Beversley need not be such a bore after all.

Edward tried not to look at the Luckets, having made certain that Susan was not with them, yet his head turned again towards that poor woman whose dull eyes stared unseeingly into space while her restless hands clawed at a black leather-bound prayer book she had picked up, though she could not read.

Edward suddenly tensed, and his heart leaped. Who was that slight figure sitting in shadow at the back of the church, her head bowed and her face hidden by her bonnet? She was dressed in the plain calico gown of a maidservant, and she was – was she . . .?

He willed her to look up and meet his eyes.

And she did. Yes, she was Susan, little Susan. The large grey eyes met his for a brief moment and then looked down again.

Edward experienced a tremor, an increase in his heartbeat. He saw again a cheerful, ragged little girl defending Goody Firkin; a serious-faced child with a thirst for knowledge, almost trampled underfoot by his horse; a charity child outstripping her betters at school; a girl with a shadow in her eyes, glimpsed in the fields at haymaking and harvest time.

And now she was here again, older, taller, her body rounded into a woman's shape. Was it possible that those wretched supplicants for parish relief were her family? Yes, he recognised them, the surly man, the cross-eyed boy – and that poor lost-looking soul was her mother, incredible as it seemed. Edward longed above everything to help Susan, to assist her and relieve her of anxiety in any way he could.

As Susan silently repeated the words of the 'Our Father', she sensed an unspoken command, and against her will she raised her eyes to the Calthorpe stall and the dark blue gaze fixed intently upon her. She recognised Edward, the younger son now grown to manhood, strong and ruddy-complexioned. He was smiling, and she knew it was for her alone. Just for a moment their eyes met, then Susan hastily lowered her head for shame: he too would witness the public spectacle this morning.

When Dr Gravett passed the Luckets' pew on his dignified progress up the aisle, the sour smell of unwashed flesh assailed his nostrils, and he frowned in revulsion; the verger should have warned him. Another time the applicants would have to wait outside in the porch. He glared at the sexton, who gave the signal for fiddles, flutes and voices to begin.

'Let us, with a gladsome mind,
praise the Lord, for He is kind.
For His mercies ay endure,
ever faithful, ever sure!'

94

The rector cut them short after four verses, and, taking his place at the lectern, began to intone Morning Prayer. The General Confession, Absolution, Lord's Prayer, Versicles and Responses followed in brisk succession, and the rector settled into his high-backed chair to endure the sung Venite and Te Deum. He then read the parable of the talents from St Matthew's Gospel, extending it to include the preceding parable of the wise and foolish virgins, as not inappropriate for the occasion. As the people stood for the Creed, he purposefully ascended to the carved oak pulpit and cleared his throat. It was time at last for the main business of the morning.

'"For unto every one that hath shall be given, and he shall have abundance: but from him that hath not shall be taken away even that which he hath."'

He paused and closed the book. 'Three servants were each given a sum of money by their master. An unequal amount, representing the unequal share we each receive of this world's goods.' He looked around the church. All eyes were upon him. 'It is not the will of the Almighty that we should all start out with the same inheritance, and even if that were the case, a few years would bring about inequality. The hard-working and thrifty would prosper while the shiftless and idle would spend what they had and be reduced to poverty.' He took a breath, and his voice deepened into judgemental sternness. 'And there are those present here this morning who have squandered their money in habits of idleness and intemperance. They must surely feel a sense of shame.'

Complete silence had fallen on the congregation, and some heads turned towards the malodorous strangers from Lower Beversley.

Edward looked down the length of the nave to where Susan sat with bowed head, and anger rose within him. Must she always suffer for being born a Lucket?

Worse was to come.

'It is my unhappy duty this morning to point out an example – and likewise a warning – of the dire consequences of improvidence,' the rector continued. 'I take no pleasure in doing so, I assure you, but rather sorrow. May we all heed and learn from the fate of those who have come to beg from the prudent and provident this morning.'

Sighs and shivers passed over the assembly like a chill wind, and feet shuffled uncomfortably. The four Luckets sat dumbly in their pew behind the font like a row of miscreants in the stocks. Bartlemy lowered his black head, but Dolly continued to stare straight in front. Joby gazed at the floor, and Jack might have been looking anywhere.

Polly shrank back between her companions on the maids' bench. Osmond thought that her painful blushes were due to his bold appraisal of her, and his desire increased.

Edward saw Susan's head drop still lower, and he seethed with rage; how much longer was she to be tortured by this pompous old fool?

The harangue went on for a further half-hour before the steeple clock struck twelve and the rector stepped down, having ordered the applicants to stay behind after the service to receive an agreed amount from the church wardens. He raised his hand in the final blessing, and the singers began Psalm 100. The worshippers scraped their feet, and the rector commenced his stately walk down the aisle. Ignoring the row of beggars, he lifted his heavy chin above his swathed cravat, and looked straight ahead.

Which is why he did not see the warning glare in Doll Lucket's eyes as she slowly raised her right hand, clutching the prayer book. Drawing back her arm like a bowman taking aim, she threw the black leather-bound missile at the rector's head with all her strength as he passed. It caught him on the left temple, landing with a force that would have done credit to the leather-covered ball that the men whacked with their bats on the green.

The rector's yelp of surprise and pain went unheard, drowned by an unearthly shriek from Doll. She opened her mouth and howled like an animal, again and again, building up a blood-curdling wall of sound. Her bony frame shook with the effort, her face was hideously contorted, and her upraised hands were clenched.

The people stood motionless, unable to focus their thoughts, though one or two superstitious souls fell to their knees in terror that an unclean spirit had got into the Lord's house.

For it was a howl of the doomed, the damned, the trapped, a sound of fury and without hope. Nobody who heard Doll that Sunday morning ever forgot her helpless despair, and when at last men began to shout and women to wail, the general uproar came as a relief, a sound of familiar human voices – frightened voices maybe, but not demented. Not like the madwoman.

The wordless yells ceased at last when Doll's voice cracked and hoarsened; she could protest no more, and collapsed in a heap on the floor behind the font.

Nothing that Susan had imagined had been half as bad as this. Though trembling in every part, she forced herself to rise and go towards the font, though as she neared Bartlemy she stopped and drew back. Glancing to where Polly was sitting, she could not see her sister, and stood helplessly where she was, unable to focus on any course of action.

The situation was saved by Widow Gibson, who came bustling up with an unstoppered dark bottle of pungent-smelling salts, which she held under Doll's nose. She then turned on Bartlemy.

'What be the matter wi' ye, man? Move yer carcass and get them boys outside, can't 'ee?'

With his departure Susan could move to help her mother, and together she and Mrs Gibson hauled the half-fainting Doll up off the floor and laid her along a pew.

Dr Gravett was staggering in the aisle, clutching at his head as a thin trickle of blood ran down on to his neckcloth. The sexton recollected his duty and helped the rector into the vestry, followed by Mr Turnbull, who was thankful to leave the care of Mad Doll to the handywoman.

Mr Calthorpe, Justice of the Peace, stood up in his stall. Raising his voice, he ordered the church to be cleared forthwith, and beckoned to his agent.

'That woman must be put under restraint. Edward, take care of your mother and sisters.'

The two men strode down the aisle towards the group gathering round Dolly, and Edward followed close behind them, thinking only of Susan.

'She must be charged with common assault and taken to Belhampton Gaol straight away,' announced Calthorpe.

'Gaol? Oh, *no*!' cried Susan, her hand going involuntarily to her throat.

To Calthorpe's surprise, Edward added his voice to hers.

'Show mercy, sir, and let her be taken to the House of Industry, not prison – please, Father!'

Calthorpe stared, not displeased by his son's compassion.

'Very well, but she must be taken there at once. Have the carrier summoned to take her on his cart.'

Widow Gibson seemed the obvious choice of attendant to accompany Doll on the open cart, and the bailiff was bidden to sit beside carrier Dick – there was only one Dick now, the father being dead – in case assistance was needed. As the cart rolled away from the church gate the old handywoman beamed at the onlookers: it was her moment of glory.

And so Doll Lucket travelled to her last home, the place she would never leave.

The rector was carried home in his own phaeton with Miss Gravett, suitably bandaged and reassured that he was in no danger of rabies. It was even whispered by some that he had got what he deserved.

After the congregation had departed to marvel on the morning's events over roast meat, Susan realised that Polly had slunk away with the Bever House servants, and might not even have seen her sister in the church. Susan was left standing alone in the porch, leaning her aching head against the cool stone and wondering what she should do. Farmer Bennett had stormed out during the uproar, taking his wife and family with him.

'There's to be no more truck with any o' them Luckets,' he ordered, and when Marianne tearfully pleaded on Susan's behalf he told her to shut her mouth and stop mooing.

The steeple clock struck one. Miss Glover should have returned from Little St Giles by now, and

Susan's only hope was to beg for lodging at her cottage until another maidservant's place could be found, perhaps somewhere away from Beversley. In trying to do her duty that morning, she had lost her livelihood, the very roof over her head. It was so unjust! Feeling weak and drained by the ordeal, she sank down on the low stone bench and buried her face in her hands.

She did not notice the movement at the entrance to the sunlit porch, but a light touch on her shoulder made her look up with a start.

'Susan! I did not know that you were still here,' Edward began, hesitating when he saw her mournful eyes, hastily lowered. 'I beg your pardon – Miss Lucket. Your mother will be looked after at the – by the . . .'

Words deserted him as he beheld this girl at close quarters, alone with him after all the hubbub; and the tender concern that she glimpsed in those intense dark blue eyes finally unlocked Susan's pent-up emotion. She could no longer hold back the tears she had kept in check until now.

The truth was that his kindly meant reassurance about her mother underlined her lack of daughterly love; there was even a kind of relief in knowing that Mad Doll would be safely out of the way. Was this her punishment for not loving the mother who had betrayed her? Homelessness and hunger?

Edward's reaction was mixed. Sorry as he was to see her distress, it was his happy chance to comfort her, and seating himself beside her on the weathered stone, he put a tentative arm around her, gently drawing her head on to his shoulder.

'Susan – sweet Susan, don't cry. I can't bear to see you unhappy.'

This must surely be a dream! *Edward Calthorpe* here beside her, holding her close against him and speaking kindly as a brother might. What a difference it made! Strength seemed to flow from his encircling arm; the very feel of his light jacket, unbuttoned on a summer's day, and the softness of his lawn shirt proved that he was real. She breathed in his wholesome maleness, a blend of healthy warm skin and hair that was sweetly pleasing to her senses, not like — but no! She must not let *that* besmirch such a beautiful moment as this.

Not a breeze stirred in the deserted churchyard. The shady yews filled the air with their aroma, and there was no sound but the drowsy hum of insects among the seeding grass-heads. Together they watched as a pair of white butterflies circled round each other before coming down to alight on a lichened headstone warmed by the June sun. Susan and Edward sat motionless, neither daring to break the spell by a word or movement; their very breath was soundless, though Susan sensed the rise and fall of Edward's chest as she leaned lightly against his shoulder. She closed her eyes. Oh, that time might stand still and let this moment blend with eternity . . .

At length he gently withdrew his arm from her shoulders.

'Let me offer you assistance to get home, Miss Lucket.'

She had to tell him.

'I ha' nowhere to go, sir. I been working at the Bennetts' these four years gone, but now they won't have me. I – I was told to stay out o' church this mornin', but I disobeyed Mrs Bennett and went.'

He nodded, unsurprised. 'I see, Susan. You disobeyed out of loyalty to your family. So do you want to return to them now?'

'Where, sir, the Ash-Pits? Never, I'd die first. That be no home o' mine.'

Startled by the emphasis of her words, he thought of Bartlemy's surly scowl, and hastened to reassure her.

'Then let me accompany you back to the Bennetts' farm, and I'll speak to Thomas Bennett.'

She wiped her eyes with the back of her hand.

'That'ud be very good o' ye, sir,' she whispered, wondering how much he knew of the farmer's sullen temper.

'Come, then, give me your arm and we'll walk over there. And you must call me Edward, for I want to be your true friend, Susan.'

They stood up, and she smoothed her hands over her creased gown. Her bonnet strings were unloosed, and it slipped down over the back of her head. Edward bent down to pick it up, replacing it on her head and coaxing a few wayward strands of hair back under it. Smiling, he tied the strings in a bow under her chin, and she looked up in blushing surprise, unused to such brotherly kindness; and he was also entirely respectful to her as a woman, which gave her an assurance of perfect safety.

They walked out of the churchyard and across the green. There was nobody in sight as they crossed the bridge and took the path beside the paddock field where a few horses grazed. When they came to a gap in the hedge with a stile, he asked if she would like to walk through the field; nimbly he vaulted the stile and held out his hand to assist her. She carefully raised the skirt of her gown as she mounted the horizontal bar and stepped over the top one, looking down at his laughing face.

'Go on, Susan, jump – I'm here to catch you!'

So she flung herself forward, her gown flying out as she fell into his outstretched arms. There was a strange exhilaration in being caught and clasped against him, and she could not help but respond to his loving look. With him at her side the afternoon was transformed into a shimmering idyll of cloudless blue sky and lush green pasture from which the horrors of the morning receded. Was she really here, walking with Edward Calthorpe, exchanging shy, wordless glances? It seemed unbelievable, yet there was no doubt of his liking for her. Past and future were forgotten: never had she been so happy as at this present moment.

The harsh cry of a corncrake close at hand made them both start, and Edward drew her towards him.

'The corncrake is no great singer, is she, Susan? Yet today I find her sweeter than any nightingale because I hear her with you beside me.'

They stood together in the middle of the field, and Edward took hold of her hand and looked deeply into her grey eyes, questioning, searching: he longed to kiss her.

But the moment was lost.

Looking beyond his shoulder Susan stiffened at the sight of the huddle of the Ash-Pits; she thought she saw a black figure lounging in the sun, a blot against the green. And there were her young brothers, idle Jack and wiry Joby, left motherless and cut off from their sisters by the dark shadow that lurked nearby.

Susan gasped in dismay and drew back from Edward. He turned his head to see what had caught her attention, but could see nothing but the tall hedgerow and the lane beyond.

'Dear Susan, what troubles you? Have I said something untoward?' he asked anxiously.

''Tis no fault o' yourn, sir,' she muttered, turning away. ''Tis just – my mother an' everything.'

For there were things he must never hear, never know about. The very thought of him knowing was too horrible to imagine. But the spell was broken, the idyll dissolved; when he reached for her hand again she began to walk ahead.

'Dear Susan, forgive me. Of course you are grieved for your poor mother,' he said, increasing his pace to keep up with hers. 'Only let me be your friend and do what I can to help you. I'll ride over to the House of Industry and bring you news of her, take messages—'

''Tis good o' ye, sir, but there be no need – thank ye.'

She marched on, struggling with angry tears at this spoiling of a perfect afternoon; she saw the shadow stretching down the years, and could not foresee a time when she would ever be truly free from the taint of it.

When they had ascended the track up to the Bennetts' farmhouse they found the front door open and heard the sound of voices within. In response to Edward's pull on the bell rope they were confronted by a gaping Bet, who shook her head at Susan and dropped a clumsy curtsy to young Mr Calthorpe.

'Is it possible to see Farmer Bennett or Mrs Bennett?' he asked politely.

'Bide 'ee here while I fetches missus,' answered Bet, adding aside to Susan. ''Tis all up an' down here. Young missus ha' come over from Pulhurst wi'out warnin', an' her such a size as 'ee never saw!'

Mrs Bennett stepped into the hall looking

harassed, and in no mood to curtsy to Gertrude Calthorpe's younger son. Her first thought on seeing her disobedient maidservant was one of relief.

'Good day to you, Mrs Bennett,' began Edward. 'I have returned Susan Lucket in the hope that you may be prepared to overlook her – er—'

The farmer's wife cut in sharply. 'I fear that my husband is set against the whole family after what happened this morning, Master Calthorpe and, his temper being hot, there'd be little to gain by talking until he be cooled somewhat.'

She then turned to Susan, and saw that she had been crying. The girl was also dusty and tired – and her stomach must be empty, thought Mrs Bennett; and at once her need of a sensible maidservant over-rode all other considerations, including her husband.

'My Sally be here, and she'll stay until she's delivered,' she told Susan. 'Young Percy's out o' his mind with worry, for she's sadly swollen with the dropsy and weeps all the time. There'll be no peace till the child's born, that's for sure.'

Susan immediately understood.

'Oh, Mrs Bennett, I could help ye take care o' her!'

'That you can, Susan, none better. I hold naught against you on account o' your relations, but the less the farmer sees o' you, the better. We must make up a bed for Sally in Marianne's room – young madam'll have to go into the smaller one next to it. Stay upstairs till things have settled a bit, and I'll get Bet to bring you up some bread and cold meat.'

Susan nodded, pulling off her bonnet and pre-paring to start work at once. She glanced gratefully at Edward, whose duty had been done. He bowed to Mrs Bennett and said he hoped for early news of the safe arrival of a grandchild. With a last loving look at

Susan he took his leave, and went home to face his mother's reproaches and his sisters' cold contempt.

Lying on her attic mattress that night beside a snoring Bet, Susan relived the events of the day. She thought of Doll, now confined to the place she had always dreaded, and of the precarious lives of the boys. She thanked heaven that Polly at least was in a good place.

But it was Edward, her rescuer and champion, who returned again and again to her mind; so far above her, yet he treated her with the courtesy due to a real lady. She recalled his gentle touch, his encircling arm, his clean wholesomeness; and she remembered the way his eyes had lingered on her face.

But then a foul shadow had intervened to spoil their innocent happiness. The secret shame endured for so long had clouded Susan's attitude towards men, and she shrank in dread from that gross coupling that took place between male and female. What she felt towards Edward Calthorpe was almost the same kind of distant devotion that she felt for her Lord and Saviour Who, Miss Glover said, should be loved above all others.

Yet one thing she knew for certain: whatever the future might hold, the memory of this glorious afternoon in Edward's company would remain, to relive and rejoice over in her dreams. It could never be taken away from her.

Chapter 10

As she helped her mistress to prepare the bed-chamber where Mrs Twydell would give birth, Susan remembered that she had been taken on as maidservant at the time of this daughter's wedding; now it was the turmoil of Sally's approaching delivery that had saved her from dismissal. She felt a special sense of commitment towards the young matron, and looked forward eagerly to the birthing, though it soon became clear that she would have new and exacting duties in connection with it.

When Mr Twydell brought his wife home to her mother because he could no longer cope with her tears and peevishness, Mrs Bennett's anxiety was offset by relief at having Sally under her own roof. Mrs Coulter, who had delivered all five of Sarah's children, was now engaged to deliver the first grand-child, thought to be due in mid-June, though Sally's size suggested that her pains could start at any time. At the end of a week there was no sign of travail, though poor Sally had a catalogue of discomforts and seemed to be swelling before their eyes. Marianne proved quite unsuitable as a nurse, and was dismissed in favour of Susan's quiet and capable presence in the sickroom, where Sally moped with her feet raised on a pillow and her wedding ring hanging on a chain around her neck because her fingers had become as puffy as her face and ankles.

'Oh, I'm that fatigued, Susan, in this heat,' she

moaned. 'My gown's too tight – my slippers won't fit
... Oh, pray fetch my mother. I feel a tightness round
the child's head. Oh, why am I suffering so?
Something must be wrong, I know it!'

'Courage, Sally,' Mrs Bennett would entreat her
several times a day. 'This child will be born in due
time, like any other.'

Sally responded with a loud belch of wind from
her displaced stomach, and bewailed her bloated
appearance.

'Percy's coming over this evening, and I can't bear
for him to see me like this! I was happy when I first
began to show the child, but now my belly has grown
so large that I can hardly sit on the chamber pot –
careful, Susan, hold on to me or I shall wet on the
floor. Oh God, I shall die before the child be born. I'm
sure o' it, this will end in death!'

Raspberry leaf infusions were ordered, and broths
and jellies made from calves' feet; but Sally resisted
most of Susan's coaxing, and pushed the dishes
fretfully aside.

'You must think me a thankless creature, but I feel
so *ill*,' she wept. Most of the time she stayed in her
room, resting or padding around in an ungainly
manner, very different from the proud young bride
of four years ago. Susan soothed her as well as she
could, bathing her blotchy face in cool well water and
waving a big feather fan lent by Marianne.

When Widow Gibson called at the back door with
a poultice made from boiling the root of the mother-
wort, Mrs Coulter dismissed her impatiently, and
suggested gentle out-of-door exercise, so in the
cooler air of evening Sally was taken outside and
walked along a short garden path, supported by her
mother and Susan.

'Help me! Hold on to me, I can't move for the cramp in my leg – it's *agony*!' she cried after a few steps, and the three of them stood helplessly in the middle of the path. The farmer had to be summoned to carry his daughter indoors, and he vented his dissatisfaction on Mrs Coulter.

'I don't know why Sally makes such heavy weather o't,' he grumbled. 'Her mother was never in such a case as this.'

'Mrs Twydell has the dropsy, and that makes it harder for her,' answered the midwife defensively.

'Then get on wi' what ye're paid to do, woman, for Sally says it be nigh on ten months since—' He broke off for the sake of propriety.

'That midwife be now too old for such work as hers,' he muttered to his wife.

The days dragged by to midsummer. When Sally started complaining of a blinding headache Mrs Coulter ordered her to lie flat on the bed with the curtains drawn; not a word was to be spoken above a whisper in the room. Mrs Bennett was at her wits' end, and Susan realised it was essential that she at least should stay calm.

One afternoon Marianne peeped round the bedroom door.

'Susan!' she whispered with a meaning look. 'Who d'ye suppose has just called on us?'

'Hush, Miss Marianne, y'r sister ha' just fallen into a doze. I'll come out.'

In the passage she found Marianne full of girlish flutter.

''Twas Mr Edward Calthorpe, Susan, with an invitation to a midsummer party and picnic by the lake in Wychell Forest – well, it *was* to be midsummer, but they have to wait on Mr Henry

Hansford, who's still away at sea. There'll be carriages and cold provisions and a tent to sit in—'

'Ssh!' Susan glanced toward the bedroom. 'That be nothin' to do wi' me, Miss Marianne. I must go back to y'r sister.'

'No, wait, Susan, that isn't all,' went on Marianne excitedly. 'He asked specially for you, and gave me his compliments to pass on. Oh, my! Such a gentleman, and such polite manners!'

Susan stared. The name of Edward Calthorpe had the power to make her heart leap, even during this worrying time; and to think he had called and asked after her . . .

'Don't you want to hear his message, Susan? He said to tell you that he and Parson Smart rode over to the House of Industry last week and saw Mad D— I mean they saw your poor mother.'

Susan gasped. 'Did he?' She was quite unable to picture a meeting between Edward and Doll.

'Yes, and he said to let you know that she seems to be settled well enough, though a bit wandering in her thoughts. Oh, Susan, I'm sure he's in love with you!'

It was like having a deep secret shouted out for everybody to hear. Susan's heart missed a beat, but she shook her head in quick denial.

'Oh, *no*, Miss Marianne, he's just good an' kind – and now I must go back to Mrs Twydell.'

'Oh, Susan, I would *so* like to go with the party to Wychell Forest! D'you think that my mother will let me?'

'Hush, here comes Mrs Coulter,' said Susan, as footsteps reached the top of the stairs and the midwife limped towards them, leaning on the apothecary's arm and followed by Mrs Bennett. Susan accompanied them into Sally's room and

110

stayed while they appraised her; Mrs Bennett then went downstairs and the midwife conferred with Mr Turnbull outside the bedroom door. It was not completely closed, and Susan strained her ears to catch their muttered comments.

'I be half-minded to put my forefinger in and tear the bag o' waters with my nail,' the woman confided. 'In general I don't hold with interference, but it might just start her off.'

'But if the pains did not follow, she'd be leaking water and in a worse case.' Turnbull sounded doubtful.

'But it might relieve some pressure. My dread is that she may start throwing those fearful fits, as sometimes happens when there be so much dropsical swelling . . .'

The midwife lowered her voice and Susan could not heart the rest, though Turnbull groaned.

'I am inclined to ask Dr Parnham to come over from Belhampton to see her,' he said. 'Twydell can afford his fees.'

'Hm. These man-midwives are overzealous in their use o' butchers' tools,' murmured the midwife. 'They're not willing to wait and give Nature a chance.'

'But Dame Nature may betray us while we wait upon her, madam! Believe me, I do not doubt your skill, but what would you do if she started having fits?'

'And what would the man-midwife do, Mr Turnbull, and her not even started in travail?'

Susan cupped her ear to catch his low reply. 'And if we lose the child, or the mother, or both, madam, and her husband asks why I never sent for Parnham?'

'We'd be harshly judged, I agree, Mr Turnbull,' sighed the woman. 'We have a choice of evils, and not for the first time.' She sounded disconsolate, and Turnbull's voice softened.

'You are in pain, madam, and that makes you melancholy. Take heart, for you are much respected as a mistress of your craft.'

Susan then heard Mrs Coulter confiding her fears.

'I may not practise my craft much longer, for the hip-gout grows worse and I must take a stick to get about. I can't mount even the mildest o' mares, and soon I'll only be able to attend those who can send a gig or donkey-cart for me. Besides, the business o' birthing troubles me more as time passes, and women in peril such as we have here – they cause me much grief, and doubt o' my own judgement. I'm getting too old, Mr Turnbull.'

More muttering followed, and then the apothecary came to a decision.

'Look, I will bring two ounces of castor oil, to be well mixed with freshly squeezed orange juice and given to Mrs Twydell at first light tomorrow. The violent emptying of the bowel may stir the womb into its duty.'

So the next morning Susan lightly held Sally's nose between thumb and forefinger until the nauseous mixture had all gone down.

'Now drink some water and breathe deeply, Mrs Twydell,' begged Susan, praying that the oil would not be vomited back again. She opened a window to let in a breath of air, and Mrs Bennett sat down to read aloud from the *Hampshire Chronicle* in a vain effort to divert Sally's mind.

She threw the newspaper aside when Sally called urgently for the commode-stool and sat weightily between her mother and Susan, groaning as her bowel churned. A gurgling eruption of wind and liquid matter filled the room with an overpowering smell.

'That's right, Mrs Twydell, you hold on to us and don't mind a few farts,' Susan said comfortably. 'We all ha' to let 'em go sometimes, even the Queen when she sits on the stool!'

Unpleasant as the purging was, it achieved the desired effect, for by midday Sally began to feel regular board-like tightenings of her abdomen, quarter-hourly at first, then every ten minutes. By six o'clock her mother was counting five minutes between them, and Sally was holding her breath with each seizure. Farmer Bennett willingly got out the three-seater, first to fetch Mrs Coulter and then to bring Mr Twydell over from Pulhurst.

Mrs Coulter's preliminary examination of the neck of the womb confirmed that the head of the child was presenting but was still quite high up. As she withdrew her two fingers, there was a gush of cloudy fluid: the waters had broken.

'The child's head faces towards the mother's front instead o' the back,' said Mrs Coulter, and Susan gathered that this was not welcome news.

'It means that travail will be longer, especially as it's her first,' sighed the midwife. 'Either the head will turn round before it comes forth, or it'll come out facing upwards – but the first is more likely, and it takes more time.'

The whole household waited up until the early hours of Midsummer Day, but when there were no developments the farmer ordered them to their beds, leaving only his wife and Susan to take turns at sitting up with the midwife and her charge.

113

When Mrs Coulter laid her ear against the abdominal dome to hear the child's heartbeat, Susan asked if she too might listen, and the thrill of hearing the rapid pit-a-pat-a-pit-a-pat-a was like the revelation of learning the alphabet. The sound was most clearly heard on the right side, and the midwife pronounced it to be strong and regular.

The pains continued throughout the night and the following day. Bread and meat were sent up to the bedchamber, and Susan gave Sally sips of water and fruit cordials between her pains. Mrs Coulter showed her how to rub Sally's back with long downward strokes and a circular movement at the base of the spine. It helped to ease the discomfort to some extent, but Susan noticed the midwife wincing with her own constant pain from the diseased hip joint; her eyes were ringed with fatigue, and Susan persuaded her to take a nap in Marianne's room while she took over the stroking of Sally's back, pressing her palms into the lower curve and softly murmuring encouragement.

In the mid-afternoon Mrs Coulter decided to do another examination.

'I don't do this without good reason, Susan, for 'tis painful to the woman and makes for a greater risk o' childbed fever – but I need to know how much the ring o' the womb be opened after all these hours.'

Lubricating her right hand with goose-grease, she thrust her fingers into the birth-passage while Susan stood on the other side of the bed, holding Sally's hand.

'The child's head be still high, and the ring be hard and thick,' said the midwife in disappointment. ''Twill scarce admit three fingers as yet.'

She withdrew her hand and said under her breath, 'Were it not for the dropsy I'd get her out o' bed and walk her round the room – but as things are I'd better send out for Turnbull again – not that he'll have any better ideas than I.'

Nor did he, though he looked grave.

'We can but wait and hope that the ring will dilate, madam, and that she may have strength enough to deliver the child when 'tis fully opened.' He frowned and pursed his lips. 'I think 'twould be a good idea to have the opinion of Dr Parnham. His Chamberlen forceps might shorten her ordeal.'

Mrs Coulter shook her head firmly. 'Give her time. I've never called in a man-midwife yet.'

'Can you not ease my poor Sally's pain at all?' asked Sarah Bennett, openly disregarding the Church's prohibition on relief of pain in travail. 'A little sweet wine in warm water?'

He shook his head. 'No, I am completely against the use of alcohol in childbirth, having seen the results of it in the House of Industry. It makes the mother stuporous and unable to bear down when she should. And babies are slow to cry.'

However, he produced a small dark bottle of opium tincture, with instructions to give three or four drops in water sweetened with honey, and to repeat the dose at Mrs Coulter's discretion. Thanks to this Sally gained a little relief, though her sleep was disturbed by the frequent need to sit on the chamber pot to pass tiny trickles of urine.

Mrs Coulter's head drooped while Sally dozed fitfully, and Susan was emboldened to whisper a question.

'What did Mr Turnbull mean about Dr Parnham's – what did he say – *forceps*?'

The midwife pulled a face. ''Tis a device like a great pair o' tongs by which the man-midwife may grasp the head o' the child and pull on it, to draw it forth from the womb. Ugh! I would as soon open up the belly to take out the child, though 'twould surely cost the life o' the mother.'

Susan was both horrified and fascinated. 'Why, has that ever been done, Mrs Coulter?'

The midwife shrugged. 'Aye, on very rare occasions, to save the child. 'Tis said that the Roman Emperor Julius Caesar was removed from the womb that way, and that his mother's belly was stitched together and she lived – but that's as may be, Susan. I would never dare do it, not even as a last resort.'

That evening Mrs Bennett demanded that Marianne should come and take over Susan's duties to enable the maidservant to rest for a few hours, but the younger sister's horror at the sights and smells, Sally's irritability and Marianne's clumsiness proved an intolerable combination, and Susan was recalled to bathe Sally's face and hands without splashing the sheet, and hold a glass of water to her lips without spilling it.

As the midsummer dusk fell it was clear that the pains were getting weaker and less frequent. Mrs Coulter yawned, shook her heavy head and secretly prayed for the strength and right judgement to see this young mother through to a happy outcome. She thanked God for the sensible Lucket girl.

'The womb's tired and taking a rest, Susan,' she said. 'It has gone into inertia, as the doctors say. There'll be no progress without the pains, but 'tis my belief that this is Nature's way o' giving the woman some respite – her and those who wait with her,' she added half under her breath.

The hands of the green marble clock on the mantelpiece pointed to twenty minutes to eleven.

'Then let's take what Nature offers, and you an' Mrs Bennett go to bed,' answered Susan, alarmed by the older woman's grey features, exhausted by pain, anxiety and sleeplessness. 'I'll stay here along o' Mrs Twydell – don't worry, I'll call ye if she needs ye.'

And so for a few night hours there was an uneasy silence over the farmhouse. Alone with Sally, Susan curled up in a blanket on the floor as she had done as a child in the roost at Ash-Pit End. She slept in snatches, getting up at intervals to make sure her charge was resting, and quietly placing her ear to the belly to hear the child's heartbeat.

As soon as she lay down again, weird and fantastic images passed before her eyes. She was with her mother, who was giving birth to Joby by the light of a guttering candle while the pale, silent faces of her three lost brothers looked on – Bartle, Will and Georgie, floating past in the darkness like dis-embodied souls. Then Edward Calthorpe was riding on a tall horse, coming to rescue her from some kind of danger; but before he could get to her she fell beneath the wheels of the Bever carriage and would have been trampled into the dust had it not been for Miss Glover in a grey silk dress and bonnet, hauling her up into bright sunlight and kissing her.

'You are the best pupil in the class, Susan!' she cried.

And then there was Edward again, coming towards her in the cornfield, holding out his arms as she ran up to him and was encircled in his arms, clasped against his chest; she felt the softness of his shirt, smelled his delicious cleanness, heard his whisper as he held her strongly, safely. 'Sweet Susan, do not cry – dear Susan!' She could hear his heart beating as she lay against him.

And then – *horror*! A hateful, intimate sensation of pain, of shame, a hideous dark shadow spreading over the cornfield like a blight. Edward had disappeared, leaving her alone in terror, and she dared not turn round for fear of seeing two lustful red eyes beneath black brows. She screamed and struggled – and sat bolt upright in Sally's bedchamber. In the half-darkness before dawn she saw that Sally was also sitting up on the bed, and calling out in panic.

'Help! Help me, my pains are upon me again, harder than before. *Help!* Mother, where are you?'

Susan struggled to her feet just as Mrs Bennett came into the room, summoned by her daughter's cry. Mrs Coulter, stupid with sleep, limped painfully behind her, and a loud, unconcealed fart escaped from her before she could control her tired muscles. Susan tried to pull her thoughts back to reality.

'Oh, why will not the child come out?' cried Sally. 'Oh, that my belly might be cut open and let it be taken from me!'

Susan could not help glancing at Mrs Coulter, remembering their earlier conversation.

'Hush, Sally, y'r baby'll come out the proper way, now that y'r pains ha' started again, and ye've had a good rest,' she said confidently, and Mrs Coulter embarked wearily on another examination.

'If the ring be no further opened I'll send for Turnbull again,' she told them, 'and then he may call for Dr Parnham if he pleases and the husband agrees.'

While the midwife thrust her hand into the moist cavity between Sally's splayed thighs and Susan held the writhing girl's hand, Sarah Bennett read aloud from the Book of Common Prayer, choosing Psalm 116.

'"The sorrows of death compassed me, and the pains of hell gat hold upon me:"' she read, glancing towards the bed. '"I found trouble and sorrow. Then I called upon the name of the Lord; O Lord, I beseech thee, deliver my soul."'

The words hung on the air while the midwife's fingers probed.

'The child's head has come down, that's for sure,' muttered Mrs Coulter, her eyes tightly shut as she concentrated on an entirely tactile examination. 'And yes, there's the ring round it – I can feel it at the front but not at the back. Praise be to God, 'tis almost fully open. There, there, my sweet dove, not so much further to go now,' she said to Sally, who gave another despairing wail as her muscles hardened again.

'How much longer, Margaret?' implored Sarah Bennett: the age-old cry of the birth-chamber.

'Ah, if I could answer that question every time I'm asked it, I'd charge a fee for't, and be rich as well as wise,' replied Margaret Coulter ruefully. 'Ye'd best carry on reading, Sarah.'

Mrs Bennett picked up the book. '"The Lord preserveth the simple: I was brought low, and he helped me."'

Susan reached for the cup of water to hold to Sally's lips.

'"For thou hast delivered my soul from death, mine eyes from tears and my feet from falling. I will walk before the Lord in the land of the living."'

Mrs Bennett could read no more, but covered her face with her hands. Susan remembered Miss Glover's firm faith in the Almighty, and began to repeat the Lord's Prayer quietly. The two older women joined in, and Sally repeated the final 'Amen' two or three times.

Mrs Bennett always said later that their prayer was answered, for as the midsummer sun rose on that Thursday morning, Sally's groans took on a different sound: from helpless wailing, she now began to grunt and strain.

'Quick, I need the commode-stool again!' she cried in panic. 'Help me to sit on it now, or I shall make a stink!'

Susan's thoughts flew back to the cold and dark of a February morning when as a child of seven she had helped her mother at the birth of Joby.

'Is it a great stinking turd, Ma?' she had asked as Doll gasped and pushed down.

She now saw Mrs Coulter turn her eyes heaven-ward in thanks.

'No, sweetheart, I doubt ye need the stool now. 'Tis the child's head ye feel pressing down,' she said. 'Don't be afraid, 'tis a good sign. I'll take a look to make sure.'

She and Susan separated Sally's legs and when the next pain began the midwife pointed out to Susan the distension of the female parts, the slight parting of the fleshy-lipped opening, and a glimpse of what the watchers longed to see. Mrs Bennett leaned over to share the first sight of a dark, shiny glimmer through the slit before the pain subsided and the curtaining folds hid it from view.

'There it is – the top o' the head,' breathed Margaret, while Susan thrilled with anticipation and Sarah wept for joy. It was nearly six o'clock.

'Come, Margaret, we must get her to sit up and push hard. I have a sheet to tie to the bottom of the bed—'

'No, Sarah, we need to see a lot more than that before she spends her strength,' replied the midwife.

'She must save it for the last great efforts. Be patient, Sarah,' she added kindly. ''Twill be born within another couple o' hours.'

But it took longer than that for the head to descend, and when they listened to the child's heartbeat, it was noticeably slower. The foetid odour of stale sweat filled the room, and Susan's head swam; the hands on the green marble clock blurred and cleared; half-past six, seven, half-past seven, eight; the sun had been risen four hours when Sally began the final expulsive efforts. Sitting up against her pillows she pulled on a sheet tied to the end of the bed as she strained down.

'That's my good girl – push down as if ye were on the closet-stool – come on, push again, we can see the head, give another push, Sally, give another heave down . . .'

When Margaret Coulter's tired, husky voice gave out, Susan took over the encouraging and exhorting, with Mrs Bennett adding her impassioned pleas to her daughter, begging her to keep going and not to lose heart.

'I can push no more, for God's sake, I tell you I *can't*!' gasped Sally, her face congested and her lips bruised and bleeding from biting. Susan rolled up a handkerchief and placed it across Sally's mouth between her teeth to bite on.

Half-past eight. The child's crown, swollen and spongy, was now filling the outlet at the height of a pain, and the mother's delicate skin was stretched to paper thinness.

'She will tear below for certain,' whispered the midwife, and Susan's heart ached for Sally's inescapable agony.

'Let me die, for I cannot push – let me die . . .'

Sally's face was ominously blue, with a white circle round her mouth.

Susan impulsively threw away the sheet, which she saw was of no use, and guided by her memory of the past, she placed Sally's hands behind her drawn-up knees.

'All right, Mrs Twy— all right, Sally, just grip y'r knees when ye get the pain and pull on 'em. Never mind about the pushin',' she said.

Twenty minutes to nine. The damp, dark circle of the child's head slowly advanced. Margaret Coulter and Susan Lucket exchanged a nod: they were partners working together to save two lives. Birth was about to take place, and Death was waiting to snatch Life away. Susan's courage rose like a flame at the challenge.

With a final surging contraction the head was born. The face was bluish-purple, with squashed features, and the crown elongated as if it had been stretched. The eyes were open, and Mrs Coulter quickly wiped them and placed a forefinger in the mouth. First one shoulder was born, then the other, the arms flopped out limply, and the rest of the slippery, blue-tinged body of a large male infant appeared, followed by a brisk loss of blood. Mrs Coulter spread a huckaback towel on the bed and received the baby upon it. Sally gave a long-drawn-out sigh, and her mother hardly dared speak.

'Is he . . .?'

Margaret Coulter blew upon the child's body.

'Come, little man, give me a cry, for the love o' God,' she muttered under her breath. She flicked her fingers against the soles of his feet, and gently blew upon him again. She placed two fingers on his chest and nodded when she detected a slow heartbeat. She wrapped him in the towel, and placed her mouth over his nose, sucking out moisture, and then blew directly into his mouth.

The baby stirred faintly. He gave a spasmodic gasp. He wrinkled his nose. His legs jerked up in a convulsive movement. He flexed his arms. His chest rose, drawing in air, and when it came out it made a weak, grunting sound. And again. And again.

'Praise be to God, he lives,' Sarah Bennett groaned in her relief. 'But his head, Margaret – has he got water on the brain?'

'No, no, Sarah, he has had a hard journey and his head's pressed out o' shape,' replied Margaret, tying and severing the umbilical cord. ''Twill improve in a day or two. Here, take him. I must attend to his mother.'

Following the expulsion of the after-burden, Sally had lost a quantity of blood and lay wax-pale and still, her breathing rapid and shallow.

'Her muscles be too weak to stanch the flow,' whispered the midwife to Susan, fearing that the new mother's life might yet flow out with the haemorrhage. She thrust a pad of sheep's wool into the passage and held it there, telling Susan to straighten Sally's legs and raise them together on a pillow taken from under her head. Within another minute the bleeding had diminished to a thin trickle, and Susan silently echoed the midwife's prayer of thanksgiving.

'She must be left to sleep now. Take the child to another room and let him rest in his cradle,' ordered Mrs Coulter, her voice shaking with fatigue. 'He'll need a wet nurse, Sarah, so ye'd better send for young Jenny Kyte over at Crabb's cottages – she'll be glad to share her milk. Let the father see his son, and

I reckon it wise to have him baptised before the day's out.'

Susan took the baby to Marianne's room and gazed at him with reverent awe. This was the Twydell baby that she had helped to bring into the world! In her exhilaration she forgot her tiredness and had little patience with Marianne's tears.

'What a horrid, horrid business, Susan! No modesty! No dignity! A woman might as well be a farmyard animal. How can any decent woman want to be a midwife?'

'Hush, Miss Marianne, and just be thankful that y'r sister be delivered at last. See here, y'r little nephew – ain't he a fine big lad?'

'Ugh! How can you say that when his head is such a fearsome shape? He'll grow into an idiot, for sure,' wailed the new aunt.

'F'r shame, Marianne, arter all y'r sister ha' been through!' Susan's grey eyes flashed as she spoke. 'Mrs Coulter says she ha' seen many such heads, and it'll be as round as a ball by tomorrow – and so 'twill be, my sweet little lad, yes, so 'twill be!'

She gently kissed the baby, whose skin was now pink, though his feeble little sighs and grunts touched her heart, and turned her back on his hysterical aunt. An upbringing in poor, overcrowded conditions had made Susan immune to the sort of squeamishness that Marianne showed. In her pity and concern for Sally Twydell, she had felt no revulsion over a natural – if exceedingly painful – bodily process. What Marianne saw as crude and undignified was for Susan a matter to be dealt with sensibly and practically – and for such a reward! A new life beginning, a first breath drawn: surely there could be nothing more wonderful than to attend a woman in childbirth, to help and comfort her throughout the pain and to care for the helpless newborn child.

Susan discreetly watched as Mrs Bennett showed the baby to Mr Twydell when he came up to see his wife. Sick with worry over her, he tried to smile at the squashed-looking object whose snuffling grunts reminded him of a piglet, and confirmed that he was to be called Samuel. When Dr Gravett arrived for the christening, Susan was present at the short ceremony in the parlour, and took Samuel from his grand-mother to show to his young aunt Bessie, who at nine years old was somewhat overwhelmed by all the strange happenings, not to mention the alarming sounds from Sally's bedchamber over the past three days.

Though the birthing was accomplished, Susan's duties were by no means ended. Sally took some weeks to recover and Samuel's care was shared between Susan and the young wet nurse, whose own baby daughter was said to resemble Osmond Calthorpe.

Susan felt that she had passed an important milestone in her life; the village school had been a first step for her, and the Bennett farmhouse was the second. She was now conscious of her own enhanced status in the household, and the farmer's wife had been unreserved in her thanks.

'I'll never forget what you did for my Sally all through this terrible time, dear Susan. You've been like another daughter to me,' she sobbed, flinging her arms around the girl's neck. 'And Margaret Coulter says she doesn't know how she'd have got through without you. In fact she told me that she thinks you'll be her successor one day – the Beversley midwife!'

Susan's heart lifted in exultation as she heard this, for Mrs Bennett had put into words an idea that had been taking shape in her own mind, something she hardly dared to think about, let alone to hope for.

Yes! More than anything else she wanted Mrs Coulter's prophecy to come true.

Chapter 11

Polly Lucket watched with mournful eyes as the Bever carriage rolled out of the stable-yard, taking Mr and Mrs Calthorpe and their daughters to Wychell Forest, followed by their sons on horseback. The big farm cart had already left with three menservants and two maids in charge of the tent and provisions. Polly had begged and pleaded with Mrs Martin to let her go with them, but the housekeeper knew Mr Osmond's predilection for pretty maid-servants, and the girls accompanying the party had been chosen for their strong arms and plain looks.

So Polly pouted as she hung out washing on the line in the stable-yard, while observing the retreating backs of the Calthorpe brothers, Osmond so tall in the saddle, his fair hair caught with a black ribbon at the neck. She could just picture Miss Rosa Hansford simpering at him today by the lake, and wondered if he would be tempted to return her smiles for want of any better diversion. It just wasn't fair!

A few minutes later her ears caught the sound of rapidly approaching hoof-beats. She turned her head and gave a cry of joy when she saw the rider coming back through the archway.

Mr Osmond! Polly guessed that he had turned back for no other reason than to see her and speak to her without his brother overhearing. She stood fearlessly in his path as the horse galloped straight towards her, as with one hand he reined in slightly, leaning over in the saddle at a dangerously low angle. He swerved to pass within inches of her, swooping down like a bird of prey: she felt his breath on her face and heard his words.

'I shall return and have thee, pretty Polly – wait for me!'

In a flash he had straightened up in the saddle and dug his heels into the horse's flanks. A flying hoof threw up a stone quite close to Polly's upturned face, but neither he nor she considered the risk he ran. Polly's dark eyes sparkled with excitement as she watched him gallop away for a second time, disappearing from sight under the archway.

I shall return and have thee, pretty Polly – wait for me!

Polly understood exactly what the words meant, and was already woman enough to know that she had a hold over Osmond as long as she refused to be bedded. It gave her an intoxicating sense of power, and she danced up and down the yard at the thought of the saucy answers she would give him, the sport she would have in making half-promises and then evading his claims. Their different stations in life gave an extra dash of spice to the game, and Polly knew she could keep the upper hand as long as she played her cards right and did not yield. Standing there among the flapping sheets and shirts, she hugged herself for sheer delight.

In his pursuit of Polly, time was not on Osmond's side, for he was soon to become an army officer. Thanks to his Oxford background, even without a degree, a place had been found for him at the Royal Military Academy at Woolwich for a short period of training in the conduct of an officer, and his only fear was that the American upstarts might be crushed before he'd had a chance to distinguish himself in their defeat. He already saw himself leading a company of men with cannon and musketry against the rebels, and a military tailor in Belhampton was engaged to make his uniform: a red coat with brass buttons and epaulettes, two pairs of white breeches, a cloak and a tall peaked and braided hat. White leather gloves and a pair of very stiff boots had been delivered at Bever House, and he could hardly wait to show himself off in Belhampton with fellow officers waiting to be summoned to the depot at Winchester.

His parents' thoughts on the matter were less sanguine, and there had been a very unpleasant scene when Mr Calthorpe had first broached the idea to his wife. Gertrude was terrified at the thought of her first-born crossing the ocean to go to war, and it was only when Osmond himself became fired with enthusiasm that she had reluctantly accepted the inevitable, eased by her husband's assurances that the war would be over within another year, and that there was little or no danger.

Calthorpe was well aware that in this he had spoken less than the truth, and he was troubled. In spite of what Lord North and his party said, the colonists were proving to be unexpectedly firm in their insistence on 'No Taxation Without Representation', and were proudly calling themselves the United States. Gertrude would never forgive him if . . . But what else could he do with a boy who was no longer a boy and showed little or no sense of responsibility? It was costing a fortune to equip him for a military career, while the estate was burdened by rapidly rising land taxes to pay for the war.

The frown lines deepened between Calthorpe's

eyes, for now Edward had got this crazy idea that he was in love with a maidservant from Lower Beversley, the daughter of a madwoman who had nearly put out the rector's left eye. Gertrude demanded that he remonstrate with the boy, who in some ways was even more resistant to reason than his nonchalant elder brother.

'A word with you, Edward.'

'Sir.'

'You have greatly offended your mother.'

'I had no such intention, sir, as I tried to tell her—'

'Your intentions may have been good, Edward, but it was one thing to defend the maid in her distress and quite another to go gallivanting across the fields after her like a lovesick ploughboy. And you do her no service, for she is far beneath you and has bad blood, as was only too clearly demonstrated in the church. It is most unfortunate, I know, but—'

'I love her, Father.'

The quiet declaration broke in on Calthorpe's homily, and pulled him up short. He shook his head and sighed.

'You think so now, Edward, but 'tis a boy's love, and you will see the folly of it in time. I am not unsympathetic – in fact I commend your concern for the girl – but I have to insist that you show proper respect to your mother, and remember our position in Beversley. Do you hear me?'

Edward gave the slightest of bows. 'I hear you, sir, and I'm sorry I caused distress to my mother, but time will show whether this be a boy's love or not. I know that there will be no other girl for me but Susan – and she too is deserving of respect for the way she has learned her letters and raised herself from low beginnings. She is a virtuous maid, and will not shame us, Father.'

Knowing as they both did that Osmond had fathered at least two bastards on village girls, Calthorpe could think of no answer to this.

'I understand you, Edward, but have a care for the girl's own sake if you truly feel as you do for her.'

Edward nodded.

'And where is she now, this girl – Susan, isn't it?' asked his father in a more conciliatory tone.

'In service at the Bennetts' farmhouse, sir. It was to plead for her reinstatement that I walked over there with her after that commotion in Great St Giles. The farmer had dismissed her just because of her mother.'

'And Mrs Bennett agreed to take her back?'

'At once, sir. The – er – birth of a grandchild appeared to be imminent, and Susan was received with open arms.'

Calthorpe nodded. 'I see. Good.'

'Thank you, Father.'

'Hm. Well, just bear in mind what I – what we have agreed, Edward.'

He had held out his hand and Edward grasped it warmly.

Susan tiptoed into the sickroom and suggested that she should take over at the bedside.

'I ha' some sheets to hem, an' may as well do 'em here as anywhere, Mrs Bennett. How is she?'

'Sleeping. Her skin is cooler, but she's so weak, Susan, so *dull*,' came the mournful reply. 'She cares for nothing, not her husband, not me, nor even the baby she bore in pain. It's been three weeks now.'

'Ah, but she be much better than she was, Mrs Bennett. All the swelling ha' gone, and she no longer

131

raves. She just needs more time to get her strength back.'

'You're a good girl, Susan.' Sarah Bennett heaved herself out of the chair. The air was hot and humid, and even with the window wide open the drawn curtains made the room seem stifling.

'Is Marianne in?' she asked.

'No, she be out walkin' somewhere. Poor Miss Marianne! She's mopin' 'cause she's not wi' the party by the lake in Wychell Forest.'

'No, Susan, she is *not*.' Mrs Bennett sounded impatient. 'How could I possibly let the silly girl go on her own? The farmer and Tom have no liking for such jaunts, and I have to stay with my poor Sally. If Madam Calthorpe had invited the Smarts I might have let Marianne go, but I suppose the parson looks too much like a scarecrow, and his Betsy too patched and darned. It'll be a dull enough party, I dare say, with the men all arguing about the war.'

Susan looked up with a half-smile. 'I dare say Miss Glover can argue as well as any o' them.'

Left alone with the sleeping invalid, Susan settled into the chair and resisted the temptation to close her eyes. She had not had an unbroken night's sleep since the baby's birth. Sally had fallen victim to the dreaded childbed infection, and had lain with a raging fever for days on end. Mrs Coulter had to postpone stitching the long tear of skin and muscle between the two passages, and it had become inflamed and suppurating, with a foul-smelling discharge. An uneasy silence, full of fear and anxiety, had hung over the farmhouse, tainted with the very smell of death, and broken only by the cries of the two babies.

The curtains stirred a little, and Susan heard young

Tom Bennett's voice down in the yard, prophesying rain.

A sudden gust blew the curtains inwards, and Susan glanced quickly at Sally. To her surprise the girl's eyes were open, two hollow caverns looking straight at her.

'How long have I lain here, girl?' she asked in a feeble but clear voice. 'Where have you taken my baby? I want to see him and hold him.'

'Yes – why, yes, Sally – Mrs Twydell – I'll get him f'r ye this minute,' stammered Susan, hastily rising.

Outside on the landing she called over the banister. 'She's askin' f'r Samuel!'

While Mrs Bennett hurried up the stairs, Susan fetched the child from Jenny Kyte's arms and carefully placed him in Sally's. Her pallid features brightened at the sight of him, and her sunken eyes shone with tender maternal love.

''Tis like as he were newly born, and this her first sight o' him,' whispered Susan to the grandmother.

'Praise be to God, she's ready to be a mother to him at last!' answered Mrs Bennett, wiping her eyes on her apron.

As if to mark the moment, a vivid flash of lightning illumined every window in the house. Mrs Bennett and Susan moved in close to the bedside, and Sally enfolded her baby protectively as a tremendous thunderclap reverberated down the valley. More flashes and rumbles followed, and within minutes a deluge of rain was unleashed; windows had to be pulled shut and doors closed against the pounding arrows. Marianne came running up the track holding her hat on, her gown soaked and clinging.

'Oh, think o' the picnic party caught in such a storm!' she cried. 'The danger o' being struck by—'

133

'Never mind about them. Your sister has returned to the land o' the living,' said Mrs Bennett reprovingly. Tom was sent over to Pulhurst with the good news, and a happy Mr Twydell arrived to sit at his wife's side, oblivious to the downpour.

Later that evening Mrs Bennett took Susan aside.

'You must take a holiday tomorrow, Susan, for you've worked without a break for weeks on end,' she said. 'You can go and visit your mother at Belhampton, or call on your sister. I tell you what,' she added as an idea struck her, 'Marianne can stay here with Sally, and I'll take out the three-seater and do some business in the village. And you can come with me.'

A holiday! Susan's spirits rose, and though she had no wish to visit the grim workhouse where Doll languished like a dark memory, she longed as always to see Polly. But how? She could hardly go up to Bever House and ask to see their maidservant Lucket.

Once again the answer was to call on the friend who had always been ready to help her.

Seated at her writing table in the house that had become known as Glover Cottage, Sophia wondered whether to send a note of thanks to Mrs Calthorpe on the day following the Wychell Forest picnic. Or would a tactful silence be more appropriate after such an unmitigated disaster?

While she thought it over, her maid, Tess, announced a visitor.

'Susan! I cannot think of anyone I'd rather see. Come, sit down and let us talk. There is so much I want to hear!'

Susan responded gratefully, for she had been rehearsing what she would say: how she would tell Miss Glover that she had a holiday, and longed to see Polly.

But first it would be polite to enquire about the picnic party.

'Miss Marianne was that sorry not to be there, Miss Glover – she wouldn't even ha' minded the storm! Did ye get very wet?'

Sophia shook her head ruefully. 'Ah, Susan, the storm was not the only cause for regret yesterday – but never mind that now. It's *you* we must talk about. Mrs Coulter has given me glowing reports of your skill and good sense at poor Mrs Twydell's confinement. How dreadful to be in travail for three days with a ten-pound baby! And Mrs Coulter being sadly afflicted with the rheumaticks, she told me that she would never have got through without your aid. I am convinced that the Almighty sent you to be there for both mother and baby – and midwife.'

Susan felt her colour rising, but the praise was sweet. ''Twas a hard time, Miss Glover, an' Mrs Twydell ha' since been laid low wi' the childbed fever, but she's over the worst now.'

'Praise God for that. And how is the child?'

'Ah, Samuel be the sweetest babe, Miss Glover. He ha' big blue eyes an' a fat little belly—'

She broke off in confusion, but Sophia smiled and nodded for her to go on.

''Tis a joy to hear you! I know that you spent hours at the bedside so that poor Mrs Coulter could get some sleep. Oh, you were surely meant to be there!'

Susan looked down at her hands. 'I was glad to be there, Miss Glover,' she said simply.

'And do you know what else Mrs Coulter said to

135

me, Susan? She thinks that one day you will take on her mantle and become the Beversley midwife! What are your thoughts on that?'

Susan replied in a low voice. 'I'd like that to be true, one day.'

'And so it will be, I'm sure. How right I was to send you to learn your letters – and 'twill also be my privilege to send you to Dr Parnham for his course of lectures to midwives, so that you may obtain a licence.'

'Oh, Miss Glover, *will* ye?' Susan's eyes widened in happy expectation.

'Ah, but not for several years, Susan. You are much too young as yet, and besides, there is a very important requirement before a woman can practise as a licensed midwife. She must be married and have first-hand experience of childbirth.'

All the eager hope in Susan's eyes vanished immediately.

'But I shan't ever be married, Miss Glover – I ha' no liking for't!'

Sophia laughed gently. 'How can you say that, Susan? Most women get married sooner or later, and you will think differently in a year or two. How old are you now? Eighteen? A careful, modest girl with pleasing manners – you are sure to catch the eye of a respectable tradesman or a farmer's son—'

'*No*, Miss Glover, don't say so, f'r I *never* shall!'

Susan's painful blush and the violent shaking of her head convinced Sophia that the subject had been broached too early for a girl who had seen little evidence of happy family life at the Ash-Pits, and she did not pursue it.

What a daft baggage she must think me, Susan chided herself, and tried to make some sort of apology.

'I'm sorry, Miss Glover, but I'd sooner live like yeself, wi' no husband, beggin' y'r pardon.'

Sophia gave her an odd look, and Susan hoped she had not been impolite. It was time to speak of Polly.

'Mrs Bennett ha' given me a holiday, an' I'd like above all to see me sister Polly, Miss Glover – but I don't know when she may leave her work, so I've come to ask ye what to do. I do long to see her!'

She clasped her hands together, her grey eyes pleading, and Sophia was put into a dilemma. If anybody deserved a simple wish to be granted, it was surely this girl, but it was a bad time to be asking favours of Bever House.

'I'm not sure that I can get permission for Polly to be allowed out today,' she said, knowing that Gertrude would be in a furious mood, and to approach Mrs Martin directly would be too risky; she would be sure to be seen calling at the kitchen door. She was about to suggest that the sisters might be able to meet after Divine Service on Sunday, when Tess came in to announce that Mr Edward Calthorpe was at the door.

'Edward? Oh, good, show him in, show him in!' said Sophia, rising from her chair to greet her cousin. Susan also hastily got to her feet and curtsied. Edward's pleasure on seeing her was unmistakable and unconcealed.

'Cousin Sophy – and Susan too. What a very pleasant surprise! I am doubly fortunate,' he said with a smile, taking a chair. 'First of all I've come to enquire about you, Sophy. I trust you have not caught cold after the storm? You should have seen her standing up in her pony-trap in the rain, Susan, like a drenched Boadicea!'

Susan had no idea what a Boadicea was, but smiled

and nodded, hoping she looked more composed than she felt.

'Thank you, Edward, I am perfectly well,' replied Sophia. 'How are your parents and sisters?'

He looked again at Susan as if unable to take his eyes from her, and then replied, choosing his words carefully.

'My mother is naturally disappointed about some aspects of yesterday, Sophy. It was a great pity Henry was not able to get home in time to join the party. Selina was melancholy at his absence.'

Sophia inclined her head. 'Of course.'

'And if Henry had been there he would have poured oil on the troubled waters of disagreement over the progress of the war. As it was, I blame myself—'

'Oh, *no*, Edward, it was I who should not have contradicted the rector when he spoke against Mr Fox's policy of making peace with the colonials!' insisted Sophia. 'I'm sure your mother holds me to blame for what happened.'

'Old Gravett talks a great deal of nonsense, Sophy, and 'tis high time he was contradicted. No, the fault lay with my brother Osmond. If only he were not so boastful, so arrogant, talking as if the 67th Hampshire Foot Battalion would go in and crush Washington at a single stroke – it was he who so annoyed the squire. The Hansfords must be worried every hour of the day about Henry, and to listen to that nonsense was the last straw! So don't reproach yourself, Sophy, for *I* should have tackled Osmond and drawn his fire away from our guests.'

Edward gave a self-deprecating grimace, but then smiled and went on, 'Ha! Did you see my brother's face when the squire rebuked him? And then he looked to Father, but found no support in that quarter, so stormed off and rode away, leaving poor little Rosa Hansford as dejected as Selina!'

Sophia glanced at Susan, who was hanging on every word.

'Perhaps we should leave the matter there, Edward,' she began, but he turned to Susan and continued the catalogue of misfortunes for her entertainment.

'And then Sophy took young William Hansford off to see the family of otters further down the bank of the lake, Susan, and what did he do but get his hand bitten by the bitch otter who distrusted his interest in her cubs!'

'Did *anything* go well, sir?' asked Susan politely.

'I can't think of anything – can you, Sophy? And as if we were not already surfeited with pleasure, there is another important social event in the offing – a great ball at Bever House, no less, to be held in September, when Henry will certainly be home. In fact my mother intends to use the occasion to announce Selina's betrothal to him.'

'A *ball*, Edward?' asked Sophia, frowning. 'At such a time, with Mr Hansford and Osmond both on active service?'

'That's the official reason for it, Sophy, to honour them both. The army and the navy!' He lowered his voice as he leaned towards Susan. 'That does not include me, sweet Susan, for I have another year at Oxford, by which time we are all assured that the war will be over.'

Sophia's ears were sharp, and did not miss the endearment. 'And if it is not, Edward?'

'Then 'twill be the navy for me, cousin, but I hope not, for I have other plans.'

And again Sophia observed his sidelong glance at their companion, and her shy smile in response.

'Who will be invited to this ball, Edward?'

'Everybody who is anybody in the country, Sophy, or who *thinks* they are somebody,' he replied, laughing. 'I would escape from it if I could, but we shall have to put a good face on it, cousin, and dance with each other as a last resort.'

In spite of his tone of wry amusement, Susan sensed a certain tension in the air. Miss Glover looked as if she were about to say something but decided against it. Instead she asked Edward if he could suggest a way that the Lucket sisters might meet.

'They see so little of each other these days.'

A rather embarrassed exchange followed, as Edward knew his mother would never encourage Susan to come near Bever House, and he also knew his brother to be besotted with Polly, which boded no good. Then he had what he thought was a bright idea.

'Would you and your sister care to go over to the House of— to Belhampton one afternoon, Susan, to visit your mother? It would be my pleasure to drive you in the gig, and wait for you.'

Sophia heard Susan's sharp intake of breath, and saw the inner conflict reflected in her face.

'If ye please, Mr Edward, I'd rather not go.' Her eyes were fixed beseechingly on Sophia as she spoke.

'Very well, Susan, of course you need not go,' replied Sophia with a quick look at Edward that warned him not to pursue his offer. If the girl did not want to see her poor, afflicted mother in such a place, it was hardly surprising, but Sophia had long sensed something deeper behind Susan's attitude towards

Doll, ever since that sudden flight from the Ash-Pits four years ago.

For Susan, Edward could hardly have made a more unwelcome suggestion. She was beginning to see her future life taking shape and leaving the hated past behind; to be reminded of Dolly languishing unvisited in the workhouse made her uneasy, yet she shrank from contact with her. There was an unforgotten pain, an unhealed hurt in remembering Doll's devotion to her sons while sacrificing her daughter to shameful misuse, and Susan had no feeling left for her but an appalled pity. If only such memories could be blotted out for ever! Dear and noble Edward, she thought sadly, thank heaven he would never know of the dread, the revulsion, the sheer terror that still came back to her in dreams. She had heard with enormous relief that her former home was no more, for Bartlemy and Jack had disappeared, some said to Portsmouth to join the navy, which had need of men and boys on the lower decks. Joby, a cheery lad with an honest, open face, had moved in to the forge, where the blacksmith praised his way with frisky horses.

Edward acknowledged his cousin's look, and cursed his own insensitivity. Longing to speak with Susan alone, he now offered his arm to attend her to her next destination.

'Actually, Edward, Susan is being collected from here by Mrs Bennett,' explained Sophia. 'And besides, she and I have a few more matters to discuss this morning.'

Edward was clearly disappointed, but wished them both a pleasant day, and held Susan's hand for an extra moment while he looked deep into her eyes.

'I look forward to being of service to you when I

141

can, Susan,' he told her, and read her answer in those shining grey depths.

Sophia missed none of this silent exchange, and firmly bid her cousin good day, though she promised herself to have a very straight talk with him in private at an early date.

Meanwhile she felt she should give Susan a friendly warning, and set about it without preamble.

'Sit down, Susan, for there is something I must say. Forgive me, but I could not help noticing a certain freedom in my cousin Edward's manners towards you. He is a fine young man, a gentleman in fact, but he was wrong in this matter, and did you no favour. I commend you for your own modest behaviour, for this should not be encouraged.'

Susan instinctively protested against this censure of one who could do no wrong in her sight.

'But Mr Edward ha' been so good an' kind to me, Miss Glover. I know he's a gentleman and far above me, but I can't help bein' obliged to him.'

She flushed as she spoke, and Sophia feared that she might have offended her young friend.

'Please, Susan, understand that I'm not blaming you – though I have to blame Edward a little for not considering your feelings more. It is as well that he will be going back to his Oxford college in the autumn.'

She brought her chair close to Susan's and laid a hand upon the girl's bowed shoulders.

'Listen to me, Susan – I say this only for your happiness. Mr Edward is young, he is subject to his parents, and in no position to make any kind of commitment, even if you were on an equal social standing with him.'

'I know it, Miss Glover, ye don't ha' to tell me,'

muttered Susan, looking away and biting her lip. 'I ha' no ideas o' marryin' any man – not Master Edward nor any other.'

Her obvious uneasiness confirmed Miss Glover's suspicions as to the state of her affections, and on a sympathetic impulse Sophia decided to share a certain matter of her own.

'Susan, let me tell you something,' she said gently. 'You are not alone in this. I understand how you feel, the dreams and the disappointment.'

This was so unexpected, coming from the lips of Miss Glover, that Susan raised her head and looked at her blankly.

'Yes, Susan, I too have let myself foolishly dream of one who is not for me,' went on Sophia earnestly, 'and I have had to pray to accept the Lord's will on the matter. As you must also do.'

'But ye're a *lady*, ye could marry where ye please,' said Susan, though she had never thought of Miss Glover as anybody's wife, and found it hard to imagine.

'You are quite wrong there, Susan. I am not a *lady*, but a bastard with no legal standing in the world. I happen to have money, thanks to my grandfather's bounty, but that is all. Without it I would be nobody – perhaps a maidservant like yourself, or a sempstress like my mother.'

Sophia Glover's exertions on behalf of the poor, especially the women and children, had made her highly respected in Beversley; she was seen as old Lord de Bever's granddaughter rather than an illegitimate offshoot. Susan had never considered her origins, nor the fact that she seemed to have no relations but cousins; this fact now struck her for the first time.

143

'But, Miss Glover, ye're the most – everybody looks up to ye an' thinks the world o' ye,' she said, floundering in her search for the right words, and wishing she could express herself better. 'This gentleman – why can't ye marry him if he – if he's the one ye like?'

'For the very good reason that his affections are engaged to another, Susan,' came the quiet reply. 'And there are other reasons why he is not for me, just as Edward Calthorpe is not for you. So you see, we can share in this, even though we may not speak of it. And we must pray for each other, Susan, as well as for ourselves and – those we care for in secret.'

'Oh, I will, Miss Glover, that I will!'

And for the first time the two women embraced, warmed by a new closeness in their greater knowledge of each other. It was another step towards equality.

Chapter 12

When the invitation arrived at the Bennetts' farm-house, Marianne seized on it eagerly.

'There is to be a ball at Bever House!' she cried. 'And we're all invited, even Bessie! You must take the lace off my Sunday gown, Susan, and sew it on to my green silk.'

'I ha' better things to do than sit around stitching at your gowns, Miss Marianne,' said Susan, briskly piling newly washed linen into a basket. Marianne scarcely heard her.

''Twill be such happiness to go to a real ball! I wish I had one o' those big waving ostrich feathers to sew to my cap!'

'Why don't ye wear a cock's tail-feathers like the Miss Smarts ha' sewn on to their bonnets?' asked Susan tartly as she hurried off upstairs. Since Mrs Twydell had returned to Pulhurst with her baby, Mrs Bennett spent a great deal of time visiting her there, and Susan's household responsibilities had increased.

Marianne's excitement was short-lived.

'Your father won't go hobnobbing with the Calthorpes and their grand friends,' said the farmer's wife, 'and neither will Tom. Bessie's too young to stay up so late, and my dancing days are over. And you can't go unchaperoned.'

'Oh, Mother, make Tom go and take me with him – he *must*!' wailed Marianne on the verge of tears. 'I couldn't go to the pleasure party at Wychell Lake

145

because o' Sally's confinement, and now I'm to miss the ball. It's not fair!'

'Shame on you, when your sister came so near to death,' her mother reproved her.

'But, Mother—'

Mrs Bennett frowned and gestured for silence. She felt that becoming a grandmother had aged her ten years, and she was not inclined to give way to a scatterbrain like Marianne.

However, she received different advice from an unexpected quarter on her next visit to Pulhurst.

'Let her go, Mother,' said Mrs Twydell. 'She's had a dull time of it this summer, with all the upheaval I've caused.'

'But she can't go alone, Sally!'

'Then you must defy Father and go with her. Let my sister have a little pleasure before she has to face the truth about women's pains.'

She sighed as she spoke, and Mrs Bennett understood only too well; so she allowed herself to be persuaded, and an acceptance was sent on behalf of the mother and daughter, with polite excuses from the others. A message was returned from Bever House offering an overnight room for them and their maid; Marianne's joy was unbounded.

'You will be our maid, Susan, and help me to dress – and then you may go and have a merry time below stairs with your sister, and stay up as late as can be. Oh, my!'

This struck a chord with Susan, who had only managed a brief meeting with Polly after church one Sunday afternoon – a mere half-hour's walk around the village green within earshot of another maidservant appointed by Mrs Martin to make sure that Polly met nobody but her sister. The idea of a

146

whole night under the same roof seemed too good to be true. And Mr Edward would be in the house, too . . .

Acceptances poured in at Bever House. Old county families who in previous years might have declined the attorney's invitation were now prepared to condescend to him and his lady. There was a craving for pleasure and diversion with the war in its fourth year with no sign of victory. In Beversley the net was cast wide to include the Bennetts, the Smarts, the Turnbulls and Mrs Coulter as well as the rector, whose sister had apologetically taken to her bed, causing him a great deal of inconvenience, though the apothecary's face was grave when he visited her.

Lieutenant Henry Hansford was expected daily on home leave before setting forth across the Atlantic on a troopship at the end of September. He had not yet officially spoken to Selina or her father, and Mr Calthorpe suspected that he wanted to wait until the war was over; but Gertrude thought that an announcement should be made before he left for America, to make Selina's situation clear to other would-be suitors. Mr Calthorpe intended to have a frank talk with the young officer as soon as he returned from Portsmouth.

Preparations were going ahead in the kitchen, where Mrs Martin was engaged in much baking and broiling, while her husband strutted in a green baize apron, overseeing the cleaning and polishing of silverware, glass and plate. Martin was in high good humour, and had plans for a below-stairs entertainment that would be as memorable as the one upstairs. As he went about his duties he hummed a

147

little tune to himself, which grew into a patriotic ditty with a rousing refrain.

'It wants but dancers now to turn it into a right fine gallop!' he declared proudly, and a fiddler was brought in and paid out of Martin's own pocket to play 'The Red and the Blue' in the servants' hall on the night of the eighteenth.

Mrs Bennett took the reins of the three-seater with Marianne and Susan on either side of her. It was a fine, mild September evening, and Susan resigned herself to Marianne's excited chatter.

'There'll be that many brother officers o' Mr Calthorpe and Mr Hansford, that I dare say the young ladies'll be asked to stand up for every dance!' she said eagerly. 'Now, what'll I say if a gentleman offers his arm to take me into supper? Should I accept, or say that I'm with my mother?'

Half of Hampshire seemed to be converging on Bever House. Footmen stepped forward to open carriage doors for the more exalted guests, and the Bennett ladies were taken in charge by a pock-marked maidservant who led them up three flights of stairs and along a passage to a room with four low wooden beds.

'There be two other ladies to share the room wi' ye, an' yer maid'll sleep wi' the Bever maids,' said the girl, bobbing the briefest of curtsies.

'Yes, very well, we shall be quite comfortable, I'm sure,' said Mrs Bennett, taking off her cloak. 'See to Marianne, Susan. I've learned by now how to do up my own buttons.'

Polly Lucket was carrying up another loaded tray to the dining room where the sideboard was already laden with pies and cold meats. She eyed the main drawing room where music was playing, and thought she heard Master Osmond's laugh above the buzz of conversation; she had strict orders to return at once down the backstairs, but could not resist a quick peep in through the open door.

She gasped at the brilliance of the glowing candlelight, the gliding movement of the dancers, the beribboned gowns of the ladies and the red and blue coats of the officers as they performed a stately minuet. There was no sign of Osmond, but Mrs Calthorpe was approaching, and Polly beat a hasty retreat.

The musicians had been playing for nearly an hour, and one of them was attracting a certain curiosity among the guests. Three violins and two clarinets were augmented by a drum to give a martial flavour to the lively tunes, but who was the lady in grey silk seated at the pianoforte beside them? Playing alongside hired musicians? Surely not!

In fact Sophia was quite enjoying herself, and her position on the elevated dais gave her a good view of the assembled company. When Mr Calthorpe had asked her that day if she would agree to play in place of the pianist, who had injured his hand, she had consented willingly enough, having no great liking for an evening of polite conversation and an occasional dance with some admiring bachelor who had heard of her fortune, or a married bore doing his duty by Lord de Bever's granddaughter. She enjoyed playing, especially the country dances that were still the favourites; she watched as couples crossed, pirouetted, formed circling quartets that reversed and interwove with each other, touched hands, brushed shoulders and still managed to exchange remarks and glances as they returned to their first positions.

She saw Mrs Bennett and her daughter enter this scene of glowing light and colour, to be received by Mr and Mrs Calthorpe. They then found seats by the wall where they could view the dazzling spectacle of gowns, jewels, and feathered turbans such as were seldom seen in Beversley. In an adjoining room card tables were set out, and Sophia saw Mrs Coulter hobbling towards Mrs Bennett to invite her to try her hand at Speculation. The farmer's wife politely shook her head: her place was with her daughter, at least until the girl was asked to dance.

Marianne was smiling shyly in the direction of the Calthorpe sisters and Rosa Hansford, but they were taken up with the uniformed officers, and Osmond was surrounded by bright-eyed girls vying for his attention; Rosa's simperings behind her fan had so far failed to attract his notice.

Her brother was in the middle of a knot of blue-coated naval officers at the far end of the room, but his tall figure could not be hidden and Selina Calthorpe quickly tracked him down.

As Henry led her on to the floor to join in the dancing, he suddenly caught Sophia's eye. His look of astonishment gave way to a smile of recognition that lit up his face. Sophia responded with a slight raising of her eyebrows, and saw him speak to Selina, who also looked in her direction as she replied.

He's asking why I'm playing instead of dancing, she thought, and forthwith applied her attention to the keyboard. He would never know that Sophia mentioned him daily in her prayers, that he might be

150

kept safe from the perils of the sea and dangers of warfare. And also that he might be happy in his choice of a wife.

There he was again, looking across the room over Selina's head, even as he talked with her.

' 'Tis gracious of your cousin to play for us, Selina, for surely a member of your own family should be dancing.'

'Oh, 'tis a spinster's lot, Henry, to make herself useful where she can!' answered the young lady unconcernedly. 'Sophy is much taken up with good works, though she has an ear for music, and I dare say would rather play than dance!'

She leaned herself against him lightly as he led her down the line; she was determined not to show disappointment at his replies to her father's discreet questions. As Calthorpe had suspected, Henry had no wish to enter upon a betrothal while on active service. It would not be fair on any young lady, he said, to be asked to wait for a man who might never return. Mr Calthorpe had told Selina that Henry's sentiments did him credit, and advised patience, though Gertrude still pinned her hopes to the ball, for surely Selina had beauty and wit enough to bring the squire's son to a declaration!

Yet Henry's attention seemed oddly distracted, and his eyes were directed towards the musicians rather than on his partner.

Creeping down the backstairs, Susan recognised the little figure ahead of her, returning from the dining room with an empty tray.

'Polly? It *is* you! Oh, Poll!'

'*Sukey!*'

The tray was dropped and clattered down the stairs as they embraced.

''Ee looks that fine an' tall, Sukey, Oi hardly knows 'ee!'

'So do you, Poll, as neat an' pretty as ever I saw!'

'Aye, 'tis a good life here, Sukey, Oi tells 'ee!' giggled her sister. 'Oi never in my life had such merry times, an' the best o' it is –' she took Susan's hand and put her lips close to her ear – 'young Master Osmond ha' eyes fur none but Oi!'

Susan's smile faded a little, knowing what she had heard of the elder Calthorpe brother's ways with maidservants.

'Take care, Poll. Don't let him do what he shouldn't,' she said anxiously.

'Not Oi, Sukey, fur Oi likes to tease un!' laughed the young coquette. 'Though to tell 'ee truth, Oi loves un dear!'

'Don't go an' tell him that, Poll.'

''Course Oi won't. Tell me, Sukey, ha' ye got a sweetheart?'

'No, an' I don't want one, neither,' replied Susan firmly, thinking Polly as giddy as ever and too pretty for her own good.

'That ain't what Oi heared, Sukey,' returned her sister slyly. 'Master Edward ha' bin in his ma's bad books 'cos o' chasin' 'ee all over Beversley. Be that true or not?'

'Never say it, Poll! Mr Edward be good an' kind, but that's all that he . . .' She faltered, and Polly gave a shout of laughter.

'Sukey, 'ee be blushin'!'

'Don't be daft, Poll.'

'I ain't daft, 'ee be blushin' even more. Lord bless

152

us, Sukey, don't 'ee wish we was upstairs 'long o' them fine folks, dancin' the night away?'

'That I do not, Poll. I'm happy just to be wi' my little sister again. We'll sleep side by side tonight, like when we were children.'

Polly returned her sister's loving look with a quick warning.

'Oh, don't speak o' them old times, Sukey. The maids here don't know about –' she lowered her voice to a whisper – 'They don't know Oi be daughter to her as went fur the ol' rector in church, an' got sent to the workhouse. Oi told 'em Oi be an orphan. Come on down, Sukey, we got a fine table spread, an' a fiddler to play fur dancin'!'

With arms around each other's waists they went down to join the company in the thickening air of the servants' hall where the door was still open to the warm blue dusk, and the evening star could be seen above the tops of the beeches.

Sophia's fingers flew over the keys, and she saw out of the corner of her eye that Mrs Bennett and her daughter had sat unnoticed for half an hour on small, hard chairs, and their smiles were becoming rather strained. While whirling feet passed and repassed them on the parquet floor, and muslins and silks revolved around red and blue uniforms, not a glance was spared for Marianne, whose shoulders drooped as she sat with fading hopes; Sophia's heart ached for her, especially when a scrap of conversation drifted up to her ears from a nearby group of young people chattering between dances.

''Pon my word, there are some fine rosy-cheeked country girls here tonight!' observed a flushed army officer, mopping his brow after a particularly energetic gallop with Caroline Calthorpe, who answered with a kind of apology.

'You must understand, sir, that our mother is very kind to the village girls, and she has invited whoever is halfway pwesentable in Beversley. So I must ask you to be kind too, and go and dance with that poor girl sitting over there with her mother. They have been vainly twying to catch the eye of any passing gentleman for the past hour – though I must warn you that when she stands up her feet are monstwous bwoad, so be on your guard, sir!'

The officer glanced briefly in Marianne's direction, and joined in Caroline's girlish laugh as she lowered her lashes prettily. Sophia winced at such unkindness, and trusted that Marianne would never hear of it.

She noticed that Osmond was looking frankly bored and Edward was talking with Henry and a determinedly effusive Selina. He was frowning, and Sophia wondered if he had overheard his younger sister's remark.

Suddenly he left the group and went over to pay his respects to Mrs Smart and her two sons and one daughter who had walked up from the parsonage in Lower Beversley, having no conveyance. The parson, as usual, had more pressing demands upon his time; besides which he had no decent frock coat to wear to a ball.

As Sophia spread out the music of 'Sir Roger de Coverley' in readiness for the next dance, she saw Edward bow to Miss Lizzie Smart and hold out his hand in invitation; the young lady at once accepted and joined him in the line-up of dancers.

And then to Sophia's great satisfaction Mr Simon Smart strolled over to the Bennett ladies, and bowed to Marianne. The girl raised tear-filled eyes to meet the honest features of the parson's eldest son, a well-built young man apprenticed to a wheelwright in Belhampton and none the worse for an austere upbringing.

It warmed Sophia's heart to see Marianne's wretchedness turned to joy as Mr Simon led her into the set. And it did not end there, for they both danced together again and again, and Mr Simon escorted both mother and daughter in to supper, while his brother Andrew took care of Mrs Smart and their sister. The young couple seemed to be dancing on clouds; the awkward, large-footed Miss Marianne was transformed into a radiant beauty, and Sophia wondered whether one or two of the uniformed gallants might be wishing they had seen this charmer first!

Below stairs the temperature was rising. The groaning table had been plundered, and now it was time to set the benches against the wall and for the fiddler to step forward. Candlelight gleamed on the rows of pewter vessels and copper pans as Martin stood up and addressed both Bever House staff and the visitors.

'We now be ready to begin the dancin', and I've got a new one fur ye tonight. I'll sing the words while ye tread the measure in the style o' our country dances. Up on yer feet, then, fur "The Red and the Blue"!'

The fiddler played the opening bars and Polly was seized round the waist by a footman, who had been hovering near, waiting for his chance to claim her. Martin began to sing in a full-throated baritone.

'A soldier bold in coat of red, when bugle calls
  him off to fight,
Away in far Americky, his musket puts the foe
  to flight;
Sound the drum-beat up and down, raise up the
  flag, the day is won,
Clap hands, clap hands, clap-clap-clap-clap, his
  lady's lonely wait is done!'

The refrain was soon picked up and sung with
gusto:

'Hand in hand go down the line, the lady's little
  slipper trips –
Take the moment when it comes, and taste the
  sweetness of her lips!'

The lively music and patriotic sentiments had an
immediate appeal, and sets of eight were quickly
formed. Visiting lady's maids and coachmen were
drawn in to gallop up and down the clapping rows
while the fiddler's arm flew in and out.
   The second verse was equally well received.

'A sailor brave in coat of blue, when duty calls
  his ship must go
To rebels in Americky, the French and Dutch
  and Spanish foe;
Dance the horn-pipe up and down, raise up the
  sail and plough the foam,
Clap hands, clap hands, clap-clap-clap-clap, his
  lady waits his coming home!'

A surge of voices took up the refrain:

156

'Hand in hand go down the line, the lady's little
   slipper trips –
Take the moment when it comes, and taste the
   sweetness of her lips!'

It was an instant triumph for Martin: a new country
dance was born. Couples skipped down the lines,
circled round and re-formed the sets; clod-hopping
stable-boys and burly coachmen flung their arms
round the waists of the female servants in a bobbing
of blue and white gowns and aprons. Susan gave a
sharp cry of alarm when she was dragged into the set
by a grinning red-haired stable-lad, who bellowed
the refrain in her ear.

The open door beckoned, and the quicker wits
soon realised that if they went out through it into the
yard, they could re-enter through the kitchen door
and return to the hall along a narrow passage, past
the butler's pantry, still room and agent's office. Not
only did this diversion allow a welcome breath of air
under the star-lit sky, but it gave them a chance to
carry out the advice given in the refrain; the men
were not slow to take the moment when it came, and
the air was filled with delighted shrieks from lips
whose sweetness was found mightily pleasing.
Blushing faces reappeared in the hall to continue
dancing, while others slipped out; 'The Red and the
Blue' seemed set on course for the night.

Upstairs the musicians were at supper, but Miss
Glover remained at the piano; only a handful of
couples were dancing, among them the indefatigable
Mr Smart and Miss Bennett. Windows were flung
open to let in the cooler air, and a sound of merry-
making floated in on it, an insistent rhythm of voices,

feet and fiddle in marked contrast to the music upstairs.

'What good cheer they are having down there, dancing out of doors!' exclaimed Osmond, and, intrigued by the exuberance of the sound, he went to the landing and along the passage to the backstairs, followed by a sizeable number of the younger people, oblivious to Mrs Calthorpe's dismay. Soon they were pouring down the stairs to the servants' hall, where Osmond stood in the doorway, his light blue eyes roving over the stamping couples until he saw the girl he sought.

'All right, fellow, 'tis time to give way to a better man,' he said, dismissing the footman and seizing Polly in his arms.

'Come here, little Poll, and teach me the words of this song that has so fired you all – and I shall teach you something better, by God!'

Polly's eyes sparkled as he interwove his steps expertly with hers, and she raised her clear young voice in the refrain.

'Hand in hand go down the line, the lady's little
    slipper trips –
Take the moment when it comes, and taste the
    sweetness of her lips!'

'Ah, you're the sweetest, softest little creature, my own Polly,' murmured Osmond, nuzzling his mouth against her neck.

But Polly was by no means ready to succumb. Her sense of power in their master-and-maid relation was too intoxicating to throw away lightly. She was happy to go on playing a waiting game, to keep him pleading and adoring. Linking arms and smiling as she sang, young Polly Lucket skipped down the line of dance with her gentleman admirer, the happiest girl in Hampshire.

The stream of young people from upstairs joined hands with their partners and formed new sets for 'The Red and the Blue', taking full advantage of the diversion through the stable-yard. Osmond soon led Polly along this route to claim the sweetness of her lips, but she made sure that they always followed the others back to the hall.

Susan was having difficulty keeping her partner at arm's length; she had steeled herself to stay calm and enter into the spirit of the occasion, but when he led her out into the yard with a crowd of other flushed and giggling pairs, his drink-laden breath assailed her nostrils, awakening hateful memories.

'Oi see'd 'ee as soon as 'ee come in,' he told her, grinning. 'Sez Oi, it ain't only the pretty uns who untie their gowns an' let us feel 'em, all nice an' warm—'

He pressed himself hard against her, and she turned her face away. At first she thought it was his hand boldly exploring low down on her belly, but then realised that both his arms were around her waist and that it was his hardened male member nudging her through layers of fustian and cotton.

An uncontrollable terror seized her, a choking panic that seemed to rise up in her throat like the smell of crushed bracken fronds mingled with the stink of a man. She remembered the hoarse grunts, the stickiness between her thighs: she was once again a fourteen-year-old girl kicking out and clawing, desperate to get away from this pawing oaf.

'No, no, *stop it*, Oi won't have 'ee, Oi will *not*, Oi tells 'ee!' she protested, her voice rising to a scream.

'Hey, what the – aah! stop it, yer mad besom – *aah!*' roared the lad, ducking her blows to the derisive cheers of other couples in the yard. Thrusting her aside, he then received another and harder blow: a box on the ears from Mr Edward Calthorpe, who had suddenly appeared in the yard.

'Be off with you, lout. Take your hands off the maid, or you'll answer to me for it!'

The lad took to his heels, leaving Susan to face her rescuer and ready to die of shame at being found in such a situation, flushed and dishevelled. Had she but known, her appearance enchanted him, and he had to restrain himself from seizing her in his arms on the spot.

'My own Susan – how came you to be here in such company?'

She burst into tears. 'Mr Calthorpe – oh, Mr Calthorpe!'

All her rage and fear dissolved, together with the loathsome memories that had given rise to her wild words. She turned away from Edward, putting her hands up to her face. It was too much for him to resist, and while the dancers skipped past them with curious looks, she found herself enfolded in his arms and listening to his gentle, soothing words.

'Sweet Susan, do not cry. The fellow has gone.'

Held against his heart, her body ceased trembling; she drew a couple of deep breaths to steady herself.

'You are safe now, Susan. I beg your pardon for the treatment you have received from one of my father's own outdoor servants. He will be whipped for it.'

'Don't be too hard on him, f'r he be no different from most of 'em, Mr Edward,' she muttered, knowing full well that many of the maids would be more compliant. 'It's just that I can't bear to – to – oh!'

There was a further gush of helpless tears, and he took a fine white handkerchief out of his pocket.

'I would not have you troubled for the world, Susan,' he said, thinking how meagre were his words to convey his longing to shield her from all harm.

She wiped her eyes, and recollected where they were. 'I must go back indoors, Mr Calthorpe. My sister'll be looking f'r me.'

He smiled. 'Isn't that your sister on the arm of my brother over there? She does not appear to be searching for you, Susan!'

It was true. Polly and Osmond galloped happily past them with eyes only for each other.

Edward stepped back and bowed gravely to her, his blue eyes twinkling as he held out his hand.

'Miss Lucket, will you grant me the honour of this dance?'

As in a dream she took his hand and, facing the direction of the other couples, she stepped lightly with Edward Calthorpe along the stable-yard, in through the kitchen door, across to the dark, wainscoted passage and along it, emerging into the music-filled servants' hall. He led her back into the set she had joined with the red-haired boy, and partnered her as the dance began again. The maid who only minutes before had screeched and fought like a madwoman was now smiling and blushing with pleasure; he twirled her round, first one way and then the other, crossed and recrossed with the other couples in the set, and when he led her hand-in-hand down the line to the clap-clap-clap-clap of the rhythm, she seemed to float on air. She reached up to touch his hands and form an archway for the rest to troop under, and so long did they gaze into each other's eyes that they had to be prompted to drop hands and go down to their position at the bottom of the set. On and on went the dance, and by and by Edward led his lady through the door into the yard where the air was fresh and cool upon their faces.

His hand was on her shoulder, and his fair head leaned towards hers. She inhaled the wholesome smell of clean, warm flesh above the gauze cravat, now loosened by his exertions. She sighed and swayed towards him: their noses briefly touched before his lips found hers. A stray lock of his wavy light brown hair fell forward and caressed her forehead as Edward Calthorpe kissed Susan Lucket full on the mouth.

She offered no resistance, but gave herself up to this moment out of time. He was a prince, and she his honoured subject. The sensation was as far removed from her previous experience of man's mastery as east is from west, as heaven is from hell; it was the *cleanness* of Edward that put him immeasurably above the common run of mankind – or rather Susan's perception of the male sex, distorted as it was. His gentle good manners made him more like a god than a man in her eyes, a being to be worshipped but not feared, adored but not desired in any fleshly sense. The innocent fantasies she wove around this man involved no more than such a chaste embrace as this, the tenderness of a kiss that made her sigh with happiness. Anything of a grosser nature was not to be imagined; the very thought of it brought a blush to her face.

As for Edward, he was ready to declare himself then and there, to tell her that he wanted no other girl for his wife and that they would be married as soon as he got his degree, with or without his father's consent. They would live in Belhampton, in a couple of cosy little rooms near to the attorney's office where he would work as a junior partner. He *must* speak and tell her of his love before some rustic got to her first. Now was surely the moment . . .

In spite of all her good intentions Osmond's kisses and fondlings were having an effect on Polly, aided by a considerable intake of barley wine. She had awakened in him a fierce desire that would stand for no further delay, and he had taken her hand and pulled her across the yard to the path that led down to the beech grove.

Alone with her lover among the dark trees Polly was excited but confused. She had been hoping for an opportunity to relieve herself, but Osmond had never once let go of her hand. She hiccuped as he propped himself against the broad trunk of a tree and held her close to him; her kerchief had come untucked from her bodice, and he pulled it out of the way.

'Kiss me again, dearest Poll!'

Her legs trembled uncontrollably as his hands encircled her little breasts, and she felt him trembling too as he bent his head over the firm white flesh. Then he raised his lips to her mouth, and clinging, swooning, drowning in his arms, she gave herself up to his demanding kiss.

'You'll let me come to you, Polly – God knows I want to be within.'

He reached down and tugged at her gown, pulling it up above her knees, and she made an effort to restrain him.

'Oooh, no, Mas'r Osmon', Oi mus'n't let 'ee . . .'

But the barley wine was taking effect, and the stars

above them whirled round to the strains of 'The Red and the Blue'. Her feeble protest was silenced by kisses, and she giggled as she collapsed against him; he let himself slide down the tree trunk until he was sitting on the ground, and Polly ended up astride his thighs, her legs splayed out on each side. Through the trees the lighted windows of Bever House swayed as if under water, and she too swayed on her perch while Osmond fumbled with the buttons of his breeches. He drew her close against him, and she sighed and smiled sleepily.

'Press hard against me, Poll – I'm rising for you, by God! Open your legs wider and let me— *Damn!*'

Osmond groaned and swore as his body rushed ahead of his plans for a slowly mounting climax of pleasure with his pretty little Polly.

'In God's name, I cannot hold back. Quickly, Poll, quickly! *Now!* Damnation, I'm spending too soon, by hell!'

Burying his head against her shoulder, he gripped her little form as his body heaved and shuddered. Polly felt a huge hardness against her woman's parts, quickly followed by a warm oozing; then the hardness was gone, and she was left spread-eagled, her skirt above her hips: and then, merciful relief . . .

He laughed ruefully. 'That's finished that, little Polly. I was too quick, or not quick enough. I've spent, and you've missed me! Never mind, we have it still to come. I'll make it up to you, by God!'

Polly swayed and smiled happily, bathed in a warm river of comfort; it flowed and flowed around her as if it would never stop.

Osmond's voice broke in sharply on her dreamy state.

'Why, you dirty little vixen! I lose my seed too

164

soon, and what do you do but sit there and *piss* all over me, by God!'

It was true. Poor Polly's gown was soaked, as were his unbuttoned breeches and the edges of his shirt and military jacket. Polly was bewildered by his change of attitude. What had become of the overwhelming desire he had shown not five minutes ago?

His indignation turned to loud, guffawing laughter.

'Damn me, Poll, I'll have to say I pissed before I could unbutton, and my father will rail at me again for a drunkard. Get up, Poll, and pull down your petticoats – come on!'

A damp, shivering, giddy Polly was half-led, half-dragged back to the house, staggering on the uneven paving of the stable-yard as her father had done more than a decade earlier. She clutched at Osmond, who continued to laugh and curse by turns, finally pushing her in through the kitchen door and disappearing before he was seen with a drunken maidservant.

But in fact they were both seen.

'Polly!' cried Susan, disengaging herself from Edward's arms as he was about to declare his love. 'Oh, my poor Poll, what ha' that damned man done to 'ee?'

Polly turned unfocused eyes on her sister and gaped stupidly. A wave of shame and dismay swept over Susan, not only for Polly's condition but that Edward should be a witness to it; her first thought was to get Polly up to the maids' sleeping quarters above the laundry, out of sight. She accepted Edward's assistance to help carry the girl up the narrow stairway, but after muttering her thanks she begged him to leave them at once.

165

'Ye mustn't be seen here, Ed— Mr Calthorpe. 'Twould mean more trouble f'r us all. Be quick an' go!'

He had no choice but to obey, sick at heart and full of anger against his brother.

Alone with Polly in the maids' room, Susan removed the wet gown from the unresisting girl and put a cotton nightshift on her as she lay on her straw pallet under the slanting ceiling.

'Poor, silly Polly, I fear the worst for ye,' she said grimly.

Polly hiccuped, yawned and turned over on her side. 'Mas'r Osmon',' she murmured thickly.

'Devil take Master Osmond and all such who ruin poor girls like yeself, Polly.' Susan's voice was low but cold as ice. She was quite certain that Polly's maidenhead had been breached, a calamity that could have dire consequences; it was a reminder of the unbridgeable gap between the Calthorpes and themselves.

With the drawing room practically emptied of dancers and the musicians not returned from supper, Sophia was still at her post, supplying music for the few couples on the floor: Mr Andrew Smart and his sister, Lizzie, were dancing a minuet with his brother, Simon, and Miss Marianne, while Mrs Bennett looked on with fond approval. Parson Smart might be poor, but the family was respectable enough, and Simon was a good worker who would support a wife and dependents by the sweat of his brow, owing nothing to other men's favours. The farmer might not be too pleased, but if this evening's business came to anything, Sarah Bennett was confident that she would be able to talk him round.

166

The hired musicians returned and lounged in their seats, nodding appreciatively at the tireless lady pianist whose nimble fingers continued to run up and down the keyboard.

When the tall, blue-coated officer entered the drawing room, Sophia was immediately aware of him. He was alone, and made his way straight towards the musicians' dais.

He must be looking for Selina, she thought, and was about to suggest that he try downstairs, but he stopped and spoke to the musicians, who nodded respectfully and picked up their instruments to accompany the minuet.

Sophia would have gone on playing, but Henry Hansford had stepped to the side of the pianoforte and was looking at her with a strange intensity.

'Miss Glover, you have not stopped playing all the evening,' he said. 'I insist that you break now, and leave the seat you have occupied so long.'

'I beg your pardon, Lieutenant Hansford,' she answered pleasantly, her hands still on the keys. 'I am sure I have enjoyed the evening as well as anybody else here tonight.'

'I am glad to hear it, but my own enjoyment will not be complete until I have danced with you, Miss Glover. Will you do me that honour?'

Sophia caught her breath momentarily: she was conscious of a tremor in the region of her heart, and a need to hide her own feelings. Mr Hansford was some years younger than herself, and, more importantly, was as good as betrothed to another – her own young cousin Selina. She smiled and shook her head.

'Thank you, Lieutenant, but I am not dancing tonight.' She spoke in the composed manner for which she was known, but he appeared not to hear her, for he quietly closed the lid of the pianoforte and leaned upon it, looking down at her.

'But I am asking you to make an exception in my case, Miss Glover. I shall soon be in the thick of war once more, and do not know when I shall return. I ask you again, will you dance with me? I beg you not to refuse.'

Sophia took a breath, looked down at her hands and then raised her eyes to meet his. Without a word she rose from the piano and took his hand. He bowed and led her to join the other two couples on the floor, where there were more smiles, more bows and curtsies, and the stately dance continued.

This was entertainment indeed for Mrs Bennett, sitting on the other side of the room.

'D'you see what I see, Margaret?' she asked the midwife, who had come to sit beside her.

'I do, Sarah – and the way he turns his head to look at her.'

It was true. As soon as the couple took their first steps, he looked straight into her eyes and said, 'Sophia.'

So then she knew. There was no need to pretend or try to persuade herself otherwise. He had chosen her, and there was no other. Her blue eyes shone softly in the candlelight, which caught the glossy ringlets at the nape of her neck, and the hired musicians stared in surprise at their pianist, wondering why they had failed to notice earlier how beautiful she was.

'How old would she be, Margaret?' asked Mrs Bennett.

The midwife closed her eyes as she worked out dates. 'Must be twenty-eight – no, twenty-nine years since that poor little sempstress died in childbirth. And what about him?'

'The Hansfords' first was born dead, and then she had Henry two years later, that was before I had Tom,' calculated Mrs Bennett. 'Yes, he must be around twenty-four, and old for his years, being in the navy. It's not such a wide gap, Margaret.'

'And a much better choice,' answered the midwife sagely.

For the couple under discussion everything was changed – or rather, everything was revealed.

'I have been blind for so long, my Sophia – 'tis *you* I have been dreaming of all these months at sea. 'Twas you all the time, and I did not know it!'

She turned her head to look up at him, and everything he longed to see was there in her eyes. And all for him.

With Susan and Polly gone from the scene, Edward was filled with a bitter resentment towards his brother; he almost hated Osmond for the selfish lust that took no thought for consequences, and which had interrupted his own precious time with Susan. Coming upon Osmond with a group of army officers on the stairs, he faced him squarely.

'I want a word with you, Brother.'

'Why, what a face you have on you, Ned! Has your virtuous little maidservant given you the slip?' grinned Osmond.

'I promise you, Brother, if you have harmed that young Lucket girl, I'll knock you down – nor will I ever forgive—'

'What do you mean, Neddy? God knows I haven't touched the girl – or any other tonight,' replied Osmond with a short laugh, while the others looked on uncertainly.

Edward turned his back on them with a gesture of

contempt, and having no further interest in the ball, he went out to the stables and saddled his horse for a solitary nocturnal ride across the common. He tried to think of Susan, but she evaded him. Her face was pale and dim and far away.

The fiddler was still playing in the servants' hall, though Martin's voice had long given out. Selina Calthorpe stood irresolutely in the doorway, trying not to show her irritation. Henry had come downstairs and danced a couple of measures of 'The Red and the Blue', but now there was no sign of him. The young lady's determination to be bright and gracious was coming under increasing strain. Where on earth had he gone? Her cold blue eyes assured her definitely that he was not among the dancers, where her sister, Caroline, was cavorting with a sweating redcoat. Selina impatiently turned her back on the scene.

It was too bad of Henry – unless of course he was talking with her parents at this very moment. Ah, yes, maybe that was it! She lifted her skirts to run up the stairs to the drawing room, where a minuet was being played.

There were only three couples on the floor – good heavens, that Bennett girl was still hanging on to the parson's son! – and Sophy must have gone for a belated supper, for the piano was deserted.

Mrs Bennett nudged her companion. 'Look over there, Margaret.'

The shock on Selina's face when she realised that Henry was dancing with her cousin was a sight to remember. At first she told herself that he was just being kind, and regretted her earlier remarks about Sophy's spinster status and good works. She would

170

tell him that she had not meant any spite by it, and might even say she was sorry.

But then she saw him looking at Sophia as if he could not take his eyes from her face. When their hands touched in the course of the dance, he raised hers to his lips in an impulsive movement, the gesture of a lover.

Selina Calthorpe was not in the picture.

Mrs Bennett nodded significantly at her companion. She would have a fine tale to tell Sally on her next visit to Pulhurst!

Leaving Polly sleeping, Susan made her way back to the room allocated to the Bennett ladies. Weary and dispirited, she braced herself to listen to Marianne's account of the ball.

She had not long to wait. Marianne opened the door and seized her in a rapturous hug.

'Such company, Susan! Such dancing! It has been the happiest night of my life,' she exclaimed joyously.

'Yes, yes, Marianne, you can talk about it later,' said her mother. 'Go and fetch your bonnet and cloak, Susan, for we're going home. There has been a change o' plan. I'm taking Mrs Smart and Miss Smart home in the three-seater, and Marianne will walk with Mr Simon and Mr Andrew. I shall not be sorry to sleep in my own bed,' she added, glancing down at the straw mattresses.

Susan saw how the land lay. 'And am I to return wi' ye?' she asked, dismayed at having to desert Polly. Mrs Bennett noticed her anxious look, and realised that the maid would also have to walk; on this occasion the farmer's wife was inclined to be lenient.

'You may stay overnight with your sister if you like, Susan, but you must come back at first light.'

'That I will. Oh, Mrs Bennett, thank ye – an' I'm glad Miss Marianne enjoyed the ball!'

Susan lay down beside Polly in the crowded room with five Bever maids and two other visiting lady's maids beside herself, sprawling on straw pallets and sharing blankets.

'Be ye feelin' better now, Poll?' she whispered.

'Oh, Sukey, Oi done a terrible thing,' came the reply in a small, flat voice that confirmed Susan's fears.

'What'd he do to ye, Poll? Can ye remember?'

'Some o' it, not all. Oh, Sukey, Oi be too ashamed to tell 'ee what Oi did!'

Titters arose from the Bever maids, who knew about Polly's special relationship with young Master Osmond, and Polly began to sob.

'Oh, Sukey, it be hard fur poor girls who don't know the fancy ways o' ladies an' gen'lemen!'

'I reckon it ain't hard to guess what he done!' mocked a voice in the darkness, followed by more giggles.

'Hush, Poll, there be no use in talkin' now, 'tis too late. Just pray that ye be not in trouble.'

She stroked the curly head that lay in the crook of her arm until the sobs turned to gentle snores. Within half an hour all the rest were asleep, and Susan was left to ponder in the darkness over the dangers that lay in wait for her silly little sister, Polly.

But her last thought was of Edward, who had said he would not have her troubled for the world.

And had kissed her so sweetly upon her lips.

172

Chapter 13

A heavy cloud of heartbreak and anger hung over Bever House on the Saturday morning following the ball. Mrs Calthorpe kept to her bed, attended by her personal maidservant, Jael Ferris, who also glided into Selina's darkened room from time to time with wine and water.

Edward had spent a few sleepless hours on his bed, wrestling with his troubled thoughts; his one idea was to declare himself to Susan Lucket and claim her affections. How soon could he ride over to the Bennett farmhouse, and what should he say to the farmer and his wife? Unknowingly he missed an opportunity to speak to Susan alone that morning, for she had woken at daybreak, taken whispered leave of her sister and walked back to the farmhouse with only her confused reflections for company.

For Susan now acknowledged to herself that she loved Edward Calthorpe, and could not deny that his attentions gave her a tremulous joy. How could she not rejoice, knowing she was admired by the man she had worshipped from a distance ever since they were children? Yet Miss Glover's warning came back to her, not to allow herself to dream of anything more: it would be quite unheard of. And there was her dread that Polly might be in trouble because of Edward's elder brother. Susan felt nothing but scorn for the man, and had no cause to think highly of the rest of the family, which was another reason why she should not dream of *him*, why she must do as Miss Glover advised, and pray to overcome such forbidden thoughts. And yet . . . the sensation of his lips on hers last night had nothing to do with reason.

At the farm, Marianne greeted her with an ecstatic account of her own triumphant evening at the ball, and equally happy anticipation of courtship to come. Susan's head ached as the girl prattled on, but she tried to smile and show interest in Mr Smart's many virtues, until Mrs Bennett suddenly broke in.

'And how did you find your sister, Susan?'

Susan might have replied politely that Polly was well, but found that she could not speak. Tears filled her eyes, and she could only shake her head. Mrs Bennett gave a sympathetic nod and did not repeat the question, though she put two and two together, and like Susan she made five. If that silly little creature was with child she would be turned out of Bever House, as Jenny Kyte had been, and have nowhere to go but the House of Industry, thought the farmer's wife. The Calthorpes would never accept any blame for her condition, nor would they offer her a penny of support.

Shortly before noon Marianne's happiness ended abruptly. A gentleman walking up Bennett's Lane turned out to be Mr Simon Smart calling to offer his compliments to Mrs and Miss Bennett, but he did not even get over the threshhold. The farmer called out to him from the adjoining field, demanded to know his business and ordered him to turn round and go back to finish his apprenticeship and stay away from a girl who was much too young and foolish to be talking of courtship.

Marianne's floods of tears plunged the house into gloom, and Mrs Bennett took her up to her room where she comforted her as well as she could. Susan was ordered to take over in the kitchen, filling a basket with bread, cold meat and cheese for the outdoor labourers, along with a large jug of ale, and to take it down to the field where the plough was already turning over the stubble after harvesting.

And this was the situation when Edward Calthorpe arrived. He was shown into the family parlour where he stood hat in hand for a quarter of an hour; nobody seemed to be around but a gaping Bet, who had answered his knock. Susan had caught a distant sight of him riding up the lane on her way back with the empty basket, and her heart leaped with joy and fear and hope and despair – for she knew that it was herself he had come to see. Trembling, she crept in at the kitchen door and stayed there, washing utensils at the stone sink, sending Bet out to fetch more water.

When at length Mrs Bennett entered the parlour, she gave a start at seeing young Calthorpe. Bet had mumbled something about 'The gen'leman be here,' and she had assumed him to be Mr Simon. With Marianne's sobs in her ears, she had put off the moment of encounter, not knowing what she could say.

She apologised for keeping Mr Calthorpe waiting, but when he asked to speak with Susan Lucket, her mouth tightened.

'We don't allow our maidservants to spend time alone with gentlemen under our roof, Mr Edward,' she said, her tone implying that the ban applied as much to Calthorpes as to any others.

'But I have a need to speak to her, mistress,' he insisted, wondering how firm he should be if his request was denied.

'You could have seen her this morning before she returned from Bever House,' said Mrs Bennett unhelpfully.

He checked an exclamation of annoyance, for he had not known of Susan's overnight stay.

'What is your business with her, Mr Edward?' She made him feel like a schoolboy, but in fact Sarah Bennett was on her guard and, remembering Polly, she faced this young Calthorpe with the distrust she felt towards the whole family.

Edward hesitated. He had come prepared to lay his heart before Susan, but laying it before Mrs Bennett was a different matter. He decided on complete frankness.

'I have come to tell Miss – to tell Susan – to ask her to marry me when I am able to support her, Mrs Bennett.'

The farmer's wife reached for the nearest chair and sat down. A Calthorpe talking of marriage to a servant girl!

'D'your father and mother know?' she asked.

'Not yet, mistress. I want to secure Susan's promise to wait for me. 'Twill be two years before I can start practising as an attorney.' Edward felt a kind of relief, almost thankfulness, in confiding in a woman who had Susan's interests at heart.

'Your honesty does you credit, Mr Edward, but you and the maid are very young. She may not care to be tied to a promise for so long. Besides . . .'

The parson's son had been dispatched with a flea in his ear, and yet here was a Calthorpe come a-courting their maidservant. The irony of it was not lost on Mrs Bennett.

'Besides, I have a duty to the maids in my care, Mr Edward.'

'Then let me tell you, mistress, I love her with all my heart, as God sees and knows.'

It was impossible not to be touched by the words and the way in which he spoke them. Mrs Bennett had to make a decision.

'I'll go and tell the girl that you're here, Mr Edward,' she said, 'but if she doesn't care to hear you, or wants not to be left alone with you, 'twill be as she wishes.'

He bowed his acceptance of this.

When her mistress came in search of her, Susan shook in every limb, and Sarah felt obliged to offer the kind of advice she would give a daughter.

'Mr Edward seems a civil enough young gentleman, and I believe he means what he says now, Susan – but you are both much too young, and his family would never – I mean he can't defy his parents on account of you. And with this war on, it's no time to be making promises that can't be kept.'

'Oh, that be just what Miss Glov— what I think meself, Mrs Bennett,' Susan answered gratefully. 'But he be the best o' men, even if I can't have him,' she added, leaving Mrs Bennett in no doubt of her true feelings.

'D'you want to bid him farewell, Susan, or shall I send him away like the farmer sent Mr Simon?'

Susan hastily smoothed her gown and straightened her cap, following her mistress into the parlour. As soon as Edward saw her, he was at her side.

'Susan – oh, my love – er, good day to you, Miss Lucket,' he said, catching Mrs Bennett's warning look.

Susan automatically curtsied. 'Good day to ye, sir.'

'Susan knows your errand, Mr Edward,' said Mrs

Bennett. 'There's to be no talk o' promises until the times are better and you're both older.'

'But I must speak to her!' pleaded Edward, looking first at one and then at the other. 'I have to return to Oxford next week, and cannot go without telling her of my intentions.'

Sarah Bennett decided to be kind.

'I'd better go and see what that idle girl's doing in the dairy. It won't take me more'n five minutes, then I'll be back,' she told him with a meaningful glance at the long-case clock on the wall.

As soon as the door closed behind her, Edward seized Susan's hand and held it to his lips.

'Dearest Susan, I have come to tell you of my love for you, and to ask if you will wait for me,' he began, but when she raised her troubled grey eyes to meet his, he could not hold back. His arms went round her as if of their own volition, and he drew her head down against his shoulder. His voice shook as he uttered the words he had rehearsed.

'A year from now I shall have a degree, Susan, and may then start to practise as a junior attorney – and after another year I'll be able to take a little home for us in Belhampton.'

She cut in quickly, almost fearfully. 'Oh, Mr Edward, how can it ever be?'

'Believe that it can be, Susan – and tell me – oh, please tell me that you love me!' Edward had no knowledge of lovers' talk, but spoke from his heart. 'If you can but love me, I would wait for ever.'

Susan's thoughts whirled. On the one hand she heard his words with incredulous joy, while on the other caution and common sense told her that this was utter folly, and could never come to reality, for all the reasons already given. And there was something else too, something deeper and darker that she could not name and did not even want to think about.

Without raising her head she murmured his name under her breath. 'Edward.'

'Susan – my own sweet Susan.' He put his forefinger beneath her chin and gently raised her head so that he could press his lips to her forehead. 'I'll have none other in the world but you, Susan.'

She could not answer straight away, but struggled to compose herself, to quieten her agitation.

'Susan? Have I your answer?'

How should she answer? How could she *not* answer, with Edward's arms around her, his face so close that she could feel the warmth of his skin. How could she be calm and sensible?

She could. And she was.

'I can tell ye only one thing f'r sure, Edward. Whatever happens, even if we can't ever be – if I can't have ye, Edward, I'll have no other. Not ever. Ye have my word on't.'

'My sweet Susan! Then you'll be my wife in the course of time, for *I* will never have another. Never.'

Again she raised her face to look into his. Their eyes met and his lips found hers in a brief but infinitely tender kiss.

When Mrs Bennett returned after exactly five minutes, he took his leave, not unhappily, for he had Susan's promise echoing and re-echoing in his ears. And in his heart.

As for Susan, she clung to the memory of their farewell – his words, his touch, his look, his kiss – but she dared not look too far into the future. Edward loved her today, and that had to be enough.

*

When Lieutenant Hansford called at Glover Cottage that morning, there were no reservations placed on the promises exchanged between himself and Miss Glover; the meeting was in every way a happy affirmation of what had passed between them the previous evening at the ball. His love was declared, and her response was all that he could desire. Their only sadness was the prospect of his early departure to America to face the dangers of a sailor's life in wartime.

For the remainder of his leave the pair were frequently seen together in Beversley. Sophia was briefly received by the squire and his lady, though Mrs Hansford did not make a return visit to Glover Cottage. Relations between the squire's family and Bever House were strained for a time, as the very name of Sophia Glover threw Mrs Calthorpe into a hysterical rage; she was seen as having deliberately set out to steal Henry from Selina.

Nevertheless the newly betrothed pair visited other homes in Beversley, and entertained Parson and Mrs Smart to dinner at Glover Cottage. They also called at the Bennett farmhouse, where Sophia passed on some very welcome news to Susan, which was that one of the Bever maidservants had told Miss Glover's kitchen-maid that poor little Polly Lucket was crippled with belly-cramps at the time of her monthly flow. Susan's thankfulness was so great that she forgave Miss Glover for changing her mind and becoming betrothed to the man she had admitted to foolishly dreaming of – now revealed to be young Mr Henry Hansford, friend of the Calthorpe brothers and linked with their elder sister. Until now.

*

Polly Lucket's encounter with Osmond in the beech grove had been such a shaming experience for her that she could not bring herself to face him following the ball. No amount of smiles and teasing on his part could bring her again to his side, and right up to the day of his departure for Woolwich she took evasive action every time she saw him loitering near to her. This only inflamed his desire, and he consoled himself with the prospect of future pursuit of his pretty little Polly.

Only it was taking a deuced long time, by God!

When all the leave-takings were over, autumn seemed to come in overnight with whining south-westerly winds that stripped the trees and sent the leaves flying across sodden fields; the last swallows and swifts hastily departed.

It was noticed that Miss Glover threw herself into parish work with even greater energy after the lieutenant's departure; there was a new youthfulness in her step, a fresh sparkle in her ready smile. The only change in her circumstances was that Mrs Coulter moved into Glover Cottage, where the pony-trap was always available to take her to women in travail. The midwife's rheumaticks had become worse, and she had been late arriving in the birth-chamber on at least two occasions.

It was clear that the time had come to train a decent, able-bodied woman to be an assistant to Mrs Coulter and take some of the work from her shoulders.

But who? Nobody among the mostly unlettered mothers of large families had the time to spare, nor did they have the necessary skill and judgement. Widow Gibson was good enough for Lower

Beversley, but not for attending tradesmen's wives, who could pay for the services of a properly licensed midwife. In the whole of the village Sophia could think of nobody remotely suitable.

When Mrs Coulter herself suggested Susan Lucket, Sophia was quite shocked.

'But she is a *maiden*, Margaret, a girl not yet twenty!'

'She has a wise head on her shoulders, Sophy, and keeps it there when other, older women have been known to give way to panic. And she has a natural leaning to the work.'

'I agree she is a very capable girl, but she has no experience of childbirth,' Sophia pointed out.

''Tis generally held that a midwife must have borne a child in wedlock, Sophy, but I have long observed that a woman in the pain of travail will accept anybody who can relieve her, whether it be a man like Turnbull or a drunken creature such as delivers the bastards in the House of Industry. I tell you, Sophy, I thanked God for Susan when Sally Twydell suffered such grief, for without her I'd have fallen with exhaustion and lost my good name. She saved that mother and child as much as I did.'

The midwife heaved herself out of her chair and reached for her stick. 'I need to go to the close-stool, and my joints move but slowly.'

She hobbled to the door, wincing as the inflamed hip joint took the weight of her body.

Sophia sighed. The poor woman did not always get to the privy in time to save her skirts from a wetting, and there were dark patches on some of the chairs where she had sat. Tess wrinkled her nose when Sophia told her to sponge the seats with a cloth wrung out in vinegar.

182

The shortening days and weeks went by, and then quite suddenly the matter was decided by the dictates of circumstances or, as Sophia saw it, the will of the Almighty.

When the landlord of the Swan sent word that his wife had begun her travail one wet Sunday afternoon, Mrs Coulter's face fell. She had been in pain all day, and Mr Turnbull's tincture of opium had made her sleepy and stupid without much easing the red-hot needles of pain in her hip. Sophia wrapped a warm sheep's fleece over the affected part and helped her up into the pony-trap. They jolted down the track towards the turning into Mill Lane, but before they reached it a ragged-breeched boy of about ten came running from Crabb's cottages.

'Missus! It be me ma, her sent me ter fetch 'ee!' he shouted to the midwife.

'Mercy on us, 'tis the Dummet boy,' she groaned. 'His mother's due with her seventh. Whatever shall I do, Sophy? The one at the Swan'll probably take longer, but how can I leave her?'

Sophia thought quickly.

'Tell your mother I'll send help to her within the hour,' she told the boy, turning the pony towards Mill Lane. 'I'll put you down at the Swan, Margaret, and then go on to the Bennetts' farm and ask for Susan Lucket to come to the Dummet woman. 'Tis the best we can do, and I pray it may go well. Gey-up!'

The pony trotted briskly along the muddy lane, sending up a shower of clods on either side. The landlord came out to assist Mrs Coulter's slow and painful descent, and Miss Glover continued on to the farm.

'Susan! You're to come quickly. Miss Glover needs

you,' ordered Mrs Bennett excitedly. 'Leave what you're at, and fetch your cloak.'

Miss Glover stood in the parlour, her cape and bonnet dripping.

'Good day, Susan. I need your services as midwife.'

She proceeded to explain about the two women brought to bed at the same time, and Mrs Coulter's infirmity.

'I shall be with you at the bedside, Susan, and none will dare speak amiss. Come, there is no time to be lost.'

'Go and comfort Mary Dummet as you comforted my Sally,' urged the farmer's wife. 'You'll come back with a fine tale, I don't doubt!'

Seated beside Miss Glover in the trap, Susan looked out upon the already darkening fields with a sinking heart. What should she say on entering the birth-chamber? Suppose the woman's husband turned her out?

Miss Glover's face was set and unsmiling as she silently prayed for courage. Familiar as she was with the lives of the Beversley poor, she had hitherto been excluded from the mysterious rites of childbirth by her spinster status, and now here she was, unprepared with any knowledge of this great matter, accompanying a young girl from a notorious family to attend a woman in travail.

Lord Jesus Christ, have mercy upon us and all women in need of Thine help, she silently implored.

They reached Crabb's Lane and turned towards the huddle of low-roofed dwellings, their candle-lit windows glowing faintly. A burly farm hand approached, calling through the drizzling November dusk.

'Mrs Coulter?'

'Good evening, Dummet. Mrs Coulter has had to attend another birthing, so I have brought young Miss Lucket to help your wife,' answered Miss Glover with all the authority of a visiting gentle-woman.

'Good evenin',' he said doubtfully as they climbed down. 'Ye'd better get inside. Her be huffin' an' haa-in', the way she allus does when 'tis gettin' near.'

'Good. Take care of the pony and tether him,' ordered Sophia.

They entered a small, stuffy room that smelled of bodies, candle-grease and baked potatoes. Children's faces, pale and large-eyed, seemed to stare from every dark corner.

The two visitors climbed a narrow, boxed-in stair-way to a single room where the children's pallets lay piled at one end and the matrimonial box-bed stood at the other, with Mrs Dummet writhing and moan-ing upon it. A short cotton shift scarcely covered the huge dome of her belly. Two neighbours sat beside her, and the room reeked of porter, the strong ale that was supposed to enrich the blood and ease the birth-pangs, while ensuring a good milk supply for the child.

Miss Glover removed her cape and bonnet, nodding to Susan to do the same.

'How long has she been in pain?' she asked.

'Nigh on two hours, missus,' replied the older of the two women with a disapproving look at Susan.

'Very good,' said Sophia, feeling nothing but dismay. 'Take our wet clothes and lay them together.'

Susan sensed their hostility towards herself, and it had the effect of making her resolve to prove them wrong. Holding her head high she approached the

185

bed. Mrs Dummet lay gasping, her matted hair clinging to her forehead in damp strands.

'Take a rest afore the next pain comes, Mrs Dummet,' said Susan softly. 'Let y'rself go all loose an' limp. Lay quiet an' still, and just breathe in and out, in and out, that's the way.'

The two women muttered to each other.

'Not much good tellin' her ter lay still when any fool can see that she got the pains on her and needs ter start pushin'. What do a wench from the—'

'Hold your tongue, goodwife!' snapped Miss Glover with unusual asperity. 'Take away that chamber pot, and bring it back empty.'

The women looked mutinous, but the older one told the younger to do as they were bidden.

Mrs Dummet began to heave and moan again as another pain seized her muscles, and Susan gently turned her over on to her left side. Sitting down beside her on the bed, she began to rub the woman's back with long, sweeping strokes, then in a circular movement just above the cleft of the buttocks. She spoke quietly, repeating the words over again and again.

'Don't hold y'r breath, Mrs Dummet, let the air go in and out, in and out. That's the way – breathe in and out, in and out – good, that's very good. Has the pain gone now? Then let y'rself go limp on the bed, and rest till the next one.'

Her repeated phrases and the stroking movements of her hands began to produce a relaxation of the woman's body, with a consequent easing of fear and tension. A calmer atmosphere prevailed in the room. Sophia Glover watched in wonder.

'What be y'r name, Mrs Dummet?' asked Susan. 'Mary, is it? Take heart an' trust me, Mary, and all will go well wi' ye.'

She smiled into the woman's face, and their eyes met: in that moment she and Mary Dummet became partners. Having scarcely met before this day, there was now a lasting bond between them.

A stout wooden box-cot was at hand with a length of linen and woollen covers. Susan asked for the string and scissors such as Mrs Coulter used to sever the belly-cord, and the women were sent to fetch a bowl of warm water. The news quickly spread that poor Mary Dummet was giving birth without a midwife, attended only by a spinster who knew nothing of women's mysteries and the Lucket girl – yes, a *Lucket*, believe it or not! Things had come to a sad pass in Beversley these days.

Within half an hour Mary Dummet's groans turned to the characteristic expulsive grunts, and Susan could see the top of the baby's head at the height of pain. A clean towel was spread between the mother's parted thighs, and within another ten minutes she was safely delivered of her seventh child, a little daughter whose robust first cry was a signal for great relief and rejoicing. Susan placed her in her mother's arms, and Sophia Glover almost fell on her knees, such was her awe at what she had witnessed. She thanked God that she had been privileged to assist at this miracle.

Flushed and perspiring, Susan did not dare to relax until the baby's arrival had been followed by the after-burden, that strange object like a lump of ox's liver. She remembered how at Joby's birth it had been cooked and eaten by the hungry Luckets.

And then she looked around and saw that she was no longer an unwelcome intruder, but the heroine of the hour. Mary was laughing and embracing her, as was Sophia, and the two neighbours had stopped

187

muttering and joined in the general chorus of praise. Miss Glover called Dummet and the children upstairs to see the new baby, and above the child's lusty cries Susan heard herself referred to as Mistress Lucket.

It was a moment of triumph, and she rejoiced that the birthing had been easy, with no unforeseen dilemmas. At eighteen years of age she had attended a woman in childbirth as the only midwife, and a healthy baby now lay in the mother's arms. Come what may, Susan now knew that her destiny was assured. She was indeed the future Beversley midwife.

Mistress Lucket.

Part III: 1780–1783

Midwife

Chapter 14

There was no market in Belhampton on the blowy April day that Mr Turnbull drove across the common with his two passengers; apart from meeting a one-eyed beggar woman and two army officers on horseback, they had the road to themselves.

Little was said on the journey; each of them was deep in thought about the coming interview with Dr Parnham, the renowned man-midwife. Susan Lucket had formally applied to be enrolled as a pupil at his next course of lectures to midwives, and he had agreed at least to see her, accompanied by Miss Glover and the apothecary.

As Mrs Coulter's assistant over the past sixteen months, Susan had attended ten women in childbirth. She still lived and worked as a maidservant at the Bennetts' farmhouse, but when a summons came to attend at a birthing, either by messenger or the arrival of Miss Glover's pony-trap, she was at once released to go to the more urgent duty, and Mrs Bennett eagerly awaited her return with news of the outcome: was it a boy or a girl? How long was the travail? How had Mistress Lucket been received? The farmer's wife took a certain pride in the fact that the young midwife lodged with her, and messages from Glover Cottage had to pass through her; on occasion she herself had taken Susan to where her services were required, and stood by offering advice and comfort to the prospective grandmother and other relatives.

Mr Turnbull had quickly come to rely on Susan's judgement, and consulted with her as an equal, forgetting her youth and maiden status because of her seemingly intuitive knowledge of women's business, a minefield that gave him more grey hairs than any other of his professional duties. And because she was unmarried, untrained and unlicensed to practise, and therefore in a vulnerable position, he had agreed to Miss Glover's request that he plead her cause to Dr Parnham, seeing that Mrs Coulter was in too much pain to make the journey of five miles each way along an uneven track. As they neared Belhampton, however, Turnbull's resolution began to waver, and he wondered how he would stand up to possible rigorous questioning from the surgeon.

Miss Glover, on the other hand, appeared calm and confident, smiling encouragingly at Susan from time to time; betrothed to the squire's son for a year and a half, she remained a model of useful, contented spinsterhood. All her former reservations about the propriety of Susan acting as a midwife had been overcome, and she was more than willing to pay Dr Parnham's fees for the course of tuition, and the licence that would be granted to Susan on its completion. She had provided the girl with a handsomely bound book in which to record her deliveries, and had sent to London for a copy of Dr George Counsell's textbook, *The Midwife's Sure Guide*, which, although published some thirty years ago, was full of sound advice to such midwives who could read it. Susan had painstakingly copied every detail of her first notebook into the larger one: the names and addresses of the women she had attended, with their dates and times of birthing, together with a few notes on the deliveries, and she had brought it with her to show Dr Parnham. She also had a letter in Margaret Coulter's painful scrawl, testifying to her natural competence at midwifery and unblemished character.

She now returned Miss Glover's smile and raised her eyebrows in a little gesture that said what will be, will be. Whether or not the good doctor agreed to take her on as a pupil, she would continue to practise as an unlicensed midwife in Beversley through sheer necessity, there being no other to assist the ailing Mrs Coulter.

Just before they reached the outskirts of the town they passed the House of Industry looming behind a row of poplars to their right. Susan turned her head to the left, not wanting even to look at the stark three-storey building in sullen grey stone. For almost two years Doll Lucket had languished there, and was becoming something of a legendary figure of whom weird stories were whispered.

Sophia noticed the closed expression on Susan's face, but refrained from making any remark about her relationship to Doll, perhaps for fear of the response.

The track now straightened, widened and became the road into Belhampton. A little further on it divided two ways, one to the market square and the other curving uphill to a cluster of handsome dwellings standing in their own gardens. Turnbull reined in before one of these, a tall red-brick house with classical Queen Anne gables.

A trim maid showed them into a book-lined study with a large desk, several high-backed chairs and a half-circle of smaller ones. Sophia sat down and Turnbull motioned Susan to a chair, where she sat clutching the woven straw bag that held her register of births.

She stood up again when the door opened and a well-built man of between forty-five and fifty entered. He was of middle height, comfortably rather than fashionably dressed, and wore a light grey wig with curls at the temple and a short queue at the back. His sharp eyes seemed to take in the three of them at a glance.

'Good morning.' He bowed briefly to Miss Glover, who inclined her head.

Turnbull began nervously, 'Good morning, Dr Parnham. I trust that you—'

'Is this the girl you told me of, Turnbull? By my faith, she's scarcely more than a child. Has she really attended women in childbirth?'

'She has indeed, Dr Par—'

'Then 'tis no wonder I hear stories about Beversley,' cut in the doctor with a short laugh, sitting down at the desk and indicating the circle of chairs.

'This is where I give instruction, and discuss methods of securing a good outcome when the child is in the breech and other less common positions,' he told them. 'I teach the use of the birthing forceps to the doctors, and impress upon the midwives not to delay sending for a doctor when the situation is beyond their skill.'

Susan gave a slight nod, recognising this piece of advice from *The Midwife's Sure Guide*. Parnham glanced at her.

'So, what do you want me to do with this solemn-faced girl, Turnbull? I am at pains to understand why you have brought her here, for she is ten or fifteen years too early for the business I speak of.'

When Turnbull hesitated, Miss Glover answered for him.

'Indeed, Dr Parnham, we should scarcely have gone to this trouble had we not been convinced of Miss Lucket's outstanding ability,' she said a little impatiently. 'I can vouch both to her skill and also to the desperate need of it in our village. Mr Turnbull and I are here to recommend her on behalf of the women of Beversley for your course of instruction.'

The apothecary felt uneasy about how the doctor might react to this straight-talking spinster; he was very conscious of the man's condescension in agreeing to see them at all.

'Miss Glover, I don't think—' he began, but Parnham cut him short.

'Miss Glover? Ah, yes, I have heard you highly spoken of for your good services to Beversley. Am I to assume that it was your idea to bring this child to me?'

Sophia answered him coldly. 'This child, as you call her, is neither deaf nor dumb, Dr Parnham, and may be addressed directly.'

Turnbull gasped, but Parnham duly nodded towards Susan.

'Very well. What have you to say, miss?'

Susan looked him straight in the eye, her fingers gripping the straw bag. 'If 'twere not f'r Miss Glover, sir, I'd still be nothin' but a poor maidservant. She had me taught my letters, and ha' defended me agin them as object to me attendin' on women, sir.'

The doctor's eyebrows went up, and his lips formed a circle, as if he were about to whistle.

'Indeed? I admire your gratitude to the lady. And are you as zealous at your craft as she says? Do you consider yourself a midwife?'

'I wish to become so, sir,' Susan replied in a low tone but clearly.

195

'Even though you are so young, and not yet a wife yourself?'

'I've attended ten women, sir, an' put all their babies into their arms.'

Susan realised that she felt at ease with this man, not in the least intimidated by his manner, as was poor Mr Turnbull. She took the register out of her bag and handed it to him.

'One o' these had a child in the breech, sir.'

'And was that child born alive, miss?'

'She was that, sir, crying straightway.'

'And how old is it now?'

'Coming on eleven months, sir.'

'And is it weaned and growing?'

'She is, sir.'

'And does it show any wits?'

'She smiles an' calls out to her mother, an' crawls on all fours, sir.' Susan smiled at the thought of the pretty little girl at the village bakehouse. ''Twas an easy birthing, sir, even though in the breech, 'cause the mother'd had children afore her.'

'And why should that make a difference, miss?'

'Why, sir, the older ones opened up the way an' stretched the birth-passage f'r her. 'Tis when a first child be in the breech that there be most danger to its life an' wits.'

Parnham was more impressed by the girl's honest admission that the birth had been easy than if she had seized the opportunity to boast of her skill at managing a breech delivery successfully.

'And have any of your ten women been so long in travail and so wearied that their pains have faded away?'

'Yes, sir, one or two,' replied Susan, thinking of

Mrs Twydell and another whose travail had seemed never-ending.

'And how did you deal with this inertia of the womb?'

'By doing nothing, sir, which is very difficult,' she replied promptly. 'Mrs Coulter do say 'tis Nature's way o' giving the mother respite, an' so I let her sleep if she can, an' give her water or fruit juice sweetened wi' honey. I talk to her cheerfully, and get her to sit on the chamber pot – and I wait, sir. And by an' by the pains ha' come back.'

'Ha! Did you hear that, Turnbull? *Masterly inactivity*, eh? This girl's been well taught. Remember, though, miss, the longer the travail, the greater the danger to the child.'

'Yes, sir, and I'd send f'r a doctor if there was one to call, or talk it over with Mr Turnbull, sir. Meanwhile I'd listen to the heartbeat – the baby's, I mean – and try to be calm and hide my thoughts from the woman.'

'Humph! 'Tis a pity you are not a wedded wife of thirty, else I would certainly take you on as a pupil. Tell me, have any of your women swelled up with the dropsy?'

'One, sir,' she replied, again thinking of Sally Twydell. 'An' a few others've have swollen ankles an' fingers, but not as bad.'

'And what might happen to such a woman as she nears her time?'

'I've heard o' the mother's malady, sir, an' the risk o' fits, a danger to both mother an' baby, though I ha' never seen one.'

'Have you heard of the epilepsy?'

'I don't think so, sir.'

'Or the falling sickness?'

197

'Oh, yes, sir, there was a poor boy when I was a child, he used to fall down where he stood, an' kick an' grind his teeth an' bite his tongue. He got taken to the workhouse – the House o' Industry – when he got bigger.'

'Indeed he did, and he's there to this day, poor Gus,' replied the doctor with a sigh. 'And that's the kind of fit that these dropsical women can get. Pray that you never see one, for they're terrible to behold.'

Susan was silent. Parnham smiled and folded his arms.

'Well, miss, you are a promising candidate, but ten years too young, and you want a husband. You have no experience of childbirth yourself, and that is considered a great lack, is it not?'

'No more a lack in me than in yeself, sir.'

Turnbull nearly groaned out loud, while Miss Glover lowered her face, either to spare a blush or hide a smile. The doctor's eyebrows shot up.

'You have a ready tongue, maid, and I judge you a quick learner. Beversley will have an excellent midwife in another decade. But you must understand that I cannot train a girl so young, and a maiden.'

Sophia Glover could not restrain her disappointment. 'Miss Lucket already practises as a midwife in Beversley without benefit of formal training, Dr Parnham, simply because there is no other to do this work save for an elderly invalid and a handywoman of doubtful repute. And she will have to continue to practise, whether licensed or not, for the women do not ask to see a piece of paper signed by you when they need her skill. I have assisted her, and know how highly regarded she is by women who care nothing for her youth.'

Susan flashed a grateful smile to her as Parnham acknowledged this rebuke.

'True, Miss Glover, a woman with her pains upon her would not object to a circus bear in the birth-chamber if she thought the creature could ease her woe. But I'm not prepared to put my own reputation at stake by licensing a mere maid in a profession that needs maturity and discretion.'

Turning to Susan, he went on, 'However, you have satisfied me with your answers and general demeanour, Miss Lucket, and I hope to see you again as a married woman when a few more years have passed. Thank you for bringing her to see me, Turnbull. I shall remember her and recognise her again. I wish you good day.'

As he rose from his chair, Susan made a last attempt to plead for herself.

'If ye'd but give me a fair course o' instruction, Dr Parnham, even without the licence, ye'd be doin' good service to the mothers an' children o' Beversley. As Miss Glover says, I ha' to do the work 'cause there be no other to do it – but I need to increase my knowledge, sir.'

Parnham frowned and seemed about to speak, then changed his mind and turned away from them, pacing the length of the room and back again, his hands clasped behind him, appearing to be deep in thought. The three of them waited in silence while he considered the matter, and Susan pictured him pacing in the same manner when weighing up the situation at a difficult birthing.

When at last he sat down at the desk and spoke again, his tone made it quite clear that this was as far as he was prepared to go.

'Listen to me, Miss Lucket. The House of Industry,

the place you call the workhouse in Belhampton, has a number of birthings within its walls each year, mostly bastards to servant girls and women of the lower sort who have gone there because of their condition. No respectable gentlewoman can be persuaded to attend these poor wretches, and I have long felt concern for the younger ones among them, with only an old tippling gossip at hand in their hour of greatest need. Some indeed are whores who may be infected with the clap, but –' He glanced at his hearers, whose shocked faces reflected their awful realisation of what he was about to propose. 'But if you, Miss Lucket, would be willing to take up residence as a nurse in the infirmary of that place for a period of – let's say a twelvemonth – attending the women as midwife, you would gain more experience of the harder side of life than in five years outside of it. And if you can stay there without losing heart or giving up your intention to be the Beversley midwife, you would convince me of your true commitment, and I would admit you to my course of lectures here without payment. What have you to say to that?'

Susan looked Dr Parnham straight in the eyes and did not flinch, though she heard Sophia's gasp of indignation, and felt her friend's hand on her shoulder.

'Do not agree to it, Susan,' Sophia whispered, loudly enough for the men to hear. 'Wait a year or two, and we'll try again. I do not ask this of you – and in any case, we can't spare you.'

Sophia knew that it was not the privations of the House that Susan most dreaded; it was the prospect of living under the same roof as Mad Doll, and while the true reason for this had never been made clear,

Sophia knew, or thought she knew, that Susan simply would not be able to bear it.

Mr Turnbull nodded his agreement with Miss Glover: he thought it an unreasonable condition to make.

Susan took a deep breath and answered clearly.

'Thank ye, Dr Parnham, f'r y'r offer. I'll take it, an' move into the House o' Industry as soon as the guardians please.'

Sophia turned to her in astonishment. 'A year, Susan, in that awful place? May God have mercy on you and give you strength, my poor friend!'

And for the first time Susan saw tears in her eyes.

Dr Parnham also saw what consternation he had caused, and the way Miss Glover swept out of his study without another word. Susan, on the other hand, curtsied and bid good day to this man who knew nothing about her and the extent of her aversion to the place where he was sentencing her to spend a year.

Her thoughts turned to Edward, now a midshipman on the same troopship as Lieutenant Hansford somewhere on the high seas, witnessing scenes of heaven only knew what carnage, facing the danger of shipwreck and death from the deadly American long rifles. What were her morbid fears compared to the perils he had to endure?

If this was the way to fulfil her ambition, then this was the way she would follow. And when she became the licensed Beversley midwife, Edward might present her to the Calthorpes with less apology than for a poor maidservant.

Edward. He who had vowed that he would have no other but herself, his love would surround and sustain her, even within those grim grey walls.

Chapter 15

Osmond had passed another wretched night of pain and sleeplessness.

'For God's sake, Mother, go to church and leave me to myself, can't you? I will say my prayers alone here.'

Gertrude Calthorpe stood irresolutely beside the four-poster bed. Her son's eyes were ringed by dark circles, and there were two deep vertical furrows between them, etched by the mysterious ache he suffered in a leg no longer there. He had wept in the night for the loss of it, grinding his teeth and burying his face in the pillow; Berry, the manservant, had lain awake on his mattress in the corner of the room, pretending not to hear until his young master had shouted to him to fetch more claret.

The decanter was empty again now, and in response to his father's tentative protests Osmond replied sharply that a couple of glasses were necessary to give him relief from the darting pain that shot down his right leg to the foot.

'But my boy, there is no limb there,' said Mr Calthorpe, gesturing helplessly towards the stump beneath the bedclothes.

'Whether the limb be there or not, Father, I tell you it still hurts me like the deuce,' returned Osmond, grimacing as the stump gave an involuntary jerk.

'Then I shall ask Turnbull to make up more of his opium mixture,' declared Calthorpe.

'Ugh, that foul-tasting, bitter stuff! A glass of good red wine gives far more ease, and 'tis a damned sight kinder on the palate. Oh, for God's sake, Father, send Martin down to the cellar, and then take my mother to church. I've had my fill of her weeping and wailing.'

He turned his head away from his parents' troubled faces, and muttered an obscene oath. Calthorpe winced, and took his wife's arm.

'Let us do as he says, my love, and don't give too much weight to his hasty words. 'Tis only to be expected in a man of four-and-twenty who has borne such a crippling loss.'

Gertrude nodded dumbly, wiping her eyes on the handkerchief she always kept tucked in her sleeve. He tried to comfort her as they went downstairs.

'We must pray that his sacrifice for his country will prove to be—'

'Oh, I care nothing for the hateful war!' she burst out angrily. 'I grieve only for my first-born son, my poor Osmond – oh, my son, my son!' And her tears began to flow again.

'Come to church, Gertrude. The carriage is below, and the girls are waiting for us.'

Calthorpe had to hide the grief in his own heart. It had been almost six weeks, and the strain was telling on them all. If only Edward were at home to cheer and encourage his brother; if only a way could be found to end this ghastly waste of manpower and the drain on the country's resources. Osmond's army days were over, and he was undoubtedly recovering, but his ill-temper had to be endured by both family and servants, and cast a gloom over the whole house.

*

Seated in the family pew, Calthorpe tried to pray, but during Dr Gravett's interminable sermon his thoughts strayed back as they always did to the ordeal that had begun on a beautiful day in May, when a villainous-looking messenger rode up to Bever House on a half-starved horse and demanded payment for the care he said he had taken of Captain Calthorpe, lately returned to Portsmouth on the *Blackbird* with scores of other wounded men; he was now lying in an inn, said the man, robbed of all his possessions and with no means of getting home.

The best horse had been hastily saddled and Berry sent on ahead with money, clothes and provisions, while Calthorpe followed in the Bever carriage with Jude and Mrs Ferris. Never would he forget the journey, the low company and coarse laughter at the inn, the sight of his son lying near to death in a filthy room – and the smell of the leg. It filled the room and then the carriage, it clung to clothing, upholstery, hair and skin, the very stink of corruption. The Calthorpe sisters and servants shrank back from it when Osmond was carried into Bever House, and when Gertrude fell on her knees beside the gaunt figure lying on the litter, she fainted clean away.

Mr Turnbull was sent for, and dressed the unsightly swelling on Osmond's forehead, though he did not dare to unwrap the stained and oozing bandages from the leg. He recommended a military surgeon in Winchester, who was at once sent for, and only Berry and Mrs Ferris were allowed in the sickroom besides Osmond's parents. Crushed pine needles and yew were scattered on the floor and burned on the fire, while sprigs of rosemary were hung up to sweeten the air, but to no effect; the stench permeated the house from attics to cellar.

The surgeon arrived the next day, a short, bald man with no wig, and carrying his instruments in a folded leather bag like a carpenter's tools. He removed the bandages and revealed a seething mass of grey maggots feeding on the dead tissue. Calthorpe recoiled, putting his hand over his mouth; there was a line of demarcation around the calf, below which the flesh was black and decomposing. It was obvious that the leg must be taken off before the poison spread all over the body, and the stricken father nodded his consent.

The fire was made up, the surgeon's instruments were set out on a table, the cautery iron heated in the fire, and Osmond was strapped to the bedstead. Mrs Ferris made up a mixture of French brandy, opium and honey to let him sip at intervals; she was the only woman in the room, with Turnbull and Berry to assist. Calthorpe held his son's hand throughout the operation, including the endless minute when the leg was sawed through above the knee. Turnbull handed over the red-hot cautery by its leather-covered handle, and a hiss of steam went up as it touched the raw flesh. The surgeon deftly stitched the skin across the stump, having left a flap on the inside of the thigh. The desperate remedy was accomplished, and that night Calthorpe quietly buried his son's leg in a corner of the churchyard at Great St Giles.

Looking back now on that dreadful day, Calthorpe was convinced that Osmond began to recover from the very hour that the leg was removed; slowly and gradually his appetite improved and he gained strength. The sore on his head healed over, his bowel and bladder control returned, and now he was sitting up and taking notice of his surroundings, though he seldom smiled.

For as Osmond's general health improved, so did his ability to think clearly and see his situation as it really was and how it would be for the rest of his life. He saw the blankness in his sister's faces as they stood at his bedside, and when the Hansfords visited with Rosa and William the four of them had sat and stared as if he were some kind of freak at a fair, or so it seemed to him. Rosa had crocheted a black silk cover like a bag to put over his stump, and left it lying on the bed; Mrs Ferris had whisked it away, and it had never appeared again.

Friends did not know what to talk about, for there were so many subjects that had to be avoided: fox-hunting across the downs, shooting parties in pursuit of pigeon and pheasant, the ballroom floor; there could be no return to the saddle or the dance for Captain Calthorpe, pride of his regiment and heir to Bever House.

There had been one visitor who had brought him a little diversion, a change of direction for his thoughts, even some good-natured disagreement. Miss Glover had not crossed the threshhold of Bever House since the night of the ball nearly two years ago, but she now walked purposefully up to the front door and asked to see her cousin Osmond. Mr Calthorpe welcomed her gratefully, and Gertrude said she no longer cared one way or the other if Osmond consented, and so Sophia was shown into the sickroom. When Osmond saw her, he yawned and shook his head impatiently, expecting to be bored by more canting such as he got from the rector.

Sophia sat down beside him and took a book from her bag.

'Have you read any of Mr Fielding's novels, Osmond? I've brought this copy of *The History of Tom*

Jones – it is said to have greatly shocked the sensibilities of Dr Johnson!'

'What? You may read me a little of it, Sophy, for I can't give my mind to the printed page,' sighed Osmond, idly reflecting that his cousin was not a bad-looking woman. No wonder Henry had been so taken with her, though it had been hard on Selina to be jilted. Still, what did it matter now? What did anything matter?

But by degrees, reading short passages aloud to him from the rollicking tale of Mr Jones' adventures, and leaving out what she thought too improper, Sophia had engaged his attention long enough for him to remark that she had been a damned sight more entertaining than most. He painfully shifted his position so that he was facing her instead of the opposite wall.

'Pour me out another glass, Sophy, and pass it across. All right, go on reading, don't stop.'

Jael Ferris appeared at the end of an hour with Osmond's medicine and a silent glance of dismissal for Sophia; it was time for the patient to rest. Sophia took her leave with sombre thoughts: suppose Henry were to suffer the same fate – or worse?

She found Mr Calthorpe eagerly waiting to speak to her, and followed him to his study, where he closed the door and asked her to take a chair.

'God reward you, Sophy, I cannot tell you how deeply obliged I am. Nobody else seems to know what to say to the poor boy – I certainly do not.'

'Cousin Osmond,' she said, laying her hand lightly upon his arm, 'talk to me. Tell me all about Osmond.'

And for the next hour Calthorpe truly unburdened his heart for the first time.

'It was the very worst day of my life, Sophy, when

we got the news. I had to order my wife to stay at home, though she clamoured to come with me in the carriage. Poor Gertrude! In the end she gave up her own personal woman, Mrs Ferris, who proved to be invaluable. She knew how to deal with those rogues in the tavern, that slattern who was supposed to be caring for Osmond. Oh, Sophy, when I saw him lying there . . . Berry had washed him, but he looked like death – and the smell of that leg – oh, my God. My God!'

His voice broke, and Sophia held his hand in both of hers. 'I was praying for you, Cousin, as was everybody in Beversley,' she said quietly.

'Yes, I know, and your prayers have been answered, in that my son still lives, and is getting stronger. If only he could have peace in his mind, and accept the changes that must be made in his life! As we journeyed home in the carriage I held him in my arms with his head resting on my shoulder – and again when he lay helpless under the hands of that surgeon – and I have never loved him more than at those terrible moments. But now my son must walk with a peg leg and a stick, he who was so handsome and upright . . .'

And here Calthorpe broke down completely and sobbed aloud. Sophia rose and put her arms around his shoulders, holding him until the storm had subsided.

'Patience, Cousin Osmond – have patience and hope,' she urged. ''Twill take time for him to accept the changes there must be. He may yet be able to mount a horse again – it has been known. Put your trust in the Almighty, as we all must in these times.'

'God bless you, Sophy, I am so thankful to see you

in Bever House again,' he said, kissing her hand in gratitude.

Osmond heard the bell tower of Great St Giles strike eleven. Divine Service was about to begin, but without the tall, commanding figure in his red coat and high peaked hat, catching the eyes of the women. He groaned aloud. *That* Captain Calthorpe had had two legs. Now he was a cripple, shut away from the eyes of the congregation in their Sunday best; he pictured the bench on which the maidservants sat in the north transept, and little Polly blushing at his bold glances . . .

Polly. What a confounded bungling he had made of his opportunity with her when he had been a whole man. Many a time he had lain in his hammock on the other side of the Atlantic and relived the memory of her soft young flesh straddled across his overshot member; how many times had he longed to be soaked again in the warm stream that had flowed from her little overfilled bladder! Recalling that incident had brought him to a pitch of solitary release on more than one occasion. What a damnable fool he had been to berate the sweet innocent as he had done then! Now he would give anything to be able to go back to the beech grove on that September night. It would have a different ending, by God!

Was that a step in the passage outside? He listened. Berry must have been reprieved from Divine Service because of his young master's needs – and indeed he was needed, for the decanter was again nearly empty.

'Berry!'

There was no reply, no obedient footsteps.

'Berry, are you skulking out there? Fetch me a—'

He stopped short with a gasp as a slim, dainty figure silently slipped round the door, which stood ajar.

'Yes, Master Osmond? What be it 'ee wants fetchin'?' asked a pert little voice.

'*Polly!*' He heaved himself up on the bolster. 'Oh, Polly, is it really you? Shouldn't you be at church with the others?'

'Why, do 'ee want me to go back there?' she asked with a delightfully saucy look, though her heart leaped at the sight of her master, so pitifully pale and thin.

'Oh, Polly, you sweet little thing, are you real?' He feasted his eyes on her hungrily, forgetting every other thought as she came to his bedside. 'How did you escape my mother's eye? Have a care, Berry may be around somewhere.'

'Don't 'ee worry, master, Berry an' me ha' come to a – an understandin',' she said, tapping the side of her nose. 'Oi went to church wi' the other maids, but Oi crept out o' that little door in the transep' afore the ol' rector come in. Berry be below, keepin' a watch fur 'ee an' me.'

'Is he, by God! I didn't think he'd take such a risk.'

'Ah, Berry be a good'un, an' cares a lot fur 'ee, Master Osmond.' She did not add that the man had heard him weeping in the night for his lost leg, and caught his broken words as he sighed for 'Polly – my pretty little Poll.' It had been one man's pity for another that had led to Berry's collusion with the maidservant, who now laughed merrily.

'Dearest, sweetest Polly, an angel must have sent you to me,' he murmured, overcome by such a wave of love and gratitude that his voice trembled. 'Quick, a kiss – a kiss now, to prove that you're real.'

She took hold of his outstretched hand, and he seized hers, kissing it fervently; and then he drew her to him and kissed her lips, lingering, tasting the sweetness. She smelled a sourness, a taint of sickness on his breath, but took no heed, so much did she long to please him.

'Shall I draw the bed-curtains, Master Osmond?' she whispered when at last he stopped to draw breath.

'Ye-es, but you know I'm not yet well, Poll, and my leg that has gone still hurts as if 'twere there. I must take care, Poll.'

He spoke awkwardly, apologetically, suddenly alarmed at being called upon to do a man's work on a bed of pain in a sickroom. He knew that he needed shaving, that his skin was loose and flaccid like an old man's where he had lost weight; and the unsightly stump was hardly an object to arouse a young woman's passion. He was nervous – he, Osmond Calthorpe of all men, was afraid he lacked the prowess to take an eighteen-year-old maid.

But he reckoned without Polly's love, which had never faltered and which she had saved for him, rejecting the advances of all other would-be sweet-hearts, and there had been many. She had nightly kneeled to pray for his safety: 'Ye knows how dear he be to me, Lord, every last bit o' him!' She too had pondered over the disaster in the beech grove, and had learned from listening to the other maids talking of their amorous swains. She knew that what had gone wrong on that occasion was due to his over-eagerness and her drink-clouded ignorance, and she was now ready to cope with the practicalities of love-making, though with her hero in his present state, she realised that success or failure depended on her –

she whose only aim was to give him pleasure, for she had no wish to tease him now. She was completely sober and had taken care to relieve herself before coming to his room, where love made her bold.

She quickly untied her gown, letting it fall to the floor, revealing the plain cotton shift beneath; she pulled back the coverlet and got in beside Osmond as he lay on his back in his nightshirt. Their bodies touched, and both trembled a little. Polly sniffed the heady mixture of sweat, pine needles and red wine, and sensed his uncertainty and self-doubt; it touched her heart, rousing her to a tender desire for him more than a display of male mastery would have done.

'I am not the man I was, Poll—'

'Hush, my own dear love,' she whispered, stopping his words with her lips against his. The long, clinging kiss that followed, both consoling and arousing at the same time, quite took Osmond's breath away; he felt the blood surging through his veins in response to her delicious softness, and a flush spread across his sickroom pallor. Polly's lips touched his nose, his eyes, his ears, his neck, and her breath quickened in unison with his own.

'Polly, my sweetheart, my pretty little darling . . .'

She smiled confidently as she drew his head down to her breasts, pushing aside the cotton shift so that he could fasten his lips on each rosy nipple in turn. They hardened under his touch, just as his own vital member was slowly, very slowly, rising with the onrush of blood into its vessels.

'Do you know how to assist this fellow to perform his proper duty?' he asked her breathlessly, taking her hand down further under the covers until her fingers closed around the phallus.

'Be this what 'ee means, Osmond? Do 'ee want me to touch him, my love?'

'Yes, yes, Poll, I do. Can you kiss him? That's even better.'

He closed his eyes and sighed out his mounting tension as her curly head lowered to obey. Loving him as she did, she showed a dexterity that was not due to experience but sprung from her fervent wish to please him: her instincts led her unerringly to do what most women need to be taught if such is required of them. Polly's fingers lightly touched and tickled the two eminences behind the now proudly lifted spear of his passion.

'Ah, Poll, that's right, that's it, that's what's needful, this, *this* is what I've been dreaming of. Oh, Polly, my little, little Polly, 'tis the very bliss of heaven . . .'

He groaned for pleasure, and at just the right moment, not too soon and not too late, Polly took her hands and lips away from his manhood and carefully arranged herself above him, a leg on either side, parting the fleshy curtains of her maiden's cave with her fingers.

They sighed as she sank down upon his upright member.

But to their mutual dismay he could not enter. Her virginal hymen proved unexpectedly resistant to penetration, and after two failed attempts Osmond had to open up the way with an exploring forefinger.

'Forgive me, Polly,' he said thickly when she gave an involuntary cry and gritted her teeth as he tore through the delicate membrane. Willing though she was to admit him, the forced entry caused her such a sharp stab of pain that she thought she would faint. But again love came to her aid and stifled her protests as the blood flowed, staining the sheet. If it had been any other than her beloved Master Osmond doing this to her, she could not have borne it.

He found that he had been somewhat discouraged by the delay, and wanted further assistance from her to regain a full erection, now that he had made his way clear. So again Polly set to work with fingertips and lips, and he closed his eyes and sighed, not noticing her white face and drooping head.

'Now, Polly, you may mount your steed again, and this time he will take his rightful place.'

His voice was faint and distant in her ears; no sooner had she resumed her position than he thrust upwards into her sore cavity and she clung helplessly to his heaving frame beneath her, listening to his mounting sighs and moans that reached a climax of release within half a minute. The stronghold was breached, the river flowed, and seconds later he collapsed in limp exhaustion, unable to bear her weight or the return of the phantom pain in the jerking stump. When she rolled off him sideways, he howled in agony.

'In Christ's name, Poll, have a care for that damned leg, for it hurts like hell!'

She was all penitence, and the tears she had managed to control during her own ordeal now sprung to her eyes for him.

'Oooh, Oi be that sorry, Master Osmond. Forgive me, Oi wouldn't hurt 'ee fur the world!'

He winced and clenched his teeth, his pleasure quite overtaken by a dismaying anticlimax of discomfort. The fact that Polly had not achieved the satisfaction he had enjoyed by reason of her efforts did not occur to either of them. He took a gulp of wine from the glass she handed him, and fell back on the bolster with a long sigh.

'Don't look so sorry, Poll – you've done me more good than all of Turnbull's physic.'

'Oi be that glad to hear 'ee say so, Master Osmond. Gi' me another kiss, my love—'

A knock on the door caused them both to freeze into stillness, holding their breath until they heard Berry's low voice.

'It be but ten minutes to midday, Mr Osmond. They'll be back from church any time arter twelve.'

Their time was up, and they had to part hastily. Polly got off the bed and pulled on her gown.

'Where be me cap? Goodbye, dear Master Os—'

'Make haste and go, Poll. Come again to me when you can.'

She slipped out of the door, and he lay back on the bed, falling asleep almost at once. He dreamed that his leg was restored to him, and that he was again inside Polly, riding her with proud abandon, thrusting again and again into her welcoming cave, while she laughed aloud with glee at his strength and power.

When he awoke the bed was soaked with urine, and Berry had to help him to sit out on a chair while Mrs Ferris changed the sheets. Jael's black eyebrows rose slightly at the sight of the bloodstains, but she made no comment.

Back in bed, clean and refreshed, Osmond rejoiced. It was surely ironic, he reflected, that after such a long wait to take possession of Polly – it was just six years since she had first come to Bever House as a laundrymaid – it had taken the tragic loss of his leg to bring her to his bed.

Having given herself in love to Osmond at last, Polly lost the power she had retained for so long. She now had to obey his commands, close her mind to danger, to consequences and everything but her desire to make her master happy. Berry was forced into co-operation with the lovers, and had to leave the bedchamber when Polly crept in at midnight; he returned at dawn to make sure that she left before the household was stirring.

The maids who shared Polly's room observed her nightly absences, but nothing was said in the hearing of Martin or his wife, who were answerable for the good behaviour of the servants.

Yet Polly's nocturnal wanderings remained undiscovered as the weeks went by, and she and Osmond accepted their amazing good luck without any suspicion that they were being protected.

Only Berry knew of the brooding presence that watched over their comings and goings, and gave him his orders: and he often wondered when Jael Ferris slept, if ever.

Chapter 16

The Belhampton House of Industry had been built a quarter of a century earlier to shelter the destitute and provide them with useful occupation. The original intention had been good, but in practice the workhouse system had become a byword for penny-pinching charity, a last resort for the unwanted members of the community who could not help themselves. The aged man or woman with no family to offer support, the cripple, the idiot, the unmarried mother and her child, along with the unfortunates who could not earn a living for any reason – the blind, the born deaf and therefore dumb, the epileptic – all found a home of sorts within its walls. Apart from delivered mothers and orphans sufficiently grown to find work in the world outside, few ever left except in a plain unmarked coffin on a short journey to a pauper's grave. And there were many such funerals, especially during the winter months.

One of the inmates in the spring of 1780 was Rose. She was not yet fifty but prematurely aged after a life of poverty and the loss of every child born to her. She had been brought to the House with an advanced canker of the left breast, and spent her diminishing days in bed, shunned by the other inmates because of the foul smell of the lesion, which had to be dressed every day.

The new nurse had been given the unpopular task of 'seeing to Rose', and the two women immediately

217

discovered a fellow feeling to their mutual advantage; in fact Susan later said that Rose had helped her to weather those first few weeks under the rule of Mrs Jarvis, otherwise known as 'Mother', who was in charge of the mothers and babies. Mrs Jarvis was not at all happy to give up her position as midwife in the House, and declared war on the newcomer from the start.

This all provided diversion for Rose, who loved hearing workhouse gossip and eagerly awaited Susan's daily visits.

'How's that poor young gal gettin' on, her as was makin' such a sighin' an' sobbin' last night?' she asked as Susan filled a basin with salted water and set out pads and bandages.

'Hannah's likely to give birth some time today,' answered Susan, who had sat up during the night hours with the sixteen-year-old girl but had been banished when Mother Jarvis came in after breakfast.

'Poor lamb! Be she in danger, do 'ee reckon?'

'I don't think so, Rose. She's young an' strong. Old Mother Jarvis be in great danger, though – o' being strangled by my two bare hands afore today be done!'

Rose chuckled weakly, and Susan gingerly removed the malodorous dressings of yesterday. She marvelled at this woman's stoic endurance, her capacity to share a conspiratorial joke, even in her dire condition. There was only a spreading greyish mass where her left breast had been, though she felt little pain from it; there was more discomfort from the hard lumps in her neck and armpits.

'Bain't as sweet as lavender, eh, gal?' she said wryly as Susan dabbed and mopped, forcing herself not to gag over her task for Rose's sake.

'How be that one who the doctor put them tongs on, Susan, to pull the poor baby out? Last week, wa'n't it?'

'Mm. She's feeling a bit better now, and the babe's bein' suckled by another.'

Susan frowned as she spoke. Dr Parnham's birthing forceps were blamed for the high incidence of childbed fever and infant deaths in the House, and it was said that he used the workhouse mothers to practise his infamous methods. In Susan's opinion it was Mrs Jarvis's lack of basic cleanliness during and after birthings that was more likely to be the cause of infections; and when a mother died, the baby was almost certain to follow if no wet nurse was available.

'Can't 'ee get rid o' the ol' besom by sendin' her to swig gin wi' Mistress Croker?' suggested Rose with a grin.

'I can try,' replied Susan grimly, carefully applying fresh pads to the area. 'Those two like nothing better than to get together and say how I be no good as a midwife because I ha' never had children – not like Mother Jarvis, who's had nine.'

'An' buried five on 'em,' added Rose. 'An' how be the poor orphans here, Susan? That idiot boy and little Dorcas an' the rest?'

'God help them, Rose, it breaks my heart to see the way they ha' to work, poor mites. Even them as can only toddle, picking up cotton waste off the floor o' the workroom. Mind you, I ha' plans to do something f'r those children.'

'Be that so, Susan?' asked Rose, seeing the determined gleam in her eyes. 'What be 'ee goin' to do?'

'I want to start teachin' them their letters, Rose, just

as I was taught, so that the brighter ones may learn to read and write.'

'Lord save 'ee, Susan, what'll they read? And what'll they write on? There be no books in this place, nor slates.'

'Ah, but I shall go to a good friend o' mine, Rose, the lady who had me taught my alphabet. She'll get me some reading-books an' slates when I tell her o' the need f'r them.'

'Would yer friend be that lady in Beversley – her as takes the midwife out to the women in a little pony-trap?'

'That's the one, Rose, Miss Glover. If 'twere not f'r her I wouldn't be here today.'

'Oi wouldn't thank her fur that if Oi was 'ee! But Oi thanks her fur *me*,' she added as Susan picked up the pail of discoloured dressings to be burned outside in the yard.

'There ye be, Rose dear. 'Tis done once again.'

'Once more, once less, gal. Oi doubt as 'ee'll ha' to do it fur much longer.' Her faded eyes rested on the girl with affection. ''Ee be a good'un, Susan, an angel in this place – the only one as can bear to come nigh me.'

Susan gave her a sip of water, spread pine needles and rosemary leaves around the bed, and looked with tenderness upon the dying woman.

'Ye're me best comfort here, Rose,' she said simply.

Rose smiled. 'Ah, 'ee must ha' got a sweetheart to comfort 'ee better'n Oi can,' she answered with a knowing look. 'One o' they cocky apprentice lads in Belhampton, eh?'

'No, Rose, nothin' like that,' answered Susan, but her eyes betrayed her. Rose was right in one sense, for it was the knowledge of Edward's constancy that consoled her. She was conscious of his loving thoughts winging their way across the miles, surrounding and upholding her, just as hers went out to him in his danger and hardship. Because of him, she found the courage and determination not only to survive but to succeed.

Rose saw the faraway expression in the grey eyes. 'Ah, Oi reckons as 'ee got a fine gen'leman who's bidin' un's time to speak,' she said softly. ''Ee deserves summat better'n what there be in here.'

She lay back on the bolster and closed her eyes. 'Mind 'ee comes an' tells Oi how poor little Hannah goes on.'

'That I will, Rose. Have a rest now.' She leaned over to kiss the hollow cheek.

Out in the passage leading from the women's dormitory Susan suddenly stood still and listened. She caught the sound of a low murmuring at the other end of the passage, on the landing by the stairs. Her heart sank and she instinctively drew back as she saw a shadow fall across the wall, followed by a grey figure fluttering towards her, mumbling and wringing its hands. She pressed herself against the wall, hoping that it would not accost her, and held her breath while two vacant, empty eyes looked briefly into her face as if searching, yet showing not a glimmer of recognition. Then the woman went on her way and Susan watched her disappear round a corner.

Mad Doll was always worse just before the full moon.

The stifling birth-chamber reeked of spirits, and the girl lying on the mattress was nauseated and glassy-eyed.

'Stay wi' me, Missus Lucket, don't 'ee go away agin,' she begged at the sight of Susan.

Mother Jarvis glared. 'Don't 'ee come here fussin' an' foolin',' she barked. 'Her bin makin' a great pother, but the lazy cow won't push. What her needs is—'

'Aaah! Help me, missus, help!' cried Hannah, her broad features contorted in a grimace that bared her teeth and screwed up her eyes against another onslaught of pain.

'Come now, Hannah, breathe hard, puff and pant like *this*,' said Susan, going to the girl's side and showing her what she meant by taking a series of quick, panting breaths.

Mother Jarvis shouted her derision. 'Call 'eeself a midwife, an' all 'ee can do is huff an' puff! What her needs is to heave down wi' her great belly an' push it out – as 'ee'd know if 'ee'd bin through it 'eeself!'

The handywoman constantly taunted Susan for her youth and unmarried state. Her own ideas of midwifery were based on old customs slavishly followed, in contrast to Susan's practice of dealing with each stage of travail as it occurred, adjusting her management accordingly. Now she tried to ignore her tormentor.

'Take a sip o' water, Hannah,' she urged, but the girl made a sudden clumsy movement and the cup was knocked over, spilling its contents. Mrs Jarvis jeered.

'No good givin' her watter when what her needs is a swig o' gin – summat to deaden the pain, as 'ee'd know if 'ee'd bin through it!'

Susan rolled her eyes up in exasperation. How on earth was she to get rid of the old hag? Rose's suggestion came to mind, and she forced a smile.

222

'Surely 'tis time f'r ye to take a rest, Mother Jarvis,' she hinted. 'Ye bin here all the morning, and Hannah's not ready to give birth f'r an hour or more yet.'

This approach met with a suspicious 'Huh!'

'Why don't ye take a cup o' tea with Mistress Croker?' went on Susan. ''Tis a fine day, ye could sit outside, the pair o' ye, on the bench in the yard.'

The woman's eyes glinted. The Master's wife kept a kettle on the hob and a bottle in the cupboard.

'Hm. Maybe a little walk'd clear me head, arter bein' cooped up here all mornin' – but mind 'ee gets that girl movin', or her'll still be layin' here an' mooin' this time termorrer.'

Susan sighed with relief as the woman waddled away, and threw open the sash window to let in a breath of air. Hannah stirred and moaned.

'How much longer'll it be, missus?'

The eternal question. Susan smiled and shook her head.

'There never was a travail that didn't come to an end, Hannah. Don't worry, I'll stay with ye now, and we'll get through it together.'

By four in the afternoon the pains were coming hard and close on each other, and Susan could see the small circle of the child's head. She got ready to assist Hannah through the final stages, but to her utter vexation Mother Jarvis returned, slurred of speech and unsteady on her feet. And noisily abusive.

'Get her pullin' on the rope, yer fool! Call 'eeself a midwife, and don't even know how to get a woman bearin' down!'

A thick knotted rope was attached to a post embedded in the floor of the birthchamber, for women to pull on as an aid to pushing. Susan hated it, and refused to use it. She could have screamed at the handywoman, but knew she must control herself for Hannah's sake.

'Look, Mother Jarvis, please go away and leave me to deliver this baby in my own way—'

'Damn yer eyes, Oi'll ha' ye thrown out o' the House!' snarled the woman, staggering to the bedside and thrusting a fat elbow into Susan's side just as Hannah began to yell with another pain. It was impossible to stay aloof and dignified in such a situation, and Susan calculated that in her gin-soaked state Mother Jarvis should be reasonably easy to topple. And it had to be done at once, because she was raising her arm and shaking her fist in Susan's face.

Susan acted. She shot out her left leg between Mrs Jarvis's feet, and at the same time hit out at the raised fist with her own bunched knuckles.

It worked. The woman shrieked and lost her balance, landing in a heap of petticoats on the floor. Susan stood above her, her grey eyes flashing.

'Now will ye take yeself off and leave us alone, d'ye hear?'

Mother Jarvis's caterwauling echoed through the building.

'Oi'll send fur the Master, Oi will! Oi'll have 'ee up in front o' the Justices!' she hiccuped, struggling to get up, but her foot was caught in her skirts and she howled the louder.

'Help, help! Oi be ravished! Oi be murdered!'

The noise brought the House Master from his workshop, accompanied by a cowed maid-of-all-work, Mag. Croker was a stout, broad-shouldered man who could turn his hand to carpentry and plastering; unable to read or write, he had been appointed by the guardians as being unlikely to defraud them, and because he had a shrewd wife, the true voice of authority in the House.

Croker now stood awkwardly on the threshhold of the room. This was women's business, and he wished they would conduct it in a more seemly way.

'What be ye doin' down there, Mother Jarvis?'

'Help, Master, help me! That Lucket crittur be attackin' me. Her be crazed like her mother!' screeched the handywoman, flailing her arms and still trying to extricate her foot from the folds of her petticoat.

Croker turned away in embarrassment. 'Go an' fetch Mistress Croker, quick!' he ordered Mag. 'And come away, Lucket. Leave Mother Jarvis to see to Hannah.'

Hannah's eyes widened in panic. 'Don't send Missus Lucket away! Oooh! Aaah! The pain be comin' agin – help me, help!'

Her screams added to the din, and Susan could not make herself heard, though she remained at Hannah's side, holding her hand.

When Mistress Croker came panting along the passage, she gestured to her husband to stand back while she took in the situation with her little piggy eyes. Bending over, she gave the handywoman her arm and hauled her to her feet.

'What's the bother, Jarvis? 'Tis only one more slut givin' birth to one more bastard to feed,' she muttered crossly, though she seized the chance to score over the tiresome new nurse.

'Out o' this room, Lucket, or 'ee'll be up afore the guardians fur this.'

'Take care, her was sent by the doctor,' cautioned Croker.

'Oi care not if her was sent by the devil, her's done

nothin' but make trouble. D'ye hear me, miss?' She advanced towards Susan. 'Get out.'

Susan's blood surged in her veins: she literally felt her sinews hardening in her determination to stay at Hannah's side. Let them just lay a finger on me, and they'll find out what I can turn into, she resolved grimly, remembering her attack on Bartlemy, likewise the red-haired stable-lad on the night of the Bever House ball.

And yet her voice was calm when she spoke to the terrified girl on the mattress.

'Don't worry, Hannah. I'm here and I'll stay wi' ye, no matter what they say.'

'Well said, miss. My arrival is timely, I see.'

A new voice broke in on the scene. Nobody had seen Dr Parnham coming up the passage behind the Crokers. He now advanced into the room, a formidable figure in riding jacket and boots. Susan could have wept with relief.

'Dr Parnham, thank God!'

He raised his eyebrows. 'Was I summoned by a supernatural agency, then? I had no intention to come this way when I set out on the mare. What's happening here?'

He glanced at the girl on the birthing mattress. 'Ah, yes, poor Hannah, 'tis about time. Is she pushing? Well, attend to her, miss, attend to her. The rest of you may leave us. Thank you!'

And in less than half a minute he had guided both Mistress Croker and Mother Jarvis through the door, none too gently. Mag was sent to fetch hot water in a pitcher, and the door was firmly closed. He turned to Susan.

'Right, miss, now is my chance to see you at work. Carry on.'

For the next twenty minutes Susan encouraged and instructed Hannah without interference or interruption, but the girl was tired and progress was slow.

'Oi can't push no more, missus!' she gasped.

'Yes, ye can, let yeself go loose and limp between the pains, Hannah. Save y'r strength f'r when the pain be upon ye.'

Laying her ear low down on the belly, Susan listened to the baby's heartbeat, and found it slowing as a pain began; she heard it gradually picking up speed when she listened immediately after a pain. She looked at Parnham, who had not said a word all the time he had observed her.

'Dr Parnham, there's something I've often thought about when the child's head be slow coming down, as now.'

'Really, miss? And what's that?'

She drew a deep breath. 'With the head so low and the pains so hard, it be but the tightness o' the opening that keeps it back. In the end the skin'll tear behind, and then there'll be room enough for it to come through.'

He nodded. 'A fairly obvious statement, miss, but true, as you say. So . . .'

'So, if I were to take my scissors, sir, and cut the opening where 'tis most like to tear – at the back – wouldn't that make room sooner, and shorten the time f'r mother and child? And wouldn't it be easier to heal than a jagged tear?'

He smiled into her eager face. 'Quite right. By my faith, you're a regular little Trotula! Did you ever see this done?'

'No, sir, but Mrs Coulter told me she's done it when the delay was great, and Mr Turnbull ha' seen yeself do it.'

'That's right. I make such a slit as you describe before applying the Chamberlen forceps to the head, to make more room for manoeuvre. I am loath to cut this girl's perineal muscle, though.' He looked thoughtful.

'I ha' often thought it'd shorten an overly long time o' pushing, sir – even when not using the forceps, I mean.'

'Hm, yes, but it should not be done without good reason, and only when the child's head is hard against the outlet, otherwise you do but create a bleeding point,' he answered.

'This child's heartbeat is slowing,' she added, lowering her voice, while Hannah's moans continued.

'Oi *can't* push any furder, Oi tells 'ee, missus!'

Parnham came to a decision. He would give this extraordinary young woman an opportunity to test her theory.

''Tis not something I teach midwives to do, but would you like to attempt it while I'm here to guide you, Miss Lucket?'

'Yes, indeed, if ye please, sir.'

'Good, then have your scissors at hand. Now, wait for a pain to start, and place your forefinger just within the opening, thus, to shield the child's head from the blades. There, that's right. Now, when the pain is at its height, take your scissors and make your cut *here*, at an angle, directed away from the back passage, like this – *now*.'

Guided by his finger, Susan closed the blades of the scissors firmly on the stretched skin, and cut a slit about two inches long from the back of the vaginal opening, just as the child's head was being pushed down by a contraction. Parnham told her to keep her palm pressed against it, using a wool pad to stem the

228

oozing blood. Her heart thudded with apprehension: might she have cut the girl for no good reason? The head remained unborn at the end of the contraction.

'Wait for the next one, miss. We may have made the cut a little too early. The right timing is crucial with this. Now we must wait and she must push.'

To their mutual relief, two more contractions brought the head thrusting through.

'Well done, Signora Trotula,' murmured Parnham as Susan wiped the child's face and put her forefinger in the mouth. Shoulders, arms, trunk and legs followed swiftly with a gush of water and blood, and Hannah was the mother of a daughter.

'Ye can hold her just as soon as I ha' tied and cut the cord, Hannah,' smiled Susan, thankful beyond words at the success of her experiment.

'And here comes the after-burden,' said Parnham in satisfaction. 'How is it with the child?'

The baby answered for herself with a series of ear-splitting howls that drowned Susan's reply.

'In God's name hand it to the mother, else we'll be deafened!'

A smiling Hannah held out her arms, and while she gazed in wonder at her baby, Susan had a question for the surgeon.

'Why d'ye call me T-Trotula, sir?'

'Ah, she was a learned woman doctor at the University of Salerno some six hundred years ago,' he replied. 'She did great things for women and their babies, like making a cut to widen the outlet – just as you have done, my dear, just as you have done today. But now you must mend that cut, so fetch some strong linen thread and a large sewing needle.

He stood behind her as she put in the stitches, with Mag holding Hannah's hand.

'Be quick and firm, place the stitches deep – three or four will suffice,' he told her. 'There now, 'tis done – and all thanks to you, signora!'

Before he left he took a look at the woman who had been delivered by the forceps a week before, and advised that she should start suckling her baby.

'Get her to drink a couple of glasses of porter a day – no spirits, mind – and see that they all have water to wash themselves. Good!'

He left by the back door, having tethered the mare in the yard. Susan saw him out, and he laid a hand on her shoulder.

'I had no thought of doing this place a service when I sent you here, Madam Trotula, but that is what I have done,' he said seriously. 'You will change everything for these poor women, and I will support you. On that you may rely.'

He rode away, looking back to smile and wave to her, and then she ran up to the dormitory to tell Rose of Hannah's good news and what had happened in the birth-chamber.

But Rose never heard it. Just as the new baby had drawn her first breath, she had quietly drawn her last, and Susan could not wish her back to a world that had treated her so cruelly.

Parnham's words proved to be true, for Mistress Lucket ousted Mother Jarvis from the birthing room, and as the weeks went by it was remarked that women recovered more quickly from childbirth, more babies survived, and there were fewer cases of childbed fever. Susan's insistence on clean linen and the use of soap and water at every birthing was quoted outside the workhouse walls, and with Dr Parnham as her champion, her authority grew steadily. With the help of Miss Glover and money donated by the surgeon, she began to hold classes to teach the orphans their letters, turning a deaf ear to the ridicule of the Crokers and Mother Jarvis.

However, they had early discovered her most vulnerable point, and used it to humiliate her whenever they could.

Mad Doll.

The flitting apparition that haunted the House was held in awe by the inmates. There was no escaping from the grey figure that drifted daily and nightly along passages and up and down stairs, suddenly appearing in doorways or standing unnervingly at a bedside. Stories were told of her that were to become part of workhouse lore for a century to come.

Susan felt herself stiffen whenever Mad Doll appeared. Although she tried to hide her feelings and treat the deranged woman with kindness, always defending her against teasing and ridicule, her own unease showed sufficiently for her enemies to note it and sneer in her presence. Had they but known it, their gibes were less painful to Susan than her own secret revulsion towards the poor creature who had borne her, the mother she could neither love nor forgive. The very sight of her was a hateful reminder of everything that Susan shrank from remembering.

And she could never tell a soul.

Chapter 17

The post-chaise approaching along the Portsmouth Road was a moving cloud of chalky dust; the hair and uniforms of the two naval officers sitting aloft were white with it, and at intervals they spat it out over the side.

Two miles short of Beversley, Lieutenant Calthorpe turned to his companion in eager impatience.

'Let's get down, Henry, and walk 'cross country. 'Twill be the best way to our journey's end.'

First Lieutenant Hansford grinned, for he had been about to say the same thing. They called down to the coachman to stop, picked up their rolled sailcloth bags and leaped to the ground, where they struck out across farmland, through ripening corn that shimmered in waves under the July sun. Every step they took brought new pictures into view – a still group of red and white shorthorns in a meadow dotted with tall ox-eye daisies; half a dozen fine fat sows with their piglets, let loose to root in an oak plantation; every aspect of the rural scene gladdened the eyes and rejoiced the hearts of men lately released from the harsh confinements of life at sea.

They reached a tree-crowned summit of rising ground from where they looked down at the familiar valley; on the far side stood the beech grove, and behind it Edward could see the red chimneys of Bever House. Somewhere down there in Beversley was his sweet Susan, perhaps at the Bennetts' farmhouse, or attending a woman in childbirth; or she might even be at Glover Cottage, consulting with his cousin Sophy and Mrs Coulter.

'Susan, my own dear love, if I did but know where you are, I'd be straightway at your side,' he murmured under his breath.

His friend either heard the words or guessed at them, for he clapped him on the shoulder. 'Call with me at Glover Cottage on your way up, and see if Sophia has news of a certain young lady's whereabouts!'

'Gladly, Henry – and wherever she is, I shall go there before I show myself at home,' replied Edward, his heart leaping at the possibility of seeing his darling so soon, perhaps within the hour.

'Good! Let's go down and cross the Beck by the flour mill, and go up through Crabb's Lane to the main street. Come on!'

They hoisted their bags on to their shoulders, and were down by the Beck within a quarter of an hour.

At twenty-two the younger Calthorpe brother looked much older than the Oxford graduate of a year ago, when he had enlisted in the navy. He had felt there was no choice, with Osmond and Henry engaged in the war that had dragged on from year to year, and after an abbreviated training at the Portsmouth Naval Academy he had been recommended by Lieutenant Hansford to be rated as a midshipman on a troopship where half the crew had never wanted to go to sea: they were pressed men.

With Henry as his commanding officer, Edward had learned fast. His dark blue eyes were sharper and deeper-set, and his skin was roughened by all weathers and the salt of air and diet. His limbs had hardened into a muscular agility that matched the

233

knowledge he had acquired, the brutal sights he had seen: the gaunt, unshaven faces, the hoarse shouts from the lower decks where punishment lashings exposed the bones beneath the flesh. Edward had learned to steel his heart where once he might have tried to intervene; discretion was often the better part of valour in the King's navy, especially in time of war. Far from desiring to serve their country, men deserted at the first opportunity.

Gone for ever was the reticence of Edward the boy; the man now home on shore leave knew exactly what he wanted from life, and was determined to claim it without unnecessary delay: before he returned to sea in three weeks' time with the two stripes of a lieutenant, he would be married to Susan Lucket.

Susan! The memory of her sweet face had so often come between him and the life around him, shielding him from its baser effects, and not only aboard ship. There were temptations enough in a seaport where drink flowed freely and the favours of town women were not only cheap and available but actively thrust upon callow youngsters. And only Edward knew how close he had come to succumbing.

It had been a fine spring evening when he had walked up out of the port to the wooded hill above it, simply to get away from tavern company. A young girl had followed him, and as soon as they were alone among the trees she had sidled up to him with a pretty smile and said she was tired of walking. Would the young gentleman sit down with her? He had rather awkwardly agreed, and when they were seated on the tussocky grass, he had asked her name. Her voice was soft and beguiling.

'Oi be Meg, sir, an' Oi knows well how to pleasure a fine young gen'leman like yeself, sir.'

And within half a minute she had guided his hands around her waist and pressed her rosy lips to his mouth. It all happened so quickly, and he was taken by surprise at his body's response: the instant hardening as his blood surged, the immediacy of his desire to take what was being so freely offered.

He returned her kiss, and let her lead his hand inside her bodice to touch her flat little chest. His other hand seemed to find its own way under her skirt and between her warm thighs as they sank down together on the ground.

'Oh, Meg . . .' His breathing had quickened with his pounding heart, and he closed his eyes as she found his lips again. While his senses reeled in the moist warmth of her kisses, he felt her prying hands busily unbuttoning his breeches in a curiously practised way, as if she had done this many times before and was in a hurry to get to the point of her business with him. He shuddered to recall how close he had come to taking her there under the whispering leaves; but it was the touch of those nimble hands that made him stop and seize them. They were a child's hands. He looked at her bare feet, also very small to belong to a girl engaged in such trade as this.

'Meg – Meg, how old are you?' he asked hoarsely.

'Oi'll be fifteen come midsummer, sir, but Oi knows well how to—'

Edward sat up sharply, realising with a shock that he had been about to ravish a child.

'We must stop this, Meg,' he gasped. ''Tis sinful, and with such a little maid as you are—'

'Don't 'ee worry, sir, 'ee ain't the first,' she assured him cheerfully. 'An' Oi knows just what gen'lemen—'

'May God forgive us, and myself more than you, Meg!' Horrified at such wickedness, Edward leaped to his feet, aware of how foolish he must look. Yet conscience-stricken as he was, he felt he had an obligation to remonstrate with her and try to persuade her to turn away from a life that would surely destroy her if she persisted in it.

'Listen to me, Meg. How long have you been – er – pleasuring?'

She gave him a wary look. 'Not long, sir.'

'And do your parents know about this?'

'No, they be in the country, sir. Oi live wi' me sister Jenny an' her little girl, two year old. Jenny works at the Bishop's Table, that be an inn down there, sir –' she gestured towards Portsmouth below them – 'an' Oi be larnin' to do the same as her, like, to pay fur me bed an' board, sir.'

'Good God! And do you not know the dangers of such a life, girl? The harm to your health, your character, your – your immortal soul?'

'Oi dunno about me soul, sir, but me belly'd be better fur a slice o' bread an' bacon,' she retorted, straightening the thin kerchief over her narrow shoulders. She was disappointed at the way her handsome bluecoat had turned out. Trust her luck to get a canting preacher!

A wave of self-disgust swept over Edward. What a despicable hypocrite he must look, straight from the pages of Molière, doing up his buttons and brushing the dead leaves from his jacket after he had come so near to using the services of this poor child-whore!

'Come, Meg, and I will take you back to the Bishop's Table and speak to your sister.'

He held out his hand to help her to her feet, but she pouted and gave him a sidelong look.

'There be little joy in goin' back wi' nothin' in me pocket, sir.'

He delved into his own pocket and drew out a handful of silver and copper coins. Her eyes widened.

'Be them all fur me, sir? Oooh! Jenny'll be that pleased! Thank'ee, sir, Oi thanks 'ee well!'

Stowing the coins away in a little purse beneath her skirt, she reached up to kiss him in childish delight.

''Ee be a right good'un, sir!'

And turning quickly on her bare heels, she ran off down the hill with her prize money, leaving Edward to ponder on the fate of girls like her, sick with remorse when he thought of Susan, and how he had so nearly betrayed her.

And yet the encounter with Meg had been a reminder of his frequent longing to hold Susan in his arms as his lawful wife. His manhood would rise at the contemplation of how it would be when he took her to bed; how often he secretly imagined melting her virginal whiteness in the flame of his passion, until they were blended together into one flesh . . .

Henry's voice broke in on his thoughts. They had come up Crabb's Lane and reached the main street, where Miss Glover's cottage stood back from the other dwellings in its pretty garden.

'Oh, Edward, I am half afraid she will be out – and half afraid that she will be in.'

'Then, Henry, you must go and find out!'

She was in – and the joy in her eyes on beholding Henry was all that he could have wished. Edward turned away as his cousin and his good friend embraced each other, but after a moment or two she called out to him.

'And Edward, dear Cousin Edward, how good it is to see your face again!' She held out both hands to him. 'I take it you have not yet been home?'

When they assured her that this was their first port of call, she advised them against mentioning this when they reached their respective homes, for fear of offending their parents.

'But, Sophy, I have come to ask for news of Susan Lucket,' explained Edward. 'Is she at the Bennetts'? And does she still assist Mrs Coulter?'

Sophia hesitated for a moment, and then asked him to step into the parlour with her.

'I had better have a little talk with you, Edward, if Henry will excuse us. I will tell you what you have clearly not yet heard about Mistress Lucket.'

'What is it, Sophy? Pray tell me at once – is she not well?' he asked in alarm.

The news of Susan's changed circumstances was soon told, and Edward was thunderstruck.

'*What?* In heaven's name, *why*? How came she to be shut up in that godforsaken place?'

Sophia told him about Dr Parnham's proposition, to his great indignation.

'How dare he subject her to such degradation?'

'My dear Edward, I can see that you have been changed by life at sea, and your Susan is also changed. She is no longer the poor child from the Ash-Pits, nor maidservant in a farmer's household. She is a skilled and capable midwife, and has quite transformed the infirmary at the House of Industry. Dr Parnham speaks very highly—'

'But, Sophy, I have come to offer her *marriage*. She cannot stay in there!'

'Hear me out, Edward,' ordered Sophia with a touch of the nursery governess in her expression. 'Susan is training for work of essential importance to Beversley. Mrs Coulter grows daily more infirm, and needs a successor. Susan has a strength and

238

inner resource that I am sure is God-given.'

She paused and clasped her hands together on her lap. Even in his anxious concern for Susan, Edward could not help but be struck by the lively sincerity that shone in her clear blue eyes. He had never previously thought of his cousin as a beauty, but now she seemed to glow from within.

'There is something of the wise woman about her, Edward, though she is but a maiden, and there are those who object to her doing such work, for propriety's sake.'

'Then I can be of use to her, Sophy, for I can bestow on her the protection of my name. I soon have to go back to sea, so if she wishes to continue at that wretched place and learn from that confounded doctor, she will do so as Mrs Edward Calthorpe. And then nobody will dare to object!'

'Ah, Edward, I can see that you mean what you say, but there will be great objections to such a marriage, especially now that—'

She checked herself. Edward must go home and find out for himself how things were. 'I wish you success in your hopes, Cousin, but please do not tell your parents straight away. Let them enjoy one night of your company, and go to visit Susan tomorrow.'

'Very well, Sophy, I will deny myself until tomorrow morning,' he told her reluctantly. 'But I shall not waver, not for any reason. And now I had better leave you, or Henry will say I am no friend of his! Good day to you, Sophy.'

They kissed, and Sophia hoped that her smiles hid the unease she felt as she watched him walk away. Then she turned and held out her arms to Henry.

*

As soon as Edward crossed the threshold of Bever House he sensed trouble, though his father greeted him with joy.

'I cannot tell you how happy we are that you are sent safely home to us, Edward!' he said, while Selina and Caroline's tearful embraces alerted him to ill news. Just for a moment, for a split second of time, he thought Osmond must be dead, but in his mother's welcome all was explained. He listened in mounting horror as she told of their sorrow, and took himself to his brother before even changing his dust-whitened clothes.

Osmond was sitting out on the terrace at the back, a table with a decanter and glasses at his side.

'How you are changed, Ned! I declare you've doubled in size,' he remarked on beholding the broadened frame and weathered face. 'No doubt of it, the navy offers the easier option.'

Edward let this pass, and said that he thanked God for his brother's survival. He soon discovered that the invalid ruled the household, with family and servants deferring to his every whim, and the atmosphere dependent on his swings of mood from day to day. They all looked to the younger brother to dispel Osmond's gloom and revive his hopes for the future.

Edward now understood why Sophia said that he should keep his wedding plans to himself on this first day at home.

After dinner the brothers talked about their experiences of service life, and Edward did his best to be encouraging.

'You will do him more good than anything else,' said Mr Calthorpe when Osmond had been taken to his bed, having imbibed a fair amount of wine.

Edward's conscience pricked at the thought of how soon he planned to desert them all to wed his Susan; he felt that he could not deceive his father any longer.

'Are you walking out with the dogs, Father? If so I will come with you.'

'Ah, I shall be glad of that, Edward,' came the heartfelt answer, and the two of them set out to walk around the boundary of the estate in the cool of the evening.

'You are just what Osmond needs at this time, Edward.'

The moment of truth had come.

'Father, I have something to tell you, and you will not be pleased. I have but three weeks of leave before I must return to sea on the *Bucephalus*, and during this time I must marry the girl I love. You know her name, Father – Susan Lucket. She works as a midwife in the House of Industry, and tomorrow I shall ride over to Belhampton and ask her to be my wife – and when we are united, I must spend what precious time I have with her. Oh, Father, I am sorry, but I have to put Susan first. I have loved her all my life.'

It had been said, and Edward stopped speaking and looked at his father to see the effect of what he expected would be a bitter disappointment. They walked on for several yards in silence, and then Calthorpe stopped and laid his hand on his son's arm.

'I cannot give you my official approval, Edward,' he said heavily. 'Your mother will be heartbroken, and will have no good to say of your intention. Life will not be easy for you, either now or in the future.'

'But, Father, I am prepared for difficulties – maybe poverty at first – but Susan and I will live thriftily

241

after the war, when I start to practise. And if I should not return—'

'My son, do not say it, I beg you!' Checking the rising tide of emotion in his voice, Calthorpe went on quickly, 'After the trouble we have had with your poor brother, my attitudes are somewhat changed, and I wish for nothing but my children's happiness, Edward. Your mother will never receive your – your wife at Bever House, but I think I have always known that this would happen, and as your father I wish you well.'

'Thank you, Father. That means a great deal to me.'

'And shall make it my business, privately, to ride over and visit your wife from time to time. I should go to that place more often anyway, seeing that I am on the Board of Guardians.'

Edward was overcome by this unexpected sympathy, and felt a rush of affection towards his father, whose sufferings of the past two months had left their mark.

'God bless you, Father, from my heart. I am truly sorry to cause you and my mother distress at such a time.'

'I know, my boy, I know. And I shall not forget that her – that Susan's children will be of my own blood.'

Nothing further was said, but their brief, silent embrace told more than words could have done.

At the breakfast table the next morning Edward felt that he might as well have pitched a cannonball into the room. Gertrude Calthorpe gave a shriek and dissolved into angry tears, Selina and Caroline were contemptuous and Osmond merely baffled.

'You can have the girl, can't you, Ned, without having to marry her, surely?' he muttered in a low tone. 'No need to let her trap you for life! Come, there is still time to stop and consider your future.'

'Don't expect me ever to receive her at Bever House,' raged Mrs Calthorpe. 'You will have no standing in the county with that low-born girl as a wife. You should hear the complaints I receive from respectable women who are deeply shocked that an unmarried girl dabbles in practices that no decent woman should even speak of, matters I would not repeat in front of your sisters. You will share in the shame of it if you marry her, and it will fall upon us all.'

'On the contrary, Mother, I shall raise her to the status of a married woman, so that she may practise her craft without giving rise to such spiteful gossip,' Edward retorted.

'And can't you see that she has trapped you for that very reason, just to serve her own ends?' shrilled Gertrude.

'Look, Mother, Dr Parnham and Cousin Sophy have the greatest praise for—'

'Yes, oh, yes! Thanks again to that bastard cousin of yours who gave the wretched girl ideas above her station in the first place – and tricked Henry Hansford away from Selina – oh, she has been the curse of this house! Oh, go away, go away, and leave me alone, for heaven's sake!'

Her voice rose hysterically, bringing a couple of maidservants hurrying in. Edward felt there was nothing to stay for, so saddled his horse and rode off to Belhampton and the House of Industry. He had waited long enough to see the dearest girl in the world.

Chapter 18

Charles Parnham could not make up his mind. It was his habit to spend two mornings with his students and two or three visiting his patients, though there was no set pattern to his working day because of the summonses that came in at all hours. Records and correspondence had to be dealt with when time allowed, and he had planned to spend this morning at his desk.

There were two women nearing their time at the House of Industry, and Parnham considered riding over to see how they did. He knew that there was not the slightest need for him to do so, because *she* would look after them and let him know of any untoward developments. He could rely on her absolutely.

He reluctantly took up his quill, wishing that a messenger would call him to a bedside. This must be the effect of Elizabeth's death, he thought: his patient wife had suffered years of encroaching muscle weakness, resigning her dreams of motherhood to the barren sickliness that claimed her while he was increasingly away from home, attending more fortunate wives.

Poor Elizabeth. He had engaged two extra women servants to ensure that she had every care and attention, and he had been a faithful husband, though it was more than a decade since he had shared her bed. She had never complained about her lot, and he had always assumed a cheerful manner in her presence, never talking of the sometimes joyful, sometimes tragic scenes in which he had to play his part.

Whereas little Trotula shared every aspect of his work.

Charles sighed heavily. Self-doubt and regret were added to the dull pain of grieving, and only God knew how he had felt on that morning six weeks ago when the maidservants had called him to Elizabeth's side at dawn, to find that her life had quietly ebbed away in sleep. He had felt shock, yes, sorrow and distress, of course – but something else, which he was only now able to acknowledge to himself: he was free.

If he chose to do so, he could ride over to the Belhampton workhouse and visit whomsoever he pleased; and if the gossips wagged their tongues about the young, unmarried midwife – and he suspected that Croker and Jarvis already did – well then, there could be a remedy for it.

Charles Parnham drew himself up short: his thoughts were racing on ahead like a galloping horse, and his wife hardly cold in her grave. It was important to preserve his usual daily habits during this early period of widowerhood, he told himself; it was not a time to give way to impulses, to rush headlong into any new situation.

He must wait. Yes, of course, he must wait . . .

To the devil with waiting.

He dropped the pen and rose from his desk. Within ten minutes he had saddled the mare and turned her head towards the place that drew him like a magnet.

'Now, children, pay attention, all o' ye, and that means Jemmy too. Everybody look this way, and we'll say the alphabet together.'

245

The dozen children sitting along each side of a trestle table on forms provided by Dr Parnham began to recite in ragged chorus.

'A, B, C, D, E, F, G . . .'

From then on they became less sure, and Susan had to prompt them: 'H, I, J, K, L, M, N—'

When she stopped, their voices straggled off into silence, and they stared uncertainly at her and at each other. Except for seven-year-old Dorcas, who continued through to X, Y and Z with a dogged seriousness that made Susan long to hug her and tell her what a clever girl she was; only that would not be fair on Toby, who was too scared to open his mouth, and Nan who had a hare lip and would never speak clearly. Not to mention Jemmy, who was twelve but could only scribble on his slate with less understanding than the youngest in the class.

When, with the backing of Dr Parnham, Susan had persuaded the House Master – which meant Mrs Croker – to let the orphans leave their menial tasks on two mornings each week, the children had not known what to expect and it had taken Susan an hour just to tell them about the wonderful signs that could be written on the slates supplied by Miss Glover.

'And we don't only write them down, children, we can *say* them too. Let me tell you the sounds that the letters make!'

The gradual awakening of interest in their dull eyes had been more reward than Susan had ever dreamed of. Always ordered to keep quiet, the children were cautious at first in their attempts to make the sounds that she gave to each letter, but as she encouraged them they grew bolder and each one in his or her own way began to respond. And Susan in her turn responded to them.

Nobody has ever wanted these children, she thought. They have never known love. How different from the pupils at the village school, and what would Mrs Bryers make of these, who have only me to teach them?

And yet . . . maybe I'm right for them, after all. Perhaps they need somebody like me, who was set apart from the other pupils at the school. Yet I was determined to learn, and now I'm passing on what I learned to others!

Listening to these children of the workhouse, underfed and uncared for, reciting the magic sequence of letters, their little faces alive with achievement, she found herself reliving her own discovery of the alphabet. Her duty had become her joy.

'That's very good, Dorcas. Now we shall all repeat what Dorcas has just said for us. Ready? O, P, Q, R, S, T, U—'

'Missis Lucket, Missis Lucket! 'Ee's gotta leave the childer an' come to Mrs Croker, quick!'

Susan frowned as Mag burst into the room looking wild and scared.

'What is it, Mag? What's happened?'

'Her says 'ee's to come quick, missis. A gen'leman be come, an' mus'n't be kep' waitin'!'

Susan's eyes widened. Dr Parnham? He would not bring her from her class without good reason. Her heart began to beat faster, for she dared not name her hope.

'Come quick, missis. Un be a fine brave gen'leman in a blue coat wi' gold buttons all down in front!'

Susan drew a sharp breath: yes, it might be!

'I must leave ye f'r a while, children. Write down the letters on y'r slates till I return.'

The class was held at the very back of the House, and she followed Mag through the workroom and two stone-flagged passages to get to Mrs Croker's sitting room at the front. The door was open, and she heard voices.

'Will 'ee take a cup o' tea, sir? Or a glass o' porter?'

'No, thank you, I wish only to see Miss Lucket.'

Yes, it was his voice! Edward Calthorpe *here*. Her legs shook. Mrs Croker poked her head out of the door.

'Where be that fool Mag? Ah, there 'ee be, Miss Lucket. Come in. 'Ee's got a visitor.'

Susan entered the room, and there he was, snatching off his tricorn hat and holding out his hand to the trembling girl dressed in the unbleached calico of the workhouse, a cap of the same material framing her face.

His own sweet Susan's face.

'Su— Miss Lucket, I thank God for the sight of you. It has been so long a time,' he breathed.

She had lowered her eyes, but now raised her face to his, alight with a joy that she too was unable to hide.

'Ye be home from the sea, Mr Calthorpe.'

Such commonplace words, so softly uttered as she held out her hand to take his. In one swift movement he raised it to his lips, and she felt the warm pressure of his kiss upon her fingers, saw the hunger in the dark blue eyes that held hers. All their love and longing was revealed in that meeting of hands and eyes, and Mrs Croker literally gasped in astonishment.

Edward quickly turned to her. 'I need to see and speak with Miss Lucket alone. Is there somewhere we may talk unheard?'

248

'To be sure, yer honour . . .' began the woman, but Susan lightly touched him on the sleeve.

'I ha' left a class o' children, Mr Calthorpe,' she said in a low voice. 'Come with me to see them, and then I'll walk outside with ye.'

The housekeeper bristled, her huge mobcap bobbing up and down. 'It be time they childer was set to summat useful, 'stead o' wastin' time slate-scrapin'!'

'I must go to them,' Susan repeated to Edward, and he at once took her arm to accompany her. She smiled, for she wanted to share her children with him before she dismissed the class.

Leaving Mrs Croker to fume, she led him under a brick archway into a large, high-ceilinged room where men and women sat at looms. They ranged from the young and crippled to the old and feeble: destitution was their common lot. Edward noticed an apparently able-bodied youth with a bruise on his forehead who looked up and raised his hand to Susan in greeting.

'Good day to ye, Gus,' she said, returning his smile. An old woman called out to her in a cracked voice.

'Blessin's on 'ee, pretty child! Don't let un lead 'ee astray, same as un did to me!'

'Shut yer mouth, yer ol' fool,' growled a weary-looking man whose face was furrowed by pain, and Edward saw with a pang that he had a wooden stump in place of his left leg. It reminded him of his brother's grievous loss, though at least Osmond was not incarcerated here. What surprised Edward most was Susan's easy acceptance of these poor unfortunates; she seemed to know them all by name.

They passed into a kind of junction where there

were several doors, and one of these led into a small, bare room with one high window. Here the children eagerly awaited her.

'Missis Lucket, Oi said 'ee'd be back!' smiled Dorcas happily.

'Oi can draw great A an' B, Missis Lucket,' chirped a thin boy with red wrists protruding from frayed sleeves.

'Well done, Toby, and now you must remember them,' smiled Susan, while Edward stared in dismay at their pale faces and undersized bodies. He was used to seeing wretchedness among the lower ranks in the navy, but these were *children* – or rather grotesque parodies of childhood: a girl with a hideous hare lip, an idiot boy scraping his slate with a squeaky slate-pencil that set Edward's teeth on edge. And yet Susan seemed to see nothing amiss.

'You must put away y'r slates now, children,' she began.

'Aw, missis, don't 'ee send us away!' begged one or two, and Susan glanced at Edward.

'If I may finish their lesson, Mr Calthorpe, I shan't be long.'

Impatient as he was to be alone with her, he nodded his consent, unable to refuse; and also he sensed that she wanted him to share something of her life in this place.

'Jemmy, fetch a chair f'r Mr Calthorpe.'

The oldest boy lurched to his feet and opened a door that led into a steamy room from which came a babble of voices and a smell of root vegetables boiling with bones.

'Leave that chair where it be!' screeched a woman, but Jemmy emerged grinning and holding up a wooden chair that Edward took from him.

'Pray continue with the lesson, Miss Lucket,' he said. She flashed him a grateful look and, turning to the children, she asked who could write a great A like Toby and which letter came after it. Who could write that? And the next one?

Edward was soon riveted by what he saw and heard: how they all enjoyed the lesson in their various ways, and benefited from Susan's interest in them, just as he rejoiced in the lovely sidelong looks she sent in his direction. He forgot that these were workhouse bastards and orphans, and saw them as she did, children starved of love and attention.

But then something happened to remind him of where he was.

Suddenly the door to the passage gave a click. The latch was slowly lifted, and Susan looked towards it, her smile fading. It slowly swung open, and when Edward saw the apparition standing there, a shiver ran down his spine. He had forgotten about Susan's mother still imprisoned in this place, and here she was, pointing straight at him with a bony forefinger. Hollow, empty eyes stared out of a skull-like head, and grey hair escaped in wisps from under her cap. Glancing at Susan, he saw the momentary recoil in her grey eyes; it immediately vanished, and she clapped her hands twice to get the children's attention.

'Sssh, everybody, ye know that poor Dolly won't hurt ye. Don't cry, Nan – and Jemmy, sit down at once!'

For Jemmy had leaped to his feet, and was jumping up and down, flapping his arms and making faces at Mad Doll. Reluctantly he sat down, thrusting out his lower lip in defiance.

With her mouth firmly set, Susan went over to the open door.

'No, Dolly, ye can't come in here while I'm teachin',' she said firmly but not unkindly. 'Go along, Dolly, go along now.'

She shut the door and went straight on with the lesson, though Edward saw that she was shaken. There had been no love in her eyes, nor even the friendly acknowledgement she had given to the paupers in the workroom.

While he was trying to define her attitude towards Mad Doll, another interruption occurred: Mag rushed in again from the direction of the workroom.

'Missis! Missis! Gus be fallen in a fit again, missis!'

Susan rolled her eyes heavenward, glancing at Edward before hurrying off with the maid-of-all-work. He could hear shouting and banging, and Susan's calm voice raised above the uproar. He rose and followed the noise, and when he reached the workroom he stood appalled at the scene before him.

The young man called Gus was writhing on the floor beside his loom, his face livid, his eyelids fluttering and his mouth stretched in a ghastly grimace as his head banged up and down on the wooden floor. His arms and legs jerked as if on strings, his teeth were clenched and his tongue protruded through them, bloody and frothing.

'My God, he's biting it in half!' thought Edward, horrified when he saw Susan kneeling beside the thrashing body.

'Why didn't ye put the spoon between his teeth?' she asked the cowering onlookers. 'Can somebody help me roll him over on his side?'

Edward rushed to her assistance, kneeling and hauling the unconscious Gus over on to his left side, revealing that the man had wet himself.

'For heaven's sake take *care*, Susan!' cried Edward

252

when she reached into Gus's pocket and drew out a wooden spoon wrapped in a piece of towelling. She proceeded to insert it at the side of his mouth, between his back teeth. His flailing arm landed a blow on her shoulder, and Edward at once grabbed both his arms.

'Careful, Edward, don't use any force!' she warned. 'He'll settle down in a minute or two, and fall asleep. Mag, fetch me his cushion. I've told ye all so many times, there's nothin' to be afeard of; poor Gus never hurts anybody but himself.'

Sure enough, Gus's movements subsided within a couple of minutes; his badly bitten tongue was released, and the bluish tinge of his skin turned to pink. Mag brought the pillow, which Susan arranged under his head, and covered him with a blanket taken from under his chair. She carefully tucked it round him as he lay on the floor, breathing deeply and regularly.

'Ye really *must* all try to remember what to do when he has a fit,' she told the onlookers briskly. 'There's no need f'r all this panic.'

Edward could hardly believe his eyes and ears as he followed her back to the makeshift schoolroom; this time she dismissed the children, telling them to leave their slates on the table.

'At last we are alone, dearest Susan, and you must hear me,' Edward said, taking her hands in both of his. 'I ask only to talk with you, without interruption from Gus or the children or – or any of the poor souls under this roof,' he insisted, not wanting to mention her mother.

She gave him a rueful smile. 'Ye can see how it is here, Mr Calthorpe. These poor children—'

'Call me Edward, Susan, and listen, for 'tis my turn

now, and I will be heard. I warn you, I will not leave this place until I have spoken and received an answer. Is this the best place to talk?'

She shook her head. 'Come with me, an' we'll walk outside.'

She opened the door leading to the passage, and nearly knocked over Mrs Croker, who had her ear against it. Edward would have laughed at the woman's discomfiture if he had not been so impatient to hear the words he longed for. He followed Susan through a scullery full of brooms, mops and buckets, and out into the cobbled yard.

'How do you endure this awful place, my Susan?' he asked, but she merely shook her head, thinking how much sweeter it smelled since poor Rose's death.

He seized her hand. 'I have no time to waste, Susan. Yesterday I returned from the war at sea, and have but three short weeks before I go back and join the *Bucephalus*, to sail for America with troops and provisions. And I want you to be my wife before I leave. Oh, Susan, hear me!' he implored as she closed her eyes as if in disbelief. 'I offer you a husband's love, my name, my life – everything I have.'

She had lowered her head, but he put his hand under her chin and raised her face until her eyes were forced to meet his.

'Do not refuse me, Susan. If I should not return from the war—'

'Oh, don't say it, Edward, don't even think on't,' she begged with a shudder, and the words were music in his ears.

'But it must be faced, Susan. If I were to perish at sea, I'd die happier as your wedded husband, and you would still have my name. Cousin Sophy has told me of the difficulties you have with your work because you are not married.'

'That's true, Edward,' she agreed, lifting her head. 'The women themselves don't mind me, 'tis others who speak agin me an' would stop my work – only I ha' got a good friend in Dr Parnham.'

'Then marry me, Susan. Ever since I first saw you in the stable-yard when we were but children, I have loved none other but you. Cousin Sophy has told me of your work here, but what I have seen today exceeds everything. Think of it, you could stay here and carry on your good work until I return when the war's over. Only say you will have me, my own love!'

She trembled against him but remained silent.

'What have you to say, Susan? Answer me, I pray you!'

When she spoke her voice was so low that he had to bend down to hear.

'Y'r family wouldn't like it, Edward, an' the rector wouldn't go agin them.'

'What? By heaven, I'll marry without their liking, and find a man of the cloth to marry us, I care not in what church!' he replied vehemently. 'Whether by Romish rites or in one of Mr Wesley's new chapels, we shall make our vows to each other before God. Oh, Susan, my own darling, make no more objections. Take pity on a faithful lover and let us be man and wife!'

And throwing his arms around her there in the yard, he held her close to him, so that she felt the strength of his body against her, the warmth of his breath on her face. There was no doubting his love, nor was there doubt in her heart that she returned it. Mrs Bennett had warned her two years ago that a boy's love would not last, but now he had returned to

255

her as a man, offering a husband's love and protection. And the title of Mistress Calthorpe would have to be acknowledged by the scoffers of Miss Lucket. Even if he did not return from the war – and her mind reeled away from such a dreadful possibility – she would carry on her work as a respectable widow, able to support herself and any child of their union.

A child of their union. Edward Calthorpe's child.

And there lay the reason for her hesitation. To give birth to this man's child would be happiness beyond her dreams, but it was the thought of the marital union that she could not envisage. Deep in the recesses of her memory was a dark place where a monster still lurked, never thought about except in shameful and terrifying dreams. And in encounters with Mad Doll.

Yet there was no reason why Edward should ever know – God forbid! There were no outward marks left by the past, only that uncontrollable fear of what happened between a man and a woman. She had never thought of Edward in that way.

But how could she deny him anything, he who had loved her for so long? And why should she deny herself the pride of being his wife? Surely all would be well when they were married. She murmured a silent prayer for guidance, for a confirming sign.

And a sign was given, or so it seemed, almost immediately.

'Ah, Madam Trotula, I did not think to see you walking out with a gentleman – and an officer of the King's navy, no less!'

Charles Parnham spoke cordially to hide his sudden dismay. He had walked round to the back of the House to avoid Mrs Croker, and had planned to slip quietly into the classroom; but as soon as he saw the young officer with his arms around Susan, his spirits plummeted. How little he really knew about this girl – only that poor Mad Doll was her mother, and that the family had been miserably poor. This young man was not likely to be a relative.

To Edward's extreme chagrin, Susan withdrew herself from his encircling arm and smiled in the most natural way at this intruder.

'Dr Parnham! Oh, I be that *pleased* to see ye, sir!'

She held out her hands, which the doctor took, raising his eyebrows slightly. Her companion's annoyance was not lost on him. This sailor lad wishes me to the devil, he thought. Can he possibly read my mind?

He smiled politely as Susan introduced them.

'Dr Parnham, this is Mr Edward Calthorpe o' Bever House. He be – he is in the navy, and is cousin to Miss Glover.'

'Lieutenant Calthorpe,' amended Edward coolly. Parnham bowed.

'Oh, Edward, this is my friend Dr Parnham who does so much to help women in childbirth – he teaches doctors and midwives on the subject. In Belhampton,' she added eagerly.

What a rare little beauty she is, thought Charles Parnham. And this young officer is in love with her. Well, well.

How that man's eyes rake over her, thought Edward; he must be old enough to be her father, and I do not trust him an inch.

'I thank Mistress Lucket for her compliments, and return them,' said Parnham, looking straight into Edward's unsmiling eyes. 'I would never have believed that a poor girl of her age and background could be so wise in judgement and natural skill. In truth, sir, I have never known a better practitioner of the midwife's art, even though she lacks a husband. Can it be that you think to make good that lack, Lieutenant? Forgive my intrusion at such a moment. Good day to you both.'

He turned away, intending to return to his lonely desk, but Edward was incensed at what he saw as a gross discourtesy.

'Stay a moment – I do not care for your tone, sir!'

Parnham turned round. 'Indeed, Lieutenant?'

'Who gave you the right to speak so disrespectfully of the lady I intend to marry?' demanded Edward. 'Yes, sir, you are looking at Mrs Edward Calthorpe as she will be within days, and I'll thank you to address her with the honour due to a lady!'

Susan gasped and tried to protest, but Charles Parnham walked back to them, holding out his hand to Edward.

'Well said, Lieutenant Calthorpe, and I thank you. You and your lady have all the apology that I can offer. I humbly beg your pardon, mistress.'

Edward was not inclined to be won over, but Susan's pleading smiles and her innocent daughterly regard for the doctor persuaded him to take the proffered hand. Parnham looked steadily into his eyes.

'I congratulate you, Lieutenant, you have chosen well, whatever the world may say, and I'll warrant it will say a great deal. Any assistance I can give is at your disposal. Good day.'

He left them quickly, and Edward looked thoughtfully at his retreating back. Then he drew Susan to his side again.

'Your doctor friend wishes us well, my love, so let

us be married as soon as it can be arranged. I will consult with Cousin Sophy about a church in Belhampton. So what do you say?'

Susan's answer was in her shy smile, but Edward made her speak, and when she whispered her fatal *yes*, he kissed her upturned face reverently, unaware of Mrs Croker and Mrs Jarvis gawping from an upstairs window.

'Missis Lucket! Missis Lucket!' called Mag from the scullery door. ''Ee'd better come to her wi' the scar down her face. Her say her be gettin' hard pains in her belly!'

Chapter 19

The interior of the Wesleyan Chapel at Belhampton was cool and clean, with whitewashed walls and long rectangular windows of clear glass. Plain wooden pews rose up in shallow tiers on three sides from an uncarpeted space before the unadorned altar, and the only decoration was supplied by the words of the Lord's Prayer painted in a single line around the walls; two earthenware vases filled with garden flowers added a touch of colour.

Edward stood beside his groomsman Henry Hansford at the side door. It was a quarter to ten, and they were as yet alone in the chapel. They were both in uniform and conversed in low voices.

'May it not be very long before I am doing the same service for you, Henry,' said Edward.

'The war will have to end first,' sighed his friend. 'I am trying not to envy you your more persuadable lady.'

A man entered, hat in hand, bowed briefly to Edward and took a seat at the back.

'Dr Parnham, the man-midwife,' muttered Edward.

'Oh, is that he? Sophy speaks highly of him, and says he has great admiration for your Susan's skill.'

Edward did not reply.

'Who on earth are *that* ill-favoured pair?' asked Henry as a man and woman came in and sat down at the front.

'The Crokers – the workhouse Master and his wife,' replied Edward in distaste. 'Susan says it was Parnham's idea to invite them to witness the validity of her marriage.'

'Is her sister coming?'

Edward's mouth tightened. 'No, she has not been given leave. But oh, see, there is her brother Job! He must have walked all the way over the common. Susan will be pleased to see him.'

But Joby Lucket had not walked the five miles from Beversley; he had come with Mrs Bennett and Mrs Marianne Smart in the three-seater. Edward stepped forward to greet the ladies warmly.

'This is an honour, Mrs Bennett,' he said with a bow.

'You have more than proved your words, Mr Edward, and I wish you all the happiness you deserve,' beamed the farmer's wife. 'Susan was a daughter to me when my Sally lay at death's door, and I shall stand as her mother today.'

At five minutes to ten the minister appeared with his book open at the appointed place, and beckoned the two gentlemen to come forward.

At three minutes to ten a slight flurry at the entrance caused heads to turn, and a rather flustered Mr Turnbull came in with Mrs Coulter leaning heavily against him, her face tense with pain. He guided her slowly to a front pew and sat beside her, her walking stick across his lap.

Somewhere a clock struck ten, and all eyes turned to the door through which Miss Glover would bring a servant girl to be married to a Calthorpe of Bever House. A sigh went up from the small gathering as the two women appeared, both dressed in grey, but whereas Miss Glover's gown was entirely plain, the

261

bride's had white lace at the throat and wrists. She wore a pretty straw hat with a silk ribbon, and carried a bunch of pink and white roses.

As soon as Susan entered the chapel her eyes were fixed upon Edward. She did not see the others, not even Joby, but walked straight towards the man who had chosen her for his wife. They stood together before the black-coated minister, and the marriage ceremony proceeded: Susan Lucket became Mrs Edward Calthorpe in the presence of her brother and friends. There was no music or homily, and when the gold ring was placed on her finger she trembled and turned very pale. Edward put his arm around her, and the simple service ended with a prayer that the new husband and wife would heed the word of God throughout their lives. They walked out of the chapel into a small paved court, and the attendants followed; there were greetings and embraces, especially between the bride and Joby, and with her former mistress from Bennetts' farm. Mrs Coulter kissed Susan and told Edward he had gained a prize.

'There's none I'd rather hand over to than you, Mrs Calthorpe,' said the old midwife with satisfaction. 'And now nobody can call you spinster!'

Mrs Croker noted the absence of the groom's family, but with the squire's son and Dr Parnham on hand to give their support, she kept her curiosity to herself and pushed her husband forward to shake hands with the happy pair.

At Dr Parnham's invitation they all trooped or rode up the hill to his house, where a good table awaited them, laden with cold mutton, new bread and bacon, fruit tarts and just enough wine and small beer to refresh them before they journeyed back to their homes and workplaces.

At least I have given my Trotula her wedding breakfast, though a more favoured man stands at her side, thought Charles, shaking hands with Edward and promising to watch over the welfare of young Mrs Calthorpe during her husband's absence.

He then produced his wedding gift, which took them completely by surprise: a smart little two-wheeled trap drawn by a young and well-behaved brown pony.

'His name is Brownie, and he will take you wherever Mrs Calthorpe pleases. The choice of wedding-trip is yours,' said the doctor, patting Brownie's neck and adjusting the new bridle and reins. 'And there's a basket of provisions for your dinner.'

Edward and Susan stared at the trim equipage.

'My wife and I are greatly obliged to you, sir,' said Edward.

Parnham bowed.

'Would you like to go to Wychell Forest, Susan, and walk beside the lake?' asked Edward in sudden inspiration.

'I've never been that far, Edward,' she said with shy eagerness, and Parnham experienced a pang. She'd agree to go to the North Pole if he suggested it, he thought.

'Then you shall go today, my love, thanks to Dr Parnham.'

'My humble privilege, Lieutenant,' murmured the doctor, dismissing envy as the most contemptible of the seven deadly sins.

Susan saw Joby looking longingly at the trap, and remembered that he too had never seen the forest and lake. The boy had come to her wedding, and she longed for him and Edward to know each other like brothers. It would be a great treat for him if . . .

Edward also noted the look on Joby's face, and a sharp struggle ensued between his better and baser natures. After all, there would be the night with all its happy fulfilment, and the following ten days and nights at the Belhampton inn where they were to spend the remainder of his leave.

'I don't suppose Spooner expects you back at the forge, Job,' he said, and the grateful smiles of the brother and sister were his reward for sharing his wedding-trip with his young brother-in-law. His sacrifice was not lost on Parnham, and the officer rose considerably in the doctor's estimation.

So it was settled, and the couple took leave of their friends with Joby squeezed in beside them. The twelve-year-old lad thought he had chanced on paradise, for he bathed in the lake while his sister and her husband roamed hand-in-hand through the woodland glades, and they all shared the contents of the food basket sitting on the bank.

Susan leaned her head on Edward's shoulder, and he drew her close.

'This is the happiest day of my life, Mrs Calthorpe.'

'Mine too, Edward,' she whispered, though in fact it all seemed to have the unreality of a dream, as if it were happening to a person other than Susan Lucket. If only time could come to an end now on this perfect July afternoon, so that they might wander through the forest for ever and ever, with no nightfall and no tomorrow – Heaven's eternity could hold no greater bliss.

But afternoon passed into evening, and the light began to change. They climbed into the trap for the seven-mile journey back to Belhampton; Joby fell asleep, his head nodding in time to the pony's trot, as shadows lengthened and crept across the fields.

Edward put him down at the turn-off to Beversley, then headed towards Belhampton and the Bull Inn.

Susan opened her eyes and smiled at him. His heart seemed to melt.

'Soon, very soon now, you will be my wife in very truth,' he whispered, and a tremor ran through her frame.

The landlord's wife was all smiles and curtsies, waving away the chambermaid and insisting on attending to Mr and Mrs Calthorpe herself. A boy was called to take care of the pony and secure the trap in the yard. When Edward requested that supper be served in their room, she at once led them up the open stairway that ascended from the dining room. A loud burst of laughter exploded from the market traders and soldiery at the tables, and Edward felt conscious of lewd glances following them up the stairs.

'There now, all ready fur ye!' said the landlady proudly, ushering them into the best bedchamber.

Susan was confronted by a great four-poster bed, a table with two chairs, a washstand with a pitcher and basin, and a row of brass hooks along the wall for cloaks and hats. The fireplace, empty on a summer evening, was surmounted by a carved mantelpiece on which an unlit candle stood between two expressionless china dogs.

'I'll bring up yer tray straightway, ma'am, an' if there be anythin' lackin', there's the bell rope by the bed. I like me guests to be comfortable. Ye've got a lookin'-glass over there, see . . .'

Susan took off her hat, overwhelmed by the size and grandeur of the room. Edward poured out two glasses of Madeira wine, but Susan had little appetite for food.

'Alone with you at last, dearest,' he murmured, loosening the gauze cravat at his throat. 'How I have longed for this moment!'

He stood behind her as she sat at the table, his arms encircling her shoulders. She remembered the Prayer Book's admonition to new wives, that they be amiable and obedient to their husbands, who stand in relation to them as Christ does to his church.

Merciful Father in Heaven, give me the grace to be a wife to him. Let me return his love as I should.

She let her head fall back against his chest while he gently stroked her hair.

'You are weary, my love, and no wonder after so long a day.' He laughed softly. 'That is a good enough reason for us to retire early.'

She turned her head to receive his kiss, and heard his wordless sigh of contentment. She felt his questing lips at the back of her neck, pushing aside the light brown tendrils that had escaped from the hairpins – and she realised with dismay that she needed to relieve herself. There would be a chamber pot under the bed, but how could she sit on it in front of Edward?

As if he read her thoughts, he straightened up and went to draw the bed-curtain on the further side, so that he was hidden by it.

'I shall sleep on this side, Susan, and you lie nearest to the window,' he said, and stooping down he drew out a pot from under the bed.

'There is another one of these on your side, Susan,' he added with a hint of a chuckle in his voice. 'The curtains will save us both from being overlooked by the other.'

Suitably screened, Susan pulled out the pot on her side, but at first her muscles refused to relax. She undressed, her fingers fumbling with buttons and the strings of her petticoat, and put on her plain white nightgown. She at last managed to use the pot, washed her face and hands, loosened her hair and combed it through. Then she got into the bed, pulling up the covers and turning the sheet down under her chin. How strange was this intimacy, so unimagined in her chaste dreams of Edward!

When he emerged from behind the curtain in his long nightshirt, he gazed upon her with something approaching awe.

'How beautiful you are, my Susan,' he marvelled. 'I cannot think of anything more desirable to my senses – and I have waited so long – so long . . .'

He recollected that he should first kneel beside the bed and give thanks to his Maker, and while he did so, Susan also prayed desperately.

Let me do my duty as a wife. Let me love him as he desires, O God!

Rising from his knees he got in beside her and without hesitation reached out to enfold her in his arms.

She at once felt the thrust of his hardened member through two layers of cotton, and stifled a cry.

The bed-curtain on her side was not drawn, and enough daylight lingered at the window for them to see each other's face.

And he saw fear in eyes that were wide open and alert, as if to danger.

'Why, Susan! You are surely not afraid of me, my love?' he asked tenderly, lightly stroking the side of her face.

She tried to speak, but her throat was constricted, and no sound came from it. Every muscle in her body was in a state of tension as she fought to stay still, stay calm, to be submissive to the husband she adored. In spite of a superhuman effort to conquer the clawing panic rising up inside her, she could not even shake her head in answer, let alone speak. She tried to smile, but her face was paralysed. Only the two round pools of her eyes still regarded him, wary and unblinking, reminding him of a wild woodland creature – a rabbit caught in the gleam of a poacher's lantern, a fieldmouse shrinking before the blood-thirsty stoat, helpless to escape.

Edward released his hold on her and reached out to feel for the hand nearest to him. It was cold and damp.

'Susan.'

Her icy fingers gripped convulsively at his hand.

'Speak to me, Susan. I am your husband and closest friend from this day. Something is troubling you, and you must tell me what it is, so that I may help you.'

She heard his words but could not reply. Inside her head a furious conflict was raging. She longed with all her heart to respond to him as a good wife should, and her desperate prayers were like silent screams for help.

O God, why can't I love him? Hear my prayer and let me, let me, let me love him, O Lord God!

But an irrational, ungovernable terror had her by the throat and would not set her free to love her husband. She was suffocating in a green and brown tangle of bracken fronds, and a sickening smell filled her nostrils.

Edward began to reproach himself for assuming that a midwife with extensive knowledge of women's mysteries would know what to expect. Yet why should his sweet Susan be different from any other girl about to surrender her virginity? He cursed his lack of forethought, and searched for the right words to tell her of his love. The Book of Common Prayer supplied him with the vows he had made to her that day.

'*With this ring, I thee wed,*' he quoted, kissing the third finger of her left hand. '*With my body I thee worship.* Dear Susan, how much do I long to worship thee!'

She shivered uncontrollably, and instinctively curled up into herself like a hedgehog before a predator, drawing up her knees and flexing her head.

This was no maidenly bashfulness; she was literally quaking with fright, and in consequence Edward's desire began to ebb as he faced the reality of her fear. He withdrew from her, chilled and bewildered.

Turning on his back, he stared up at the canopy above them. He had thought he knew Susan Lucket, her courage and resourcefulness, her quickness at learning and her remarkable skill at midwifery. He had seen for himself her authority in the workhouse, her kindness to the wretched souls imprisoned there; she was not afraid of them, so why should she fear the attentions of her lawful husband, so soon to return to sea? He resolved to be patient but persistent.

'Susan, my own dear wife, you must tell me what is troubling you, and I will do what I can to help. Any sorrow of yours is mine also.'

When she felt him move away from her, her tautened muscles began to soften a little, and tears filled her eyes. Such goodness, such patience on his part, deserved some sort of an answer. She sought for a convincing explanation of her unwifely reluctance, but there was nothing for it: she would have to tell him a lie.

'Edward – dear Edward, I . . .'

'Yes, Susan? I am listening.'

'I – I fear to be with child – I mean o' bein' left with child after you ha' gone back to sea.'

The words were uttered so softly that he had to ask her to say them again.

'I be feared o' bein' with child, Edward. I couldn't work, and ha' no home but the House. Your family wouldn't – oh, Edward, I dare not!'

A frank burst of tears followed the words, and Edward's spirits sank. He had defied his family, alienated his mother and sisters, perhaps for ever, and neglected to comfort his brother – only to be refused his conjugal rights by her for whom he had made the sacrifice. He had seen himself as a father, passing on his seed to another generation through the body of the woman now lying beside him, legally wedded in the sight of God and man; this woman who now wept and shook with fear at the very thought of bearing his child.

'Do you mean that you never want to be a happy mother of children, Susan?'

'No, Edward, I – yes, I do, but not yet, not until the times are better. Miss Glover—'

'Ah, yes, my cousin Sophy,' he cut in. 'She has refused to marry Henry until the war is over.'

He frowned as he considered the implication. Henry Hansford had confessed his envy of Edward's 'more persuadable lady', but what difference was there? One insisted on postponing marriage, the other refused her necessary duty within it. Surely Susan could have told him of her fears before the ceremony?

Looking back on his proposal he wondered if he should have allowed her more time and opportunity to talk about her own feelings. He suddenly thought of Meg, the child-whore who had so nearly seduced him. He remembered her busy little fingers undoing his breeches and covering his mouth with her soft, warm kisses. And the effort he'd had to make to refuse her.

He closed his eyes and lay silent for some time. All right, then. If self-restraint was demanded of him, so be it. His love was greater than mere desire. And Susan might be right after all, for to leave her with a child and then to fall in battle or drown would surely not be right or fair. Had he been merely selfish?

At length he turned and spoke quietly to her.

'It will be as you wish, Susan. I love you more than anything else in the world, as God knows. Nothing has changed with me.'

His quiet words were like a sword-thrust through her heart.

'Forgive me, Edward. As God sees us, I love none other—'

'Hush, Susan, enough has been said tonight. Let us sleep now.'

He put his arm under her shoulders and drew her head close enough to kiss her forehead. She nestled within the circle of his arm, and he saw the tears drying on her cheeks as she closed her eyes and seemed to fall asleep.

This was not the wedding night he had dreamed of, but he still had his sweet Susan for wife, the girl he had loved for years and whose trust he could never betray. He recalled stories he had heard of other unsuccessful first attempts, either because the bridegroom had been too drunk or the bride's maidenhead too resistant to be broken through. Not under any circumstances could he ever force Susan.

No, he must be patient and philosophical. One day the war would be over, bringing better times. When they were together in their own little home in the future, there would be time enough to talk, and he would help her to come to him in love and without fear.

'Sleep well, my darling,' he whispered as night settled over Belhampton and the sounds of the inn became fainter. The warm July night stole upon his senses, and a drowsy curtain of sleep descended upon him, bringing oblivion.

But Susan lay awake beside him for hours, full of helpless rage against the fate that had set a barrier between herself and her beloved husband.

For she had never loved Edward more than at this hour, when his natural desire for her had awakened dark memories of fear and hatred.

And unforgiveness towards her mother.

Chapter 20

Osmond stirred in the pale light that filtered through the curtains. Polly's dark head rested on the inner curve of his elbow, gradually numbing the arm on which it lay; the loss of sensation was beginning to penetrate to his brain, giving rise to a terrifying dream in which he lay bound to a table while a surgeon with a monstrous bald head was sawing through his arm at the elbow joint.

Osmond struggled and tried to shout for help, but his mouth was gagged. His face twitched and he moaned aloud, shaking his head from side to side. Suddenly he wrenched himself free of sleep, and sat up with a cry, sharply withdrawing his arm from under her head.

She had been deep in exhausted slumber after his insatiable demands on her young body, and she now sat up beside him.

'What? What be . . .?' She gave her head a shake to clear it.

'Devil take it, Poll, my arm is as dead as my damned lost leg. Ugh, such dreams! Give it a good hard rubbing for me, do.'

'There now, my love, 'twas but an ol' dream, nothin' to vex 'ee,' she soothed, slapping his arm to restore it to tingling life, and gazing anxiously at this pallid young man who took his fill of her with such ferocity night after night. She squinted towards the clock on the table.

'Lord, it be nearly six – they'll all be risen over there! I'll ha' to go, Osmond,' she muttered, slipping off the bed and reaching for her shift and kirtle. Another stolen night in her master's arms, and who might she meet on the way back? She'd sometimes seen that old Mrs Ferris prowling around in the dawn.

Halfway down the corridor she stopped, thinking she heard Mrs Calthorpe's voice behind the door of the main bedchamber; then she scurried on, down the stairs and into the little writing room from which she left by the window, dropping down on to a wall and from there into a lupin bed, and so round to the stable-yard and the back entrance.

Jael Ferris emerged with a sigh of relief and closed the window, refastening the sash.

The maids had been up since half-past five.

'Mrs Martin been askin' fur 'ee, Polly. Oi told her 'ee didn't want no breakfus',' said one of them, and Polly pulled a face, for it was true, she felt slightly sick. She knew the risks she took, and hoped and trusted that the vinegar-soaked pad of lambswool had done its preventive work. To find herself with child would be a disaster, but how could she refuse her beloved Osmond in his sadly crippled state? Gone were the days of teasing half-promises and merry chasings; she now longed only to please him.

There were whispers and rumours of a different kind in the servants' quarters. They all knew that Master Edward had packed his bag the day before and left for Belhampton, leaving his parents wrapped in gloom. At midday Lieutenant Hansford brought a letter for Mr Calthorpe, and later Miss Rosa Hansford came up to see Miss Caroline; the two girls shook their heads over the shocking news that soon became common knowledge.

Mr Edward had been married that morning to the girl known as Susan Lucket, who worked in the House of Industry. She was now Mrs Edward Calthorpe!

As she took in this amazing news, Polly's heart leaped for joy. Good old Sukey! And if the elder Lucket sister could become Mrs Calthorpe, why not the younger? Poor Osmond was not likely to find a wife among the haughty county families now; no, what he needed was a patient, loving girl, able to anticipate his every need, someone to comfort him and chase away the demons of the night.

Polly's bright eyes softened. Even his mother would have to admit that she was the only girl for Osmond in his present state. So even if she *was* with child, it need not be a calamity; on the contrary, it could be the deciding factor that settled Osmond's choice of a wife.

Or so reasoned pretty, foolish little Polly.

With the war going badly for Britain, the women of Beversley eagerly turned to the happier subject of young Mr and Mrs Calthorpe, who were often to be seen driving through the village in their new pony-trap during these last days of July.

Both Edward and Susan were surprised by the number of invitations they received. Cousin Sophia opened her home to them, Dr Parnham gave a dinner for them, as did Mr and Mrs Turnbull; Mrs Bennett welcomed them into her parlour, and good Parson Smart rejoiced in little Susan Lucket's change of fortune.

'Ye've done more for the paupers in that wretched

House than any of us, Mrs Calthorpe,' he said between coughs.

Edward was continually impressed by the high esteem in which his wife was held, the praises heaped upon her in so many homes, from the Dummets of Crabb's cottages to Mrs Grimes at the bakehouse; entering many humble dwellings, he learned a great deal about the lives of the villagers.

Everybody noticed the young wife's loving manner towards her husband, the way she handed him his teacup and hovered dutifully at his side, her devotion displayed in every movement. Mrs Coulter declared that it was the prettiest sight in the world.

When the newlyweds were formally invited to take tea with the squire and his lady, Susan was not at first inclined to accept.

'Oh, you must go, 'tis only polite,' Sophia assured her. 'Henry and I will be there. 'Tis Mrs Hansford's way of showing their acceptance of your marriage, and proves that she is not under the sway of Edward's mother,' she added significantly, for everybody knew of the unrelenting silence from Bever House.

Nevertheless, Susan found the atmosphere a little strained, and sat with downcast eyes while Mrs Hansford poured tea and exchanged sedate pleasantries with her future daughter-in-law. Rosa's cold blue eyes roamed curiously over the girl who had been brought up in the Ash-Pits and worked at the House of Industry, yet had so inexplicably captured Osmond's brother.

Dr Gravett sat gloomily eating cake and balancing his cup on his knee. Life at the rectory had lost many of its comforts since his sister had taken to her bed and grew weaker daily. Another Miss Gravett, a niece from Winchester, had come to keep house for them, and was not inclined to pander to the rector's imagined ills as poor Amelia had done.

The squire and his elder son talked with Edward about the high price of livestock and the shortage of available manpower on the land, while William, a robust lad of sixteen, had been told to wait upon the ladies and the rector.

All conversation was suspended when a maid-servant announced that 'Mr Osmond Calthorpe be come to call.'

Susan's face tightened, Rosa's flushed, and Edward rose at once to go to his brother's assistance. Osmond had asked Berry to help him hobble out of the house unseen by his parents, and to drive him down in the gig. He was in high spirits at his success, and manoeuvred himself between the chairs while making gallant remarks to the ladies as befitted a wounded hero.

'I vow you have made me quite envious of my brother, sister Susan!' he declared, but his smile was not returned, either by his new sister-in-law or his cousin Sophy. Certain facts cannot remain secret indefinitely; it was whispered that Osmond had a maidservant to warm his bed, and Sophia knew from her maids that Polly Lucket had become skilled at climbing in and out of windows. Susan knew nothing of this, living away from Beversley, but her former experience of Edward's brother had made her wary of him, and she hoped that he had now lost interest in Polly.

'I have been trying to persuade my father that I should go to the garrison at Winchester and take up duties there,' Osmond told the company. 'Though 'twould be a sad change for a Captain of the 67th

Hampshire Foot to wield a pen instead of a musket!'

He complimented Rosa on her pretty sprigged gown, and ingratiated himself with Dr Gravett by inquiring about Miss Amelia. Edward too was subjected to his persuasive charm.

'By God, you've done well, Ned, I have to admit it,' he said in a low tone to his brother as the party broke up. 'What would I give for such an adoring little wife as yours! But alas, I have an heir's duty to put other considerations before my own.'

Edward looked towards Susan, who stood waiting for him at the door.

'May we not invite Osmond to dinner with us at the Bull, my love?'

Her mouth was a straight line, but she bowed to her husband's wish. 'By all means name a day, Edward.'

'Excellent! So do come and dine with us, Osmond, let's say Monday? I have to return to Portsmouth on Wednesday.'

Susan nodded in response to her brother-in-law's bow, but could not share her husband's pleasure as they drove back to Belhampton.

'Dear Susan, we are unacknowledged by my family, so it means something to me that Osmond wants to visit us,' Edward said gently. 'He has been so close to death, and my father believes that suffering has improved his character. I am grateful for your forbearance, my love.'

'He's your brother, Edward, and nothing'll change that. I'll be civil enough, even if I don't ha' much to say.'

'Oh, sweet Susan, you are an angel,' he said fondly, putting his free arm around her as they drove across the common. She let her head rest on his shoulder,

278

trying not to think about her distrust of his family, especially his brother.

Or of her own miserable failure as a wife.

Osmond never kept his dinner engagement at the Bull.

On the Friday morning a hastily written note arrived from Sophia, asking the young couple to come over at once to Glover Cottage, where a distraught Polly Lucket had appeared on the doorstep just as Great St Giles' clock was striking six. Sobbing and shivering, she had gasped out a story of being flung from the door of Bever House.

'Her was jus' waitin' fur a chance to be rid o' me, Miss Glover. Now Mr Edward's gone an' married Sukey, her's turned agin me an' thrown me out!'

Sophia saw with horror that there were cuts and bruises on the girl's face and arms. She had been severely beaten. Sophia took her in and personally bathed her swollen eyes and the red weals all over her body. Bread and milk was brought for her breakfast.

'I will send for your sister and brother-in-law, Polly, and you will have to tell us exactly what happened. Remember that the truth will always come to light in the Lord's good time.'

It seemed only too clear that Osmond's illicit dalliance with the maidservant had been discovered, and that the girl had been punished for the misdeeds of both. Sophia's sense of justice was offended, though she could not exempt Polly from all blame.

In fact she might well have been as speechless as Gertrude Calthorpe had been when she had gone to her son's room and found him and Polly in the very act of fornication. When she recovered her breath she

279

had screamed and hit out at the naked girl with her bare fists until Jael Ferris had rushed in to drag Polly away. She had found a maid's blue gown to throw over the girl, and within minutes had put her out into the stable-yard, telling her to go to Miss Glover, that well-known rescuer of disgraced maidservants.

Susan and Edward drove over from Belhampton as soon as they received the message. The two sisters fell upon each other in a tearful embrace, and Sophia sent them upstairs to talk while she and Edward discussed the situation in the parlour.

''Tis the usual story, Cousin,' she told him in her direct way. 'Your brother has been pleasuring himself with this silly girl for some time, and now your mother has found them out.'

'Are you truly sure of that, Sophy? Does Polly admit as much?' asked Edward, acutely embarrassed by this development and its effect on Susan.

'Good heavens, do you think the servants haven't known about it for weeks?' replied Sophia impatiently. 'Let's hope that Polly is not with child, for Osmond cares nothing about the girls he ruins – think of Jenny Kyte, who had a bastard daughter and was wet nurse to Mrs Twydell's baby and others until her milk dried up, and then she took herself and the poor child to Portsmouth. Her younger sister Meg has followed her there, though scarcely more than a child herself, and from what I hear they both sell their bodies to sailors in ports. 'Tis shame to your brother indeed!'

She looked severely at Edward, who had gone very white.

'Good God, Sophy, do you say so? The young sister was called Meg, you said?'

'Yes. Why, have you come across her? They came

from Crabb's cottages, and their parents are broken-hearted,' went on Sophia relentlessly. 'And it was your brother who started that train of evil with his careless lust, and so ruined two girls' lives, and cares nothing for the child he fathered. But come, Edward, I must not chide you with Osmond's conduct, we must speak of the matter in hand.'

She thought his stricken look was due to her revelation of Osmond's misdeeds, while he was inexpressibly thankful that she could not read his thoughts; was it only four months ago since that spring evening when he had come so close to taking Meg's unripe body to satisfy his own lust? He burned with shame now at the memory.

'So what is to become of your sister-in-law, turned out of her place and destitute?' asked Sophia. 'She may stay here until somewhere else can be found, though in truth I have no need of another maid. I've taken in many over the years, most of them in need of Mrs Coulter's services. God grant that Polly be not another such.'

Edward took her words as a personal reproach.

'I will make a payment towards her board while she is here, Sophy.'

'Why, are you your brother's paymaster? No, Edward, you are returning to heaven knows what dangers at sea, as is my betrothed Henry. You need every penny to ensure that your wife may not be in want if – if you have left her with child. Your obligation is to her, not to her sister.'

He was silent. It was a kind of consolation to know that his unfulfilled marriage was a secret shared only with Susan.

'Come, Edward,' said Sophia briskly, 'we shall have to put on braver faces, for I hear the sisters coming downstairs. We have had tears enough for one morning.'

And so it was settled that Polly should stay at Glover Cottage until another place could be found for her, preferably away from Beversley.

'I hear that Mrs Twydell of Pulhurst is again with child, and may need extra help in the house,' said Sophia. 'I will make enquiries through Mrs Bennett.'

Polly's face fell at the thought of being so far away from her sweetheart, but Susan told her quite firmly that she needed to be removed from the scene of her disgrace.

'Cheer up, Poll, ye could ha' fared a deal worse, and we're obliged to Miss Glover yet again,' she added, though her fury against the Calthorpes rose anew at the sight of her sister's injuries. After such brutal treatment she felt that Polly should not be scolded further, and if this scandal finally separated her from the menace of Osmond, it might even prove a blessing.

On Monday morning the Bever carriage was seen leaving the village with a trunk secured aloft, heading towards Winchester. Inside sat a silent Osmond with his father. When the carriage returned in the late afternoon, only the senior Calthorpe was within. The news quickly spread that the young captain had rejoined the garrison, some said as an instructor of new recruits, while others revealed that he was to be a recorder at courts martial. Less kindly voices gave him the office of keeper of stores.

On his way back, Mr Calthorpe ordered Jude to drive to Belhampton and stop at the Bull Inn. Once inside he asked to be allowed to pay his respects to young Mrs Calthorpe, to whom he apologised for the lateness of his visit. He offered the Bever carriage to take Edward back to Portsmouth on Wednesday, and suggested that Mrs Susan might like to travel down with her husband and return in the carriage. Susan respectfully declined, however, and said she would say farewell to Edward at the inn before returning forthwith to her duties at the House of Industry.

In fact Susan could not bear the thought of stepping into the Bever carriage, so great was her contempt for Edward's mother and brother.

Edward woke suddenly in the early hours of that last night at the inn. His wife lay with her back towards him, sweetly enclosed within the larger curve of his body, her head beneath his chin, her hair spread over the shared bolster. She breathed softly and rhythmically as he silently kissed her temple and smoothed the hair back from her forehead with his right hand. His whole being yearned with love and longing, and he pressed himself against her back, feeling their thighs touching. His heartbeat quickened, and he was aware of his rising desire, of his manhood thrusting towards her. Hardly daring to breathe, his fingers closed on the thin cotton of her nightgown, slowly drawing it up, trembling at the feel of her bare flesh. His unruly member leaped beneath his nightshirt like a separate part with a life of its own, disobedient, deaf to reason and caution.

'Susan.' His whisper was scarcely audible. 'Susan, my own darling wife.'

He leaned forward to kiss her cheek, and she stirred slightly, murmuring his name. He was lost: he could hold back no longer, but seized her in his arms, his hands meeting across her breasts.

'Oh, Susan, Susan!'

283

She smiled in her dream, murmuring his name again. 'Edward.'

He drew her more closely against him, his heart pounding in his ears.

Then came a breath of fear.

'Edward?' It was a question.

Then, 'Edward, Edward, help!' It was a shout: she was calling to him to come to her aid, to save her from the beast that had risen up out of the darkness of night.

A choking smell of crushed bracken overwhelmed her, so nauseating that it almost took away her breath; coarse fustian scraped against her legs, and to her unspeakable horror a length of hot remembered flesh pushed at her from behind, separating her thighs, defiling her, forcing her into desperate defence.

She reared up in the bed, a raging fury of arms, legs, hands, feet, nails and teeth: frantic cries burst from her throat.

'Stop, *stop*, I won't have 'ee, *stop*, I tells 'ee – no! No, never, *never*!'

And with a scream and a violent kick at the beast, she leaped off the bed and ran to the window where she crouched cowering beneath its ledge.

'Don't 'ee come near me no more – no more!'

Edward underwent a rapid adjustment of emotions. His desire instantly vanished in the shock of her reaction to it, and was followed by a deep pity for her distress. This gave him the wisdom to stay calm and to take his time with the terrified child that she had become.

He sat up in bed and spoke slowly and quietly.

'Do not be afraid, Susan. I am your husband, and I love you. I shall not harm you. Come to me, Susan, there is nothing to fear.'

It was too dark for them to see each other's face, but she could see him holding out his arms to her; his eyes reflected what little light there was from the curtained window.

'Trust me, Susan. I shall not hurt you, I promise. Come back to bed, dearest.'

Her ears heard his words, and her heart heard the love in them. Slowly, very slowly and keeping her eyes fixed upon the faint gleam of his own, she straightened up and stood against the window. Then she moved towards the bed and his outstretched arms. Taking hold of his right hand, she climbed gingerly back into bed beside him and lay down on her right side, still watching him. He pulled the sheet up over her and laid himself down again, carefully avoiding any contact apart from their clasped hands.

They lay in silence for a long minute while he waited to hear if she would give him an explanation, some reason for the violence with which she had rejected him.

''Twas a dream, Edward. Aye, it must ha' been a dream,' she murmured at last, pleading with him to reassure her that this was so. With a heavy heart he gave her that assurance.

'All right, my love, 'twas but a dream.' He entwined his fingers with hers. 'Go to sleep again, dear Susan, you are safe with me.'

'I know, Edward, I know.' She heaved a long sigh, and he continued to soothe her with gentle words, stroking her forehead and imagining the trustful smile that he could not see.

'Sleep now, sweet Susan – go to sleep again.'

Under his loving touch she obeyed, drifting back into peaceful slumber after the terror of nightmare.

But Edward lay awake in a turmoil. An idea that

had been lurking on the edge of his consciousness for days now began to take dreadful shape, turning from a suspicion to a near certainty. He thought he had probably found the reason for his wife's strange behaviour.

The words she had uttered in terror were practically the same as those she had used to the red-haired stable-lad who had pestered her on the night of the ball, when he had rescued her.

Stop it, I won't have 'ee, no, no, never!

So unlike the Susan he knew, yet now she had spat the same words at himself.

But had she? Had they really been meant for him? Edward did not believe so; he could not.

No, he was by now fairly sure that he had found out the truth. He knew that female workers were sometimes at risk in the fields at the end of the day when there was nobody around to witness wicked deeds against them. Some scoundrel, some black-hearted rogue must have laid his filthy hands on Susan and attempted to ravish her.

Attempted to ravish?

Had she in fact been ravished and robbed of her maidenhead? Was she afraid of him discovering her shame?

Edward could have groaned aloud to think of such violation of her innocence – even of her childhood, perhaps, for he recalled seeing a shadow in her eyes when she was only about twelve years old. Only then he had been too young to understand it, and had put it down to the hardships of poverty and the loss of her young brothers. That such an evil should befall his sweet Susan was beyond imagining.

And this was their last night together; only a few short hours remained before they had to part, perhaps for ever. He could not spoil that time by asking her distressing questions about such a memory. One day, if he was spared to return to her when the war was over, they would have all the time in the world to lay the ghosts of the past. He would ask her in love to tell him everything, and he would absolve her from all blame. Then they would be free to be man and wife in the deepest, truest sense.

But now was not the time. The first light of dawn was already streaking the eastern sky, and he must soon rise and prepare for the journey, leaving his beloved wife alone.

With infinite tenderness he cradled her sleeping form and put his lips to her forehead, as lightly as the touch of a moth's wing.

She did not stir.

Chapter 21

Susan had taken to walking out with the orphans in the afternoons. There had been a series of warm, mellow autumn days, and she loved to see the children chasing each other across the springy turf of the common where harebells danced in profusion among the heather. The fresh air brought colour to wan cheeks and a sparkle to eyes used only to drab surroundings, though by four o'clock the smaller ones were beginning to tire, and Susan led them back to the House for tea in her room.

For her life had changed since her marriage, more than she had ever imagined it would. Her new title exacted deference from the likes of the Crokers and Mrs Jarvis, who knew that the heir to the Bever estate was a one-legged cripple, so far without lawful issue; and who could tell whether the younger brother might one day lord it over Beversley with his wife at his side? This Mrs Calthorpe might then be in a position to grant them favours – or, putting it another way, she might remember slights and take her revenge.

She now had her own comfortable little sitting room with a fire to boil a kettle over, and her pony had a stable at the back where the trap was kept. A modest monthly income paid to her by Mr Calthorpe's agent enabled her to buy tea, sugar and muffins to toast and spread with butter when she and the children got in from their walks. She drove herself into Belhampton to purchase linen to make nightgowns, shirts and smocks in place of coarse woven calico for the children; the newly born were protected by soft flannel, which was made up into vests for the older children by female inmates who could sew. Stories had begun to circulate about the pampered lives of the paupers, and Dr Gravett preached indignant sermons from the pulpit about the lax state of affairs, though Mr Calthorpe, also on the Board of Guardians, remained silent.

All this brought Susan a measure of satisfaction, and the children's affection was precious to her, taking her mind off other matters, like her secret shame about the way she had treated her husband during their short time together. There was one memory – had it really been only a dream? – that especially troubled her: what exactly had happened during their last night at the inn, when she had found herself cowering beneath the window in the grip of a frightful nightmare? She recoiled from reliving the incident, for fear that it might not have been a dream at all . . . Edward, as always, had been so good and kind.

Edward. Her husband. He wanted children one day, and she wanted to bear them, and therefore she would have to do her obedient duty as a Christian wife. But when would she be free from that unreasoning terror? Somewhere deep inside her she knew that one day Edward would have to know the truth. Yet that was unthinkable. Impossible.

So while Susan Calthorpe worried about her husband's safety and prayed that he might be saved from the many dangers that surrounded him, there was a part of her that feared his return.

And Mad Doll's haunted eyes still made her blood

run cold, a constant reminder of the shadowed years.

'Missus Calthorpe! Doctor be here to see 'ee!' called Mag. 'Do 'ee want they childer took off 'ee?'

Susan rose at once, her eyes alight with pleasure.

'No, no, Mag, they can stay. Good day to ye, sir!'

'Good afternoon, Madam Trotula. I looked for you and your brood of chicks on the common, but you were not to be found, so I have pursued you to the Palace of Ease.'

''Tis good to see ye, sir. There're no muffins left, but will ye take a cup o' tea?'

'Gladly. So these young people have been stuffing themselves with muffins! Good heavens, whatever is the world coming to?'

His beaming face belied the irony of his words, and Toby, Dorcas and Nan grinned back at him with a boldness they would never have shown a few months ago. He hung his hat on the back of a chair, and drew it up beside Susan, taking the cup she handed to him.

'And how is everybody in the House of Hope? How are the ladies-in-waiting? And Hannah's child, is it still thriving?'

'*She* feeds well, sir, and holds up *her* head,' Susan corrected him. It was a joke between them that he never gave babies a gender. 'Hannah's milk is still good, and she ha' hopes o' finding a place as nurse to some newborn child. D'ye know o' any mother in Belhampton or around who might take her in, sir?'

'Ah, Mrs Calthorpe, you are always sending me off on nursemaid's errands. 'Tis no wonder I am often late for my classes, and keep my students waiting!'

The children giggled at the woeful face he put on, his good-humoured pretence that Mrs Calthorpe ill-used him. Susan realised that they enjoyed the warm and easy understanding between herself and Parnham, in which they caught a glimpse of the family life they had never known: a father's indulgence, a mother's tender care, a sense of belonging.

Charles felt it also, watching Susan as she boiled the kettle again, her face flushed by the small fire. Keeping the children with them was a way of stopping gossiping tongues, he surmised; all very well, but it made it hard for him to find out how she really did. Two months after her wedding, Parnham was uneasy about his Trotula. He knew of course that she lived in constant anxiety for her husband, and yet . . . he still felt that something was not quite right, and it troubled him. Although his own foolish dreams had come to nothing, he still enjoyed his privileged position as her trusted friend and champion.

Meanwhile he drank the tea she had poured for him, and sitting there in the stuffy little room, inhaling the steam from the kettle, the odour of undersized bodies and the lingering aroma of toasted muffins, Charles Parnham wished himself nowhere else on earth.

And should his Trotula find herself a young widow when all the carnage was over, she need not fear poverty or the rejection of Bever House, because . . .

He frowned, and ordered such forbidden thoughts, like Satan's whispers, to depart from him.

Both Mrs Bennett's older daughters were with child, and while Mrs Marianne Smart looked a picture of health at four months, Mrs Sally Twydell was full of apprehension; she was due to give birth at Christmas, and greeted her mother and sister with sighs and groans when they visited her.

'I'm getting the dropsy in my ankles again, Mother, and have to sit on the pot every half-hour – and oh, the palpitating of my heart!' she groaned, making Marianne feel quite guilty for keeping so well.

'How is the young Lucket maid getting on?' asked Mrs Bennett, simply to change the subject.

'Oh, don't talk to me about the stupid girl,' answered Sally fretfully. 'She has not half the sense of her sister, and slouches around in a dream. It was too bad o' Miss Glover to pass her off on to me in my state of health, and she'll be sent away soon if she doesn't mend her ways.'

'Oh, please try to keep her, Sally, for Susan's sake!' pleaded Mrs Bennett. 'She has trouble enough, with Edward away at the war, and his mother bearing such spite against her. That's why they threw Polly out, y'know, after five years o' service at Bever House.'

Mrs Marianne stayed silent but looked knowing, having heard quite a different story.

'But the girl's bone idle, and so *silly*, mother! She has not the least idea how to behave in front of company. And the other day Percy found her fast asleep in his study, if you please, snoring her head off. He was furious, I can tell you.'

'Good heavens, is the girl not well, Sally?' asked Mrs Bennett as a thought struck her. 'Can you not send for her and let me see how she looks?'

Mrs Twydell rang the bell for tea, which was brought in by a smart maidservant who smiled and curtsied.

'My mother wishes to see Polly, so send her in to us,' said Sally languidly.

One look at the bloated features and thickened

waist was enough for Mrs Bennett, and in the ensuing babble of raised voices and recriminations, she felt obliged to take the Lucket girl back to Beversley in the three-seater.

As soon as Mrs Bennett was shown into the parlour with a tear-stained Polly in tow, Miss Glover feared the worst. She ordered Tess to take the girl into the kitchen while Mrs Bennett sat on the same cane-bottomed chair used by Edward on his last visit to his cousin, when Polly had been turned out of Bever House. Now Sophia heard the sorry sequel.

'And when my Sally sent for her, the little baggage tried to deny it, Miss Glover, though she shows plainly enough, and must be four months gone if she's a day.'

'Yet Mrs Twydell had not noticed?'

'My daughter is much taken up with her own expected child, and doesn't see as much as I'd ha' done,' admitted Mrs Bennett. 'There was an upset, such sobbings and sighings that I said I'd bring her back with me – and 'tis my belief she'd better go to the House o' Industry and let poor Susan – Mrs Calthorpe – take care o' her.'

Sophia frowned. 'I shall talk with Mrs Susan first, and see how she feels. Meanwhile I'll keep the girl here and send word straightway to Osmond Calthorpe at Winchester, to ask what he intends to do about his child.'

Mrs Bennett's eyes narrowed. 'I doubt ye'll gain much from that quarter, Miss Glover.'

'I may surprise you, goodwife,' replied Sophia, her blue eyes flashing. 'If he tries to deny his part in the business, I shall apply to my cousin his father to pay for her board here, and let the shame of it be told all over Beversley, that she is with child by Osmond. Let Bever House deny it if they can!'

Mrs Bennett allowed herself the glimmer of a smile at this declaration, though she shook her head. 'But what grief for my Susan, so soon after her marriage!' she sighed.

Sophia sent for Polly, who came in eyeing them warily.

'Well, Polly Lucket, what have you to say for yourself now?' asked Miss Glover. 'You must have known about this when I sent you to Mrs Twydell as maidservant.'

'No, Miss Glover, Oi di'n't ha' no idea then!' protested Polly. 'Oi had me flow at the end o' June, same as usual, so Oi be not yet three months.'

'You don't deny it, then, Polly? You are certainly bigger. And have you the sickness?'

'Oh, aye, Oi spue most mornin's, an' don't want no breakfus', Miss Glover.'

'And who is the father of your child, Polly?' asked Sophia, suppressing her natural sympathy until she had tested the girl.

'Oh, Miss Glover, Oi never ha' bin wi' anybody but Master Osmond!'

Her tears began to flow, melting Sophia's heart.

'Very well, Polly, I shall send to my cousin Osmond to tell him of this.'

The tears gave way at once to a wide smile of surprise and joy. 'Oh, Miss Glover, that be so good of 'ee! As soon as un knows, un'll come to marry me fur certain, just as Master Edward married Sukey! Oi knows it, Miss Glover!'

'Do not count on it, Polly,' said Sophia gravely. 'You had better not hope for more than a little money, at most.'

She and Mrs Bennett exchanged a significant look. 'Go and wash your face now, Polly, and Tess will give you some supper.'

Mrs Bennett's relief at having managed to get rid of Polly was considerable. Two breeding daughters were enough worry, without having a servant in the same way. Tying her bonnet strings under her chin, she took her leave with many expressions of gratitude.

But Sophia was left in a melancholy mood, and spent the rest of that evening contemplating what repercussions there would be, and what might lie ahead for foolish Polly.

And she thought of Susan, whose husband faced the same dangers on the high seas as Henry, with winter coming on.

And she spared a few thoughts for herself, now in her thirty-second year, and looking every day of her age.

The next morning she set off in her new chaise for the House of Industry, and on the way up the track to the common she met Dr Parnham on his mare. He reined in alongside her.

'Good day to you, Madam Glover. If you're on your way to Belhampton, could you call on Mrs Susan at the House? I think she would welcome a visit from a wise woman friend. There is not much good company at the Palace of Ease, for all its daily luxuries.'

Sophia smiled at his intentional irony. 'As it happens, I am on my way to visit her, Dr Parnham.'

'Excellent! I know she'll be pleased to see you,' he beamed.

'Though I fear there is no good news for her,' added Sophia, and noticed that his sharp eyes were immediately alert.

'What is it? Has there been news of her husband?'

He almost glared at her from under anxious brows, and she hesitated, feeling that she had no real right to publish Polly's disgrace, certainly not before Susan was told.

'Speak, madam! What ill news have you for her?'

Sophia was not used to being commanded in this way, but she reasoned that he would know soon; it was not worth an argument.

' 'Tis her sister Polly, an empty-headed girl who finds herself with child,' she said briefly, picking up the reins to be on her way.

But to her astonishment he dismounted and laid his hands upon the side of the open chaise.

'Go on, go on, madam – with child by whom? Is the man named? Tell me, I beg you,' he added, somewhat less curtly. 'I am Mrs Calthorpe's true friend, and will give her what help I can.'

'It is not for me to say, Dr Parnham,' said Sophia a little stiffly, but he cut in with a repeated request that he be told.

'Is there any chance of marriage for the girl?'

'No chance at all,' she said, and quickly deciding that everything would soon be revealed, as she herself had promised Mrs Bennett that it would be, she lowered her voice and leaned towards him.

'The man is Osmond Calthorpe, Edward's brother and heir to the Bever estate.'

She was quite unprepared for his blazing reaction. '*What?* Oh, God damn the Calthorpes, what trouble for my poor Trotula! To the devil with him! Devil take the whole cursed tribe of 'em!'

Sophia was taken aback at his vehemence, and wondered if he knew that he was speaking of her only relatives, thought she broadly sympathised with his view of them at that moment. It was time to move on, she decided, so leaving him to rage, she seized the reins and urged the horse up the track towards the common.

Why should a man of Parnham's standing be so affected by a silly maidservant's disgrace? she wondered. By all accounts, he met plenty of them at the House. And what was that name he had used – Trot-something? That could only be Susan, surely? Sophia considered, not for the first time, that the doctor's friendship with the young midwife was unusually close.

In her sitting room at the House, Susan stood appalled.

'Ye've brought me the news I've dreaded f'r five years, Sophy,' she said dully. 'When she went to Pulhurst and he to Winchester, I thought the danger was past – but 'twas already done. Oh, 'tis cruel, cruel!'

She put her hands to her face, and Sophia enfolded her in her arms.

'Dear Susan, 'tis bad news, but what's done is done. I shall send to my cousin Osmond this very day.'

'And what good'll that do?' Susan's grey eyes were as cold as a winter sea. 'I've never trusted that man. His father hoped f'r a change o' heart after he lost his leg, but that sort don't ever change, not as long as there be silly maids like my poor little sister. What will become o' her and her child? Oh, how could Edward have such a rake f'r a brother? Poll must come here, Sophy, to the workhouse, along o' other poor girls in trouble wi' nowhere else to go!'

And in her friend's arms she gave way momentarily to despair.

'No, Susan, listen – Polly may stay with me as kitchen-maid until Christmas. When she gets heavy and slow, she may prefer to come here and be with you. But not yet.'

'But ye've done so much f'r us already, Sophy, we'll be yet deeper in y'r debt,' Susan protested, wiping her eyes.

'My dear Susan, are we not friends?' Sophia's tone was unusually tender. 'Your natural skills are far greater than mine, and if I have been able to do you some good, I've been repaid a hundredfold. Think of what you have done in this place, a midwife to the women and a teacher to the children – and a friend to all. Take courage, dear Susan! Polly's a robust girl, and a pretty one – she has a good chance of finding a husband willing to take on another man's child. Come, Susan, put your trust in the Almighty, and think of Edward, your husband.'

Susan straightened up and began to compose herself.

'Poor Edward, I could wish that he had any other name but Calthorpe,' she muttered. 'Forgive me, Sophy, 'twas but a moment o' self-pity. Thank ye f'r offering to take poor Polly f'r the time bein'. And thank ye f'r y'r friendship.'

They embraced again. Had Susan realised, Sophia's offer was as much for her sake as for Polly's. She knew how hard Susan worked, and Polly would be a heavy extra burden.

When Dr Parnham called later that day, he added his assurances of help, and said he would find Polly a place as a wet nurse after her confinement. Warmed by the love and kindness of her friends, Susan allowed herself to be comforted in this latest misfortune; but when she visited her sister a few days later at Glover Cottage, Polly burst into tears.

'Oh, Sukey, Miss Glover sent Osmond a message, but there ain't bin no answer yet! Oi do so long to see un agin!'

Susan could not pretend to be surprised at this, but what neither of them knew was that Sophia had received a deeply insulting letter from Mrs Gertrude Calthorpe, disclaiming any responsibility on Osmond's part for Polly's condition. The girl's bad reputation was well known, wrote the lady, and any one of a number of menservants, stable-boys and farm hands could have fathered her child. Miss Glover was informed that any further communication on the subject would be ignored.

Look at it how she would, Sophia saw that there was nothing more to be done. The Calthorpes had virtually declared themselves willing to ride out the scandal, and it seemed that Mr Calthorpe consented to his wife's letter. Sophia had no more weapons to use, and told herself to pray to be delivered from the un-Christian anger she felt towards her relations.

Susan had her own secret thoughts about the bitter irony of the situation. When she considered her so-called marriage to Edward Calthorpe, her refusal to grant him his conjugal rights appeared just as shameful as unmarried Polly's swelling womb.

Winter came in with fogs and heavy skies that made the dark days even shorter, with no relief in the news from across the Atlantic. The capture of Charlestown had not been followed by further British advances, and with the French fleet lying in wait to attack troopships and the Spanish once again taking an opportunity to besiege Gibraltar, there was a growing demand for a truce with the rebel colonials. Anxiety for their loved ones perpetually plagued Susan and Sophia.

At home the decline of the year saw a deepening of rural poverty as men were lost to the land and food prices rose with taxes. The House of Industry had several new inmates.

The funeral of Miss Amelia Gravett took place just before Christmas, and a large number of villagers turned out to honour the quiet spinster whose whole life had been spent in the service of her brother, the rector, pandering to his delicate health and indulging his enormous appetite. Leaning on the arm of his niece-housekeeper in her formidable black bonnet and cape, he was heard to sigh that he had made a mistake in remaining a bachelor, which was a state devoid of comfort. Parson Smart was called upon to take the Christmas services at Great St Giles in respect of Dr Gravett's grief.

Christmas at the Bennetts' farmhouse was a time for rejoicing, with the arrival of a little daughter to Mr and Mrs Percy Twydell, after only a few hours of travail. It proved to be the last good news of the year.

Susan had done what she could to make Christmas a memorable festival for the orphans, and they had helped her to hang up branches of holly and ivy in the refectory. These symbols of the season were still in place when a visitor tugged at the bell pull and asked to see Mrs Susan Calthorpe. Mrs Croker bowed him into the little sitting room, and Susan was sent for.

As soon as she saw her father-in-law, she knew.

'Edward?' she whispered, gripping the back of a chair.

'Yes, my dear. The *Bucephalus* has been attacked by the French and sunk off Cape Fear.'

'And Edward?'

'We don't know, Susan. Many men were drowned, but . . .' His voice broke, and he made an effort to control himself. 'Forgive me, Susan, I have left my wife and daughters weeping their hearts out, but we are not without some hope. The reports are vague, but it seems the *Bucephalus* drifted for a while before she sank, and a number of men were picked up – taken out of the sea – and some may even have swum to shore, for it was not far out from land. Edward could have been one of those. He may still be alive.'

Susan walked over to the window and stared blankly out at the fading daylight. He stepped towards her, and laid his hand on her shoulder.

'We must not give up hope too soon, my child,' he said gently. 'The casualty lists will take some time to come through, and even if Edward is listed as missing, we know that he may have survived. He could be taken prisoner. He may even . . .' Again Calthorpe's voice failed, and a shudder passed through his frame. 'We must hope, and not . . .' He paused as if searching for words to encourage the silent, white-faced girl who stood very still with her back to him. 'Time and the end of this accursed war may yet bring him back to us.'

But Susan merely shook her head, and neither spoke nor wept. All she knew was that she had sent a loving husband away disappointed and uncomforted, to board the troopship and return to the war.

To his death.

Chapter 22

Even Dr Gravett could not have argued that life was easy for the paupers during February of the new year. Not since the outbreak of the white throat in the winter of 1768 had the House of Industry been visited by such a virulent infection. It began with a kitchen-maid complaining of a headache; she was told to get on with her work, and two days later she was dead. Within a week half the inmates were unable to rise from their beds, and with windows closed against the cold outside, the influenza infection rapidly spread through the stagnant air. Men and women weakened by a poor diet collapsed at their looms or fell down where they stood. Shivering and sweating by turns, the victims lay helpless in the dormitories, unable so much as to raise their heads. Some developed inflammation of the lungs, coughing and gasping for breath, and Susan Calthorpe soon learned to recognise the signs of fatality – the sunken, unseeing eyes, the bluish tinge to the skin, which lost its heat and rapidly grew cold. It seemed to her that Death himself stalked the draughty passages and stone-flagged rooms as the deadly advance continued.

Susan's first priority was the children, and when Dorcas and Toby showed signs of fever, she nursed them in her own sitting room to keep them apart from the others. Everybody seemed to turn to her for directions, and she often found the best help in quite unlikely quarters. Mag the drudge conscientiously kept up a good daily supply of fresh water from the well, and saw that it was always within reach of parched lips. With the cooks laid low, Mrs Croker took over in the kitchen, making vegetable soup, boiling and mashing potatoes and sending pans of bone broth up to spoon-feed the very ill.

Susan and Mag took turns at caring for the sick women, while Master Croker looked after the men, assisted by Gus, who had a gentle touch and was no longer avoided because of his fits, though they continued. With such numbers affected, only the most basic of needs could be attended to, and there were occasions when linen went unchanged and the dead lay beside the still living. Croker had the grim task of removing the corpses and placing them in the makeshift coffins he had hastily nailed together, to be collected by the black-draped cart which took them to a communal grave in a Belhampton churchyard.

All communications between the House and the outside world were stopped in an effort to contain the infection. Even so, Mrs Jarvis fled from the danger under cover of darkness; and there was one visitor to the afflicted House who could not be kept away.

'Missus Calthorpe! Doctor be here to see 'ee agin!' Mag's voice called up the stairs, and Susan straightened her aching back from bending over the sick women, some of whom were now struggling towards recovery. Her hair hung in untidy wisps from a limp mobcap, and her calico gown was creased from being slept in; she had not undressed for a week. Grey-faced with fatigue, she put down the basin of hot water and the towel she had been using, and descended the stairs to where Charles

Parnham awaited her. He could not hide his shock at her appearance.

'In heaven's name, let me take you away from this hell, Trotula, before the influenza gets you too,' he pleaded. 'You may stay at my house and have a room to yourself. My housekeeper and servants will show you every respect, and—'

She raised haggard eyes and shook her head. 'No, sir. I ha' lost my little Dorcas, and may lose Toby, along o' more'n a score o' the old an' feeble. How'd I sleep in a sof' bed, an' them lef' ter their fate?'

Tiredness made her revert to broad Hampshire speech, though Parnham hardly noticed in his alarm.

'But, my dear, if I were to lose – I mean I gave Lieutenant Calthorpe my word of honour that I would take care of you.'

Susan drew a long, sighing breath and gave him a hopeless look.

'There's bin no word o' Edward since his ship went down, an' he be likely at the bottom o' the sea,' she said with chilling resignation. ' 'Twas yeself sent me to this place, Dr Parnham, an' here I'll stay till the fever be past, f'r 'tis a home o' sorts, an' these be my people – an' my children. The night afore last I delivered a poor woman in such a high fever that she raved o' haymakin' while in travail, and didn't know she'd borne a son. Can I leave the likes o' her an' her child?'

'But if you should be struck down with the influenza—'

'Then let it be, sir, f'r I care not that much whether I live or not. But I ha' bid Miss Glover keep away, and ye'd better do the same, sir.'

He suppressed a shudder on hearing her fatalistic words.

'My dear Trotula, I'm a healthy man who eats two

304

good meals a day, not like these half-starved wretches who have no resistance against outbreaks of this kind.' He lowered his voice. 'But I have something to tell you. Can we talk more privately in your sitting room?'

'No, Toby be in there. Come an' walk outside in the yard, sir, where the air be better. I'll fetch my cloak.'

Out in the biting February wind, he took her arm.

'You have every reason to live, Trotula. At Easter your year in this place will be completed, and the mothers of Beversley need you – and especially one,' he added significantly.

Her tired eyes widened. 'Polly? Ha' ye news o' her, sir? Miss Glover wrote that she's heavy wi' the dropsy, and Mrs Coulter expects her to be in travail soon, though she can't be due till April.'

'That is the reason for my visit,' he said seriously. 'I called at Glover Cottage this morning, and saw your sister.'

'You saw her? Oh, Dr Parnham, tell me how she does! Is it truly the dropsy that's makin' her so big? I remember when Mrs Twydell had the same—'

He patted her hand and spoke gently. 'As you say, my Trotula, the poor girl is not due to give birth until April, but she may well start her pains earlier because of the dropsy. The sooner 'tis all over, the better it will be. But listen, there is another reason for her size. When I placed my hand upon the belly, I felt many small parts that must be limbs, and then I discovered another head, high up beneath the diaphragm. I'm as certain as I can be that she's carrying twins.'

'*Two!* Oh, my God!' Susan covered her face with her hand. 'Whatever will she do? Though bein' smaller, they should be born more easily than one large child.'

305

'That is true, though with greater risk to the infants, especially the second. But try not to worry, little Trotula, for 'tis further reason for an earlier travail. I shall not be far away if you need me.'

He looked down at her bowed head with a tenderness she did not see, and continued, 'Only, for heaven's sake, keep yourself free of the influenza fever, or Polly could be—'

Again he stopped short, and never finished the sentence. He had been going to say 'without a midwife', but feared even to mention such an awful possibility.

And he did not want to add to her troubles by revealing his misgivings over Polly, who stood in real danger of developing the dreaded 'mother's malady', which, though not common, was often fatal to mother and child. Dropsy was an early sign, and the final stage, which Susan had not yet witnessed in her short experience of midwifery, was marked by violent fits.

Charles Parnham was a worried man, yet had to hide the fact under an air of hope and assurance.

The solitary horseman reined in outside Glover Cottage, and for a full minute remained in the saddle. The collar of his cloak was turned up and his leather slouch hat pulled down against the strong March winds. The horse flattened its ears and blew down its nose in protest at the rider's indecision.

At length the man dismounted, lowering himself carefully and staggering a little, an unimposing figure on the ground. He reached for the walking stick tucked into his belt and leaned heavily on it, swinging his peg leg forward and wincing as he hung the strap of the bridle over the tethering-post;

then he clicked open the gate and limped up to the door.

Tess answered his knock, and when he asked if he might see her mistress, showed him into the parlour where he was kept waiting for several minutes. He heard doors opening and closing, footsteps running up- and downstairs and female voices calling, among them his cousin's.

When she entered, Sophia's eyes were stern and unsmiling.

'What is your business, Cousin Osmond?' she asked directly, with no formal greeting.

He leaned upon his stick and faced her unhappily.

'Sophia, I have much to regret in the matter of poor Polly Lucket, and I've come to enquire about her – and perhaps to see her, with your permission.'

Miss Glover gave the slightest of nods. 'Indeed, I am pleased to hear you say so, Osmond, but to what do we owe this tardy regret? You never answered my letter or sent her a word of comfort.'

'Believe me, Sophy, I do feel for her sufferings, whatever you and others may believe to the contrary. Every day that passes she has preyed upon my mind, waking and sleeping, and I have ridden over from Winchester to find out how she does.'

He was in pain from his aching stump, but did not want to sit down while Sophia stood.

When she replied she spoke coldly. 'Many a time that girl begged me to send for you, Osmond. I never told her about the letter I received from your mother.'

He hung his head. 'I had nothing to do with that, Sophy.'

'Yet you must have known of it,' she returned, 'for only you could have told your mother about the message I sent you.'

307

'I deeply regret that now, Sophy, and I say again, I had no part in the letter my mother sent you.'

'And yet you never sent a word to Polly.'

He sighed deeply. 'No, to my shame. May I ask how she does?'

Sophia looked grave. 'Not well. She is great with child and great with the dropsy. She has stayed here because there was an outbreak of fever at the work-house, and many of the inmates died of it. Otherwise she would be within those walls like any other destitute woman.'

Osmond winced, whether from pain or her relentless words, Sophia was not sure.

'And when a renowned man-midwife examined her last month, he discovered that she is carrying twins,' she added.

'Oh, my *God*! And is she nearing the time for her delivery?'

'Not until April,' replied Sophia, watching his face. 'But both the doctor and Mrs Coulter think she may be brought to bed earlier – they say 'tis Nature's way in such cases. Do you wish me to send you word when she is delivered?'

He gestured helplessly. 'Yes, I do, but – Cousin Sophy, you surely must know that I'm in no position to marry her.'

Sophia smoothed the front of her gown and adjusted her shawl, making no reply. Osmond leaned on the back of a chair while he put a hand in his jacket and pulled out a small leather bag.

'You have shown great kindness, Sophy, and at least let me recompense you for your trouble. There are a dozen guineas.'

He placed the clinking bag on a small table she used for writing letters. She did not touch it.

'Take it, Sophy, and use it for her and the—' He stopped and shook his head as if not knowing what to say. 'And will you allow me to see her before I go?'

Sophia was clearly undecided what to do for the best.

'I am not sure that it would be good for her,' she said, 'though if she should later hear about your visit, she would be even more grieved at not seeing you. Look here, I will send for the poor girl, but you must not upset her. Only greet her and wish her well, and then you must go.'

'Of course, Sophy, yes, I – I understand,' he muttered.

Sophia rang the bell and told Tess to bring in Polly Lucket.

The next few minutes were pandemonium.

A grossly swollen, ungainly figure waddled into the room. As soon as she saw him she shrieked his name again and again. '*Osmond!* Master Osmond! Oh, my love, 'ee be come fur me – Osmond, Osmond!' And with desperate eagerness she flung herself at him.

'Look out! Have a care, for God's sake, you'll have me over!' he cried as she grabbed wildly at his clothes, trying to throw her arms around his neck.

'Polly! Stop that!' Sophia rushed forward to drag the girl away from him, and he only managed to stay upright by clinging to the writing table.

'Oi ha' waited so long fur 'ee!' Polly wailed. 'The child presses hard upon me – me back aches night an' day. Take pity on yer poor Polly, do!'

'Don't, Poll, don't hang on. In God's name, how came you to be such a monstrous size?'

All through the bleak winter months at the army depot he had dreamed of the girl who had teased and

309

delighted him with her saucy ways, and who had come to his bed to pleasure him back to health. He remembered her patience with his peevishness, her willingness to divert him in a score of ways.

But what dire transformation was this? He shrank back as she tried to reach out to him, her face blotched, her belly grotesquely swollen.

Struggling to be free of Sophia's restraining arms, Polly caught sight of the horrified unbelief on the face of her lover, and sank back with a pitiful moan. The image of his face became obscured by a thickening web of darkness that rose up and engulfed her so that she saw and heard nothing more.

There had been no new cases of the influenza fever at the House for the past two weeks, but an air of silent exhaustion hung over the place as the surviving inmates returned to some semblance of normality. The wan-faced children mourned for little Dorcas, and Toby clung to Susan, who had brought him back from the very door of death. The greatest toll had been among the old, but there had been unexpected fatalities and equally surprising survivals; Mad Doll still wandered endlessly along the passages and stairways, wringing her hands and searching for heaven knew what, while the House Master had been the last to succumb to the infection and died within two days.

Susan was the only follower of Dorcas's small coffin, and a mere half-dozen mourners turned out to comfort Mrs Croker when she buried her husband. One of these was Mr Calthorpe, representing the Board of Guardians.

'He tol' me that the influenzy ha' got into Bever House by the back door,' the widow informed Susan on her return. 'Their housekeeper be struck down, he says, and can't raise her head from the bolster.' The new black mobcap bobbed up and down vengefully. ' 'Twill vex that mother-in-law o' yourn, Mrs Susan, fur her'll get no callers while there be fever under the roof, an' serve her right; she done nothin' fur us.'

Susan shrugged. The epidemic had left her feeling drained and curiously detached from everyday events. She cared nothing at all about Bever House and its occupants, and although her anxiety over Polly was always at the back of her mind, she was thankful that the girl was safe with Miss Glover, with Mrs Coulter at hand. Susan had calculated from Polly's last flow that the twins were actually due at the beginning of April, though Dr Parnham had predicted an earlier date.

'Nature must intervene, I think,' he had said, and Susan longed to see her sister and make her own judgement. With the epidemic over, she told Mrs Croker that she would get out the pony-trap and drive over to Beversley on the morrow.

'Oh-ah.' The big black cap nodded knowingly. 'Yer sister'll be gettin' t'wards her time, Oi dare say. And 'ee'll be away to be Beversley midwife soon, Missus Calthorpe. 'Twill be a bad day fur this House, wi' Croker and 'ee both gone.'

And to Susan's surprise the mobcap began to wobble as its owner shed real tears into her apron. Susan had no great liking for the woman, but she put a hand on the heaving shoulder.

'There now, Mrs Croker, ye'll ha' to take care o' the children f'r me – they'll miss me the most,' she said, voicing her only regret at leaving the House.

Mrs Croker raised her little reddened piggy eyes,

and was about to swear undying devotion to the orphans when there came a loud jangling at the front door, and they both jumped.

'Lord ha' mercy, who be that?' cried the widow, hurrying down the passage while Susan waited with a pounding heart.

' 'Tis yer brother, Missus Calthorpe, ridden over from Beversley, an' says 'ee's to go to Glover Cottage straight away!'

Susan ran to where Joby stood at the door, his face reddened by his ride across the common. An old horse panted beside him.

'Miss Glover sent word fur me to fetch 'ee, Sukey. Her says Polly be in a bad way,' he said bluntly.

'Merciful heaven!' Susan's hands flew to her throat. 'Be she in travail, Joby? Is Mrs Coulter with her, d'ye know?'

'The midwife be at the Bennetts' wi' Mrs Marianne. Miss Glover jus' tol' me to fetch 'ee,' said the boy urgently. 'Oi ha' to go back straightway. Can 'ee foller me in the pony-trap?'

'Yes, Joby, yes, I'll get out the trap an' come now.'

Impelled by an overwhelming urgency Susan hastily prepared to leave; the long-unexercised pony found himself once more in the shafts, and Susan's straw bag was flung on to the seat. She climbed up and seized the reins without once looking back, straining her eyes to follow Job across the windswept common in the fading light.

'Go on, Brownie, go on – good boy!'

She sighed with relief when the roofs of Beversley came into view, the glimmer of candles in windows. Within a few more minutes they reached Glover Cottage, where the front door was open and Sophia stood in the triangle of light. Only when she let go of

312

the reins did Susan realise how stiff and chilled she was from sitting in an open trap.

'Thank God – you are welcome indeed, Susan!' Sophia almost groaned her relief. 'I pray that she may take heart from the sight of you.'

Susan hurried indoors while Job saw to the trap and horses.

'This afternoon she had a shock, Susan. Osmond Calthorpe came to see her.'

'What? Why should that betrayer come to trouble her now?'

'Hush, Susan, I truly believe his conscience reproaches him – but he was shocked by the sight of her, as you will be too, and she swooned when she saw him. Now she complains of constant headache and pain at the front and the back, and Mr Turnbull says her waters have broken. Mrs Coulter was called to the Bennetts' soon after Osmond left, to attend young Mrs Smart, and I felt that you should be here.'

'Yes, oh yes, Sophy – thank ye for sendin' Joby!'

'Dan Spooner has lent him an old, broken-winded horse, and he'll stay here in case there are any messages to send. The maids will give him supper, and you too.'

'I must go to Polly straightway!' And Susan flew instinctively up the stairs to the landing and the room where her sister lay. She stopped short at the doorway and took in the scene before her.

The curtains were drawn against the dusk, and a candle threw looming shadows on the ceiling. The air had the sweetish, acidic smell of a sickroom, mixed with rosewater and lavender; a Bible lay on a shelf next to some glasses and medicine bottles. Mr Turnbull stood at the foot of the bed looking at the young woman who lay motionless in it. The once-pretty girl had become a mountain of waterlogged flesh, and her face was so swollen that her eyes were mere slits.

Susan at once felt the waiting presence of Death in the room.

Polly turned her head slowly. 'Dear ol' Sukey, Oi know'd 'ee'd come,' she said weakly, and Susan kneeled beside her. Tears welled up as she kissed the hot cheeks and took hold of the puffy hand lying on the bedcover.

'Yes, dearest Poll, I be here,' she whispered. 'How goes it wi' ye? Are ye gettin' hard pains in y'r belly?'

'Oi ha' the bitterest headache, Sukey, an' the stars spin round like on the night o' the ball. Remember how we danced an' danced?'

And in a husky, tuneless voice she began to sing: '"Hand in hand go down the line, the lady's little slipper trips –"'

Susan turned to the apothecary, who gave a helpless shrug.

'Sukey, will 'ee fetch Osmond to me?' croaked Polly. 'Tell un Oi be in great sickness, an' bid un come. Oh, Sukey, let me see my sweet master once more!'

Susan held her hand as she tried to sing the second line of the refrain: '"Take the moment when it comes, an' taste the sweet . . ."'

The words trailed off and Polly moaned plaintively, turning her head from side to side and repeating Osmond's name.

'You must put your trust in the Lord's mercy, not in the ways of men, Polly,' said Sophia gently, while Turnbull beckoned Susan to follow him from the room.

On the landing, he closed the door and spoke gravely.

314

'I fear for the babies, Mrs Calthorpe, as I cannot hear their heartbeats, and Mrs Coulter says there have been no movements for several days. The waters are foul and greenish, and all this excess water in her body may affect the brain and cause fits. We can but hope that the pains of travail will soon begin.'

'Has she been examined, Mr Turnbull?' asked Susan.

'No, not yet. Mrs Coulter had to leave in haste, and I have been waiting for you. Thank heaven you are here, Mrs Calthorpe!'

Susan remembered the apothecary's fear of the complications of childbirth, and in any case he was not allowed to perform such an examination. Returning to the room, she washed her hands and smeared the right one with goose-grease from the jar in her bag. Sophia turned back the bedcovers and gently separated Polly's legs as Susan instructed her.

Susan could scarcely put a fingertip into the ring of the womb, and could only conclude that Polly was not in true travail.

On hearing this Mr Turnbull said he would go home for the night, but that Job could be sent to fetch him at any time. There being no news from the Bennetts, Sophia suggested that Tess should sit with Polly for half an hour while Susan took some refreshment by the parlour fire. Downstairs the two women discussed the situation, and Susan wondered if she should send for Dr Parnham before it got pitch-dark.

'There seems little point in his being here if Polly is not even in travail,' said Sophia, suppressing a yawn. 'Would it not be better to send a message in the morning? Perhaps we should all try to get some rest in the meantime.'

This sounded reasonable, but Susan had felt a deep foreboding as soon as she stepped over the threshhold. She also noticed with a pang that Sophia looked white and drawn, and remembered all the months of inconvenience she had had with Polly.

'Ye must go to y'r bed, Sophy, ye look fit to drop. I'll sit wi' me sister now, and comfort her as best I can. Ye've done more f'r us than we can ever repay, dear Sophy, so I'll bid ye good night now.'

But there was to be no good night. Tess's frantic call summoned them upstairs with speed.

They never forgot the sight that met them. Polly's head was thrown back, and every muscle in her body was stiffened and jerking convulsively. Her face was contorted into a hideous grimace, with her clenched teeth biting into her protruding tongue. Flecks of bloodstained froth spurted out on to her nightgown.

Sophia covered her mouth with her hands to stifle a cry.

Gus, thought Susan at once, remembering the frequent seizures she had witnessed in the House, when Gus would fall to the floor and foam at the mouth, hurting himself and biting his tongue. She had learned to keep calm, reassure the onlookers and protect him from injury with cushions and a gag between his teeth.

'Keep her on the bed – don't let her fall out,' she now ordered sharply. 'You stand that side o' her, Sophy, an' I'll stay this side. All right, now, is there anything I can put between her teeth – a spoon? A wooden stick?'

There was a metal spoon in a cup on the shelf, and Susan quickly wrapped the corner of a huckaback towel round it.

316

'Can ye hold her head still, Sophy? That's the way . . .'

'Oh, for heaven's sake be careful, Susan, she'll bite you!' cried Sophia as Susan managed to insert the handle of the padded spoon between Polly's upper and lower teeth. It released her bleeding tongue, and she made a choking sound as blood and spittle dribbled out on to the bolster.

'Good, now let's get her over on to her side. That's better.'

The situation was under control, but Tess quaked in terror, cowering behind Miss Glover.

'Her be possessed by a demon! It's a devil inside o' her!'

'Hold y'r noise, Tess, 'tis a fit and will pass,' said Susan impatiently, though Sophia had more sympathy with the girl than she cared to admit.

Gradually Polly's convulsive movements began to subside. They saw her face turn from a livid blue to a yellowish pallor, while her limbs relaxed, her features slackened and within a minute she lay still, breathing deeply and noisily, as if snoring.

'Praise God!' breathed Sophia, sending up a silent prayer of thanks. Susan saw that her friend was trembling.

'Dear Sophy, I'm sorry ye've been frightened, but 'tis a fit such as we were warned about, an' after she ha' had a sleep there could be another,' she cautioned.

'Another? More fits? Oh, then let us by all means send for Dr Parnham!' exclaimed Sophia, aghast at the thought of a repetition of what they had just witnessed.

Susan too was shaken by the struggle with her afflicted sister, but made an effort to sound calm and matter-of-fact.

'I doubt if the doctor could do more'n we can if she has another, Sophy,' she began, but Miss Glover insisted.

'Job must go up to Bever House and ask my cousin Calthorpe to get out the Bever carriage and send to Belhampton to bring the doctor back,' she said.

Susan stared. 'I'd never ha' thought o' askin' the Calthorpes, I must say,' she said. 'But 'tis only right, o' course, seein' that Polly's givin' birth to their grandchildren.'

'And there are highwaymen and all kinds of ne'er-do-wells waiting to attack night travellers,' added Sophia, 'so a carriage should go, or at least two strong horsemen. I'll call Job.'

At thirteen Job Lucket was a well-grown lad with strong muscles from working at the forge. He at once went to fetch the ancient nag that he had been lent; Bowman was gentle but wheezy from the smoke and coal-dust of the smithy.

'Ask to speak to Mr Calthorpe, Job, and tell him I sent you,' said Sophia earnestly. 'Say your sister Polly Lucket is in danger for her life and – and the twin babies also. Beg him to get word to Dr Parnham at Belhampton. Do you understand, Job?'

The lad nodded, his steady grey eyes so like Susan's.

'I'll do that, Missus Glover, just as 'ee says.'

He mounted Bowman, heading him towards the beech grove and Bever House. When he reached the gates he rode up the drive to the front entrance and, slithering down the hollow flank, he seized the bell pull with one hand and banged on the knocker with the other.

*

Dr Octavius Gravett was feeling more than a little

put out. Surely a message could have been sent to the rectory to say that Mr Calthorpe had taken to his bed, and was unable to share a pipe and a bottle with the rector and squire as was his custom on Friday nights.

Mrs Calthorpe was apologetic, but had forgotten all about the gentlemen's arrangement.

'Mr Calthorpe has caught cold and is sweating and shivering by turns,' she said. 'I hope he has not caught the influenza. Mrs Martin is but slowly recovering from it.'

Alarmed by the threat of infection, the rector hastily bid her and her daughters good night and was about to leave when they were all startled by a sudden ringing and knocking at the front door.

'Heavens, it must be a messenger with ill news!' cried Gertrude Calthorpe, turning pale and clinging to the rector's arm. 'Stay with me, Dr Gravett, for pity's sake.'

They hurried down to the hall just as Martin drew back the bolts and opened the door to reveal the slight figure of Job standing beside a tall old horse.

'What brings you here, boy?' asked the butler.

Job looked over Martin's shoulder, straight at Mrs Calthorpe.

'If 'ee pleases, missus, bid the master send the carriage or a good rider to Belhampton to fetch the man-midwife to me sister!'

'What? Who is your sister, and who sent you to Bever House?'

Job stepped forward and showed his face clearly.

'My sister Polly Lucket be in great sorrow, and needs the man-midwife to save her. Missus Glover sent me.'

Gertrude Calthorpe could scarcely take in such effrontery.

319

'Lucket? Glover? Good God, how *dare* she ask my help for that slut of a girl! Be off with you, wretch, or I'll have you whipped for coming to a house of sickness at such an hour.'

But Job stood his ground and regarded her steadily.

'The women say Polly ha' two babes, missus, an' Master Osmond visited her today, Oi knows 'cause Oi seen un. Oi asks 'ee again to send fur the doctor.'

Gertrude Calthorpe had been making some rapid calculations, and now fairly exploded with fury.

'How dare you – how dare *she*? What lies, what wickedness! Do you say that the creature is giving birth *now*? Don't you see what this means, Dr Gravett? Selina, Caroline, do you hear? Don't you remember that Osmond was lying close to death in Portsmouth last spring, and suffered the loss of his leg on the fifth day of May? Oh, how we have all been duped! That slut of a girl must have been with child for two or three months when she took advantage of poor Osmond's weakness, planning to trap him into marrying her, just as foolish Edward was trapped by her sly older sister. Oh, my poor son, what a conspiracy to blacken his name! She came brazenly to his bed and—'

Her voice rose, and the rector began to be embarrassed by her hysteria.

'Calm yourself, dear madam,' he pleaded. 'I shall send this boy packing, and see that he gives you no more trouble.'

He turned sternly to Job. 'Do you seriously believe that this gentlewoman should order a horse to be saddled and a rider set upon him, to go five miles across the common on a moonless night, all for the sake of a shameless wench and a pair of bastards? Be off with you, impudent dolt!'

Had Octavius Gravett known it, his words were to echo in Beversley history for years to come; they burned into Job's memory for life.

He drew back. 'Then *I'll* ha' to ride fur the man, then, seein' as there be no help here, nor pity neither. Don't look fur me in that church o' yourn agin.'

He remounted Bowman's sagging back, and for the second time that day headed for the track that led up to the common. He strained his eyes to discern the way ahead when the horse reached the open country, but scudding clouds obscured the stars, and the wind whistled through the dry gorse, chilling Job's brave resolutions. He gritted his teeth and dug his heels into the horse's flanks. The expanse of heathland seemed limitless in the dark, and as they skirted an alder copse, there was a rustling followed by an agonised yelp. Job's involuntary cry startled Bowman, who lurched violently to one side, kicking out with his back legs.

'Steady, ol' feller – 'tis only a fox wi' a hare, most like,' panted Job, as much to reassure himself as the horse. He had no idea of the time, and trusted they were still heading north.

When the horse stumbled again the boy lost the reins and clung helplessly to the loose, leathery folds around Bowman's neck.

'Go on, go on, ol' feller,' he urged the sweating beast, forcing himself to keep his seat and stay alert as they stumbled on into the unending night, with no lamp to light their way and no sound but the moaning of the wind.

Chapter 23

Polly had no idea how long she had wandered through swirling space where the stars circled in their courses or suddenly shot across the night sky in a flash of dazzling light. The pain that throbbed in her head had spread out to every part, turning into a general tingling sensation that didn't hurt so much. Voices drifted around her, whispering, cajoling, telling her to sip from a spoon, go to sleep, put her trust in God and repent of her sins. The words buzzed round her head like flies, getting mixed up and in the wrong order, so that she forgot them all and clung to one word only: *Osmond*.

Where was her fair, blue-eyed prince among men, he who had smiled upon her in the Bever stable-yard, gazed across at her from his pew in Great St Giles, leaned down from his horse to her as she hung washing on the line?

I shall return and have thee, pretty Polly! Wait for me!

How she had teased him with her mischievous smiles and pouting lips. What good times those had been, while she still resisted him! And what joy had filled her heart on the night of the Bever House ball, when he had chosen her out of all the young ladies in their fine gowns. How Rosa Hansford had stared when she saw the little maidservant in her cap and apron, dancing down the line with Osmond!

Sound the drum-beat up and down, raise up the
   flag, the day is won,

Clap hands, clap hands, clap-clap-clap-clap, his
    lady's lonely wait is done!

But now he has vanished again, and Polly's memory
of the beech grove is hazy and confusing; one
moment a warm, thrilling contact with his eager
body, and then a wet disgrace and Osmond is calling
her a dirty little vixen – and Sukey has somehow
taken his place and is tucking her up in bed, looking
both sad and cross.

Ah, but everything changed when he came back
from the war, a wounded hero, thin and ill-looking,
with a leg that stunk so badly that it had to be cut off.
How she had longed to be at his side to comfort him!
But his mother kept everybody away from him
except for that old black-browed Mrs Ferris.

Until that Sunday when she had slipped out of
church: how his face had lit up at the sight of her!

My pretty little Polly, by God! – quick, a kiss now!

And she could refuse him nothing. Oh, the midnight creeping, the barefoot pattering along passages,
the return to her own quarters in the cold dawn; for
there had been no more teasing, only pleasing of the
man she adored, the lover who had taken her so
hungrily, even violently at times. She had sat astride
him, riding to heights of happiness: even when he
had hurt her she had let him have his way, biting her
lip rather than cry out. She had been his best physick,
he had told her, better than any of Turnbull's.

And now comes the wonderful news that cunning
old Sukey has actually got Edward to marry her!
Polly is overjoyed for her sister, and dreams of
becoming another young Mrs Calthorpe.

Only it never happened. Instead she was beaten
and turned out of Bever House in the early morning,

since when life had grown duller and drearier every day; first that moaning Mrs Twydell, then the weary winter months at Miss Glover's, feeling sicker and heavier with every week that passed.

And then, like a vision – *Osmond*! He had come to her at last, but when she went towards him he backed away and said she was a monstrous size – and then he vanished again, leaving her feeling worse than ever.

A gentleman from Belhampton had come and frowned at her, ordering her to lie on a feather bed in the dark. Miss Glover had read the Bible to her, Mrs Coulter had put an ear to her belly to listen to the babies' heartbeats, and Tess had grumbled about all the extra work she had to do.

And now here was dear old Sukey at her side again, with memories of that magic September night when they had danced with their Calthorpe sweethearts.

> Hand in hand go down the line, the lady's little
>   slipper trips –
> Take the moment when it comes, and taste the
>   sweetness of her lips!

But now the night is closing in after a great storm that raged around Polly, rolling the bed from side to side and sending lightning flashes through her head. Her tongue feels swollen and sore, and there is a strange, still heaviness deep down in her belly, not a flicker of the movements she has got used to. They had said that there were two babies waiting to be born, but Polly now feels too ill to care. Only let God be merciful to her, and send Osmond again for one last time – and then she will never ask for anything more.

Where be thee, my sweet master? 'Twill soon be too late.

But the only sounds that come from her throat are wordless groans. The other voices are growing fainter and further away, and Polly is sliding down towards the edge of the world.

Soon, Osmond, soon, or 'twill be too late . . .

To arrive at Portsmouth docks a day earlier than scheduled was an unexpected bonus, and although First Lieutenant Hansford was due to board another troopship at noon on the morrow, he seized his opportunity with eager joy. While other officers and crew had gone off into the town to seek what entertainment was on offer, he opted to travel four-and-twenty miles just to spend one night at home. Tired as he was after a fairly rough Atlantic crossing with a cargo of wounded men, some of whom had died before reaching port, Henry desperately needed to look upon her whom he loved more than life.

At first he had thought to hire a horse, but then he chanced to see a timber-truck departing for Wychell Forest. Trees were being felled in ever larger numbers for ship-building, and the long, low drays drawn by teams of eight or ten horses were frequently to be seen on the Portsmouth Road, sometimes blocking the way while the draymen exchanged high words with stagecoach drivers. An unloaded dray travelled much faster and needed only a couple of horses, so Henry eagerly leaped aboard. It was dark when he arrived at the forest edge, and now had to complete the journey on foot. It was some seven miles to Beversley, and once he got on the Winchester Road, Henry struck out, his strength renewed by the prospect of seeing Sophia before the day was done.

He smiled contentedly to himself. Would she have retired by the time he reached the cottage? Henry knew that she would wake at once at hearing his special knock, and swiftly come to answer, whatever the hour. She would say his name and hold out her arms to him; brief though the visit would be, it was worth every mile of the double journey.

Henry Hansford was tired; a deep weariness seemed to have seeped into his very bones. His eyes had seen enough of ghastly sights, his ears had echoed with the groans of injured and dying men. He was heartily sick of the war, and knew that there was now no hope of a British victory. He needed Sophia, the sight of her beloved face, the sound of her sweet voice. The thought of her love was balm to his mind and body, giving new impetus to his aching legs. Soon, soon he would see her again, hear her, touch her, enfold her in his arms . . .

Susan sat alone beside her sister, and the presence of Death drew closer. Polly had partly recovered consciousness, and her breathing was quiet and shallow, though at intervals she took a deeper intake of air, a sharp involuntary gasp that made Susan start; it was followed by a long, sighing exhalation.

'Ha' ye any pain, dear Poll?' Susan asked gently, touching her sister's cooling forehead.

The only answer was a slow turn of the head until Polly's beseeching eyes met her sister's. The dry, cracked lips moved soundlessly.

'Osmond . . . my master . . . Osmond.'

She mouthed the words with difficulty, as if she were using the last of her strength to beg for her lover to come to her once more. One last time.

Susan held her hand and knew that life was

ebbing. She leaned over and kissed Polly's lips.

'I'm here wi' ye, little Poll. I be right here beside ye,' she whispered, and began to say the twenty-third psalm.

'The Lord is my Shepherd; I shall not want. He maketh me to lie down in green pastures: he leadeth me beside the still waters.'

The sudden knock at the door broke upon them, shattering the silence: a knock followed by three short taps and another loud knock. *Rap!* Rap-rap-rap, *rap!*

Susan raised her head. Had Joby returned at last? Or was it Mr Turnbull? Could it possibly be Dr Parnham here already? She rose and opened the door, to see Sophia emerging from her room in her nightgown, a wrapper thrown over her shoulders.

'I will go, Susan – I will answer!' she said, her eyes alight with joyful surprise at hearing that special knock, unexpected as it was.

Susan stood on the landing and heard the front door open, the sound of a glad greeting and eager exchanges between Sophia and a man. She looked back into the bedroom and saw Polly's face: she too had heard the arrival of a night visitor.

The strangest thought occurred to Susan. Had the hopes and longings of her dying sister summoned her faithless lover to her bedside at this late hour?

As if propelled by an inner force she did not understand, Susan made her way down the stairs and stood on the bottom step, just out of sight of Sophia and her visitor.

'Henry!'

'My own Sophia, how I've dreamed of beholding your face again – oh, my darling!'

'But where have you come from at such an hour? How have you got here?'

'From Portsmouth on a timber-wagon, and I must return by tomorrow noon. Oh, Sophia, kiss me. I have so little time!'

He bowed his head over her upturned face, and their lips met in a kiss that told of their mutual yearning more than any words could have done. Her arms went round his neck and his encircled her body, drawing his cloak around to enfold them both.

They looked up quickly when Susan stepped forward, a dishevelled figure whose round eyes stared straight at Henry.

'Susan's sister Polly lies gravely ill upstairs,' Sophia told him hurriedly, feeling his arm still around her waist as if unable to let go of her. 'She is great with child – with twins, in fact – and young Joby Lucket has gone to Bever House for a message to be sent to Dr Parnham, the man-midwife.'

She became conscious of Susan's eyes fixed upon Henry. 'How is Polly now, Susan?' she asked. 'Is there any change?'

Susan forgot all rules of conventional behaviour. She had only one idea in mind, and rushed forward to seize Henry's arm.

'I took ye for Osmond Calthorpe, sir, an' so may my sister. Her mind wanders, and she's sinking fast. Come to her, Mr Hansford, come to my poor sister, I beg ye!'

'Dear Susan, Lieutenant Hansford has come up from Portsmouth today and has to return by noon tomorrow,' remonstrated Sophia. 'Dr Parnham has been summoned, and—'

'*No!*' Susan's voice rose and she gripped Henry's arm, pulling him towards the staircase. 'No! My sister be beyond human aid, an' longs only to see him who betrayed her. God must ha' sent ye, sir, so come up an' sit alongside o' her, let her see ye. Take her hand an' call her Polly, I beg o' ye. 'Twould be such comfort!'

'Susan!' cried Sophia with a half-apologetic glance at Henry, who now found a voice.

'Hush, Mrs Calthorpe, try to calm yourself,' he said awkwardly, though not unkindly. He was unable to believe his ears when he understood what he was being asked to do. 'In Miss Glover's house your sister is getting every care, but how can I, a complete stranger and a man, walk into her bedchamber? It would be improper – indecent, even – and when it got to be known, I would be censured wherever it was spoken of. Is that not right, Sophy?'

Genuinely horrified at Susan's request, he turned to his beloved Sophia for support.

But to his dismay he found none, for she had become convinced by Susan's belief that this was the will of the Almighty, and should be obeyed.

'It never *will* be spoken of, Henry,' she said with that seriousness that was characteristic of her and which especially endeared her to him. 'All of us here under this roof tonight will be sworn to secrecy – myself, Mrs Calthorpe, the two maidservants, Job Lucket when he returns, and Dr Parnham if he gets here. Only do as she says, Henry – come up to the bedside and speak kindly to this poor girl – and none will know of it but ourselves and the Lord, Who has surely brought you to this house tonight.'

'But, Sophy . . .' he protested at the bizarre turn his dream had taken.

'Do as we ask you, dearest Henry, for it is a service that only you can give,' Sophia replied, her blue eyes

329

irresistible. 'Let Susan lead the way, and we will follow. I will be there.'

Very reluctantly Henry Hansford accompanied the two women up the stairs to the landing and into the candle-lit room where the foetid air seemed stifling after the cold wind outside.

Polly lay quiet and still upon the bed, her belly like a mound under the covers. Her eyes were closed, her mouth slightly agape. Sophia motioned Henry to the chair at her side, and he obediently sat down.

'Take her hand,' whispered Susan, praying that Polly would respond.

He reached out to take hold of the limp hand that lay upon the counterpane.

'Polly?' he muttered, then cleared his throat and spoke with stronger conviction. 'My little Polly.'

She half-opened her swollen eyes and slowly turned her head towards him. Her parched lips trembled, opened, closed and opened again to form words that could only just be heard.

'Osmon' . . . master Osmon', Oi *know'd* 'ee'd come back to me.'

It was all she said, but it was enough to draw sighs of relief from the two women who watched from the corner of the room. They saw Polly look upon the man she saw as Osmond Calthorpe, returned to her at last: all the love of her heart was in her eyes.

Pity swept over Henry, and he was almost ashamed of his former gentlemanly scruples. He held Polly's hand and gently stroked the mottled skin of her face, now touched with a ghostly shadow of former beauty. Apart from her shallow breathing the room was quiet and peaceful.

I have come for thee, Polly – my pretty little Polly!

330

My sweet Master Osmond – Oi know'd 'ee'd come fur me afore 'twas too late!

She was swept up into the arms of the handsome young officer who had chosen her above all the fine ladies competing for his favour. He was her own, her very own Osmond, whirling her into the dance once again. Fiddlers' bows flashed back and forth as hand in hand he led her down the long line of dancers clapping and singing the refrain over and over again. She was as light as air in his arms, and when they danced off the edge of the world he held her closer so that she did not fall into the abyss.

And then he released her, and she soared upwards into the night sky, up beyond the circling stars, higher and even higher, into the eternal sunrise that no mortal eye has seen.

The candle guttered low in its earthenware holder, almost burned out. Drowsiness had overcome the watchers whose heads nodded and lifted again as the shallow sighs turned to intermittent gasps; the wax-pale features had slackened into blankness. Henry felt the hand beneath his own grow colder, but sat unmoving at his post, a faithful substitute.

There was a tiny spasm, a choking sound in the throat, and then complete stillness.

Susan raised her head and called her sister's name: 'Polly!'

Roused by the sound and Susan's movements towards the bed, the other watchers saw that their vigil was over.

Sophia rose and drew back the curtains, then blew out the flickering candle; the sun was not yet risen. She leaned over the bed and touched the cold forehead with her lips, then stood with folded hands.

'Into Thy hands, O merciful Lord, we commend her spirit, with her innocent unborn babes. Receive them, we beseech Thee, into Thy loving care for evermore. Amen.'

Henry rose stiffly from his chair and stood with bowed head, repeating the Amen. Sophia beckoned to him to follow her downstairs to the parlour where she rekindled the fire and put water to boil.

Susan remained alone with her sister. She kneeled down beside the bed for a while, but no prayer rose to her lips. She stood up and drew the sheet over her sister's face.

Standing at the window she watched the sky lighten above Great St Giles' tower, behind which lay Bennetts' paddock field and the track from Ash-Pit End. Another track led up from the village through the beech grove to Bever House.

'Ye trod those two paths, my poor Poll,' she whispered, 'an' look where they've led ye. Ye've more right than meself to the name o' Calthorpe, but now ye lie dead an' cold, like my Edward at the bottom o' the sea.'

And she could not shed a tear, so benumbed was her heart.

'Susan dear, you have neither eaten nor slept. At least take a little wine and hot water, and then come to bed and rest.'

Susan waved away the tray that Sophia had brought up.

'Where be my brother Joby? Do he know that his sister's dead?'

'Dan Spooner has sent a man off on a strong horse to search for Job.'

The brief reply gave Susan her answer to both questions, and confirmed her suspicions.

'I thought as much! They must ha' turned him away from Bever House, so the poor lad went off to Belhampton himself, alone in the dark on an old horse.'

'He's a strong, sensible boy, Susan, and I do not think we need worry. He will be found, I'm sure.'

'Found, yes, found dead. He's more'n likely to be lyin' out there on the common wi' his throat cut an' his horse taken by highway robbers. A fine night's work, Sophy! My sister and my brother both dead 'cause o' the Calthorpes – *ha*!' Her mirthless laugh made Sophia shiver.

'Hush, Susan, do not say what you do not know,' she said, glancing towards the bed. 'We want no bitter words in this room.'

'Why not? *She* can't hear.'

'Oh, Susan, do not harden your heart. Let the Lord be the judge of wrong-doers.' Again Sophia looked at the sheeted form on the bed. 'Shall I ask for Mr Smart to call to make the arrangements for her – her burial?'

'She's not to be touched till I ha' seen Mrs Coulter,' said Susan sharply. 'I know what I want done wi' my sister's body.'

She also knew that Miss Glover would be horrified by what she planned to do, but was fairly sure that the old midwife would understand.

'Mrs Coulter spent the night resting at the Bennetts' farmhouse, and I do not know when she will return,' said Sophia patiently. 'Mrs Marianne Smart has been happily delivered of a daughter.'

'Oh, has she? And be the mother and child both well?'

'They are, praise God,' replied Sophia with a smile,

thankful to hear the immediate concern of a midwife break through Susan's otherwise bleak ungraciousness. 'And now, dear friend, I insist that you rest. Your sister will be left where she lies now, until tomorrow.'

'Nobody is to touch her.'

'Nobody will, Susan, it will be as you wish. Come, there is a bed prepared for you.'

And Sophia, who had taken leave of her beloved Henry in the last hour, led Susan to her own room.

Lying there alone with the curtains drawn, Susan fell into a fitful doze, troubled by strange and frightening dreams. She thought she heard Polly's unborn babies screaming to be released from the womb. She awoke with a cry, hearing the hoof-beats of a familiar mare outside. At once she rose from the bed.

'I could have done nothing to save her, Trotula, but I should have been here. Why did Miss Glover not send for me earlier? I had half a mind to call yesterday afternoon, and cannot forgive myself that I did not.'

Parnham shook his head mournfully as he stood beside the dead girl. He had dressed in haste, and had not even put on his wig. Susan stood at his side, pale but strangely dry-eyed.

''Twas no fault o' yourn, sir. My brother was sent up to Bever House to ask f'r ye to be fetched, but he was turned away, so rode across the common on his own in the pitch-dark.'

'He's a brave lad, is your brother. He got as far as the workhouse before the poor old nag collapsed and fell. The widow Croker says that he has but a few bruises, no broken bones.'

'Ye saw him, sir?'

'No, the widow came over to tell me his message at first light, and I came as fast as the mare could gallop. Job had said that your sister had had a fit—'

He broke off, overcome with pity for the white-faced, dry-eyed girl.

'I remembered y'r lectures on the mother's malady, sir, but I was surprised by the violence o' the fit.'

She spoke as if discussing a stranger. He sighed heavily and put his arm around her shoulders as he framed his next question.

'Miss Glover said something about your wishes regarding her body, my dear. Is she to be buried with the babies in her womb?'

She shook her head. 'No, Dr Parnham. I want to see them afore they be buried wi' her in the coffin.'

He showed no surprise. 'Very well. I will remove them through an abdominal incision. Is Mrs Coulter in the house?'

'No, and I don't want her to be troubled now that ye're here, sir. I'd ha' done it meself, and Mrs Coulter might ha' helped, but now I'll assist ye, and the sooner the better. I don't want any other body by.'

'It will be as you wish, my child. I am ready to begin.'

Parnham could have wept for her, but was well used to concealing his feelings. He put on a clean apron from his bag, and took out a sharp knife. Susan fetched a basin of water and spread towels around the bared belly of the corpse. She watched unwavering as he made a vertical incision into the pale flesh now stiffened in death.

Susan knew from the doctor's lectures that this opening of the womb was very occasionally

335

performed on a living woman in a desperate last effort to save the child, and she remembered Mrs Coulter saying that it had been used to bring forth the emperor Julius Caesar. An unlettered Irish midwife had done it over forty years ago, Parnham had said, and successfully, for both mother and child had survived.

Although Polly Lucket was beyond human suffering, every move was made with care and reverence. There was very little oozing of bloodstained fluid as Parnham cut down through skin, muscle and the thinned wall of the womb containing the two small bodies. They lay curled together, their limbs intertwined with their cords attached to a single afterburden. First one and then the other was released, and the cords cut; first one and then the other was tenderly placed in Susan's arms, held out with a towel to wrap round each of them.

'See, my dear, they are both boys, and not a blemish on them – about ten pounds between them, I'd say.'

The babies' flesh was white, with bluish-grey areas, and their sightless eyes were open. Susan wiped them dry, and after Parnham had sewed the two edges of skin together with linen thread, she put a clean nightgown on her sister and combed out the curly hair upon the bolster. Then she laid a baby on either side, each encircled within an arm. Apart from the soft rustlings of her precise movements, there was silence in the bedchamber. Parnham longed to hold her in his arms and tell her to weep her heart out, to let the sorrow and anger find a voice, but he too remained silent.

There was a gentle tap at the door, and Susan opened it to Sophia, whose eyes widened at seeing

Dr Parnham in his apron, wrapping up his knife, scissors and needles. Then she looked at the bed, and gave an involuntary cry, putting her hands to her face.

'Oh, my God! What a sight to move the hardest heart! Forgive me, Susan, but those dear babes . . . Oh, Dr Parnham, what heartbreaking work – however can you bear it? And Susan, your sister! I'm sorry, please forgive me, but oh! Heaven have mercy on them!'

Tears spilled down her cheeks, and she sank to her knees at the bedside.

Susan spoke quietly. 'I doubt if even this pitiful sight'd touch the hearts o' the Calthorpes, Sophy – neither the man who brought her to this, nor his mother who turned her out f'r what he did to her. They wouldn't even send f'r the doctor at the end, so my brother risked his life. They don't care.'

Sophia made an effort to bring her emotion under control, dismayed by the bitter condemnation in Susan's words and tone.

'Job is safe, dear Susan. It was so unfortunate that Mr Calthorpe is laid low with the fever, for he would have listened to Job, I'm sure.'

'Maybe, but that's no help to Polly now. No, Sophy, I ha' finished with that family, and with their name. Don't call me Calthorpe again, f'r I won't answer to it.'

'Susan, my dear –' Sophia rose and put her arms around the cold, unresponsive frame – 'your husband Edward had no part in this, and loves you dearly. For his sake you must remain Mrs Calthorpe.'

Susan gave her a heavy look. 'Edward is dead, Sophy. I've heard nothin' since the *Bucephalus* went down near three months ago. If he'd escaped

337

drownin', I'd ha' heard by now. I believe meself a widow, and people may call me—'

She stopped. Having renounced the name of Calthorpe, she had no good memories of being a Lucket girl. She turned to Parnham with a grim little smile.

'People may call me Madam Trotula if they want an answer!'

Susan wiped her eyes and could think of nothing more to say, while Charles Parnham kept his thoughts well hidden. He shared Susan's view about Edward's chances of survival. Many a life lost at sea went unrecorded, and families waited while hope ebbed away and time at last provided melancholy proof that a man would never return. Charles Parnham was willing to bide his time, but that time was not yet.

Sophia found time to keep her promise to Osmond Calthorpe on that fateful Saturday, and wrote him a short letter, sending it by carrier to Belhampton from where it travelled on the post-chaise to Winchester; by late afternoon he held it in his hand. Rising at once from the officers' dining table, he called for his horse and set off for Beversley, arriving at Miss Glover's door before dusk.

Susan lay in a deep, exhausted slumber, and did not hear the door knocker, nor the sound of voices as it opened to admit him. Sophia was not inclined to allow him access to the dead woman's room, for fear of an encounter with his sister-in-law.

'Only one minute, Cousin Sophy, and I swear I will not cause you trouble. Only let me look upon her for one last time.'

Their footsteps on the stairs were quiet enough; it

was the knock-knock-knock of the wooden peg that penetrated Susan's consciousness, like the sinister approach of some dreadful fiend. She moaned with fear, and in a waking dream she heard it coming nearer and nearer until it was on the landing, right outside the door.

'Dear Lord, have mercy! Polly, Polly!' she muttered, writhing under the bedcovers. Then came the whispers.

'Just for one minute, mind – this is against my better judgement – you must keep absolutely quiet, not a word to me or to – to her, do you understand?'

And the sound of a door opening quietly and closing again.

But when Osmond saw the tranquil faces of the mother and her babies – his own sons – he forgot his promise.

'My little Polly, oh my dear love, my sweet children. Oh, forgive me, my pretty, pretty Polly!'

'Hush, Osmond, hush, for heaven's sake! She has finished with the troubles and deceits of this world.'

'But how shall I live out the rest of my life, Sophy? She died alone and forsaken, without one last sight of me. Oh, my God, however shall I bear it?'

Knowing that Polly had not died alone, but unable to reassure him because of her solemn pledge to Henry, Sophia now begged him to leave.

'Come away, Osmond, you cannot stay here. Their souls are in God's keeping. Come away now, quickly – and be quiet.'

Susan was awake now. She heard the door open and got out of bed. As Sophia led Osmond from Polly's bedchamber, she opened her own door and stood before them.

'Susan!' Sophia instinctively tried to put herself

between them, but shrank back before the blazing hatred in the grey eyes that confronted her enemy. He trembled and drew back a pace, steadying himself against the banister rail.

Susan glared at the man like an avenging angel, and deliberately let her gaze drop to his wooden peg. As plainly as if she had spoken, he knew that she intended to make a grab at his stick and kick at the peg, sending him sprawling helplessly down the stairs. He cowered before her, and a full minute passed; the three of them stood unmoving as a tableau.

Then Sophia Glover summoned up all her spiritual strength.

'Let us pass, Susan,' she commanded.

The words seemed to come from a long way off, and Susan swayed slightly; a faintness came over her, saving Osmond from her vengeance. She closed her eyes and stood aside to let Sophia assist his downward progress, one step at a time, and uttered not a word.

She did not even spit.

Chapter 24

None of his family had ever seen Mr Calthorpe so angry. For the first time in her life Gertrude actually felt afraid of him, and deeply regretted her words on the night of the Lucket boy's dismissal from Bever House, though she tried to shift some of the blame on to Dr Gravett.

Mr Calthorpe's wrath was no less daunting for being delayed. Polly Lucket and her babies had been buried in Little St Giles' churchyard for a week before the master of Bever House even knew of the tragedy. Struck down by the same virulent strain of influenza that had depleted the House of Industry, he had been scarcely conscious of his surroundings for several days, while his wife and Mrs Ferris tiptoed around the sickroom. As he began to recover it was from the servants that he heard scraps of information, and gradually built up a picture of the sequence of events that were already the talk of Beversley; Job Lucket had not hesitated to tell his tale in the village.

When Osmond rode over from Winchester to visit his sick father, Calthorpe asked him point-blank if he had any news of the Lucket girl; after a brief hesitation he had broken down and disclosed that she had died in childbirth with twins.

Calthorpe then relentlessly dragged from his wife the story of Job Lucket's request and the response to it, after which he rebuked her more severely than at any previous time in their marriage. For once she had not answered back, but had lowered her eyes and trembled before him. She wept when he spoke of the dead babies as their grandsons, and Osmond admitted that he had seen them at Glover Cottage and known them for his own. He repeated Cousin Sophia's assertion that they had not been due to be born until mid-April, but that Polly had been very ill with something called the mother's malady.

Calthorpe turned his face away from his wife's laments and his son's regrets, and asked for Mr Turnbull to be sent for. He questioned the man very closely about the circumstances of Polly's death, and learned that she had died before giving birth; he shuddered at hearing of Dr Parnham's post-mortem removal of the twins.

'It was unfortunate that you were laid low with the fever at the time, sir,' ventured the apothecary.

'That is an understatement of the case, Turnbull. My wife accuses the rector of turning the boy from the door while *he* insists that he was protecting her. No doubt they were all in great danger from a poor boy in fear for his sister's life,' Calthorpe added with grim irony.

The apothecary did not reply, for he knew of the enormous indignation in Beversley. Gertrude Calthorpe's standing was at its lowest ebb, and so was the rector's. At Great St Giles worshippers talked or snored their way through the sermons in a way that would have been unthinkable a couple of years previously. Farm workers passed by the Calthorpe ladies and their florid cleric without so much as touching their forelocks, and the womenfolk had forgotten how to curtsy, except when they met Miss Glover.

'Has – er – Mrs Susan Calthorpe returned to the House of Industry, Turnbull?' asked Calthorpe.

'Yes, but only for a short period, sir, until Mrs Coulter has moved out of Glover Cottage. The poor woman is very infirm with the rheumaticks, and is going into one of the St Margaret's almshouses in Belhampton to end her days. Then Mrs – er – Susan will move in with Miss Glover and take up her duties as the licensed midwife for Beversley. Her remarkable skill has made her greatly respected, but she is still only one-and-twenty, and Miss Glover wishes her to live at the house for the time being . . .' Turnbull coughed; he wondered if Calthorpe knew that his daughter-in-law had forsworn his very name.

After Turnbull's departure the agent came in with the monthly accounts.

'Leave them on the desk, I'll look at them directly,' said Calthorpe listlessly, passing his hand over his eyes.

'Beggin' yer pardon, sir, there's been a return o' the payment made to Mrs Susan Calthorpe this month.'

'What? Did you not send it to her at the House of Industry?'

'Yes, sir, but she's sent it back with the carrier, and there's a letter. I have it here, sir.'

The note was brief.

Mr Calthorpe,
    Here is yr Money returned. I have no need of Money from you, & sever all connexion with every Body bearing the name of Calthorpe which I no longer own.

There was no signature.

Calthorpe's head drooped back against the carved wood of his chair. The total rejection contained in the

343

few written words was more painful than he could have imagined, and the worst part was that he felt her contempt was justified. As Edward's wife she, and her sister, had been cruelly ill-used.

Edward. His son who had loved her so dearly. Oh, if Edward might return home alive and sound in body and mind, this enmity would surely be ended! Mrs Susan Calthorpe would be received at Bever House with all the status and privileges due to the wife of his son. But was there any hope left? How many months would have to pass, the father asked himself, before he must admit that Edward was indeed dead? In his weakened condition he uttered his son's name aloud, and helpless tears filled his eyes.

Susan could not believe that her year of service at the House of Industry was completed, and she made her farewells with very mixed feelings. While Mrs Croker sobbed dolefully and Mag snivelled, it was the children who chiefly touched her heart.

'I know ye'll go on bein' good, just as ye've been f'r me, children, and don't forget what ye've learned,' she told them. 'I'll come over to see ye when I can—'

She broke off, biting her lip and miserably aware that she was forsaking them. She could hardly bear to look at Toby's thin little upturned face, streaked with tears.

Charles Parnham had once again to hide his true feelings and assume a jocular manner.

'Come, come, Madam Trotula, this is the day of your release! Is it really a year since you entered these hospitable walls?'

'Yes, it is, Dr Parnham, and ye never thought I'd last a week!' she retorted. 'Ye challenged me, and I accepted – and here I still am!'

344

'Ah, yes, my Trotula, I misjudged you, but I did a great service to this place thereby,' he answered, thinking how dull and dreary his visits to the House would be without her. Aloud he promised to look in on the orphans whenever he attended for a confinement, and to keep her informed about them.

At Glover Cottage Susan continued to speak of the children she had left behind, and how she felt she had betrayed them.

'Who ha' they got now, Sophy? Who can they turn to?' she asked in real distress. 'Mrs Croker doesn't really care about them, and besides, she's a drinker. And there's poor Mag, a workhouse orphan herself, put upon and worked like a donkey – nobody to encourage her and show some interest in her – and most o' the paupers can scarcely look after themselves, let alone care about the children growing up in such a place.'

Sophia noted but did not remark that Susan made no mention of her mother, poor Mad Doll.

'Oh, Sophy, when I think o' Toby's face lookin' up at me, I know he'll haunt my dreams, poor little soul!'

Sophia could only hope that Susan would soon be summoned to a birthing to divert her thoughts, but meanwhile she racked her brains to think of a suitable woman who might be prepared to visit the orphans and even give them some lessons.

'Suppose I were to call on the rector's niece,' she wondered aloud. Miss Gravett was a very upright lady of uncertain age who always wore black and was said to watch every mouthful that Dr Gravett ate; she poured out a measured amount of wine for him and then sent the bottle away.

345

'After all, the rector is on the Board of Guardians,' Sophia pointed out.

'For all they ever see of him,' said Susan drily.

Miss Gravett received Lord de Bever's grand-daughter courteously enough, but did not linger over formalities. On hearing her visitor's errand, she nodded.

'As it happens, Miss Glover, I *have* considered doing some useful parish work – only I was thinking of something here in Beversley, not five miles away from it. Anyway, what is to prevent those two Calthorpe daughters from driving their gig over there? I dare say they can get themselves to Belhampton to buy dress material and hats.'

Such refreshing directness appealed to Miss Glover, and she chose her next words carefully.

'What an excellent idea, Miss Gravett! Perhaps you could call at Bever House and put it to the young ladies that their talents might be used to improve the lives of those poor children? Though they may not take to the idea on a first hearing, Miss Gravett,' she added hastily. 'It has probably never been suggested to them before. A second or even a third reminder might be needed.'

Miss Gravett clearly understood, for she nodded knowingly, and Sophia returned to Glover Cottage feeling reasonably hopeful.

'I've done what I can, *Madam Trotula*, and Miss Gravett has gone to stir their consciences,' she reported, smiling.

'I'm sure I wish good luck to her,' said Susan shortly, going to fetch her midwifery bag from its cupboard. 'I ha' been called to the parsonage, Sophy. Lizzie Smart's mother thinks she may be in early

346

travail. I should say Mrs Decker,' she corrected herself.

Sophia sighed and shook her head. 'Ah, yes, poor Mrs Decker. Mrs Coulter thought she'd be delivered before now.'

Lizzie Smart's hasty marriage to a corporal home on leave had left her expecting a child, and the next she heard was that Decker had been killed at King's Mountain in North Carolina, yet another defeat for Lord Cornwallis's depleted army. Lizzie had no home but the barely furnished parsonage in which she had been brought up, and no support but what her parents could offer.

Sophia stood at the gate and waved as the new midwife went off in her pony-trap. Devoted as Miss Glover had been to Mrs Coulter, she was thankful for Susan's youth and energy, as well as the friendship of one she had come to love and appreciate through their shared experiences. And yet there were certain closed doors, words unsaid and thoughts unshared: Susan never spoke of Edward, and rarely mentioned Polly. Sophia respected her friend's private grief, and did not intrude upon it; she was ready to listen when Susan was ready to confide, and not before.

Yet it was difficult not to show her own eager joy when there was news from Henry. And such news! She now took his letter from her bodice and reread it for the twentieth time.

'I dare to hope that I may look upon yr sweet face in a short while,' he had written. On his return from the latest Atlantic crossing on a supply ship he was to join a major assault on the French and Spanish blockade of the West Indies, which also looked like being lost to the new American colonies.

347

I will sail in the *Minotaur*, one of a Fleet headed by Admiral Rodney's flagship *Formidable*, but before setting out on this great Mission I shall be granted at least a week of Shore leave.

Depend upon it, dearest Love of my Life, I shall stand at yr Door one Summer day, happier than any Man alive.

Sophia kissed the letter and pressed it to her heart, picturing the moment when she would open her door and see Henry on the step, waiting to gather her into his arms. How different it would be from his last brief visit! Not that she had ever complained of the way his precious time had been spent then: she piously believed that he had been sent by the Almighty to comfort Polly Lucket's last hours, and not even his parents had known of that one night in Glover Cottage. But on his next homecoming they would have days to spend together, she thought joyfully, and that would be their reward.

Henry did not think the war would last longer than another year at most, and then they would be married and begin their new life together. A permanent home would then need to be found for Susan, and Sophia had a plan to put before the squire and rector about raising a subscription from the villagers to purchase a suitable dwelling for the Beversley midwife. Mr Calthorpe would have to be consulted, and Miss Glover was fairly sure that her cousin would welcome the proposal, even if he did not want his name to appear among the subscribers.

Flushed and triumphant, Susan placed the squalling bundle in the mother's outstretched arms.

'There ye are, Lizzie, a fine big girl – another

348

granddaughter for you, Mrs Smart – an' a playmate f'r Mr Simon's little girl in another couple o' years!'

'Thank God,' murmured Mrs Betsey Smart, who had stayed beside her daughter throughout her pains. 'I'd better go an' tell Nathaniel she's delivered, thanks to – er . . .'

'Call me Susan, f'r so ye knew me as a child at the Ash-Pits,' said the midwife. 'Parson Smart was the best friend the Luckets ever had in that hard winter. We might all ha' perished o' hunger if he hadn't gone begging Mrs Bennett to share her bread.'

'Oh, ay, he used to go out beggin' fur other children while ours ha' to make do on soup an' taters, many's the time,' Betsey Smart sniffed, and Susan heard the lingering resentment in her voice. She wished that she had not spoken, and wondered how many times poor Nat Smart had bowed his thinning head before the storm of his wife's scoldings. Betsey's life had been one long struggle to bring up a large family on the wretchedly low stipend her husband had been paid by the rector: trying to make do on less than enough food or fuel, and grateful for such gifts as might turn up on the doorstep of the parsonage.

When Betsey returned to the birth-chamber, Susan had finished putting in four stitches where she had made a cut to ease the head through; Lizzie had pushed for two hours, and the baby was large, being overdue. Miss Glover had sent a packet of tea to refresh them all after the birth, and having drank hers, Susan took her leave of Lizzie and her mother, and went down to the parson's little study. She found him on his knees by his rickety desk, and at once begged his pardon for interrupting his prayers.

His knee-joints creaked as he rose and held out his hands to her.

'God bless you, my child,' he said shakily. 'I was but offering thanks that my poor widowed Elizabeth is delivered of a healthy daughter, thanks to your skill and good sense.'

'Oh, Mr Smart, I'm that thankful that y'r prayers ha' been answered!' Susan's own emotions threatened to overwhelm her when she saw how worn he looked, his sunken cheeks and red-rimmed eyes reflecting a life spent trying to serve his flock and bear their burdens whilst living on the poverty line with a cross wife. And now Lizzie had added another helpless dependant to the family, just as the older members were leaving the nest. Yet he smiled as he clasped her hands in both of his.

'You always were a bright child, Susan, a clever little girl in spite of—'

'Dear Parson Smart, I wouldn't be here today to deliver y'r daughter if 'twasn't f'r what ye did f'r us Luckets,' Susan broke in with equal fervour. 'We'd ha' starved to death like Goody Firkin. And if I didn't thank ye then, let me thank ye now, sir!'

And on an impulse she curtsied low before him and kissed his hand, at which he looked so thunderstruck that she could have laughed. Poor, threadbare Parson Smart with his chesty cough and the dewdrop that forever hung from his nose, what an unrecognised saint! Susan was grateful to the Almighty for the chance to repay his kindness all those years ago.

Widow Gibson was hovering in Mill Lane when Susan emerged from the parsonage.

'Lucky fur 'ee Lizzie Smart was easy birthin', Dame Trot!' she grinned, and Susan did not miss the mockery. 'No need to send fur yer man-midwife wi' un's knives an' forks!'

Susan flushed, well aware that the old handy-woman knew her history from before birth, and for all her makeshift ways had been good to the Luckets in bad times.

'Yes, I was lucky, Mrs Gibson,' she agreed. ''Twas a hard pushing f'r Mrs Decker, and a fair-sized babe – but she's young an' strong, and ha' good parents to take care o' her.'

'Ay, she be luckier than many. Oi tells 'ee, young Dame Trot,' went on the old woman, leaning confidentially towards Susan with onion-scented breath, 'there'll be work enough fur 'ee an' me both if this war goes on much longer. We'll reap a fine crop o' bastards afore it be ended!' She laughed, showing the gaps in her teeth. 'Oh, ay! We'll get more'n our share o' night-sittin'!'

Susan shrugged, conscious of the contrast they must present to an observer, she in her neat dark blue gown with shawl and bonnet, carrying her equipment in a straw bag, while the other woman's stained calico apron was permanently tied around her thick skirt, like the kerchief she always wore wrapped round her head with the ends tucked in at the nape of her grimy neck.

Yet Susan remembered that this woman often worked in co-operation with Parson Smart, treating common ailments and injuries in animals as well as the Beversley poor. Once again she acted on impulse and spoke in a friendly, almost conspiratorial manner.

'I tell ye what, Mrs Gibson – two heads are wiser than one when there's trouble wi' a birthin'. If I was ever to ask y'r advice, I hope ye wouldn't take it amiss?'

The handywoman beamed. 'Lord, no, Dame Trot – 'ee can send fur me at any time!'

351

'That's good to know, Mrs Gibson. And likewise, if ye ever need another pair o' hands, ye can call on me wi' no loss o' face. 'Tis only common sense!'

She got up into the pony-trap, and drove back to Glover Cottage well satisfied. An ally is of far more use than a rival, and Susan knew that she still needed to build up a reputation in the village after a year away from it. Some of Mrs Calthorpe's friends from Belhampton and Pulhurst had mockingly referred to *Madam Trotula*, and unknowingly did her a favour, because the village had quickly adopted the title, and she was now Madam Trotula to almost everybody. It amused Sophia, who could not resist some gentle teasing. 'What do you suggest, Madam Trotula?' she would ask on all sorts of matters unrelated to midwifery, but Susan was secretly gratified by the name. It had a ring to it, as well as reminding her of Charles Parnham's friendship; he was second only to Sophia in her affections, for she knew that those two had made her what she now was, a respected practitioner of her craft. The once scornful disparagement of her youth and inexperience was now all but silenced. With Miss Glover as her patroness and Dr Parnham as her champion – not to mention such Beversley notables as Mr Turnbull and Mrs Bennett singing her praises – she had no need of condescension from local gentry.

However, there was no shortage of interesting gossip at Bever House tea-parties. Miss Gravett, a prudent spinster who could have enjoyed the patronage of Bever House with all its social advantages, had chosen instead to visit the House of Industry and busy herself with teaching the half-witted children their letters, while the poor rector had to make do with cold boiled mutton and a lonely fireside. Not only that, but the lady had actually visited the Misses Calthorpe and – incredible though it seemed – had invited them to join her in this endeavour, saying that it would be useful and rewarding work for them. Of course she had been cold-shouldered, but a week later she had called again and repeated her invitation. Mrs Calthorpe wondered if the lady could be going through a certain difficult time of life: it was known to unbalance some women.

But then had come the real marvel: the sight of the elder Miss Calthorpe driving over to the House of Industry in the rectory phaeton with Miss Gravett, going to visit the orphans and organise regular reading lessons – and to introduce them to the mysteries of addition and subtraction as well.

Sophia was so delighted with this news that she called on Miss Gravett to congratulate her on her success, and to admit that she had had no great hopes of either of the Calthorpe daughters.

'Ah, but you see, Miss Glover, I understand that Miss Selina suffered a – a disappointment a few years ago, when a faithless young man left her for another. I convinced her that the best way to forget that kind of thing is to throw herself into some kind of good work for the less fortunate.'

Sophia could think of no suitable reply to this.

'I explained that I was in a position to give advice to her on the matter,' went on the black-clad lady with a sigh. 'And I'm very happy to say, Miss Glover, that she is becoming a much more thoughtful girl, far more agreeable than that silly sister of hers and her friend Miss Hansford. Forgive me, Miss Glover, but I'm known for speaking as I find.'

Once she got over the shock, Sophia was delighted

353

to hear of Selina's new interest, and thought it a good time to visit Mr Calthorpe to begin discussing the purchase of a dwelling for the Beversley midwife, by public subscription. It had to be done quietly, without Susan finding out, and Sophia looked forward to presenting her friend with a *fait accompli* in due course.

The summer months passed. Osmond Calthorpe was spared from his duties at the training depot, and returned home to help his father run the estate. Miss Glover was just beginning to be anxious that First Lieutenant Hansford had not yet appeared, when in the last week of July he fulfilled his promise and turned up on her doorstep, his face older and more weatherbeaten, his war-weary eyes fixed on the woman he loved and longed for.

Susan tactfully found herself more often out than in during those all-too-brief sunny days when Henry could hardly bear to let his adored Sophy out of his sight, though of course his parents, sister and brother also lay claim to his precious time. He slept at the farmhouse, but the greater part of each day was spent at Glover Cottage, walking out with Sophia in the noon sunshine, talking with her in the garden and reaching out to take her hand as evening shadows gathered.

But Henry had again been disappointed in his hopes of a wedding. Sophia continued to insist that they wait until the war was over.

'You say that it cannot be much longer, Henry, another year at most.'

'But for a man on active service, each day is an eternity, Sophy. If I could go back to this stupid, wasteful war knowing that you were my wife—'

354

'Henry, when I become your wife, I don't ever want to part with you again. We shall begin our life together, and stay together – no more partings!'

He sighed and looked earnestly into her eyes, wondering if he might express to her in words the hunger of his body. Sophia was such a gentlewoman, so devout in faith, so modest in speech and manners; and yet he wanted to tell her how deep was his desire for her.

'Dearest Sophy, I am but a man as other men are, and I long to hold you in my arms as my wife, as part of my own flesh. Forgive me for even speaking of it, but you surely must have the same natural longings,' he pleaded, hoping that she would not think the less of him.

She did not. 'Yes, I long for the consummation of our love in marriage just as much as you do, Henry,' she told him in a low voice, her blue eyes downcast. 'And that is all the more reason why I say we must wait until we are free to claim what we long for. I shall bear your children, Henry, but not until we can be together to provide a proper home for them.'

She paused, thinking of Susan's important work as a midwife, and how it would have been curtailed if she had been left with a child. She thought of poor Lizzie Decker and her baby daughter, Kitty, alone and unsupported apart from what the impoverished Smarts could offer her.

'No, dearest Henry, we must be patient and wait a little longer, until the day when you come home for good. Then we may consider our own personal happiness. To rush into a hasty wedding now would be selfish. Can you not understand what I mean?'

Henry knew that there would be no changing of her mind; a woman such as Sophia Glover followed

355

what she saw as duty rather than her own desires, or his. So he kissed her again and said yes, he understood, though he could not be glad.

And he was rewarded by her next words.

'The last time we met, Henry, we passed a night together in this cottage, watching by the bedside of Polly Lucket. I shall never forget the sacrifice you made then, the hours you sat with her, comforting her in her last journey. I looked at you then, Henry, and if it was possible to love you even more than before . . . I shall remember that night all my life.'

With such reassurance, Henry vowed that he would not allow his spirits to be dampened by the postponement of bliss or by the sad changes he found in Beversley: Osmond hobbling around on his peg leg, his face hard and deeply lined; Edward's wife so vengeful against the Calthorpes that she called herself some strange outlandish name rather than use her husband's. Poor Edward! How he had worshipped her and defied his family to marry her on that three-week leave; it seemed much longer than a year ago, and the war was getting nowhere. The British forces were now split and strung out from New York to Charlestown, attacked by combined American and French troops under General Washington, and hampered by disagreements between Lord Cornwallis and General Clinton.

'The sooner a truce is declared, the sooner the farce can be ended, and our men brought home,' Henry said to Sophia one evening as they sat in the twilight.

'And the sooner we shall be married, Henry.'

They exchanged loving smiles, and he continued somewhat hesitantly, 'And now my young sister Rosa tells me that she has hopes of marrying Osmond Calthorpe, if you please.'

Sophia thought at once of Polly. And of Susan.

'Has Rosa spoken of this to your parents, Henry?'

'No, no, there is nothing to tell as yet, for he has not given her any real sign that he returns her affections. She thinks he's grown more thoughtful since that shocking business of poor Polly Lucket – and now that she's gone, Rosa thinks he seems to be ready to settle down and look after the estate, just as his father always wanted him to.'

And Rosa sees herself as mistress of Bever House, thought Sophia.

'Has she considered what it might be like married to a cripple, Henry? Osmond can be foul-tempered when that leg-stump pains him. He would not be an easy man to have for a husband.'

'I'm not sure, my love. If he really intends to be master of Bever House one day, he'll need a wife! And who would be a better choice? A girl from an old local family, acceptable to his parents, not too young or too old, someone with pretty manners, respectful to his mother, friendly with his sisters. A girl who adores him. Does not my sister fit the requirements?'

'I think that Rosa is looking too far ahead, Henry,' Sophia answered, wondering what Susan's reaction would be if an announcement was made. Henry caught her mood.

'Then we won't speak of it, darling Sophy. Kiss me instead!'

When Susan returned from a birthing that night after dark, she stopped short as she entered the door and saw two figures outlined against the uncurtained window of the parlour, unaware of her or of anything but each other. Sophia's arms were around Henry's neck, her head lying on his shoulder, her face hidden. His head was bent over hers, and as his

357

lips brushed the smooth hair, his hands slid down the length of her back, coming to rest upon her buttocks in a husbandly gesture of possession. He whispered something, and Sophia's arms tightened: she raised her head and looked up into his face, offering her soft mouth for his kiss – a long, long kiss that held all the yearning of their hearts, all the desire of their bodies, one for the other.

Susan recollected herself and proceeded quietly up the stairs, feeling that her own deep sorrow had no place in the vicinity of the lovers. It was not that she was envious of their happiness in each other – quite the contrary, she desired that Sophia be happy – and that meant Henry too. No, it was the glimpse of a deep bond of love that held no fear, a love that she had never known, had never given to Edward, her husband for whom hope was now virtually gone. He had loved her with a good man's love, as Henry loved Sophia – and she had been unable to return it in the natural way. When she remembered the bewilderment in his eyes at her strange, unwifely behaviour, it was like a sword-thrust in her heart. She now bitterly regretted agreeing to the marriage.

'Edward, dearest o' men, if only I'd followed Sophy's example, and waited, ye wouldn't ha' been disappointed in me,' she wept in the silence of her room – for this was her own secret remorse that she could not share with any other soul on earth.

As summer gave place to autumn and autumn to winter, the news from across the Atlantic worsened with the weather, culminating with the fall of Yorktown at the end of November. Not until a month later did the *Hampshire Chronicle* publish the details of Lord Cornwallis's ignominious surrender to

Washington with seven thousand men. Shocked readers learned that sixty cannon had been captured by the Americans and French.

At home the decline of the year saw a deepening of rural poverty as men were lost to the land and food prices rose with taxes. Beversley was not a happy place, and there seemed to be no good news to raise the people's spirits in the depth of winter.

And at Christmas the whole of Beversley was shocked and grieved by the sudden death of Parson Smart on the feast of St Stephen, after taking the Christmas services at Little St Giles. Years of overwork and poor nourishment rendered him easy prey to the lung inflammation that claimed him at fifty-four, and too late was his true goodness acknowledged and mourned.

'Him was born unlucky, was poor Nat Smart,' wept Widow Gibson, while Dr Gravett was heard to observe irritably that the parson could hardly have chosen a more inconvenient time to die.

Chapter 25

The humiliation of the Yorktown defeat cast a gloom over the new year, and Squire Hansford openly declared himself in favour of granting the colonies their independence immediately.

'The bloodshed has gone on long enough,' he emphatically told his neighbours over a festive dinner at Bever House.

There was an awkward silence. Such words would have been considered treasonable a few years earlier, and the rector frowned into his glass and muttered about 'those who would parley with the American traitors'.

'Easy enough for you to talk, Gravett, with no sons in constant danger of death or crippling,' retorted the squire loudly. 'Calthorpe here has sacrificed a son, and Osmond . . .' He glanced towards the heir to Bever House, who had drunk the greater part of a full bottle of port during dinner, and continued, 'All I want is to see Henry come safely home to us. I'm not willing to give up my son for a lost cause.'

Mrs Hansford hastily turned the conversation to other matters. 'I hear that May Cottage will be going on the market soon,' she remarked, and went on to explain that the widow who had leased Mrs Coulter's former home was planning to get married again to a Belhampton tailor.

Mr Calthorpe immediately thought of the sub-scription fund being raised by his cousin Miss

Glover, and made a silent mental note to mention May Cottage to her as a possible home for his daughter-in-law, the Beversley midwife.

'What is happening about the parsonage?' Mrs Calthorpe asked the rector, who frowned in irritation.

'As soon as I have found a suitable incumbent to take Smart's place, the widow must find somewhere other than church property for herself and her hangers-on, madam. There's that eldest son, the one who married the Bennett girl – *he* should shoulder responsibility for his mother. And the girl with the baby should get herself work to support it.'

Miss Selina ventured to remark that Mrs Decker might find it difficult to get employment with such a young child, but her mother frowned warningly and said that the Widow Smart could surely take care of her grandchild. What else had she to do?

Spring brought more work for the midwife, as Widow Gibson had forecast, and there were occasions when Madam Trotula's territory overlapped with the handywoman's.

'Oi reckons there'll be trouble down at Potter's when that poor Jinny's brought to bed, wi' not a body to boil a pan o' watter fur her!'

Susan stiffened at the mention of her mother's people. Her knowledge of them was sketchy, and she had not heard of anybody called Jinny.

'Where does she live, Mrs Gibson?'

'Down End – that's under Fox Hill, other side o' Foxholes Wood. There be a father an' a couple o' sons scratchin' a livin' out o' a poor bit o' land wi' a pig an' a goat, but no wumman to take care o' Jinny an' her babby, come May or June. Lily Potter died when the gal was but ten or so.'

Susan felt a curious apprehension, and dared not ask the question that the artful old woman was waiting for.

'And will you be attending this Jinny, Mrs Gibson?'

'If them sends fur me, but her'd be better off in the work'us if 'ee could get her in, Dame Trot.'

Susan hesitated. This girl could be a cousin of hers. Usually she avoided intruding on the handy-woman's rough-and-ready services to the poor of Lower Beversley and outlying areas, but Mrs Gibson was clearly asking for her help.

'I'll speak wi' Mrs Croker, and maybe go and see this girl myself,' she said. 'Good day to ye, Mrs Gibson.'

On a visit to the Widow Smart, she casually asked her what she knew about the Potters of Down End.

'They're low, unchristian folks, and Jinny's half-witted, by what I've heard,' replied Betsey with distaste. ''Tis but a tumbledown place, and the men be drinkers. I wouldn't go anywhere near them,' she added firmly.

Try as she might, Susan could not get the thought of Jinny out of her head, and on a blowy April afternoon she reluctantly set out in the pony-trap to seek her out, taking the lane that ran to the south-east along the edge of Foxholes Wood; its banks were bright with tumbling carpets of bluebells, and the pale stars of late primroses still nestled in sheltered hollows, though Susan saw little of them as the trap jolted along the narrow lane and plunged down a steep descent to a stretch of rough common land. Unkempt hedges and broken fences signalled a settlement beyond the reach of parish tithes or estate rents, and when she came to a crooked signpost

362

Susan followed Mrs Gibson's directions and turned the pony down a stony track that continued for a lurching half-mile or so to a clearing. Half a dozen forlorn hens scratched at the sparse grass, and a huge black dog growled and bared yellow teeth at Brownie. Susan reined in beside a squat, one-roomed dwelling with smoke blowing out of a hole in the thatch, and looked around with a sinking heart, unwilling to face the dog.

A sullen-faced girl appeared in the doorway. Her hair was tied up in a frayed scarf, and her ragged gown was pulled tightly over the bulge below her bodice. Susan judged her to be about eight months gone with child, so this must be Jinny. She smiled.

'Good day to 'ee, Jinny!' she called, reverting to the broad speech of her childhood. 'I be come a-visitin', so will ye chain up that brute?'

The girl's button eyes narrowed, and she did not reply.

'Call me Sukey – my ma was a Potter, so maybe we be cousins, Jinny. Be it safe f'r me to get down an' talk wi' ye?'

The girl gave the animal a vicious cuff, and tied it to a fence-post with a piece of rope. Susan stepped down from the trap and pointed towards the door, at which the girl turned and went inside. Susan took a deep breath and followed her.

The dark, barely furnished room reminded her at once of the Ash-Pits, except that it was smaller. A low fire burned on bricks in the centre, the smoke rising to a hole directly above; a black pot simmered on it with a stew of root vegetables and some rank flesh that could have been any animal or bird. Straw was scattered thinly over the earth floor, and chickens ran

363

in and out. A collection of blankets and skins in the corners showed where the occupants slept.

Susan's nostrils caught the remembered sour smell of poverty, a dire combination of want and ignorance. Her spirits fell even lower, but she hid her dismay and spoke in a friendly way.

'So ye all live here, Jinny, in this little house?'

'Oh, ah, Oi an' me Dad an' Rob an' Joey. Be 'ee come to take Oi away from uns?' asked the girl with a sudden spark of interest – was it hope? – in her dull button eyes.

Susan's mouth hardened in anger at the plight of this motherless girl who had no sweetening or softening influence in her life. How wicked were the ways of men, to use her so, with no thought of the consequences!

'Ye know that ye got a baby growin' in there, Jinny?' Susan laid her hand upon the bulge, and Jinny nodded, laying her own begrimed hand over her belly.

'Oh, ah, Oi feels it movin', Oi do. Be 'ee come to take Oi away from uns?' she asked again.

'This is no place to birth a baby, Jinny, but I'll have to talk to some people about you.' Susan saw no alternative but to beg Mrs Croker to take Jinny into the House for her confinement and for a few weeks following the birth.

At that moment heavy footsteps were heard in the yard, and the menacing outline of a man's shape filled the doorway, deepening the dimness of the room. A tremor ran down Susan's spine, and she held her breath, every muscle tensed for flight.

'Who be there, Jinny?' asked a gruffly suspicious voice. 'That ol' widder come nosin' agin?'

Susan spoke up indignantly. 'I'm the Beversley

midwife, an' I'll thank ye to get out o' the light.'

He stepped back a pace in surprise. 'Oh, ah. Her ain't needin' no midwife, not yet,' he growled, his black-rimmed eyes staring at Susan in no friendly manner. Jinny gaped from one to the other, and Susan saw no sign of caring, even of a rough kind, between the surly man and the slow-witted girl. A family of foxes might have shown more natural affection, she thought, and knew that she had to get out of this hovel without delay. She leaned towards Jinny, and the girl flinched as if expecting a blow.

'I'll be back again soon, Jinny, to take ye to the House o' Industry at Belhampton to birth y'r baby.'

'Oh, ah,' muttered the man with a nod, while Jinny simply stared after Susan as she walked out to the pony-trap, giving the tied dog a wide berth.

Mrs Croker knew that if she refused to admit Jinny, Mrs Susan would appeal to Dr Parnham, who had never been known to refuse her anything, so she gave grudging assent.

The following week Susan and a highly delighted Widow Gibson arrived one morning at Down End on the carrier's cart to remove Jinny from her life of degradation to the different privations of the workhouse. The girl's father and one of the brothers were digging over a patch of ground when they drew up, and Susan knew she had been right to hire the carrier. Young Dick was now a well-grown man, and he and the sharp-tongued handywoman were a match for any opposition. When Jinny appeared at the door she was ordered to climb up on the cart, assisted by the two women while Dick gave her a discreet push from behind. The furious barking of the dog prevented any objections from being heard, and in fact no attempt was made to stop the departure of the heavily pregnant girl. Susan breathed a sigh of relief as Dick cracked the whip and they moved off, Jinny grinning happily at her abduction. Widow Gibson turned and waved derisively at the two men, who stood glowering in the yard.

'This be as good as ridin' in the Bever carriage, eh, Jinny?' she chuckled, pleased that young Dame Trot had asked for her assistance. She had not relished the idea of delivering the girl in that reeking hovel, but a word in Dame Trot's ear had worked wonders.

'Good heavens, is the man drunk?' asked Mrs Bryers the schoolmistress when she saw Dick the carrier standing up on his cart in the main street and yelling his news like the Belhampton town-crier. A crowd rapidly gathered around him: doors opened and aproned figures appeared from the bakehouse and chandlery. Job Lucket came running from the forge, sent to find out the cause of the uproar. Not only the tradespeople were drawn to the scene: Miss Glover came hurrying out of her cottage with the eager step of a young maidservant, and when she heard Dick's message she astonished Mrs Bryers by pulling the lace cap from her head and throwing it up into the air!

It was Dick's moment of glory, the day he brought the news from Belhampton of the great sea victory that had taken place on the twelfth of April in the West Indies, when Admiral Rodney had beaten the French at what came to be known as the Battle of the Saints.

'Aye, 'tis right, Miss Glover, Rodney be the hero o' the day, an' like to be made a duke or a baron or summat. He captured the pride o' the French fleet, an' chased 'em halfway back. Gave 'em a kick up the arse, he did, beggin' yer pardon!'

Beversley rejoiced with the whole country at this successful naval battle against the French and Spanish, breaking up the blockade of the islands. Rodney's flagship *Formidable* had taken the *Ville de Paris* with Admiral de Grasse and his crew, as well as four other enemy ships, and one had been sunk. No British ships had been lost. The church bells of Great St Giles were rung and services of thanksgiving were held to mark the sea victory after a long series of defeats on land.

'This proves the supremacy of our British navy!' crowed Dr Gravett from the pulpit, though at Bever House the reaction was more muted, remembering the loss of Edward. At the Hansfords' there was joy in which Sophia shared as they eagerly awaited Henry's triumphant return on the *Minotaur*.

''Twill be a great face-saver, Calthorpe, when the peace treaty is signed,' the squire quietly confided to his neighbour, adding drily that the only lasting importance of the Battle of the Saints would be the preservation of Britain's lucrative sugar and rum interests in the West Indies.

At Glover Cottage Sophia held a little celebratory tea-party, and while the ladies were congratulating their hostess and Mrs Hansford on the happy news, Susan entered and at once saw to her dismay that Selina Calthorpe was in the company. She was the only member of her family present, but Susan felt the familiar wave of hostility and took a seat as far away from her as she could. To everybody's surprise the elder Calthorpe daughter had persevered in visiting the workhouse orphans, and had become quite friendly with Miss Gravett, with whom she was now eagerly conversing.

'Does anybody know who will be the next tenant of May Cottage, now that the widow has remarried?' asked the rector's niece.

Apparently nobody did, and Miss Glover hugged her secret knowledge to herself. The subscription fund had exceeded all expectations, and she was awaiting the revised title deeds of May Cottage from her London lawyers.

Suddenly without warning Miss Calthorpe rose and came over to speak to Susan.

'Your former pupils all talk of you often, Madam Trotula, and Toby misses you most of all,' she said politely, as if they were social acquaintances rather than estranged sisters-in-law.

This is Edward's sister, thought Susan – and he'd have approved of what she's doing, whatever her reason for taking up good works; so she inclined her head and gravely asked a few questions about Jemmy and Nan and the others. It cost her an effort, however; she could not overcome her resentment that this Calthorpe girl had taken over *her* children, though she knew this to be unreasonable of her.

'Oh, and by the way, Madam Trotula,' went on Miss Calthorpe hesitantly, as she saw Susan getting up to leave, 'there is a dispute at the House of Industry over one of the female inmates, a poor creature you brought in from Down End.'

Susan was alert at once. 'Jinny Potter? What kind o' dispute? Is she delivered?'

'Yes, she had a boy in the first week of May, an ill-favoured little monkey, according to that dreadful Mrs Croker. She wants to send Jinny home with it, but the girl says she will not go.'

'Jinny *can't* go back to that place – never!' Susan

368

shook her head vehemently, and a few ladies' heads turned in her direction. 'I'd hoped Mrs Croker could ha' found work f'r her in the House, doing the same mean work such as Mag does.'

'But, Madam Trotula, how could the girl possibly be better off in the poorhouse than living at home with her own people?' asked Selina Calthorpe, genuinely puzzled.

'Oh, don't speak o' it!' cried Susan with a rush of impatience as she thought how far removed these women's lives were from the likes of Jinny, helpless victim of a vileness that would cause them to faint clean away if they were told of it.

She got up. 'I'll ha' to go and see the Croker woman and beg on poor Jinny's behalf.'

She took an abrupt leave, and Miss Gravett observed to Miss Calthorpe that she couldn't see the Widow Croker agreeing to keep Jinny and her little monkey at the House for much longer.

'But the stupid cow be neither use nor ornament, mistress! Her ain't never seen mop nor broom, nor knows what to do wi' 'em. Her eats like a pig an' lifts her skirt to piss in the yard, never mind who be watchin'. Even that fool Mag ha' got more sense an' looks arter that snufflin' monkey better'n her!'

'But, Mrs Croker, if ye could just see y'r way to keeping her here f'r another week or two—' began Susan, but the woman was adamant.

'An' how be Oi to provide bed an' board fur her an' that monkey, out o' what Oi gits from them Guardians?'

'Oh, in God's name show some pity, widow, f'r a girl who prefers the workhouse to – to the hell she went through at Down End!' cried Susan, unable to

369

restrain herself. 'Just think, a girl growin' up wi' no mother, no woman to teach her better ways, nobody but men o' the lowest sort, who—'

She broke off sharply, and Mrs Croker's piggy eyes narrowed.

'Oh, ah? And what'd these men o' the lowest sort do to make her life such hell?' she asked with a sarcastic familiarity that made Susan's scalp prickle. 'What'd they do then, eh?'

She waited for an answer, but Susan could not possibly tell her the truth about Jinny's loveless life. She remembered what she had written to Miss Glover years ago, when begging her to remove Polly from the lurking danger of the Ash-Pits.

'She got beaten, widow, especially when they were drunk,' she answered. ''Tis the same f'r many a poor woman. She can't go back to that kind o' life wi' a helpless baby, or they'll both be at the mercy o' the brutes. Have some pity, widow!'

Mrs Croker remained unmoved. 'An' how do 'ee know her's tellin' the truth? Her ain't got that down-trodden look o' a wumman who gets beaten reg'lar. An' by the way, mistress, seein' as 'ee knows so much, do 'ee know who fathered the babby on her? *Do* 'ee?'

Susan went very pale and shook her head. She swallowed, took a deep breath and replied as calmly as she could.

'She can't go back there, Mrs Croker. If you could but keep her and the baby here f'r another week, I'll do my best to find somewhere else f'r her to go.'

They stood in the passage facing each other; behind Susan stood Jinny, and beside her was Mag, holding the Little Monkey, which was all the name Jinny's baby seemed to have.

370

This was the scene that met Charles Parnham when he strode in through the open front door. His eyes had brightened when he saw the pony-trap, for he had been trying to think of an excuse to ride over to Beversley – and now here she was!

'Ah, signora, you have found your way here again at last. How do you—'

He stopped short when he saw her face.

Mrs Croker curtsied. 'Good day to 'ee, sir,' she said obsequiously.

Susan said nothing, and until he could speak with her alone he decided to be jocular. 'Come, come, ladies, what kind of a welcome is this at a time of national rejoicing? I'd thought to find you all wearing blue ribbons for Admiral Rodney's great victory at sea!'

Mrs Croker curtsied again. 'Oh, aye, sir, but life ha' to go on here same as usual, sir.'

'So I see.' He nodded towards the gaping Jinny. 'And if you're looking for wet-nurse employment for *that* one, I doubt you'll find many doors open to her.'

Mrs Croker pursed up her mouth and looked knowing. Susan forced a smile and inclined her head towards him. 'Good day, sir.'

It was the sign he needed. 'A word with you, Madam Trotula, if you please. You will excuse us, Mrs Croker. Come, give me your arm,' he said, turning to Susan. 'Let us walk out of doors.'

Once out in the cobbled yard where Edward had asked her to marry him nearly two years ago, Susan tried to speak calmly, but her arm trembled in Dr Parnham's.

'So, my Trotula, what happy chance has brought you to the House of Hope today?'

Would her friend be able to help, she wondered.

371

"'Tis that girl, sir, poor Jinny ye saw back there. Mrs Croker wants to send her back to a wretched hovel where she'll be beaten and ill-used. I've asked if she can be kept here, at least till the baby's a bit older.'

'Ah, so that's it, eh? And the good widow does not share your pity for – what's her name?'

'Jinny, sir, Jinny Potter. I found her living miserably, and brought her here for her delivery.'

'Ah!' he said again, tightening his hold on her arm. 'And why should you concern yourself, Madam Trotula, with a half-witted creature who's going to give birth to many more bastards? What is she to you?'

Susan hesitated. 'She's a poor, mistreated girl o' slow understandin', Dr Parnham, and – and may be a relative o' mine, seein' that my – my mother's name was also Potter.'

'Your mother, my dear? Ah, yes.' It was the first time that he had ever heard her refer to Mad Doll. Their relationship had always disquieted him, as if the madness had killed all the natural love they should have shared. And even if this Jinny were related to his lovely, clever Trotula, he could not see why it should weigh so heavily with her when her unfortunate mother counted for so little. He sensed a mystery, and knew he must tread carefully.

'I will use my influence with the worthy Mrs Croker,' he said, 'but I fear for Jinny's fate in the long run, for we know the evil ways of men with a girl like that.'

She shivered, and gave him a grateful look. A grateful but fearful look, he noted, and would have given anything to fold her in his arms and openly declare himself as her protector.

'Thank ye, sir, 'tis very good o' ye.'

'Is there any other way I can be of service to you, my Trotula? You have only to name it.'

'Ye're very good, Dr Parnham,' she said in a low voice. 'Ye're my very best friend, along o' Miss Glover.'

And with that I must be content, he told himself.

'Come then, we will go back to Mrs Croker, and I will polish up my powers of persuasion,' he said in an attempt at light-heartedness. 'A little flattery can work wonders, I find. Good heavens, I think I hear her dulcet tones already! Who is she berating this time?'

'Yer lyin' slut, Oi'll ha' the truth from 'ee! Who got 'ee wi' child, then? Come on, own up this minute, who was he?'

Susan trembled violently. 'Oh, my God!'

They hurried to the spot where they had left the others, just as Mrs Croker struck the side of Jinny's head.

'Fur the last time, who laid on 'ee, yer filthy slut? *Was it yer father?*'

She got her answer, for Jinny gave a pitiful wail and threw her calico apron up over her face.

'Them ha' *all* laid inter me, missus, *all* on uns laid inter me arter supper, missus!'

'Oi thought as much, yer dirty cow, 'ee can't make a fool o' me like some—'

She raised her fist to strike the girl again, but Susan leaped from Parnham's side and elbowed her out of the way so violently that the woman nearly lost her balance.

'Stop it, *stop it*, take yer hands off her – don't ye dare touch her!' ordered Susan in a voice that Parnham had never heard before; and yet in the next

373

moment she was putting her arms around Jinny and holding her close, like a mother protecting her child from all the blows a cruel world could throw.

'Hush, Jinny, don't cry, don't mind her. Ye're not a bad girl, Jinny, not a bad girl,' she said soothingly. 'Ye couldn't stop 'em, ye weren't to blame, 'twas no fault o' yourn, poor Jinny. Ssh, don't cry, don't cry.'

Jinny dropped the apron from her face, and stared open-mouthed.

''Ee won't send Oi back to uns, will 'ee, missus?'

'No, Jinny, never, never.'

'Ain't sendin' Oi back to uns, never?'

'Never again, Jinny.'

It was an encounter between two women who had both suffered ill-usage. Mrs Croker raised her eyebrows and shot a vengefully triumphant look in Parnham's direction. His stricken face was answer enough: like her he saw and knew.

Everything now became hideously clear to him. Mad Doll, the tormented mother. Susan, the unloving daughter. The absent, never-mentioned father. An unholy alliance from which the child victim had eventually escaped.

But poor, stupid Jinny had never had the wit to escape, and his Susan was defending her in front of them all. Parnham felt a great grief in his heart, and when Mrs Croker made a move to separate the two young women, he raised his hand sternly.

'Go about your business, woman. Leave us at once.'

He beckoned to Mag, who was holding the whimpering Little Monkey in her arms while the black-capped widow flounced off.

'Give Jinny her baby to feed, Mag,' he said quietly.

'Go with Mag, Jinny, your baby's crying for you, there's a good girl.'

Susan heard the kindness in his voice towards the girl he had called a half-witted creature, and was grateful. How good this man was!

'I beg y'r pardon, sir, f'r forgettin' meself. I—'

'Say no more, my dear. You have done a good action today, and everything you said to that girl was true. No blame attaches to her – or to any other girl misused by men, be they fathers, brothers or any other brutes. I'd hang all such, by God!'

His eyes blazed, and Susan trembled as she took in the implication of his words.

Any other girl misused by men.

She looked up at this man who was her true friend, and he saw the fear in her grey eyes: fear of blame, fear of condemnation, as Jinny was condemned by Widow Croker.

And he could not let her know that he knew.

'As a matter of fact, Trotula, I had some idea of Jinny's grievous wrong when I first saw her. I have come across incest on other occasions, for it has happened all through history, as we know from the Bible and ancient writers. If anybody says a word against Jinny because of what was done to her, they will be answerable to me. Do you understand?'

'Yes, sir.' It was a faint whisper.

'Good. Don't forget it. I'll let you know as soon as I've found somewhere for the poor girl to go,' he added in the friendly, businesslike tone of a professional partner. Privately he feared he would have to take the Potter girl and her Little Monkey into his own home if nowhere else could be found.

'Thank you, sir.'

And so they parted with a smile and a handshake,

and Susan was left to ponder on the dark secret she shared with Jinny.

And the fact that Dr Parnham did not condemn the girl.

A couple of weeks later Susan had a great surprise.

'There is a letter for you, Susan, from London. It came by carrier this afternoon,' said Sophia casually.

'From London? For *me*? Whatever can it be?' Susan examined the bulky envelope, sealed with wax, lying on the table in the parlour.

'You will not find out unless you open it,' smiled her friend, handing her the paper-knife.

A bewildering sheaf of papers was revealed, including a large folded parchment document headed 'Deed of Property', and an important-looking letter in finely written copperplate. Susan turned them over on the table.

'I don't understand, Sophy. The letter is from somebody called Jamieson, and the big one as full o' long words as ever I saw.'

She frowned as she unfolded the thick parchment and saw her own name buried in a sprawling cluster of mostly unintelligible words. She began to read part of it aloud, slowly and with difficulty.

'"Whereas the said Mrs Susan Calthorpe, here-inafter to be called the Owner or Occupier of the abovenamed Dwelling, hereinafter to be called May Cottage, situated in the Parish of Beversley in the County of Hampshire" – oh, Sophy, what does it all mean?' she asked in comical display as Sophia laughed over her mispronunciations.

'Dear Susan, that is the language of lawyers, who never use one word where ten will do! Mr Jamieson is the same London attorney who acted for my

376

grandfather. But look, Susan, at the bottom of the page – see, down here.'

Susan read obediently. ' "Given under my Hand on this Fourth Day of June, Seventeen Hundred and Eighty-two" – *what* is that name?'

'It is signed by Octavius Enoch Gravett, Doctor of Divinity, on behalf of the Board of Guardians and the people of Beversley,' replied Sophia, smiling. 'And you too must sign it. Don't you see, Susan, May Cottage has been bought and presented to *you* in gratitude for your services to the women of Beversley and also at the House of Industry. Are you not pleased, Susan? Would you not like to have a home of your very own?'

Light began to dawn as Susan took in the meaning of the document that awaited her signature alongside that of the rector and Mr Jamieson.

'But *who* has bought this house for me, Sophy?'

'Lots of people! There has been a public subscription of large amounts and small, according to means,' explained Miss Glover, who knew that Mr Calthorpe had given the most. 'Take it and be thankful, dear Susan. Look upon May Cottage as a gift, and well deserved. Write a letter to the rector and to the Board of Guardians, thanking them and saying how pleased you are!'

'Oh, I will, Sophy, I will!' cried Susan, as she began to realise what a home of her own would mean. She would be able to receive friends, and Joby could visit her whenever he was free. And that was not all . . .

'You will need a couple of reliable maidservants, Susan, and a girl to scrub floors and sweep the yard,' said Sophia.

Susan stopped speaking as her thoughts raced ahead. She thought of Lizzie Decker, who had had to take work as a house servant while her mother looked after one-year-old Kitty for long hours every day. A new curate, Mr Roberts, had been installed at the Parsonage with his young wife, and the Widow Smart had been kept on for the time being as an unpaid housekeeper in return for her keep. Susan also thought of Mag, the browbeaten drudge at the House of Industry. Things were about to change for these women, she thought happily; and that for her was by far the best part of this wonderful surprise.

And Sophia Glover considered herself well rewarded for all the secret plotting she had done to bring it about.

In the same month another event took place amid much surprise and some head-shaking: Miss Rosa Hansford was married to Mr Osmond Calthorpe in Great St Giles. The ceremony was quietly conducted by the rector and witnessed by such family members and close acquaintances as were able to attend. They saw the bridegroom leaning upon his stick as he made his vows beside his kneeling bride, and heard the solemn declaration of matrimony pronounced.

Mrs Gertrude Calthorpe shed the tears expected of her and the squire and his lady looked upon their smiling daughter in her white gown and trusted that her confident expectations would be fulfilled.

Kneeling in the pew, Miss Glover prayed for the blessing of the Almighty, both on this marriage between the two families and the next one.

Which would be her own.

Chapter 26

At last the negotiations for a peace treaty were no longer rumours. Admiral Rodney's brilliant display of strength at sea had given a timely lift to morale and provided a stronger background for recognition of the colonies' independence. The fighting on land virtually ceased over the summer of 1782, and tired, devitalised troops put up their arms and looked homeward. There were forecasts of an armistice as early as September, but in fact it was to be November before the final draft was signed between Britain and the new United States of America. Peace with the old European foes had to wait until the new year, and the Spanish continued to besiege Gibraltar with unremitting persistence.

First Lieutenant Hansford's return on the *Minotaur* following the Battle of the Saints was eagerly awaited, and Miss Glover was conscious of the contrast between her own situation and that of her friend Susan, now installed in May Cottage with Lizzie Decker, little Kitty and a transformed Mag. She was talking of training Lizzie to be her assistant as the work increased, and engaging the Widow Smart as housekeeper.

One afternoon towards the end of June Sophia called at May Cottage and found Susan sitting sewing in the garden; little Kitty was toddling on the grass, holding out her chubby hands to the brightly coloured butterflies.

'I am glad to have a chance to speak with you, Susan,' Sophia began tentatively. 'You know that I still feel grief for your loss, even in the happiness of my own hopes.'

'Let's ha' no talk o' grieving, Sophy. I'm happy f'r you and Mr Hansford,' came the firm reply. 'Ye deserve y'r heart's desire, if ever a woman did.'

'You have a generous spirit, Susan, and I thank you from my heart. Only . . .' She hesitated, wondering how best to put into words what she felt was her duty to say. 'Only with your dear Edward gone, and hopes of his return all but given up—'

'He won't ever return, Sophy.'

'And accepting that sad fact, my dear friend, is it not time that you made your peace with his family? You are a person of some consequence in the parish now, and there should not be this holding on to grievances. The Calthorpes also mourn for Edward, so can you not forgive them now, and bear his name with pride?'

Susan's face was blank. 'My sister Polly had more right to bear the name o' Calthorpe than I ever did, yet she was beaten and turned out o' their house when she most needed caring for. Why should I forgive them? 'Tis they should be asking f'r it, not me.'

'My cousin Calthorpe greatly wishes to call you daughter, Susan,' Sophia persisted gently. 'He was very much involved with the purchase of this house for you, though the rector got most of the credit. And Selina would be your friend if you'd let her. As for Mrs Calthorpe and – and Osmond – I suspect it is but shame for past unkindness that holds them back.'

'And 'tis anger t'wards them as holds *me* back,' retorted Susan bitterly. 'I ha' nothing to say to

Osmond Calthorpe, nor his mother, nor that china doll he married after my sister died holding your Henry's hand. No, Sophy, my poor Polly'll stand between me and them f'r ever.'

She gripped her hands around the wooden handles of her sewing bag until the knuckles showed white, and Sophia glimpsed the pain as well as the anger.

'All right, Susan, forgive me. I pray that you may find peace one day, for Edward's sake.'

'Poor Edward ha' been set free from a marriage that was never meant to be, and brought him only sorrow and disappointment,' muttered Susan half under her breath, but Sophia heard in shocked astonishment.

'*Susan!* How can you say such a thing? If ever a man loved the wife of his choice—'

'Please, Sophy, don't speak o' what ye don't know,' begged Susan, her eyes darkened by long-hidden anguish. 'Ye're dear to me, as well ye know, and I'm truly pleased f'r ye – but there's some things as can't ever be told.'

She picked up Kitty and sat her on her lap, pointing to the tabby cat who had just appeared with her two kittens. Sophia sighed, wondering if her friend's imagination had become somewhat unbalanced by the long strain of waiting, hoping and praying for news that never came. Sophia longed to comfort her, but sensed something darker beneath the surface of the words, a warning not to pursue the matter.

The silence was broken by the sound of a horse's step and a cheery male voice at the gate.

'A charming group, indeed! Am I allowed to join in women's talk?'

'Dr Parnham!' There was no mistaking Susan's welcome and the immediate brightening of her features as she rose to greet the eminent man like an old and trusted friend. He drew up a chair and chucked Kitty under the chin.

'Good news, Trotula. I've got young Jinny settled at last, and it's a good place.'

Susan clapped her hands. 'Oh, Dr Parnham, I'm so glad to hear o' that!'

'Aye, and so am I, for she nearly drove away my cook, and none of the maids would speak to me because they were woken every night by the Little Monkey hollering while Jinny slept. I tell you, madam, I had come close to drowning them both.'

'Oh, enough o' y'r nonsense, sir – tell me where she is now.'

Susan's face was completely transformed from the wretchedness of only minutes ago. What a blessing her work was, she thought gratefully, and the pleasure of talking with one who shared her interest in it.

'Very well, madam, I will tell you. She is doing good service to a pair of hungry twins who would otherwise go unfed, for their mother lies low with childbed fever and the father is at his wits' end. Our Jinny now sits in splendid state, lacking no comfort while the babies suck their fill, along with the Monkey. I only hope that there is no truth in the old belief that children suck wisdom from the teats.'

Susan laughed. 'And does she also care for the babies, sir?'

'No, indeed! I had to place my cards on the table with the husband, as it were, and tell him that the girl has no great intellect, so his mother-in-law is caring for their other needs. The man's a Belhampton hatmaker of fair means, and as long as Jinny can be milked, her place in his household is assured, whatever the poor wretch's long-term prospects may be. But enough of her – how is it with you, Madam Trotula? I trust your practice is flourishing?'

'Enough to need an assistant, sir, and I'm teaching Mrs Decker the basic rules o' the birth-chamber. I think she'll be a quick learner and a careful midwife.

'And yet I see so little of you,' he said with mild reproach. 'You never send for me these days.'

'There haven't been that many cases o' difficulty, sir, none that I can't deal with myself.'

'Ah, my Trotula, you have grown so clever that I shall soon be sending to *you* for advice, I dare say,' he said with a mock sigh, and Susan smiled.

His tenderness of expression was not lost on Miss Glover as she watched and listened; neither was Susan's ease of manner in his company. By the time he got up to leave, Miss Glover was certain that his emotions were involved, and equally certain that Susan was unaware of it. He shook hands with them both and congratulated Sophia upon her daily expectations of seeing Lieutenant Hansford, and the good news of an approaching end to hostilities. Sophia could not help speculating about the future, and wondering if in the course of time the good doctor might propose marriage to a young midwife nearly thirty years his junior; but she quickly checked these thoughts and chided herself for encroaching on the province of the Almighty.

'Dr Parnham has shown himself to be a true friend to you, Susan,' she remarked when he had gone.

''Tis true that I wouldn't be where I am if 'twasn't f'r his defence o' me,' agreed Susan. 'But think, Sophy, who was it took me to Belhampton in the first

383

place, to meet him? Who asked him to train me up f'r a licence? Who was it?'

And they both smiled at the remembrance of that journey with Mr Turnbull, when Sophia had wept at the thought of Susan imprisoned in the House of Industry, under the same roof as poor Mad Doll.

Henry appeared in Beversley at the beginning of July, and to his great surprise found himself a hero, Admiral Rodney's representative in his own home village. The squire's eldest son had always been liked, from boyhood through to joining the navy, where his adventures had been eagerly followed. Now his popularity was even greater, and everybody wanted to shake the hand of the naval officer who looked older than his twenty-eight years but retained the friendly, open manner that had always been his chief attraction.

His romantic attachments had also provided much interest, and his choice of Sophia Glover was generally approved. She had never looked more radiant than now. Her many friends rejoiced with the future daughter-in-law of the squire, and she was seen driving out in the Hansford chaise with Mrs Hansford and Mrs Osmond Calthorpe. Her friendship with the elder Miss Calthorpe conveniently paved the way towards her acceptance by Mrs Gertrude Calthorpe and Caroline, and Sophia responded with the ready graciousness of a woman deeply in love; her heart was overflowing with joy, and there was no room for malice.

'The squire expects us to move into the farmhouse as soon as we are married,' she confided to Susan one day at Glover Cottage. 'But Henry knows that I want us to spend our first few years in this dear house.'

She looked fondly around at the home she had bought with her grandfather's bequest fourteen years previously, and Susan thought of all who had passed through its door and found a place of refuge – Mrs Coulter in her infirmity, and many a disgraced maidservant like poor Polly, who had died under its roof.

The people of Beversley took the couple to their hearts during those unforgettable summer days. Henry and his bride-to-be were invited to tea-parties, dinners and picnics, and Great St Giles was once again packed to capacity for Divine Service, because Lieutenant Hansford could be seen in the family pew; afterwards the men of the choir seized him bodily and carried him shoulder high in a triumphant procession while he laughed and protested. His sister Mrs Osmond Calthorpe added her smiles, and Henry was glad to see her apparently happy in her new life; Osmond now limped round the Bever estate daily, with or without his father, and Mr Calthorpe made no secret of his hopes that a new generation of Calthorpe children would enliven Bever House.

Henry announced that he would exchange the navy for the more settled life of a gentleman farmer, and the squire looked forward to handing over the management of the Hansford acres, the orchard and piggeries to his elder son. William, now eighteen, worked in the offices of the *Hampshire Chronicle* at Winchester, though, like his brother, he planned eventually to share their father's involvement with the Bench of Justices and Board of Guardians. Beversley now looked to Henry as the future squire, a keeper of law and order, and who better than Miss Sophia Glover at his side? It was pronounced a perfect partnership.

There was much speculation about when the wedding would be. Sophia's bright smiles promised an early date before the summer's end, but to everybody's dismay Henry was recalled to Portsmouth at the beginning of August, to take part in one more naval engagement. The besieged and blockaded fortress of Gibraltar was in desperate need of relief, and Lord Howe was preparing for a tremendous onslaught on the combined French and Spanish forces to smash the siege once and for all. It would be another boost to national prestige, and secure for Britain a better bargaining position when drawing up a peace treaty with her old European foes.

'I'll be back by the end of September, probably much earlier, dearest Sophy, and then we shall never part again. Will you marry me before I go?'

Gibraltar. It was not America or the West Indies, on the other side of a great ocean. Admiral Lord Howe was confident that the blockade would be speedily dispatched, and the highly respected Admiral Kempenfelt, 'the brains of the navy', was already aborad the flagship *Royal George* to lead the attack. This great man-o'-war now lay in harbour off Spithead for repairs and provisioning, along with over thirty other ships of the line.

Once again Sophia Glover decided to wait until Henry was finished with fighting and home for good, and the wedding was fixed for the second day of October, a Wednesday, at Great St Giles. Meanwhile Henry had the brilliant idea of taking her with his parents and brother on an expedition to Portsmouth to see the fleet. They duly travelled down in the Hansford chaise, to take lodgings at a comfortable inn where they stayed for three days; then they had to make their farewells and travel back without Henry.

'Oh, Susan, it was so wonderful, so incredible, the time of my life!' Sophia said later, for the excursion had far outstripped anything she could have imagined.

'When we stood at the sea wall and beheld the magnificent spectacle of the fleet at anchor, I simply held on to Henry's arm and just stared and stared!' she recalled. 'And the next day Henry escorted us all aboard the *Royal George*, an experience I'll never forget. He took us on the most amazing tour of the upper and lower decks.'

'Were you the only visitors, Sophy?' asked Susan, hanging on every word.

'No, that was what amazed me. There were whole families of women and children keeping company with the seamen who were preparing to sail. We saw water and provisions being taken on board, and there was a sloop with barrels of rum. In fact it was quite a carnival atmosphere! I stood and gazed up at those great tall masts and the enormous canvas sails, all furled and roped – and Henry took me to the gun-deck and showed me how those hundred guns have to be evenly balanced to keep the vessel from keeling to one side. Oh, Susan, I stood there and listened to all his descriptions and explanations, and I'll be able to picture the *Royal George* at Gibraltar – though I shudder when I think of the guns firing and those decks flowing with – oh, Susan!'

The two women put their arms around each other, and Sophia could not say more. She remembered trembling beside Henry, and his reassurances.

'This will not be a bloody battle, my Sophia, nor do we expect to lose any of our ships. 'Twill be more of a formidable show of strength to frighten the enemy and send him packing, rather than to blast him out of the water.'

The very idea of a battle seemed unreal to Sophia as she stood on a flat, steady deck in the sunshine, surrounded by water as blue as the sky and as calm as a millpond. On shore the wooded hill rose up above the port, and above them the seagulls circled lazily, their mewing calls drifting down on the clear air. What an evil thing is war, Sophia had thought with sudden conviction, though she kept her thoughts to herself as the days quickly passed, and all too soon it was time to return to Beversley.

Their last farewell was said at the quayside. He pinned a silver anchor brooch to her cloak, and she placed her little leather-bound prayer book inside his jacket, over his heart. Years of self-discipline had strengthened these two, and there were no tears.

'I shall pray every day for God's protection to rest upon you, Henry, and on all aboard the *Royal George*.'

'And I shall see you standing there on the deck beside me, my dearest love, to comfort me and give me courage. Oh, my Sophia . . .'

One last kiss, and then she had to walk away with her future relations, who had long come to value and respect her, though it had been a mainly silent party that travelled home through the bountiful Hampshire countryside, nearly ready for harvesting.

'Just think, Susan, a little more than a month and then Henry and I will stand side by side and be man and wife, never to be parted again.'

For answer Susan held her more tightly, for words had strangely deserted her.

'And who knows, Susan, this time next year you may be attending me as midwife, for be assured I'll have none but you to deliver me!'

Susan looked into the rapturous blue eyes, and tried to imagine Miss Glover, the benefactress of

Beversley and her own especial patroness and friend, in travail with the child of Henry Hansford. At nearly thirty-four a first confinement might not be easy, and they both knew about the hours of waiting, the agony, the possible danger . . .

'I would endure it all gladly, willingly, Susan,' went on Sophia, as if reading her thoughts. 'Oh, can I dare to believe such joy? Can it really be true that I shall be his wife and the mother of his child? His children?'

'Dearest Sophy,' whispered Susan, returning her friend's loving embrace. 'Dearest Sophy!'

For she could think of nothing else to say. However hard she tried, she could not envisage the scene her friend described so eagerly.

Chapter 27

Susan was certain that young Mrs Spooner's baby was in the breech position, so she was not sorry to hear that the waters had broken and the pains commenced, two or three weeks earlier than expected. A smaller baby's head would be better able to emerge from the tight ring of the womb, a known hazard with breech deliveries, especially when it was the first child, as in Mary Spooner's case.

No sooner had Susan ascertained that travail had begun and that the baby's heart was strong and regular, than a message came from Pulhurst Grange where Squire Gosney's daughter, a Mrs Knight, had also started in travail. She had made it known that she wanted Madam Trotula to deliver her.

Susan sighed. It was always the way with babies! Days would go by without a call, and then two or three would come together.

'I'll take ye with me to Mrs Knight, Lizzie, and find out how she does. If she be near delivery I'll stay till the child be born, otherwise I'll leave ye with her and go back to Mary.'

Lizzie Decker looked very doubtful. 'Mrs Knight and Mrs Gosney ha' asked for Madam Trotula, not her assistant, and I reckon they won't be happy to be left with me.'

'I'll come back as soon as I can, but if ye run into trouble they'll ha' to eat humble pie and send f'r the Pulhurst midwife,' replied Susan firmly. 'Dan

Spooner ha' been good to my brother Joby in his way, and his son's wife'll need close watching with that breech.'

Leaving little Kitty in her grandmother's charge, they headed the pony-trap towards Pulhurst. Mrs Knight was found to be in very early travail, with the ring only just beginning to open. Susan gave her five drops of tincture of opium in water, and left another dose for Lizzie to give in the night, advising the mother and her attendants to rest if they could. She then left, promising to return as soon as Mrs Spooner was delivered.

As Lizzie had predicted, the Pulhurst ladies were distinctly unimpressed at having to make do with her instead of Madam Trotula who seemed to consider a blacksmith's daughter-in-law more deserving of her attention than a squire's daughter. Lizzie took up her post and spent the night hours rubbing Mrs Knight's back, feeding her sips of sweetened water, assisting her on to the chamber pot and telling her that everything was as it should be, while praying desperately for Susan's return.

Meanwhile Susan watched beside Mrs Spooner, accompanied by the mother and mother-in-law. The travail lasted all night, and when the body of the child emerged at twenty minutes to six, the delivery of the after-coming head seemed endless; Susan steadily adhered to Dr Parnham's method, and waited until the hairline appeared at the nape of the neck before embarking on the most critical manoeuvre: too fast and there could be damage due to the sudden release of pressure; too slow and the child could suffocate through lack of air. When the head of the baby girl smoothly emerged at a quarter-hour before six, and gave a gasp, a cry and then a loud wail, both of the new grandmothers wept their thanksgiving.

Susan tied and cut the cord, handing the baby to Mary's mother while the after-burden was expelled. At her earliest opportunity she took her leave, refusing breakfast, so anxious was she to get back to Pulhurst. Dan Spooner stood outside with the trap ready and Brownie in the shafts.

Arriving at the bedside of Mrs Knight, she found that the ring of the womb had opened enough to admit three fingers, and the ensuing slow progress throughout the morning was tiring to all concerned. With the ring fully open at one hour past noon, another two hours of strenuous pushing were needed to bring forth a son of almost twice the size of the Spooner baby. Susan used her special scissors to make a widening cut in the outlet, and stitched it afterwards with linen thread.

Leaving the new mother to rest after her ordeal, Susan instructed Mrs Gosney to give the baby spring-water from a teaspoon until Mrs Knight was able to put him to the breast. She and Lizzie climbed wearily into the trap at half-past four in the afternoon, their heads aching with fatigue.

Lizzie's bonnet drooped as they jogged up the Portsmouth Road, and after turning off into the narrow lane to Beversley, Susan slackened her grip on the reins and let Brownie follow his nose to lead them home.

They did not at first hear the urgent clatter of hoofs behind them, but as they became aware of it, Susan looked back and saw two riders, one in the blue jacket and tricorn hat of a naval officer. He called out to her, coming on ahead of his companion, a rougher-looking character in a stained shirt, ragged breeches and a dirty scarf tied round his head.

'Good day to you, mistress,' said the officer. 'We're on our way to Belhampton.'

'Then ye should ha' stayed on the Portsmouth Road, sir. This way only goes to the village o' Beversley,' answered Susan a little warily, wondering if they were ruffians and the uniform stolen.

'Then we're on the right road, mistress, for we have to visit Beversley on our way,' replied the officer. 'Are you going there?'

'Aye, sir, we're returning there.' Susan stifled a yawn as she nodded, and decided that there was no cause for fear. She reined in the pony at the side of the lane to let the riders pass, but to her surprise the officer lingered, looking down at them from his tired steed as if he was wondering whether to speak further.

'You live there, then, mistress?'

'Yes, sir. I'm the midwife in Beversley.'

She raised her eyes to his face, and that was when she first noticed the black cockade in his hat, the black sash across his shoulder. A shadow seemed to fall across the sun, though there were no clouds in the sky.

'Wh-who ha' ye to see in Beversley, sir?' she heard herself enquire. Lizzie raised her drooping head and opened her eyes.

'We have a message to give to the squire there, mistress. Name of Hansford. I fear 'tis ill news.'

The skin on the back of Susan's neck started to prickle as they both stared at the messenger. The air was unnaturally still.

What day is it? thought Susan – Wednesday? No, Thursday, the twenty-ninth day of August. Sophia had said that the attack on Gibraltar was not until the end of the month. Had it already taken place?

'Tell us, sir, is it ill news from Gib-Gibraltar that ye bring?' she asked, her mouth dry.

'No, mistress, not from there. The fleet hasn't left harbour,' he said gravely. 'The *Royal George* has never left Spithead.'

'Then thank God, sir, surely—' began Susan.

But the other man drew his dirty sleeve across his eyes and cried out, 'Aye, an' her never will, not now, missus!'

'For heaven's sake, sir, tell us what's happened, what ha' ye come to—' Susan broke off, seeing tears in the officer's eyes, while his companion wept openly.

'The *Royal George* is sunk in harbour, mistress, gone down with her crew at nine o'clock this morning. It was a matter of minutes – just as if the bottom had fallen out of her.'

'God ha' mercy on us all,' breathed Susan as Lizzie began to weep. 'And the men on board – did any escape?'

'Hardly a score, it was all so quick. In fact she pulled a sloop and its crew down with her. Jim here saw it all, and should have been on board, but his escape to shore last night saved his life.'

The other man hung his head, his shoulders heaving. 'All drowned! All drowned, every man Jack on 'em. Eight hundred souls!' he sobbed.

Susan felt the blood drain from her face.

'Eight hundred? *Eight hundred men* perished?' she whispered.

'At least that number, perhaps more, with Admiral Kempenfelt and some women and children still aboard when she went down.'

'Oh, no! Oh, woe!' moaned Lizzie, covering her face, reliving the news of Decker's death; Susan put her free arm around her.

'Hush, Lizzie, think o' the sorrow to – oh, Sophy, Sophy! And is Mr Hansford known to be drowned wi' the rest, sir?'

'Aye, he be gone who were the best o' friends to me,' replied the man called Jim with another burst of sobs. The officer ordered him to go on ahead and wait.

'I'm sorry for this, mistress, but we must go on our way. 'Tis a bad day, a bad day.'

He bowed from the saddle, and urged the horse forward, rounding a bend in the lane, leaving the women sitting in the trap. Lizzie was weeping and Susan shook uncontrollably as if with an ague. She forced herself to marshal her thoughts together: it was past five, and the messengers would go up to the Hansford farmhouse. Sophia might be at home or out visiting, and although Susan shuddered at the thought of breaking the dreadful news, she wanted to be there when Sophia heard it.

'I'll get down at Glover Cottage, Lizzie, and you must go home to your mother and daughter,' she said. 'Fetch Mr Roberts from the parsonage. Tell him to come to Glover Cottage.'

When Susan arrived at her friend's house Tess let her in and said that the mistress was out visiting with Mrs Hansford.

'Though she's like to be in any minute,' she added, staring at Susan's white face and red-rimmed eyes.

'What be the matter, then, Madam Trotula?' she asked sharply.

''Tis the worst o' news, Tess,' Susan answered with a groan, sitting down heavily on a cane-bottomed chair in the parlour. 'I'll wait here until she gets in.'

'Merciful heaven, be it Mr Hansford?' cried Tess.

'Be he – be he . . .?'

'Yes – oh, Tess, what'll she do? What can we do f'r her?'

Tess burst into tears and went to the kitchen to put a pan of water on to boil. Almost at once the front gate clanged shut and light footsteps were heard running up the path to the door. Not the steps of one who has just lost the dearest love of her life.

She came into the parlour, flushed and smiling.

'My dear Susan, you look exhausted, and no wonder! I have heard all about your skilful handling of the Spooner birthing last night – this morning – and how you had to go over to Pulhurst straightway to deliver Mrs Knight! Tess, put a pan of water on to boil to make tea for poor Madam Trotula – ah, I see you have already done so. Good.'

She took off her bonnet and shawl, and went on chatting brightly. Too brightly.

'I'll tell you the oddest thing, Susan! I'd been out with Mrs Hansford, and left her on that track to the farmhouse. As I was coming back here, two riders came up, one in naval officer's uniform, and just for one moment, Susan, my heart gave a very nasty jolt. But you see, I know for certain that the *Royal George* doesn't sail until Saturday. I had a letter sent up by post-chaise yesterday, and Henry's word on it. So I wonder what their business was? Did you see them on your way back from Pulhurst, Susan? *Susan? SUSAN!*'

For Susan had risen from her chair and stretched out her arms towards her friend.

Sophia stood rooted to the spot, her eyes wide and staring. From the back of her throat came one word.

'*Henry?*'

Susan gave the slightest of nods, and sprang

396

forward in time to catch the fainting, falling body. There were no tears: the blue eyes rolled upwards, blank and sightless.

Chapter 28

While the whole of Beversley mourned for the lost hero, Miss Glover withdrew herself into an inner world of grief, and for two whole weeks stayed in her room. Susan visited daily, no matter how heavy the demands of her work, to aid the faithful Tess, who sometimes had to spoon-feed her mistress with broths and custards. While they spoke kindly to her, she spoke only to Henry.

'If only I had married you, my love, when you asked me – oh, Henry, forgive me, forgive me – if only we had been married, if only I was your wife, your grieving widow – if only . . .'

The agonised self-reproaches went on and on, until her friends began to fear for her reason. Susan would put her arms around her and beg her to weep out loud as she had done when she saw the lifeless bodies of Polly Lucket and her babies; but just as Susan had been silent and benumbed on that occasion, Sophia was now set apart by her misery, and seemed untouched by the flood of loving sympathy from the village and far beyond, the constant stream of messages and gifts.

Mr Calthorpe came, sad and anxious-looking, to sit beside his cousin. His ladies sent freshly picked flowers from the gardens of Bever House; choice orchard fruit arrived from the rectory, and honey from the Turnbull hives. Charles Parnham sent bottles of his best Madeira wine, and fresh eggs and cooked chickens were brought from Bennett's farm. Miss Glover looked upon it all but saw nothing.

When Mr Roberts from the parsonage came and read to her from the Gospels and Psalms, her response was disconcerting.

'If only we had lain together, my own love,' she said, 'I might now be with child. And then at least I'd have our baby to hold in my arms.'

Squire Hansford visited, apologising for his wife's absence, for she had also shut herself away, too much in need of comfort to have any to give. The squire's grief took the form of seething anger, and he sat and raged helplessly at the waste of his son's life. His fury was not lessened by the court martial held on board the HMS *Warspite* on the seventh of September to determine the cause of the disaster.

It was generally acknowledged that rotten timbers were the reason why a simple last-minute repair had caused a sudden inrush of water into the hold and through the lower ports. The court was told that 'a great crack' had been heard, the ship keeled over to larboard and lay with her masts flat on the water, then within another few minutes she had sunk out of sight. The verdict was that 'some material part of her frame gave way, which can only be accounted for by the general state of decay of her timbers'. The whole ship's company was acquitted of blame.

The Commissioners of the Navy tried to circulate an alternative explanation, that a freak gust of wind had caused the ship to capsize, and the renowned poet, William Cowper, was commissioned to write an elegy in which this was the reason given.

'Damned lies, damned, cowardly lies!' growled the squire. 'We saw for ourselves, Sophia, she was riding at anchor in a flat calm!'

On the thirteenth of September Lord Howe's delayed assault on Gibraltar took place, though the combined French and Spanish forces proved harder to overcome than expected. In fact young William Hansford never told his family about the eye-witness accounts that reached the offices of the *Hampshire Chronicle*, the terrible loss of life due to burning and drowning; men leapt from the smoke and flame of stricken vessels into waters littered with pieces of burning wreckage, and the survivors wept for pity of allies and enemies alike. Such accounts were not published, to spare the distress of relatives.

When Susan quietly told Sophia that the siege of Gibraltar had been lifted, she had shaken her head mournfuly.

'How cruel and wicked, to send husbands and sons to their deaths over a piece of land that is not ours.'

One morning when Susan was visiting Glover Cottage, Selina Calthorpe was shown in. She asked them to excuse her intrusion, and produced some pencilled drawings done by her class at the House of Industry, 'especially for Miss Glover'. Susan stood aside as she handed them to Sophia and pointed to one in particular. It was a rough sketch of a sailor beside a wavy sea with a ship on it, and the letter H.

Sophia gazed at it for a full minute, and when she looked up, her eyes were full of tears.

'Poor little orphaned souls,' she murmured. 'I am one with them, an orphan and a bastard with no kin, God pity us.'

Miss Calthorpe gave Susan a sideways glance as the tears trickled slowly down the pale face, the first she had shed.

'I did right to bring it, I think, Madam Trotula,' she whispered, wiping her own eyes. Susan nodded mutely, hoping that this might be the start of recovery. She still felt awkward in the presence of the Calthorpe girl who had once considered herself betrothed to Henry Hansford.

At Bever House Mrs Osmond had suffered an early miscarriage, apparently brought on by the shock of her brother's death. This unfortunate occurrence had forced Mrs Hansford to come to her daughter's bedside, and having tried to comfort her, she then went on to call at Glover Cottage.

Sophia looked up listlessly, her needlework untouched and a young kitten, a gift from Joby Lucket, playing with a tangled skein of silk under her chair.

'I had not thought to see you, madam, now that we are not to be related,' she said dully.

'Please, my dear,' began the black-clad woman, her face thin and drawn, 'the squire and I think of you as Henry's wife, because he wished it so. We regard you as our daughter, Sophia, just as if—'

She began to weep disconsolately. 'I have no comfort to give you, Sophia, but we're both in mourning for Henry, so let us mourn together – we shouldn't be apart. Oh, Henry, Henry!'

When Susan returned from talking with Tess in the kitchen, she found the two women sharing their grief at the loss of the man they had both adored, and calling each other mother and daughter.

Sophia did not again refer to herself as an orphan, and from then on she began to be seen in Beversley, driving out in the Hansford chaise and accepting the sympathy that everybody longed to give. She no longer had the energy she once possessed, and the

light had gone out of her eyes; but in her new closeness to Mrs Hansford she seemed to have turned a
corner. The rector saw her and decided that she
might now be visited without depressing his own
low spirits further; he had to be careful in his poor
state of health.

The tragedy of Henry's death and her anxiety for
Sophia had taken their toll of Susan as the year
declined. In the solitude of her room she reflected
that she had no mother figure to turn to: certainly not
in Dolly Lucket, who had stood aside and let her be
defiled. Susan knew that there were those who considered her hard and cold towards her mad mother:
little did they know the truth, she thought bitterly.

But such rancour would not do. She lifted her
shoulders and directed her thoughts towards her life
as Madam Trotula, friend of an eminent surgeon,
trusted and respected by the women who called on
her services. Lizzie Decker was ready to start
working as her assistant, and it was time to engage
the Widow Smart as housekeeper at May Cottage.

Yes! She must find her fulfilment in her work, and
nobody need know of the aching loneliness at the
centre of her life.

Christmas came and went, and the new year brought
news of the peace treaty with France and Spain;
national humiliation was set aside in rejoicing that
the war was truly over.

The end of a war means that prisoners are released
and may return home.

The weather turned colder towards the middle of
January, and there were flurries of powdery snow in
the air when Susan took to her bed at noon after
being up during the night at a birthing.

'I'm bone weary, Lizzie, and the back o' my nose is sore, as if a cold's coming on.' She sneezed, and Mrs Decker began to fuss.

'Get up to bed, Susan, and I'll bring you a glass o' wine and hot water. You should take better care o' yourself.'

Grateful for her bustling concern, Susan drew the curtains and lay down, falling asleep at once.

Just after two o'clock, Lizzie crept into the room.

'Are ye asleep, Susan?' she whispered.

'What is it? Has somebody called?' Susan sat up with a start.

'Er – yes, but – ye've got a visitor. Mr Calthorpe's here,' said Lizzie apologetically.

'What?'

'I told him you were resting, but he says it's very important, and he'll wait.'

Mr Calthorpe. What had brought him here? What fresh ill news was this? Susan was filled with apprehension, and reached at once for the long woollen wrap she wore when messengers called her from her bed. 'Tell him I'll be down, Lizzie.'

She sneezed into a handkerchief, peered at herself in the small looking-glass, and went downstairs. She stiffened at the sight of her father-in-law standing in the parlour; he looked flushed, and his eyes were unnaturally bright.

'Good day to ye, Mr Calthorpe.'

'Susan, I have a letter for you,' he said without any polite preliminaries.

She noted that he called her by her name and not Madam Trotula or Mistress. Her heart began to pound.

'I must apologise to you, Susan. This letter was brought up to Bever House, and my wife opened it, but it is for you, from a Mrs – er – Nollekens, it looks like, and it came by the hand of a traveller across the Atlantic, from a place called Chippercreek. Here, take it and read it. Edward *lives*, Susan!'

He held out a stained and crumpled envelope with a shaking hand. She took it, and sat down quickly as the room spun round her. He went on speaking rapidly.

'It's not easy to read – the woman's no writer – but the message is clear enough. Go on, read it!'

With a sense of unreality she unfolded the letter on her lap. At first it appeared incomprehensible, a jumble of oddly unfamiiar letters and unconnected words. She took a deep breath and forced herself to concentrate on each word in turn.

> Mrss Caltoorp greetin & to tell yr Good Man Edwd Caltoorp hath live above 2 Yere Prisoner to work in my Good Man his Farm & Feild but Edwd hath becom a Freind for Good he hath for us & my Good Man hath let him Free with Moneys for to berth in a Shipp to eastwd God send a flowwing Wind & safe Sail to Home Port I am yrs Mrss Walter Nollekens his Wife.

'Do you see, Susan? Do you understand what she says?' asked Calthorpe eagerly. 'Edward *did* survive the shipwreck, and must have been taken prisoner to work on this woman's husband's farm – but now the war's over and he's been set free and she says he's coming home! On his way! My son is alive, Susan, back from the dead! Have you nothing to say?'

Susan thought she was going to faint. She shook from head to foot, and could scarcely draw breath.

Edward alive. Edward coming back to Beversley, to

his family, to herself. It could not be true. She had thought him dead for so long, she had mourned for him and wept bitter tears for her failure as a wife. And now this peculiar letter. She could not believe it.

Mr Calthorpe stood leaning over her chair, his own trembling hand on her shoulder.

'Oh, Susan, think what it will be like to see him, hear his voice, touch him! And I am resolved that this will be a time of forgetting old wrongs and divisions between us. I have learned hard lessons in the time he has been gone from us, Susan – for ever, as we thought. But now you will be received at Bever House with full honour as my son's wife. Kiss me Susan. Kiss me, my daughter . . .'

But she drew back, and the letter dropped to the floor.

'No, I can't, I *can't*, it isn't true!'

Calthorpe stared in amazement. 'My dear, I can see that this has been too great a shock for you. I must allow you time—'

But she ran from the room and up the stairs to her bedchamber, and Calthorpe had no alternative but to take his leave.

The news spread around Beversley like wildfire, that Edward Calthorpe had survived shipwreck and imprisonment, and was on his way home. Everybody was happy for Madam Trotula, soon to become Mrs Edward Calthorpe again, a widow restored to wifehood, by God's mercy.

But it seemed that the midwife had taken to her bed with a feverish cold, and Mrs Decker was firm to the point of incivility in refusing to allow visitors over the step, not even closest friends.

'The poor soul must be afraid to believe that her

405

husband is alive, for fear of her grief if it be not true,' said Miss Gravett, though this explanation did not satisfy Miss Glover, who remembered the strange conversation she had had with Susan in the summer, before her own life had been changed for ever: that disclosure that the marriage had not been all it seemed, for which Susan appeared to blame herself entirely.

If it were her own beloved Henry miraculously brought back from the dead, thought Sophia, what rejoicing, what thanksgiving there would be! She sensed a mystery, but living under the cloud of her own sorrow, she did not confront her friend as she might have done in happier days, but waited for Edward's return to prove his survival beyond doubt.

As soon as Charles Parnham received the message he at once saddled his mare and rode over to call at May Cottage. It was a cold January afternoon when Widow Smart showed him into the little parlour where Susan presided over a tea-tray.

'Thank you, Mrs Smart, that'll be all,' she said firmly, and they were left alone.

'Now, Madam Trotula, you have sent for me. First tell me all about it. Is it true that young Calthorpe lives and is coming home?'

'It may be true, sir. I can't take it in. I was so sure – there ha' been no word f'r two years.'

Charles Parnham stirred his tea and knew that he was on very delicate ground; but in order to help her, he would need to know how far his suspicions were correct.

'And are you happy in the hope of seeing him again, my child?'

The small fire crackled in the grate, and a log fell

with a faint hiss of steam. He noticed how tightly she gripped her empty cup.

'I am your friend, my Trotula. Tell me, are you happy?'

Still there was no reply. Her head was bent low, so that he looked at the top of her white frilled cap.

'You do not speak, so I will attempt to answer for you,' he said carefully. 'Listen, and tell me if I am correct or wide of the mark. Now, we are both mid-wives, and in our work we daily deal with women's bodies. We look at them, we touch them with familiarity, though always with respect. Is that right, Trotula?'

'Yes, sir, I suppose so – yes,' she muttered, not looking up. Parnham sent up a silent prayer: O God, if there be a God, give me the right words now.

'But as regards men's parts, they are a very different matter, are they not? Men's bodies fill you with abhorrence – fear, dislike. Would you say that was true, my Trotula?'

She raised her eyes and looked at him with a kind of amazed relief, as if she had borne a heavy burden in secret for a long time, and then discovered that a friend had known about it all along.

'Yes, that's it, sir, that's right. Oh, my God! How did you know?'

And while he wondered how best to reply, she reached out a hand to him and answered for herself.

'Ye *know*, Dr Parnham.'

'What?'

'Ye know about me. Ye know because o' that poor girl Jinny Potter.'

'Yes, my poor Trotula, yes, I knew then,' he said heavily.

407

She gave a long sigh. 'And ye said it wasn't her fault, sir.'

'Certainly not! She was shamefully wronged by the very ones whose duty it was to protect her. Sheep-stealers are hanged, but men who do such evil as that – ugh! They go unpunished.'

There was silence for a minute or two, and then he continued with his questions.

'So, my dear, because of what was done to you in the past, you had difficulties with your married life, even though you loved young Calthorpe?'

The storm broke. She rose from her chair, clutching wildly in the air with her hands.

'Yes, yes, yes, *yes*, that's it, that's true!' she burst out. 'I was no wife to him, I couldn't – I didn't – oh, Dr Parnham, I never should ha' married him, the best o' men! Poor Sophia Glover ha' cried her eyes out f' r not marrying Mr Hansford, but I ha' wished with all my heart that I ha' never married. Oh, Dr Parnham, I'd do anything to set him free – anything – drown in Wychell Lake or hang from a tree—'

Parnham curbed his overwhelming urge to rant and rave and curse and swear, so great was his anger at what this girl had endured. He leaped to his feet and took both her hands in his.

'Hush, hush, in God's name, *never* utter such blasphemy again! Oh, *why* did you not come straight to me, my poor child? You must know that there's nothing I would not do for my clever Signora Trotula. Think of the loss to – to the women of Beversley if . . .' He paused to steady his voice. 'I knew that all was not well with your marriage from the start, and your distress over the Potter girl explained it all. Now listen carefully, I want to ask you a few more questions when you are ready, Trotula.'

408

When she had calmed somewhat, he sat her down and spoke very gently.

'There *may* be a lawful way for you to set Edward free, Trotula. Now tell me the truth, however painful it may be. Did you ever have a true union of your bodies, as husband and wife?'

'No, sir. I refused him.' She began to sob afresh.

'Hush, my child, and answer me again. Did he not enter your woman's part at all?'

'No, sir. I got out o' the bed to escape from it – I couldn't bear it, Dr Parnham—'

He seized her hands and looked straight into her face, ravaged with misery.

'Then I see a way out of your marriage, and I will do everything I can to secure it for you. Answer another question now: would you be willing to swear in a court of law before a judge that what you have just told me is true? That you and Calthorpe were never truly man and wife together?'

She looked up at him and saw the promise in his eyes.

'Why, yes, sir, if 'twould do any good.'

'And young Calthorpe, d'you think he would be willing to swear the same?'

'I don't know, sir, but 'tis certainly the truth.'

'Then he will be asked to do so, and so will you,' said Parnham with conviction. 'I will consult with an attorney-at-law, and get him to draw up affidavits. Those are written statements that you must both sign to declare that your marriage was never consummated, and is therefore null, as if it had never taken place. You would then be granted an annulment and be freed from your vows. Do you understand that, Trotula?'

'Is that really possible, Dr Parnham?' she whispered, unable to believe that it could be.

'With my support behind you, Trotula, it will be more than possible – it will be *done*, by heaven!' he assured her.

Oh, yes, he thought, he'd get it for her, if he had to go begging to lawyers, if he had to spend a fortune, if he became a laughing-stock, he would obtain an annulment for this young woman.

'Trust me, Madam Trotula,' he said emphatically. 'I'll consult with a Winchester attorney to set the wheels in motion. If Edward Calthorpe truly lives and arrives here in Beversley, I'll see him myself and explain what he has to do. Only trust me.'

'But he must never know, Dr Parnham – I couldn't bear him to know what used to happen when – when I was a child,' she pleaded.

'He never will know, my dear, nor will the lawyers. It will be said that you refused him his conjugal rights because of your enmity against his family. I warrant to keep your secret, Trotula. Nobody shall know of it but you and I.'

He was rewarded by the smile that brightened her tear-stained face, the grateful look, the hand-clasp.

'Right, you have given me my orders for the day, madam! I shall go to Winchester tomorrow, and return to speak with you again before the week is out – Friday afternoon, if not before. Farewell until then – and trust me,' he repeated again.

I was right to send for him, Susan thought, grateful beyond words. What a friend he has proved himself to be, to understand so completely, to take such trouble on their behalf. If it were truly possible to set Edward free from an empty marriage, free to marry a wife with no unnatural fears, no terrors from the past, it would be the best gift that she could now bestow on him. And he must be made to see that.

A thought suddenly struck her: what of Sophia Glover – she who had lost the love of her life – what would *she* say when she heard that Susan had knowingly cast hers away?

Two days passed, and Friday arrived. At noon Susan changed into a dark blue merino wool gown and plaited her hair to pin up under a neat little white cap with no bow but which framed her face becomingly in tiny goffered frills.

In the kitchen a tray was set with teapot, cups and saucers and a plate for fruit cake.

'When Dr Parnham arrives, show him in and boil water for tea, Lizzie,' Susan said. 'Bring in the tray and then leave us. I will call you if I want anything, but otherwise we are not to be disturbed.'

'Very well, Madam Trotula,' said the discreet Mrs Decker, who refused to speculate even to her mother about the midwife's secret matters. Susan took paper, ink and a quill pen and put them on the table in the parlour. It was not yet noon; she got out her sewing-bag and settled down to wait beside the fire.

Just after twelve came the urgent knock on the door, and Susan started: he was earlier than she had expected. Folding up her sewing, she sat bolt upright while Lizzie went to open the door.

Heavens, that was Sophia Glover's voice, surely? Susan's heart thumped. Sophy was the last person she wanted here when Dr Parnham arrived with news of his visit to Winchester. A flustered Lizzie put her head round the parlour door.

''Tis Miss Glover to see you, madam, and says

411

you're to come to the door. She's got a – a poor man with her, half-fainting and frozen with the cold!'

Susan rose and left the room at speed, saw the couple at the door and clapped her hand to her mouth.

Sophia's face was stern beneath her black bonnet.

'Help me, Susan. He came to my house seeking for you. Get a hot drink and warm a bed. He's more dead than alive.'

At first Susan hardly recognised the man whose matted uncut hair and beard obscured his sallow face; a tattered coat and breeches hung on his frame like a scarecrow's poor rags. But his sunken eyes lit up at the sight of her, and his lips moved as he tried to speak her name.

'Susan.'

The word was scarcely audible, and she was only just in time to support him before he fell to his knees. She and Sophia got him up the stairs between them and laid him upon her own bed.

For he was her lawful wedded husband.

Chapter 29

Everything was changed by Edward's return. From the moment that the two women removed all his clothing and put on a nightshirt supplied by the Widow Smart – it had belonged to the parson, and she sometimes wore it herself – he became the central point of May Cottage, around which the female household revolved.

'His parents must be told at once,' said Sophia, and Mag was accordingly sent up to Bever House with the news, and told to call at Mr Turnbull's on her way back.

By what Sophia had been able to gather, Edward had been ill with a fever that had raged on board during the uncomfortable Atlantic crossing. Already weakened by two years as a prisoner of war, when his life had been saved by the farmer's wife Mrs Nollekens, the long voyage in winter conditions and on meagre rations had again brought him close to death, and he arrived in Portsmouth a penniless beggar. It was not until some time later that his wife and cousin learned how he had been recognised by a former crew member and put on the stagecoach to Winchester. The final five-mile walk from Pulhurst in a bitter easterly wind ended on the doorstep of Glover Cottage where he begged to see Susan once more before dying.

Susan was racked with love, pity, remorse and every tender emotion, but on that first day of their reunion there was no time for words or even for tears. When Edward was settled in bed and a fire lit in the grate, she spoon-fed him with warm milk and brandy; his body warmed and he whispered her name, but no sooner did he start to revive than the Bever carriage arrived at the cottage with his parents, sisters and brother, all wanting to see him and welcome him home.

Susan was aghast at the sound of their voices below.

'Oh, Sophy, they can't all crowd into this room!'

'Leave them to me, Susan,' responded Sophia at once. 'Sit down beside him on that stool, and I will let his mother and father in to see him. The others must wait for another day.'

The Calthorpes were shocked at the wasted appearance of their younger son, and Gertrude burst into a torrent of tears.

'Oh, Edward, my poor son, he's no more than a skeleton,' she sobbed. 'Let us take him home in the carriage now, so that he may be nursed in his own room!'

'Hush, my love, he is well enough here for the time being,' Mr Calthorpe hastily interposed, knowing full well that Susan would not agree. Stepping to the side of the bed opposite her, they each leaned over to kiss the moist forehead and whisper words of encouragement to their son. Edward's eyelids fluttered, but he made no other response.

'I shall send Mrs Ferris to be his nurse,' said Mrs Calthorpe, wiping her eyes. 'She brought my Osmond back from the very jaws of death.'

'That will not be necessary,' said Sophia. 'His own wife will nurse him better than any other. She saved many lives in the influenza outbreak at the House of Industry.'

'But she has to be out attending women in childbed at all hours!' protested Mrs Calthorpe, as if Susan were not there.

'I shall be staying here at May Cottage to help care for him and to take over when the midwife has to go out,' answered Sophia calmly.

'But who will cook for him and wash his linen?' demanded the lady, her voice shriller with each sentence she uttered.

'Mrs Smart is an excellent housekeeper,' replied Sophia. 'Mrs Decker is also here, and there is a maid-servant. Rest assured, cousin, he will be as well cared for as at Bever House, and you may visit when you please – but he must *not* be upset or wearied. Now you had better leave him to rest.'

Mr Calthorpe gave her a grateful look, bowed to Susan, who had not spoken a word, and led his weeping wife from the room. Sophia followed them, and before they left it was arranged that a supply of nightshirts, linen and a sheepskin bedcover would be sent down from Bever House.

Soon after the carriage had rolled away, Mr Turnbull arrived; he hardly knew whether to rejoice at Edward's return or warn his wife of the gravity of his condition.

'The yellowness may be due to starvation, but I cannot rule out liver inflammation,' he told them. 'He must be encouraged to drink plenty of fluid-milk, cordials, a little wine – and try feeding him with bread soaked in milk, and a boiled potato mashed with butter and a beaten egg. We need to get some flesh on his bones.'

He paused and looked compassionately on the man he had known and liked from early childhood, then turned to Susan and allowed himself a smile.

'He is as well looked after as any invalid could be, madam.'

Turnbull was not the only medical man to see Edward Calthorpe on the day of his return to Beversley. Lizzie Decker appeared at the bedroom door while the apothecary was talking in a low tone to the two women, and announced that Dr Parnham had come over from Belhampton to see Madam Trotula.

Susan rose at once. 'Ah, yes, I will see him downstairs—'

But Sophia intervened, gesturing for Susan to sit down again.

'Bid the doctor to come up, Mrs Decker, and see Mr Edward for himself.'

Susan obediently resumed her seat and took hold of Edward's hand.

And that was the picture that Charles Parnham saw as he stood in the doorway: the sick man with his wife at his side, his cousin at hand and Mr Turnbull standing at the foot of the bed. He took in the situation in that one glance, nodded and bestowed a smile of sympathy upon them all.

'Heaven be thanked, Mrs Calthorpe, that he truly lives and is restored to you,' he said quietly, and glanced at the apothecary. 'If there is anything wanting, Turnbull, anything I can obtain for him, you have only to send word.'

Susan could not speak. She felt that there was nothing she could say to this man who knew and could be relied on to keep her secret. She guessed that whatever he had done about negotiating for an annulment, he would proceed no further until Edward was fit enough to be told about it, whenever that might be, and meanwhile the whole matter would have to be set aside.

Miss Glover accompanied the two men from the room and down the stairs, where they exchanged medical opinions, both favourable and unfavourable, before taking their leave.

So began a week in which Edward's life hung in the balance, when nights and days blurred into each other as he drifted down the strange and sometimes sinister pathways of delirium – always coming back to find Susan holding him in her arms, his head resting on the soft white bib of her apron. Her skilled hands now gently tended his body, washing his flesh and keeping his skin moist with oil applied to the creases of his groin and male parts. A glass jar was kept ready at the bedside for when he passed water, and Susan would carefully put it in position between his thighs and direct his limp male member into it. Sometimes he was scarcely aware of her ministrations, but in attending on these intimate needs she became familiar with his body in a way that she had previously never imagined.

By the second week in February Mr Turnbull pronounced Edward out of danger, and although he would need a long period of convalescence, he was gaining weight and strength with every day that passed. His parents continued to see him and note the improvement, and his sisters also visited. His brother, Osmond, and sister-in-law, Rosa, did not come to the cottage, but waited until he was well enough to make the short journey to Bever House. The carriage was sent for him and his wife, but Susan declined to accompany him, as she said she had to keep a close eye on a woman who had had a difficult birthing and whose baby she felt might have a stoppage.

On his return from the visit Edward was

completely exhausted, and took to his bed; it was not until the following morning that he talked of it to his wife and cousin as they sat at their needlework in the parlour. He began by quietly passing on the news that his sister-in-law believed herself to be with child again, and expecting to deliver some time in early September.

'My father is naturally happy at the prospect of a grandchild, and is sure that it will be a boy,' he told them. 'He hopes it will have a steadying effect on my brother, to know that he has an heir to follow him as landowner of the Bever estate.'

Sophia nodded gravely. She had heard about Osmond's drinking, especially since Rosa's disappointment last September.

'And did Rosa seem well?' she asked, as Susan remained silent.

'She says she is hoping to carry this one safely.'

He did not mention his own misgivings about his brother's marriage. Osmond had drunk his usual bottle of wine at dinner, and when the ladies had withdrawn, Edward had remonstrated with him at the request of their father.

'For God's sake, Ned, why d'you think I drink?' came the irritable reply. ''Tis to banish the sight of my poor Polly lying there with my two sweet sons, dead as gravestones but always with me, night and day.'

'It's time to consign that poor girl to heaven, Brother, and have some care for your wife and the child she's carrying,' Edward had urged. 'Your duty is now to the living. God has forgiven you your sins of the past—'

'*He* may have done, but *I* have not,' retorted Osmond, raising his glass again. Silent and morose when sober, he became maudlin when drunk, sighing and groaning over what could not be undone. Edward pitied him, having heard from Susan a brief account of Polly's death and Henry's secret part in it.

Sophia too kept her own counsel. Mrs Hansford had confided to her that Rosa was hurt by Osmond's mutterings in his sleep, his troubled memories of 'pretty little Polly'. Sophia prayed that the arrival of a lawful heir would end this dwelling on the girl he had loved and deserted.

Meanwhile she remarked on the improvement in Edward's looks. Susan smiled her agreement, and Edward said he must soon be about the business of making a living. When they both protested that he must not think of work for some time to come, he bid them affectionately to hold their tongues and listen to what he had to say.

''Tis time I told you something, dearest Susan, and you, too, Cousin,' he said with a sudden earnestness that compelled their full attention. 'You will have observed that I am changed by my experiences,' he began. 'In fact I have changed in every respect but one – my love for you, Susan.'

Susan lowered her eyes and Sophia remembered Henry's devotion.

Edward continued, 'When we were on opposite shores of the great Atlantic ocean and I feared never to see your face again, I began to consider how I would use my life if I was spared to return to you.'

He paused a little breathlessly, and Susan put down her sewing to move closer to him and take his hand.

'Ye always said ye'd join y'r father's old law office in Belhampton, Edward.'

'Ah, yes, and I dreamed of a couple of cosy little

rooms where we would live above the office or within easy distance of it – that was the dream, my Susan. But that's all past now, and I have lost any love I might once have had for the law.'

He paused again, his features assuming a faraway look, as if recalling a precious memory.

'Let me tell you of something that happened when I was lying sick with fever at Chippercreek, and would certainly have died if Mrs Nollekens had not defied her husband and taken me into their house.'

He stopped and hesitated as he searched for a way to describe the indescribable, while the two women hung upon his words.

'One night I seemed to leave my body and was carried up into an airy region of dazzling light, too bright to look upon. I believe that it was a foretaste of Heaven itself, and I cannot possibly convey to you what it was like, but I was in the presence of my Saviour and those who have gone ahead of us.'

'Oh, 'twas a blessed vision, Edward, given to you by God!' cried Sophia, tears springing to her eyes.

'I believe so, Sophy. And when I came back to the sorrows of this world, I knew that I would recover, but that my life must change direction. I vowed then and there to devote the rest of my time to serving God in his church in England. I shall therefore return to my Oxford college and study for ordination.'

'Praise be to God!' exclaimed Sophia, though Susan felt bewildered.

'But ye ha' studied f'r the law, Edward!'

He smiled lovingly at her. 'I have a good Bachelor's degree, 'tis true, and am well versed in the classics and proficient in Latin and Greek. This will be no bar to offering myself as a candidate for ordination, quite the contrary, and I hope to be a clerk in Holy Orders before too long. I am called to service, Susan, and must follow.'

'And when ye're ordained, Edward, will ye serve here – at Little St Giles?'

'My dear Susan, he must go where God sends him, whether here or elsewhere, and as his wife you must go with him,' Sophia told her seriously. Rising from her chair she went and kissed her cousin, and then Susan.

'I am so happy to hear your news, Edward, and will pray for your ministry – and for yours, Susan, as the wife of a clergyman.'

'But ye need to get y'r strength back, Edward, and I won't let ye go to Oxford or anywhere until ye're ready for't,' Susan told him with equal firmness, at which he laughed and said he had a scold for a wife but no complaints.

'With the good care and fattening up I'm receiving, I hope to be ready for Oxford before the end of March, though I dread the thought of parting from you again, dearest Susan.'

Parting again . . . The thought of it gave Susan a pang, not knowing for how long he would be away. During these winter weeks of nursing him, sleeping beside him as he lay in her own bed, she had experienced something very close to happiness. In his weak state there had been no question of conjugal relations, yet she had been reminded of the depth of his love, and of hers for him. Any talk of an annulment would have to be shelved until . . . perhaps until after his return from Oxford as a clerk in Holy Orders. She trusted that she would know when the time was right. It was not yet.

Then Sophia came and put an arm around her waist. 'This has been a very special time in our lives,

421

Susan. It has made a great difference to me, can't you see?'

Susan turned to look at her friend – the sweetly earnest face, the blue eyes that could be stern as well as gentle. And she saw that it was true. Gone was the pallor, the hollow cheeks with their gaunt shadows, the hopeless misery of eyes and mouth: Sophia Glover was smiling again, as if a light had been relit.

'Sophy! Oh, dearest Sophy, how would we ha' done without ye through all this time?'

'Ah, Susan, 'tis by God's grace and thanks to you and Edward, I have returned to the land of the living.'

Visitors now began to call, among them the rector, who came and told the invalid about his own wretched state of health.

'My niece has no idea of my needs as poor Amelia had,' he said as he slumped wearily on the parlour sofa. 'I've lost much weight, yet I'm hungry and parched with thirst half the time. It's all very fine for Turnbull to tell me to drink more water, but nothing seems to quench it. Yesterday I drank a pint mug of porter twice over, and half a bottle of claret within two hours of dining.'

Edward winced, and tried not to recoil from the unpleasant, acidic smell of the man's breath.

'I can see that you are leaner, sir,' he said. 'Has Miss Gravett put you on a regime of no red meat or pudding?'

'She seems to think that more vegetables and fruit will help to cure the soreness of my gums,' grumbled the rector, licking his lips with the tip of his tongue. 'And she says 'twill help the gravel. I often need to void water more than twice in an hour – and 'tis as if the piss was scalding hot.' He grimaced, and Edward had to agree that he looked far from well.

'What does Mr Turnbull say, sir?'

'I sometimes wonder how much that man actually knows about medical matters, Edward,' growled the rector. 'Half the time he seems to say the first thing that comes into his head, and is always looking at the clock when he visits.'

Dr Gravett's tendency to hypochondria was well known – in fact something of a joke in Beversley – but it now occurred to Edward that the man might have a serious disorder and nobody was taking him seriously.

'At any rate, *you* seem to have recovered well,' said Gravett, who had not visited while Edward was at his most critical. 'I hear that you are going for ordination.' He sniffed. 'Married men are better off than bachelors in the Church, though Amelia was practically as good as a wife when I was indisposed. My niece has no understanding of men's ailments, none whatsoever.'

He sighed heavily, and got to his feet, leaning on his stick. 'And you've had your cousin Glover attending on you as well, I hear. Well, young Calthorpe, I must bid you good day and wish myself half as fortunate.'

As Edward watched him shuffle out of the room, he felt that he was indeed more fortunate in every way than poor Dr Gravett.

Edward left Beversley for Oxford in the middle of March, just as the daffodils were coming into bloom. The parting was the more painful to Susan because of the secret plan she shared with Parnham and which

423

now lay on her conscience like a betrayal of Edward's love.

Lying in the narrow span of her bed meant that they slept closely enfolded in each other's arms, their slumbers sweet and undisturbed by lurking terrors.

Until that last night.

'Dearest Susan, you have saved my life, yet I have never honoured you as my wife,' he murmured, kissing her forehead and drawing her closer under the sheepskin.

'Don't speak o't, Edward, ye've been so ill – and 'tis all I want, to lie here alongside o' ye,' she whispered back. 'I want nothing more'n this.'

'Oh, Susan, Susan.'

He buried his face against her neck, and she felt his right hand stroking her back through her nightgown. She trembled as he gently turned her over and let his hand cover each soft breast in turn.

'You are so beautiful, my Susan.'

His hand was on her waist, her hip, her belly, touching her through the woollen folds while his encircling left arm rocked her with a tender, reassuring movement that filled her with an infinite longing, as if she glimpsed a distant happiness not allowed to such as she. She made herself lie still and breathe slowly while he whispered to her of his love, but when his questing fingers descended towards that place she knew so well in other women, her whole body tensed, and at once he withdrew his hand. Memories of their wedding night, the disappointment and humiliation now flooded back to them both with keen dismay; Edward remembered holding a terrified woman in his arms, and had no desire for that to happen again.

'All right, dearest Susan, all right, you have

nothing to fear. Go to sleep, my love – go to sleep.'

But it took her some time to rest in his arms and breathe normally.

One day, he thought, I shall ask her to tell me all about what happened to cause this unnatural fear. But not yet.

One day, she thought, I shall tell him how he can be free. But not now.

With the war over, life in Beversley went on as usual. Miss Glover returned to her cottage and threw herself into parish duties with much of her former energy and enthusiasm; Mrs Decker became proficient at caring for women in travail, and able to cope with the easier deliveries when several babies were born within a short space of time; and Miss Calthorpe continued teaching the orphaned children, and wondered whether she should mention to the midwife that poor Dolly Lucket had become noticeably frailer of late, an old woman at forty.

Mrs Osmond Calthorpe spent her time lying on a chaise-longue with a romantic novel. Her mother and mother-in-law spent much of their time at her side, while Mrs Ferris quietly busied herself in the background.

'Mrs Madingley of Belhampton is a midwife to gentlewomen, and delivered Lady Lyle's granddaughter last week,' said Mrs Gertrude Calthorpe to Mr Turnbull when he called to enquire about the progress of the young wife and admire her swelling belly. 'She is coming to stay here at Bever House at the beginning of August, so as to be on hand for Rosa's travail.'

The apothecary bowed and said that he had heard Mrs Madingley highly spoken of, while privately hoping that he would not be involved with the confinement. He could have wished that Madam Trotula was in charge, but that of course was out of the question; and poor Mrs Coulter was in constant pain, unable to leave her bed in the almshouse.

The news from Oxford was good, and Susan eagerly awaited Edward's letters. As Mr Calthorpe observed on one of his quiet visits to the daughter-in-law he secretly preferred in spite of her continued estrangement, Edward was no mere undergraduate. With his classics degree and excellent testimonials from former tutors, and perhaps above all for the maturity that life in the navy and as a prisoner-of-war had given him, he found himself in good standing with the Bishop's chaplain, the official who would examine him for ordination as deacon.

'This is a very different Life from when I last was here, dear Wife,' he wrote. 'Already I read Prayers and Preach in country Churches around Oxford where there is a lack for any reason, and I have been told that there is a Curacy in the offing.'

'D'ye think he means in Hampshire, Mr Calthorpe?'

'No, no – Oxfordshire. They will not easily part with him,' replied his father. 'Are you not glad for your husband, Susan?'

She was silent, and Calthorpe could see that she was troubled, though he could not hope that she would confide in him.

'I'm glad that Edward's taken up with the Church,' she said at last, putting on her bonnet and cape. ''Tis likely to bring him more comfort than the law. I must go out on my visits now, sir, so bid ye good day. Thank ye for calling to see me.'

She gave him no message for Bever House.

At the end of her rounds, Susan decided to call on Sophia and talk over a cup of tea.

'Was that the rector I saw coming from here, Sophy?'

'Yes, he has visited,' replied her friend, looking flustered.

'So did he give ye a list o' his ailments, the same as he gave Edward?'

Sophia gave a choking sound, and Susan looked at her sharply.

'Ye're upset about something, Sophy – what is it?'

''Tis not serious, but I suppose I'm feeling a little – er – surprised,' replied Sophia, clasping and unclasping her hands.

'What's *happened*?' demanded Susan in alarm.

'I have had to disappoint him, you see – the rector.'

Susan stared at her pink-cheeked friend.

'Disappoint him? How? You *don't* mean . . .'

'You'll probably laugh, Susan, but the poor man came to ask me to marry him.'

'*What?* Asked you – so soon after – oh, the bare face of him – the wicked old – oh, I can't believe it!'

Susan was so angry and offended on her friend's behalf that Sophia felt she should try to excuse the rector to some degree.

'He feels so lonely and neglected at the rectory these days, Susan, and misses Amelia very much.'

'Yes, 'cause she gave in to his whims and fancies, and had no life o' her own! And did he think ye would do the same, give up all y'r good works to wait on him hand and foot?'

'Oh, Susan, he has never been able to see his own faults, and nobody has ever challenged him about his shortcomings as a clergyman. He had seen how well Edward recovered from his illness, and thought that if he had me to look after him, he too would improve in health. That's what he said: "If you were to marry me and move into the rectory, Miss Glover, I know I would be comfortable." '

'Good God! And what did you say to that?'

'I simply told him that I would never marry. I could not bring myself even to utter dear Henry's name. He started to tell me of the advantages I would enjoy as rector's wife, but I cut him short and said I was sorry to disappoint him.'

'And what did the old wretch say to that?'

'Well, he thought I was foolish to turn down a good offer, and that I was not likely to get another at my age and with no *status*, you know – by which he meant my parentage – and he said he hoped I wouldn't regret it.'

Susan sat down and threw her bonnet on the floor. 'How dare he think himself half good enough! Oh, Sophy, just to think o' you and *ugh*!' She wrinkled her face in revulsion.

'Don't be too hard on him, Susan. I think he's truly a sick man, and ready to grasp at straws.'

'Ready to grasp at a handsome woman, you mean!'

Susan's burst of derisive laughter was heard by Tess and the kitchen maid, and did not take long to re-echo in places where the choicer morsels of Beversley gossip were recounted.

When the news of Mrs Coulter's death reached Beversley, Mr Calthorpe at once arranged for her body to be brought back for burial in the churchyard of Great St Giles. The church was packed for the funeral of a woman who had served the parish

428

faithfully throughout her long widowhood. Parson Roberts read the prayers, the rector being indisposed, and Miss Glover gave the eulogy, during which Widow Gibson wept noisily.

'We can all take comfort that Margaret has entered into her rest, freed from the burden of pain at last,' concluded Miss Glover to a general murmur of assent, and a large procession followed the bier to the last resting-place.

'Who be the gen'leman in the tall black hat?' asked young Mrs Spooner, her voice carrying above the low murmurs of the rest.

'Hush, Mary, that's the man-midwife from Belhampton, come to pay his respects,' answered Mrs Decker, frowning and glancing sideways at Susan.

When the earth had been cast over the grave and the mourners began to disperse, Charles Parnham edged his way to Susan's side. After shaking hands with Miss Glover and Mr Turnbull, he took Susan's arm and led her a little distance away among the headstones, out of earshot.

'And how goes the world with you, Signora Trotula?' he asked.

'Well enough, Dr Parnham. And yeself, sir?'

'Still at your service if and when you have need, my child.' He spoke hurriedly, searching her face. 'Your husband is to enter the Church, I hear. Do you see yourself as a clergy wife?'

Susan's face was pale and set. 'I can't be his wife, sir, f'r the reason ye know well,' she muttered in such a low, rapid tone that he had to lean his head towards her to hear. 'At some time, maybe after he's ordained f'r the Church, I'll tell him how he may be free o' me. May I call on ye then, sir?'

He sighed. 'You know you can call on me, child,

but I had hoped that you and he were – having seen your husband on the very day of his return, and his need of your devotion—'

He broke off, inwardly struggling to advise her rightly.

'My dear child, I have been thinking about you and Edward and – and this burden you bear from the past. Does he still know nothing of it?'

'No, and he must *never* know it, Dr Parnham!'

'Now listen, for I think you are wrong there. I now believe that you should tell him the full truth.'

'*No!*'

'But he has a right to be told, and allowed to make his own judgement. If he's the man I take him for, he'll be distressed, of course, but his love will be unchanged. In my experience truth is almost always better than ignorance, however painful it may be.'

'For God's sake, Dr Parnham, he mustn't *ever* know,' she insisted with controlled vehemence, and he noticed that Miss Glover was watching them.

'Hush, hush, all right, forgive me, my poor child.' He put a hand lightly on her shoulder. 'Now, I have been invited to the Hôtel-Dieu in Paris for two months, until mid-September. I'll let you know of my return in case you need me.'

He smiled and shook her hand. 'Your friend Miss Glover is waiting for you over there. She will assume you are upset for Mrs Coulter, so let her think so. We must say goodbye now, my dear, and please consider what I have said.'

'Goodbye, Dr Parnham. God bless you, sir.'

They shook hands and he turned abruptly away. Sophia looked on the point of saying something when Susan rejoined her, but refrained. Whatever the state of the doctor's heart, she was in no doubt of Susan's loyalty to her husband.

When Mr Turnbull left the graveside of his old and trusted friend, the promptings of conscience sent him straight to the rectory. He had been putting off his next visit to Dr Gravett, and now braced himself to hear the usual catalogue of woe with better forbearance.

As he was shown up the stairs by a housemaid – Miss Gravett having not yet returned from the funeral – he met a manservant carrying a chamberpot from the rector's room. Suddenly an idea came into his mind: a suspicion that the old hypochondriac might have some reason for his complaints.

'Give that to me for a minute,' he told the man. 'I have to make a diagnostic test.'

On the landing he set the pot upon a chair, and dipping his right forefinger into the urine he swirled it round and then, holding his breath, he placed his wet finger on his tongue.

There was no mistaking the taste: it was honey-sweet.

Of course. He should have guessed it weeks ago. The thirst, the loss of weight, the dry, sore mouth – all pointed to the mysterious and fatal sugar malady, described as *diabetes* by the ancient Greek physicians. The cause was not understood, and there was no cure: Octavius Gravett would die.

The apothecary felt sick and ashamed of his former impatience with a man he had never liked, but who must now face a hideous ordeal, starving to death whilst his body for some unknown reason rejected food and passed it straight through the system.

Turnbull heard the front door open, and Miss

Gravett's voice below in the hall. Putting on a suitably grave expression, he went down to break the news to her and discuss what to tell the invalid.

Even as he did so, he caught himself looking ahead: the rector would need to be replaced, and soon.

Part IV: 1783

Rectory Wife

Chapter 30

Susan drew Edward's letter from its envelope and spread it out on her lap to read again. It was dated 2 August.

'I think I did well enough before the Bishop's chaplain,' he had written. 'He gave me a Greek New Testament & set me to construe the 4th Chap: of St Paul's Epistle to Ephesians. I went tolerably through to the end, but wonder what good Greek will be to a Country Parson?'

Susan smiled and sighed; she felt she could picture the scene.

'Though there is much Good in this Chap: esp: the final Verses.'

I must look at that passage in the Bible, Susan thought, and continued to read.

'He then asked me if I wd uphold the Protestant Religion in England, and abide by the 39 Articles of the Church. The whole of it was not above half an hour. I am hopeful of taking Holy Orders in another Month, and then to see you again, dear Wife and Love of my Life. There is much to consider fr the Future. I pray fr you & ask yr prayers fr yr loving & devoted Husband, Edwd: Calthorpe.'

Susan sat in silent thought, wondering if he had yet heard of the rector's illness. Parson Roberts was taking Divine Service in both parishes, and finding his duties heavy, especially as his young wife was due to give birth at Christmas to their first child. Mr

Calthorpe made no secret of his hopes that Edward would be the next incumbent of Great St Giles.

I simply could not bear it, Susan thought despairingly. To live in the shadow of Bever House, patronised by Mrs Calthorpe and Osmond's wife would be intolerable. Edward will have to be told about the annulment, and soon. Should she write to tell him of it now? Or wait until he returned, a clerk in Holy Orders, and spring it on him? What a greeting!

Oh, Edward, Edward – would he ever forgive her?

There was a tap at the door, and Mrs Decker's eager face appeared round it.

'Yes, Lizzie, what is it?'

'My mother thinks you should know, Susan, that Mrs Osmond Calthorpe's waters broke this morning, a full month before due time, as she sat on the close-stool. Mrs Hansford has gone to her side, and the gig has been sent to Belhampton to fetch Mrs Madingley.'

Susan raised her eyebrows slightly. 'Indeed? And why should that be o' interest to me?' she asked coldly. ''Tis time ye went back to see that woman who delivered last night and lost a deal o' blood.'

Lizzie disappeared at once, and Susan heard her talking in a low tone to Mrs Smart in the hallway. She frowned and shook her head in sheer vexation at the news: there would be no other topic of conversation until that simpering creature was delivered of her child, to be followed by a daily report on its progress.

As she was putting on her bonnet and cloak to go out on her visits, Sophia called, asking if she had heard the news.

'Yes, Sophy, Lizzie and her mother always hear o'

such things the day before they happen,' Susan replied tartly.

'And d'you think the child will be in greater danger for birthing a month before its due time, Susan?'

'I ha' no idea, Sophy. Ye'd best ask that Mrs Whatshername – her they've sent the gig to Belhampton for. 'Tis no concern o' mine,' answered Susan stonily, and Sophia could have bitten her tongue.

'Oh, Susan, I'm sorry, but Rosa is Henry's sister, and would have been mine if he and I—'

'Yes, Sophy, I'm sorry too, but I care no more f'r the Calthorpes o' Bever House than they cared f'r Polly when she lay dying. And now ye must excuse me, I ha' calls to make.'

Sophia stared helplessly at her friend's retreating back. There seemed little prospect of her cousin Edward becoming rector of Great St Giles while his wife still retained such enmity against his family.

When Mr Turnbull was awakened just before midnight, his heart plummeted. He had felt apprehensive about Mrs Osmond from the start, and the arrival of a messenger on horseback confirmed his misgivings. Sure enough, as soon as he entered the birthchamber he sensed an unseen Visitor waiting in the shadows: a presence he had encountered all too often in thirty years as unlicensed physician in Beversley.

The women stood anxiously round the bed – Mrs Gertrude Calthorpe, her elder daughter, Mrs Hansford, Mrs Ferris and two maidservants. Rosa lay on her back with glazed eyes and wine-laden breath. Mrs Madingley, flushed and perspiring, could not conceal her dismay.

437

'First I thought 'twas a head presenting, then it felt like a breech, and now . . .'

She drew back the sheet, and Turnbull gave a horrified gasp when he saw a tiny arm protruding from the mother's body.

''Twas the shoulder I felt, not the breech, and the pressure has pushed this down,' muttered the midwife. She and Turnbull both knew that the head could never come through with the shoulder blocking the outlet: when a shoulder presents there is no mechanism for delivery.

Turnbull beckoned to the midwife to consult with him in the corridor outside the bedchamber.

'What is to be done? The contractions will split the womb,' he whispered frantically.

'She's not getting much by way of contractions now. The womb is in inertia,' replied the midwife.

'Then the child is trapped within her and will suffocate,' said the apothecary between chattering teeth. 'Neither she nor the child can be saved, with such total obstruction of travail. Oh, my God, woman, what is to be done?'

He remembered how Polly Lucket had died with Osmond's sons still within her womb. Was this a terrible justice being visited upon the man? Turnbull shuddered.

'She might be saved if the child were sacrificed,' whispered Mrs Madingley, and Turnbull could have groaned at hearing his own thoughts put into words. 'A hook passed in to sever the head, and then to drag forth the body piecemeal.'

Turnbull wanted to put his hands over his ears. 'I cannot do it, I would not dare, madam. Can you do it?'

'Not I, 'tis no part of a midwife's duty, I don't

438

keep hooks and suchlike. Is there a doctor we can call on?'

'There's one in Basingstoke, but – oh, if only Parnham were here and not in Paris!' Turnbull was shaking from head to foot, and Mrs Madingley saw that she would have to take the lead.

'Look, Turnbull, the child is small, a full month before its time. It may be possible to deliver it if I pull on the arm and you press down on the belly from above. 'Tis the only chance, and we must try it.'

'We shall have to tell the family of the risks, and obtain their permission,' said Turnbull, his face deadly white.

Mrs Gertrude Calthorpe was distracted to the point of hysteria, Osmond was dead-drunk in an armchair downstairs and Mr Calthorpe told them to go ahead and save the child if they possibly could, even if it meant the loss of an arm.

The midwife and apothecary approached the bed, but were halted by a cold, clear command from the tall woman at its head.

'You will not pull on the child's arm.'

Everybody in the room turned to look at Jael Ferris, her black eyes now hollow and red-rimmed from lack of sleep.

'You will not pull on the child's arm.'

'Then what in God's name are we to do, Mrs Ferris?' moaned Gertrude Calthorpe, raising a haggard face to the woman who had been her trusted personal maid and nurse to the family ever since Miss Glover had left Bever House. 'What shall we *do*?'

'Send for Madam Trotula,' ordered Mrs Ferris.

'Yes, send for her at once,' echoed Turnbull fervently.

Mrs Calthorpe glanced wildly round, then flew from the room and down the stairs to where her husband paced the hall.

'We are to send for Madam Trotula – Edward's wife – so tell Berry to go out again on Quicksilver to May Cottage, *now*!' she cried.

Mr Calthorpe shook his head. 'No, Gertrude, if we are asking Edward's wife to come to Osmond's, we must send the carriage for her. I will call Jude and go with him myself. And pray that she may show more mercy than her sister received from us.'

Turning his back on his wife, he strode out to the stable-yard, calling for Jude and the hands to wake up and get out the carriage and horses.

Susan had not slept. The summer night was full of strange and disturbing sounds: the distant yelp of a fox, the call of a night bird, the rustlings and scamperings of field and woodland all seemed unnaturally magnified. She started up with a cry when something stirred in the semi-darkness, but it was only the curtain moving in the breeze from the half-open window.

She got out of bed and went to look up at the night sky. Was Edward awake in his college room, his thoughts on his coming ordination as a priest in the Church of England? How would he receive her offer of an annulment? Would he accept his freedom to find a proper wife? Or would he refuse, and live out his life like one of those priests of the old Roman faith, celibate and childless? He was constantly on her mind.

And so was something else. What was happening at this moment at Bever House? Lizzie and her mother had murmured to each other, shaking their heads; and Lizzie had left a candle burning in the window beside the front door of May Cottage as was their practice when a call was expected.

Great St Giles's clock struck one.

When Susan heard the distant clatter of horses' hoofs, and iron-rimmed wheels, she knew that it was the sound of her destiny approaching. She stood absolutely still as the Bever carriage drew rapidly nearer and pulled up outside the cottage, its four lamps blazing in the dark.

Lizzie Decker emerged from the room she shared with little Kitty, pulling a woollen wrap over her nightgown.

'All right, I'm coming!' she called in response to knocking at the door. 'Susan, are you awake? 'Tis the Bever carriage waiting below. They've come for you!'

Susan still did not move. She seemed rooted to the spot as she heard the door being opened and her father-in-law's voice in the little hallway. He was asking for her.

What should she say?

Should she give the same reply that Mrs Calthorpe and the rector had given Joby? *Be off with you!*

When Polly lay dying with Osmond's chidren, no pity had been shown to her. Susan could now reply, *And I care nothing for Osmond's third child.*

What should she say?

Hardly conscious of moving, she found herself standing at the foot of the stairs. Mr Calthorpe was on his knees before her, pleading brokenly through his tears.

'Susan – Madam Trotula – I have come to ask your forgiveness for the wrong done to your sister, and to beg you to come to my son Osmond's wife, who is likely to die with her child if nothing can be done to deliver her. The carriage is here for you. Oh, Susan, for Edward's sake show mercy and come to her!'

What should she say?

The answer came to her quite simply. She was a midwife, a member of an honourable calling from time immemorial, bound by duty to attend women in travail: and that meant *any* woman, good or bad, a barbarian or an infidel, an enemy of England or of her own kin. The Egyptian midwives in the days of Moses had defied the Pharaoh's order to kill every Hebrew baby boy at birth, because of their sacred duty to save life, not take it. And so must she, Susan Calthorpe, save Osmond's child if she could.

If she refused, she was no midwife.

Calthorpe waited for her answer, and Lizzie stood aside, candle in hand, as Susan gave it.

'Give me two minutes to dress and get my bag.'

'Thanks be to God,' murmured Calthorpe, rising from his knees, and two minutes later he assisted her into the carriage. Jude picked up the reins and gave his clucking signal to the four horses; the harnesses tautened and creaked, and the carriage moved off. Susan thought that the whole of Beversley must have been wakened by the commotion.

During the short journey, her first in the Bever carriage, no words were exchanged, but a whole series of memories paraded through Susan's head. She saw herself as a girl of twelve, almost run down by this same carriage, and shouted at by the same coachman. That was the day she had caused Edward to fall from his horse, the day Miss Glover had offered to send her to Mrs Bryers' school. There she had been cold-shouldered by the Calthorpe girls, and Rosa had giggled and held her nose at the smelly child from the Ash-Pits. Yet their unkindness had

442

spurred her on to do better than any of them, and now here she was, more than ten years later, a Calthorpe herself and travelling in the family carriage specially sent for her.

When they drew up at the front entrance of Bever House, Susan recalled the one previous occasion she had passed through it, on the night of the ball – was it only five years ago? She and the Bennett ladies had been put in the charge of a pock-marked maidservant who had taken them up to a room with straw mattresses on the floor. Now she was received by a bowing manservant who took her bonnet and shawl; Mr Calthorpe escorted her up the main staircase and along a corridor to the room where Rosa lay. Here she was respectfully greeted by the distracted Calthorpe ladies and an exhausted Mrs Hansford. Mr Turnbull was overwhelmingly relieved to see her, and they all drew aside to allow her access to the bedside.

Mrs Madingley pulled back the sheet from the semi-conscious Rosa, and revealed the prolapsed arm, now blue and swollen.

Susan knew at once what she would have to attempt: a hazardous procedure she had never done before. She would need assistance. Turning to face the company, she spoke with authority.

'Everybody's to leave this room except f'r *you*,' she nodded to Mrs Madingley, and looked round to find a sensible, trustworthy face. 'And *you*,' she said to Jael Ferris. 'Now, I want clean warm water and towels.'

The two prospective grandmothers supported each other as they shuffled from the room with Selina. Turnbull thankfully went downstairs to talk with Mr Calthorpe over a large brandy, and Susan was left with Rosa and her two assistants, to face the greatest challenge of her career.

Dr Parnham had taught her about malpresentations – abnormal positions of the child *in utero*. He said that it was sometimes possible to turn the child to a breech position by inserting a hand up through the ring of the womb and pulling down a leg. It was called version, and had been performed by the ancient Greeks, and more recently by a Frenchman, Ambroise Paré at the Hôtel-Dieu in Paris. There were enormous risks involved, one being rupture of the womb, and the likelihood of childbed fever afterwards. It was also unbearably painful, and Susan was thankful that Rosa had been given frequent sips of wine over a long period, and now appeared to be in a semi-comatose state, with an inert womb. Version must be attempted if her life was to be saved, whether the child was alive or not; there was no point in trying to listen for its heartbeat now.

Susan recalled what her teacher had said: in a case of prolapsed cord or arm, get the woman into the genu-pectoral position, to relieve the pressure on the neck of the womb.

'Help me to get her off the bed and on to her elbows and knees on the floor,' she ordered. 'Then we must let her head go down to rest on her arms.'

Between the three of them Rosa was heaved into an ungainly position on the floor with her buttocks up and her chest down. She had to be supported by Mrs Ferris or she would have toppled over sideways.

Susan washed her hands, dried them on a towel and dipped the fingers of her right hand in the jar of boiled goose-grease from her bag. Approaching Rosa from behind, she passed her hand into the birth passage by the side of the baby's arm. The ring was

444

fully open, and Susan was able to put three fingers through it and push at the child's shoulder to make enough room to tuck the arm back inside, flexing it at the elbow.

So far, so good. Now she had to slip her hand completely through the ring and inside the womb; fortunately her hand was small, and she passed it along the side of the child's body until she found a foot – or was it a hand? Once satisfied that it had a heel, she gripped it between her index and middle fingers and drew it down through the ring of the womb, along the birth-passage and out. Mrs Madingley gave a gasp and a stifled cry when she saw it appear, and Susan continued to pull with a sustained traction until the child's buttocks appeared and the other leg came down spontaneously. The child was revealed to be a girl. Throughout this critical minute Rosa groaned in agony, and Jael Ferris never wavered in physically supporting her and giving her comfort; Susan gave all her attention to the delicate and dangerous procedure, and as the body advanced, she pulled down a loop of the umbilical cord, and noted that it was weakly pulsating.

'Merciful God, it's still alive,' breathed Mrs Madingley.

'Now ye must turn her over on to her back, so that the child's head can—' began Susan, but before the women could move Rosa again, the little body slipped out spontaneously – the shoulders, the left arm, the swollen and discoloured right arm, and then, smoothly and easily, the head came through.

And so a daughter was born to Rosa Calthorpe between two and three o'clock in the morning. Jael Ferris wept as she watched Susan sever the cord and hold the little body in her hands, softly blowing upon

445

it and discovering a feeble heartbeat. The baby's chest jerked, drawing in air, and within half a minute she gave a thin cry.

But Death had not yet left the chamber. Susan handed the baby to Mrs Madingley, and turned to the mother.

'We must get her back on the bed again,' she told Jael, and together they lifted the limp body. A brisk haemorrhage from the overstretched, paper-thin womb followed the delivery, and continued until the after-burden was expelled. Then with her left fist in the birth-passage and maintaining pressure on the belly with her right hand, Susan compressed the womb until the bleeding slackened. The twin spectres of a limp, lifeless baby and a serious loss of maternal blood were always to be dreaded at the end of a long travail; but this child was alive, though small, and with a hugely congested right arm – and the mother's bleeding had been brought under control. Susan felt a lightening of the air in the room as the the grim Presence departed.

'Turn her over on to her left side, keep her warm and let her rest,' Susan told Jael. ''Twill be a long time afore she recovers from this.'

Heaven grant that childbed fever doesn't follow on all my handling inside the womb, she added to herself, and was thankful that the child was small – scarcely five pounds, as it turned out – or version would have been impossible. Or fatal.

It was time to bring in the two new grandmothers and a whey-faced Mr Turnbull, who shook Susan's hand and could not speak for emotion. His open admiration for her skill and dexterity was followed by the praise and gratitude of the whole family. Mrs Calthorpe wept her thanks and called Susan a daughter of the house; Selina kissed her, and Caroline was clearly overawed at this elevation of Edward's low-born wife whom she must now call sister.

Susan accepted their homage with a gracious calm, though in fact she was floating in that happy state of triumph and relief that all midwives experience when a long and difficult travail ends with a live birth; and in the present circumstances her exultation was intensified by her new status with the Calthorpes of Bever House: a strange and heady sensation indeed for the girl from the Ash-Pits! She saw that the events of this night had ended the enmity between herself and Edward's family; it had been driven out by the birth of a child.

'Rosa'll need very careful nursing, and I'll come back to see her later,' she told Mrs Calthorpe. 'And the baby'll be wanting a wet-nurse to suckle her. I know a girl with a good supply o' milk above a year who's fed several babies and a pair o' twins since her own was weaned – she's slow-witted, but her milk's as good as a wiser woman's. I don't know about the baby's arm, whether it'll be o' use. We can but wait and hope.'

While Mrs Ferris promised round-the-clock care of mother and baby, Mrs Madingley quickly made her excuses and took a hurried leave of Bever House. She wanted nothing laid at her door if the mother should die of childbed fever or if the child's arm should wither and become useless.

When Susan went downstairs she was offered breakfast and whatever payment she cared to ask for by Mr Calthorpe, who threw his arms around her and called her his daughter.

'We shall be forever in your debt, Susan. Edward

shall hear every detail of what has happened this night.'

'I want no payment, sir,' she insisted, and for the first time saw Edward's father for what he was, a well-intentioned man who had done his best to shoulder the duties he had inherited, not helped by having a silly, shallow-minded wife; there was no harm in him, and she was happy to return his embrace. Even so, she was relieved not to see Osmond, who had taken to his bed overcome with emotion, so it was said.

'The Bever carriage awaits you whenever you wish to leave, Susan,' said Calthorpe, and although she would have liked to walk home in the freshness of early morning, she thought it better to accept the offer graciously; so once again she stepped into the imposing conveyance.

'May Cottage, madam?' asked Jude deferentially.

'No, Glover Cottage, please,' she said on a sudden impulse to surprise her friend with a spectacular arrival at this early hour.

But Sophia was ready and waiting, having heard from Mrs Decker about the Bever carriage being sent for the midwife, and she flew out of her door to greet Susan.

'Susan, dearest Susan, you've worked a miracle!' she cried, opening her arms to the woman of the hour. A detailed account of the night's events was demanded, and Susan spoke of her new lightness of heart now that her anger against the Calthorpes had vanished, risen like morning dew when the sun's warmth turns it to vapour; though she admitted that she had been thankful not to see Osmond.

'Ah, Susan, one day you will learn to pity him,' Sophia told her earnestly, having heard from Mrs

Hansford of his troubled nights and dreams of Polly and their baby sons, a constant, reproachful image that he vainly tried to banish by drinking.

'How proud Edward will be of you, Susan! Oh, thanks be to God that you were there to save their lives!'

And as the days passed the news from Bever House continued to be good. Rosa remained pale and languid for some time, but did not fall victim to childbed fever, and Susan put this down to Mrs Ferris's good care. The baby was named Gertrude after her grandmother, and thanks to a plentiful supply of milk from her wet-nurse, she steadily gained weight. Selina Calthorpe had been taken aback when Susan introduced the wet-nurse, a big, placidly smiling girl whose own child, now toddling, looked uncommonly like a little monkey; but catching Susan's eye, Miss Calthorpe decided not to remember certain stories last year at the House of Industry.

Little Gertrude's right arm lost its purple, swollen appearance and became soft and flaccid. A doctor came out from Basingstoke to give his opinion in exchange for two guineas, and told the parents no more than Susan and Mr Turnbull had done – that they would have to wait and see how the child's arm did. Meanwhile Susan advised stroking it, gently bending and straightening the elbow joint in imitation of natural movement.

Everything was going well. A joyful letter arrived from Edward telling Susan that words could not express his admiration, his loving gratitude; and in the circumstances of her new status at Bever House she actually began to hope for deliverance from the shadows of her childhood; that she might now leave her past behind and become a proper wife to Edward and a mother of his children. It seemed like the turning of the tide . . .

Until one day at the beginning of September when Miss Calthorpe drew her aside and said there was something she had to tell her.

'I know it's not my business, Susan, but I feel it my duty to let you know,' she said diffidently. 'If you were ever to blame me for *not* speaking—'

'What is it, Selina? What should I know?' asked Susan, suspecting some case of concealment of pregnancy.

'It's – er, it's about that poor Mrs Dolly Lucket. She's taken to her bed and Mrs Croker thinks she may be declining. I thought you ought to be told, in case you wanted to, er . . .'

Her words petered out to an awkward silence, and Susan looked so dismayed that Selina almost wished she had not spoken.

'I see. Thank ye, Selina,' Susan said at length. 'Yes, ye did right to tell me.'

She knew she would have to visit, and take Joby with her. The thought of confronting that unquiet spirit again filled her with the utmost reluctance: so many dark shadows lurked in their shared past, fear and horror and guilt and defilement.

Unforgotten and unforgiven.

In the solitude of her room, Susan covered her face with her hands. Vain hopes! What was done could never be undone.

Chapter 31

'I have to go to Belhampton this afternoon on business, Susan. Would you like to come with me?'

Sophia threw out the casual offer with a non-chalant air, as if the idea had just occurred to her.

'I hadn't thought o' going out, Sophy, but – well, I may be taking Joby over to the House one day this week or next, so I won't come today, thank ye.'

'But that's better still. I'll take you both. Two o'clock this afternoon,' said Sophia decisively.

'But Dan Spooner may be needing Joby at the forge.'

'I'll speak to Spooner and ask him to allow Job a couple of free hours,' countered Sophia, and Susan knew then that Mad Doll's decline must be known in the village, and her friend was urging her to visit without further delay.

'I don't want to give you the trouble, Sophy.'

''Tis no inconvenience. I'll set you and Job down at the House, and call for you on my way back. 'Twill give you about an hour.'

And she was gone before any further objections could be made.

Susan suppressed a shiver of apprehension. It was kind of Sophy to give up her time, but she would have preferred to drive herself and Joby in the pony-trap on this particular occasion. She had thought of going at the end of the week, and *today* gave her no time to prepare herself. At least Sophy was going on

451

into the town, and not accompanying her to the bedside: that would be intolerable.

Sophia Glover breathed a sigh of relief; pretence of any kind was completely against her nature, but her apparently impulsive offer had been carefully rehearsed, following a visit from a worried Selina Calthorpe.

'You see, Miss Gl— Sophia, I told Madam Tr— Susan about Mrs Lucket over a week ago, and she said she'd visit with her brother, but she has still not done so. I don't like to speak again.'

'And you're sure that she understood the gravity of her mother's condition, Selina?' asked Sophia, frowning.

'I tried to make it plain to her, in fact I said how I'd regret *not* telling her if – well, if poor Mrs Lucket were to die.' Miss Calthorpe looked perplexed. 'It's a strange circumstance, all these years in that place, her own mother.'

'It is unusual, but Susan's childhood was unusual, too, in a way that you and I can hardly imagine,' said Sophia loyally. 'Thank you for what you have told me, Selina, and I shall act upon it this very day.'

And within the hour she had spoken to Susan and made the arrangement without even mentioning Mad Doll.

Little was said on the drive across the common, and Sophia's attempt to talk to Joby was unproductive.

'Do you ever hear from that older brother of yours, Job? What was his name – Jack?'

Susan froze, and Joby mumbled reluctantly. 'Him went off to Portsmouth to join the navy, so he said. Never a word on him since.'

Sophia stole a look at Susan's white face, as rigidly tense as if she were going to the gallows instead of the sick-bed of the woman who had borne her.

They reached the House of Industry, and Susan and Joby got down. Mrs Croker had seen the chaise from her window, and opened the door before Susan could pull on the bell rope.

'Ah, Mistress Calthorpe, yer mother's all but gone,' she said with a suitably lugubrious expression. 'Oi'll take ye both up to see her, but her'll not know 'ee, fur sure.'

In fear and trembling of she knew not what, Susan followed the woman up the familiar wooden stairs and along the corridor to where Doll lay in a corner of the infirmary. Susan caught her breath at the sight of the shrunken frame, the face like a skull with papery skin stretched over the bone, the half-closed eyes deep in their sockets. The only sign of life was a regular rasp in the throat and a corresponding slight rise of the chest. Joby stepped back in shock, and held Susan's arm.

'Her's gone down these last couple o' days, mistress,' said Mrs Croker. 'That young Miss Selina tol' me her'd spoke to 'ee.' The little piggy eyes gleamed knowingly. 'Oi tol' her 'ee'd come if 'ee wanted, and now 'ee's come just in time, Oi reckon.'

'Thank ye, Mrs Croker,' said Susan. There seemed no point in trying to apologise or explain her long absence; the woman knew that there had never been a natural attachment between herself and her demented mother. 'My brother and I'll sit here beside her. Miss Glover'll be coming f'r us in about an hour.'

The woman watched as Susan took hold of the skeletal hand lying on the bedcover, and motioned Joby to sit down on the opposite side of the bed.

453

'Be she nearly – will her die soon, Sukey?' whispered Job, his lower lip trembling.

Susan gave a very slight nod. 'Yes, Joby, she'll soon be finished with the troubles o' this world,' she answered in a low tone. 'She won't wake or speak again.'

But no sooner were the words out of her mouth than Doll opened her eyes. They saw her lips move, and then she moaned softly. Susan leaned towards her.

''Tis all right, Ma, 'tis y'r children Susan and Job come to visit ye. 'Tis Sukey,' she added, though she did not like the associations of the childish name.

'Sukey – Sukey runn'd away – her runn'd away,' muttered Doll, shaking her head from side to side. 'Her bore with it four year, and then her runn'd away and Polly follered arter—'

Susan cut in hastily. 'Hush, Ma, 'tis Joby here beside ye – remember that little baby boy I helped ye to birth? Wasn't he a fine little feller?'

But Doll twitched her hand free of Susan's.

'Sukey? Be her here? No, no, don't let her come by!' she cried, her voice rising in fear. 'Her bore wi' un fur four year, and then her runn'd away.'

'Hush, Ma, don't fret, 'tis all right now – all right now, Ma.' Susan vainly tried to soothe her, but Doll struggled to lift her head from the horsehair pillow.

'No, no, not her! Tell her to go away – go back and mind Polly. Sukey ha' no love fur me 'cause o' what *he* done, that's why her runn'd away,' wailed the tormented woman. 'Four year!'

Susan trembled. This was agony beyond her worst imaginings, and she put her knuckles to her mouth to stifle the involuntary cry that rose to her throat. She must not give way in front of Joby, and much as she

454

longed to obey Doll and take herself away, she knew she must stay. She had forsaken this lost soul for too long, and now at her deathbed some kindness, some human compassion had to be shown.

''Tis finished and done now, Ma. Just put y'r trust in God, and be at peace,' she pleaded helplessly.

The howl that came from Doll's throat reminded them both of the terrible scene in Great St Giles on the day she had thrown a prayer book at the rector and been banished to this place for the rest of her life.

Susan stood up and laid a hand on her mother's forehead, raising her voice above Doll's demons of fear.

'God will ha' mercy on ye, Ma, and forgive all y'r sins – ye're forgiven now, Ma, 'tis all forgiven,' she said with what assurance she could command.

Doll's mouth was open, ready to howl again, but no sound came. She looked straight into Susan's face: their eyes truly met for the first time in many years of evasion.

'And I forgive ye, too, Mother.'

Doll Lucket did not speak again; after a minute there was a choking sound in her throat, then a long bubbling of air exhaled through mucus. And then there was silence.

The brother and sister saw her ravaged features soften, and her eyes stopped staring as the lids drooped. Her mouth slackened and her whole appearance assumed a marble blankness as they watched.

Poor mad Dolly Lucket was dead. Susan burst into tears.

'Oh, Joby, she suffered too – she suffered too, more'n she could bear, and I never comforted her, not once.'

'Don't cry, Sukey. Her knows her died forgiven,' said Joby through his tears, coming to his sister's side and putting an arm around her shoulders. 'See how peaceful her looks now, layin' there. Let's sit down alongside o' her an' be quiet till Miss Glover comes fur us.'

Susan longed to be gone from the place. Her tears were not so much for her mother's death as for the loss of the natural love between them, extinguished by the untellable wrongdoing of the past. She had forgiven poor Mad Doll at the end, but the harm done could never be undone. *Four years*.

And neither of them noticed Mrs Croker creep away. She had heard every word.

'*Dead*, Mrs Croker? And were Mrs Calthorpe and her brother at the bedside in time?'

'Oh, aye, mistress. The poor madwoman wept and wailed terrible when her saw 'twas Mrs Susan. Her was feared to death,' said Mrs Croker with relish, but Miss Glover had hurried away up the stairs to the infirmary. At the bedside she silently embraced Susan and stood with her head bowed to say a short prayer commending Dolly's spirit into the hands of her Creator. Joby was sniffling and Susan looked stricken, so after a few words with Mrs Croker about burial arrangements – which she said should be at Little St Giles – Sophia lost no time in removing her two white-faced passengers from the House and into the chaise.

During the drive back across the common it seemed to Susan that the light had changed from summer to autumn in one afternoon. She remained unresponsive to her friend's anxious glances, though she was aware of her concern.

Sophy's sorry for me – for me and Joby both, but doesn't know what to say, she thought. If she only knew the despair in my heart, how I could shout at this empty sky for all the harm that was done. And I can never tell a soul, not even my poor young brother, sitting there staring at nothing.

How much had he heard? Or understood? Nothing, she was sure. He could not possibly have known what Doll had meant. Not like Jack, who had certainly known and kept guard. Susan shuddered at the memory of that cross-eyed grin.

She suddenly longed to see Dr Parnham. He had sent her a letter from Paris to let her know the date of his return. He was a friend and co-worker, but much more than that: there was no need for concealment with him. No hateful secret stood between them as with the rest of the world. Dr Parnham *knew*.

Any day now Edward would return, a newly ordained priest in the Church of England, and ready to fulfil his father's earnest wish that he should replace Dr Gravett as rector of Great St Giles.

But how could she ever hope to be the rector's wife? That was the agony. She was *not* his wife, never had been and never could be.

There was no more time to delay: she must see Dr Parnham, the annulment must be prepared and Edward informed of his means of escape, just as soon as he appeared in Beversley.

They put Joby down at the smithy, and on arrival at May Cottage Mag told them that Mrs Decker and her mother were out.

'I'll come in and stay with you until one or other of them returns, Susan,' said Sophia, with a kindly glance at the adoring Mag, who went to put the kettle on.

'I ha' no need o' company, Sophy. In truth I'd rather be alone f'r a while,' protested Susan.

But Sophia was loath to leave her after the ordeal at Doll's bedside, and insisted on staying. It was to prove a fateful decision, for Susan was close to the end of her tether.

''Tis very difficult to know how to offer condolences in such circumstances as these, dear Susan, but one day you will be thankful that you were beside her at the end.'

'If ye hadn't pressed me into going over there this afternoon, I'd ha' been too late,' replied Susan wearily. 'I had no great wish to be there.'

'It is not for me to judge you, Susan. I've known of course for many years that there was a lack of love between . . .' Sophia hesitated. 'But I've also known that you had your reasons.'

'She suffered too,' said Susan wretchedly, and Sophia waited to hear some explanation of this statement, but none came.

Sophia then attempted to encourage and cheer her friend by reminding her that Edward would soon be back from Oxford, as a clerk in Holy Orders.

'And how happy he must be to know that Rosa is safely delivered of a daughter, and of your part in saving them both, to see you accepted and so much admired at Bever House! This reconciliation will give such joy to him; I know that it has brought great satisfaction to my cousin Calthorpe, your father-in-law. He will be pleased to see you as rector's wife.'

Susan's next words were like a slap in the face.

'As f'r Edward, I shall ha' to see Dr Parnham as soon as he gets back to Belhampton.'

Sophia stared. 'Why, what has Dr Parnham to do

458

with the sacred bond between you and your husband, Susan?'

'Oh, Sophy, ye're a good woman, ye're kind to the poor, ye've been the best friend I've ever had – but there are some things that can't be spoken of, and only Dr Parnham knows what they are.'

'Susan! What do you mean? *What* does this man know? Is it something not shared by Edward? For well you know that a woman should have no secrets from her husband, nor should any other man have knowledge of her that the husband has not.'

The stern disapproval in her face and voice had the effect of wrenching a desperate retort from Susan, who was sick of pretending in order to save other people's sensibilities, even her dearest friend's.

'Edward ha' never been my husband! I ha' never been truly his wife, nor can I ever be – and Dr Parnham knows a way f'r Edward to get rid o' me, and be free again – by *annulment* in a court o' law, in front o' a judge!'

Sophia's face went very white. She recoiled from Susan's blazing eyes.

'Does Edward know about this – this annulment you speak of?'

'He'll know soon enough. He was too ill when he came home, but he'll be told straightway when he returns again.'

'Told *what*, exactly?'

'What I just told *you* – that he can be set free from a woman who can't be a wife!' Susan shouted back.

'But Susan, *why*? What is it that stands between you?'

'Some things can't ever be told.'

And now at last Sophia truly began to see: to

understand the evil that she had refused to believe for years.

'You mean when you were a child – at the Ash-Pits—'

'Don't speak o' it!' Susan covered her ears.

'You must tell Edward.'

'Never. I'd die first, rather'n he should know.'

'But only the truth can set you free, Susan, don't you see? Lies and deception belong to the devil. Come, my dear, let me help you. I am a friend of yours and Edward's, and dearly love you both. Let me tell him for you.'

'Hah!' Susan's laugh was as mirthless as it was chilling. 'Oh, Sophy, if ye only knew what ye speak of, ye wouldn't offer! No, let me do the only good I can do f'r Edward now, after all the harm I ha' done him. Leave me, Sophia Glover – f'r God's sake leave me alone!'

Sophia drew back, her eyes darkened, her mouth hung open and wordless. Susan saw only horror in her friend's face, and like an injured animal that fears more pain, she turned and ran from the room.

Dismissed, Sophia walked out of the cottage without a backward glance, leaving Susan alone.

More alone than at any time since she had wept beside the sleeping Polly in the roost, mourning for her lost childhood.

But she reckoned without Sophia Glover's discernment, made keener by her own experience of suffering. And her determination that evil should not triumph over good.

Chapter 32

Having been duly examined by the Bishop of Oxford, and had his Priest's Orders signed and proclaimed at Christ Church, Edward Calthorpe considered himself the happiest man among the newly ordained clergy of his college. He was now eagerly looking forward to going home, having been absent for almost six months, and longed to discuss the future with his wife.

He had been offered a benefice in an Oxfordshire parish, and had at first been inclined to take it; he felt that the time was right to make a new start in a place where nobody knew of his wife's humble origins. After all they had been through and survived, such a move seemed good for them both: new pastures, where they might begin their married life at last, three years after their wedding.

But then had come his father's letter with the news of Dr Gravett's fatal ilness, a reminder to Edward that all plans may be subject to sudden change.

'Parson Roberts has to take Divine Service in both Churches, & cannot do his proper Duty to the two Parishes,' Mr Calthorpe had written. 'My uncle Lord de Bever had the Parish of St Giles in his Gift, & this has passed on to me as Patron, to approve appointments of Clergy. I therefore look forward to seeing you installed as Incumbent at an early date, my dear Edward, if you wd be willing to live at May Cottage the Midwife's house while poor Dr Gravett lives.'

461

And move into the rectory with Susan after his death, thought Edward, shaking his head as he firmly declined the appointment. Such close association with Bever House would be highly unwelcome to Susan, and her wishes took preference over his father's.

But hot on the heels of this news had come the joyful announcement of the birth of a daughter to Rosa, and with it the ending of the ill-feeling between his family and his wife. It seemed nothing less than miraculous to Edward, and surely an indication of God's guidance. He had therefore decided that, if Susan agreed, he was willing to abide by his father's clearly stated hopes, and become the next incumbent of Great St Giles.

Yet now, just as he was preparing to return to Beversley, this strangely disturbing letter had arrived. It was from cousin Sophia of all people, mysteriously asking for a clandestine meeting.

Let me know what Day you will arrive in Belhampton, & I will meet with you at the Wheatsheaf Inn where the Coaches come in. I beg to speak with you on a matter of the utmost Importance, having Consequences on yr future & Susan's also.

Tell nobody of this message, but send me word as I ask, and may God bless you & direct you, dear Cousin, to follow in His footsteps Who is the Way, the Truth and the Life.

I am yr most affect: Cousin, Sophia Glover.

Edward was very reluctant to go behind Susan's back, as he saw it, and to keep this meeting secret would mean not giving notice of his return to either

462

his wife or his parents. Yet he had never once had cause to question his cousin's integrity, and so wrote a reply, naming the seventeenth of September, a Wednesday, though in fact he decided to travel down the day before so as to be ready and waiting for Sophia as soon as she arrived.

Before leaving Oxford he purchased a new black frock coat and breeches, also a 'shovel' hat of the kind worn by country clergymen; the sombreness of this attire was relieved by a spotless white collar with the two starched linen bands that proclaimed his profession.

And this was the Edward Calthorpe who awaited Miss Glover on the day appointed, soon after midday when she walked into the Wheatsheaf Inn in her grey cloak and bonnet.

'Good day, Cousin Edward. I had not expected you to be here so soon,' she said in surprise.

Without ceremony he led her to a high-backed wooden bench placed sideways to the wall and adjoining an unoccupied space in a corner of the room.

'I arrived yesterday, Sophy, so as to be here to meet you.'

'How well clerical dress suits you, Edward.'

'I have not come to an inconvenient and under-hand appointment in order to talk of fashion, Sophy,' he said gravely. 'I long above all things to see my wife and discuss our future with her. I await your explanation, and then intend to be with her before this day is out.'

Sophia took her lead from his tone. Concealing her own nervousness beneath her usual composure, she nodded and commenced the speech she had been rehearsing.

'It is of her that I speak, Edward, your wife and my dear friend, Mrs Edward Calthorpe.'

'Indeed, Cousin? And what have you to say of my Susan that she cannot say to me herself?'

It was the opening she needed. She raised her eyes to him, but kept her voice low.

'Your marriage, Edward – it has not been finally made legal by the act of bodily union.'

The shocked incredulity with which he heard these words was almost palpable in the air between them. He flushed deeply.

'I have never uttered a word to a soul on this matter,' he said at last. 'Did *she* tell you this?'

'Yes, when we returned from her mother's death-bed. It was a harrowing experience for her, full of conflicting thoughts and feelings.'

Sophia paused and took a deep breath. 'Edward, how much do you know of Susan's background? Her childhood in the Ash-Pits, the poverty, the hardship – and her lack of daughterly affection towards her mother? What do you truly know about those growing years?'

Edward considered for a few moments before replying. He was obviously shaken, and she saw that he was making an effort to regain his self-possession.

'Cousin Sophy, I think I see where you are leading me, but I may be ahead of you. I do not care to discuss my wife with anybody, including yourself, but because of your special position as her friend – and that you were betrothed to my own dearest friend – I will tell you this much.'

Sophia inclined her head and waited.

'I knew of the roughness of my Susan's upbringing, of course, the sacrifices she made for her brothers

464

and sister, the loss of three brothers in a night, her father's drinking habits – 'twas no wonder that her mother's mind became unhinged. And she was not a well-guarded child, especially when working out in the fields.'

He frowned and ran his tongue around the edge of his mouth, moistening his lips before continuing.

'I have some reason to believe that Susan – my sweet, innocent Susan was – was ravished at some time by a foul brute not fit to walk this earth, and this abomination has given her a fear of the natural union between man and wife. But I am prepared to wait, to be patient and let her discover for herself that she has no need to fear, and that I do not blame her for what she could not help – or prevent. I have to wait because the poor child has not yet confided in me, understandably.'

He raised his head and faced Sophia squarely. 'So, Cousin, am I not right? Have I not anticipated this *matter of the utmost importance* that you spoke of? And for which you have taken such elaborate precautions of secrecy?'

'I cannot blame you for rebuking me, Edward,' replied Sophia sadly. 'For you are partly right in your conjecture.'

'Oh, my poor, sweet love,' he muttered under his breath. 'Oh, God in heaven, how couldst Thou have allowed it?'

'Edward, we must finish what we have begun, and then you must make a decision,' Sophia went on urgently. 'Susan's fear and loathing of – of men's bodies—'

'Stop!' he said sharply. 'I refuse to discuss my wife in this way.'

'I understand your reluctance, Cousin, but hear me

out, I beg of you. There are matters you must still hear, but not from me, and I ask your attention.'

'Does Susan know of this meeting between us?' he demanded suddenly. 'Did *she* ask you to see me.'

'No, Edward. I asked you to meet me so that I may direct you to where you may discover the truth,' replied Sophia quickly. 'There are – secret matters that I have long suspected but put to the back of my mind, but I believe now that there can be no peace or true harmony between you until these things are faced and fully known.'

'I will hear no more of this, Cousin.' He rose from the bench.

'No, stay and listen, Edward, 'tis for love of Susan I am here,' implored Sophia in rising agitation. 'I spoke to the Widow Croker at the House of Industry, and to Job Lucket. They both know more than they admit, but Mrs Croker sent me to an old handy-woman in Lower Beversley who knew the Luckets well, and attended Dolly at Susan's own birth.'

'But why ask all these people about my poor, wronged Susan?' asked Edward, his dark blue eyes flashing with indignation.

'To uncover the whole truth, Edward. And if you will hear it, you must go to Portsmouth and seek out Jack Lucket, the other surviving brother.'

Edward was suddenly alert. 'Jack? A sly-looking little fellow with a vile squint? I heard he'd gone to join the navy with that drunken father – it must have been four or five years ago. How can I or anybody find either of them now?'

'They never joined the navy,' answered Sophia. 'They became smugglers, part of an old ring that has dealt in French brandy for years, even while we were at war with France.'

'Good heavens! How can you possibly know this, Sophy?'

'This handywoman is a link in the chain, as is Dick the carrier and his father before him. 'Tis her cottage where the contraband for Beversley is stored overnight until Dick passes it on to the rectory and Bever House. Your butler Martin—'

'Ah, yes, I recall hearing something of it when we were children, though 'tis never spoken of above stairs,' said Edward, frowning.

'According to this handywoman, Jack Lucket's a messenger, a lookout for the boatmen who bring in the goods, and he passes on information about dates and times of landing to the receivers. You must give me your word, Edward, as I gave mine to her, that you will not speak of her part in it – or the carrier's.'

Edward was expressionless. 'I know nothing of the woman. And you say I should go and seek out this Jack?'

'Yes. There is a tavern called the Galleon in Stokes Bay, hard by the mud flats and frequented by the lowest sort. She said you'll need to be circumspect in your enquiries, Edward. Take gold with you but keep it well hidden. And be sure to meet Jack in a public place like this, and by daylight.'

'You have only spoken of Jack. What of the father – of Bartlemy?'

'When I asked the handywoman the same question, she said there had been no word of him for a year or more. Only Jack.'

She leaned across the settle and took his hand, looking straight into his eyes.

'Edward, you must do as I have told you. Go to Portsmouth as soon as possible, find Jack and ask him to tell you Susan's history – why she left home

467

and begged me to find a place for her young sister. I got Polly into the laundry at Bever House, you know with what final result. I have often wished that she'd gone to a humbler household.'

She sighed, and they were silent for a minute or two while Edward pondered on what she had told him. And not told.

'And you cannot give me this information yourself, Sophy?'

'No, for I am not acquainted with the full facts, and if I were I could not tell you, for reasons you may discover. You must go and find Jack. That is all I can say, Edward.'

Outside in the inn-yard the sound of rumbling wheels and horses' hoofs announced the arrival of a coach; it was followed by the sound of passengers' voices and the thump of their boxes being unloaded on the cobbles. Edward listened and frowned while trying to come to a decision, and then, without a word to his cousin, rose and went to find the landlord. Sophia sat gripping the wooden handles of her bag, briefly praying for a happy outcome to the quest she had set in motion after much anxious heart-searching. Her secret visit to the handywoman had meant pocketing her dignity to some degree, especially in bribing Mrs Gibson with two golden guineas for information about the Galleon and Jack's part in the smuggling ring. The old woman's eyes had glinted.

'Oi thanks 'ee well, mistress – an' whoever be goin' to find Jack, bid him take care un don't get a knife across un's throat – an' leave my name out o't.'

'I'll warn him to be very careful, and he won't even know your name,' she had replied.

The handywoman clinked the two coins together in her pocket.

'Oi doubts him'll thank 'ee fur what un hears, missis.'

Sophia shivered involuntarily at the words.

She now looked up as Edward returned to pick up his hat.

'There's a coach leaving for Petersfield in five minutes,' he announced. Sophia rose at once.

'Ah, you are going today, Edward.' There was both relief and anxiety in her eyes.

'Yes, I'd better go on this chase before I see Susan again,' he said shortly, thrusting a leather purse into an inside pocket. 'My box can stay here at the Wheatsheaf. I bid you good day, Sophy.' He turned to go, but she put a hand on his arm.

'Do be very careful, Edward. Here is the address of a good lodging in Portsmouth. 'Twas where I stayed with the Hansfords on that – that visit to the docks with Henry.'

She held out a folded sheet of paper, and Edward's resentment against her dissolved in the remembrance of that tragic loss of life more than a year ago. He turned back and took her hand.

'Forgive me, Sophy. I'll do as you say and seek out this brother, though I doubt he'll say aught to surprise me.'

'Take care, Edward – for her sake, take care!'

It was dusk when the Petersfield stagecoach reached Portsmouth, and Edward's landlady at the recommended lodging looked askance when he asked about the Galleon.

'That be no place for a gentleman o' the cloth, sir. 'Tis a haunt o' thieves and cut-throats who'd kill a stranger for his gold.' Edward assured her that he

469

would not go down to Stokes Bay until daylight on the morrow.

The Galleon was well out of the town to the west, at the bottom of a roughly paved incline where women were selling fresh fish at stalls along one side. It gave on to a stretch of scrubby ground littered with broken boats, bleached ropes and rotting nets where ragged urchins rooted among the debris, their shouts drifting in the autumnal wind blowing off the sea.

Edward entered the Galleon and ordered a tankard of ale from a one-eyed man with a red silk scarf and gold earring.

'What be yer business, Parson?' came the suspicious enquiry.

Edward's experience in the navy had given him a commanding manner, which he believed stood him in good stead with characters like this and two other men who sat crouched over a smoky wood fire. They nudged each other and grinned. Edward sat down and spread out a map.

'Anybody seen cross-eyed Jack around here lately?' he asked casually. 'I have gold for him if he'll show his face.'

There was immediate interest. 'Ah, Jack ain't bin around fur a while,' said the landlord, giving the other two a sharp look to silence any remark to the contrary.

'Then I must look elsewhere.' Edward raised his tankard.

'Though Oi dare say as him could be found, like.' The meaning was clear enough.

'Well, if Jack could be found and brought here by noon today, I'll double this.' Edward put his hand in his pocket and drew out three gold guineas, which he

470

put down on the shelf that held the tankards. The one-eyed landlord pocketed them at once.

'If Oi find un, who'll Oi say be askin' fur un?'

'Parson Calthorpe of Beversley in this county.' Edward set the tankard down with a flourish. 'I'll return at noon, and if Jack be not within sight from the door I shall not come across the threshhold. And I have no more gold on me now, so I'm not worth robbing.'

'Come back by noon, then, an' come alone, or ye won't get past the door,' growled the landlord.

Edward strode out of the tavern, satisfied with the impression he had given, yet with a sinking of his spirits that he could not quite account for. There was a certain shame in probing into Susan's history without her knowledge, and the very fact that Sophia had sent him this far must mean that he was to hear a horrible account of Susan's ravishment by some vile brute, or worse, a gang of brutes.

When he returned on the stroke of midday the Galleon had filled up, as if the word had got around about the strange parson with gold to give away for a sight of cross-eyed Jack.

And there he was, standing in the doorway with a wary look that combined greed with curiosity in equal measure. Edward gasped with shock, so debased had Jack Lucket become. The squint was disconcerting enough, but the broken nose and loose mouth hinted at violence and depravity in a youth of not yet seventeen, with decayed teeth like an old man's and unhealthy skin; yet something about his forehead and jaw had a look of Joby. To think that this obscenity was brother to his Susan was repellent to Edward, but he stepped forward and held out his hand.

471

'Good day to you, Jack. I'm Edward Calthorpe, married to your sister Susan. I want to talk with you and not be overheard.'

The landlord got his further three guineas and gave them a table behind a tall wooden partition, partly within sight but out of earshot of the others.

'Will you take ale?' asked Edward.

'Oi'd sooner ha' rum, mister.'

Edward asked for a bottle of rum, clearly Jack's regular tipple, and ale for himself. Once they were seated he extracted a leather purse from an inside pocket and put it on the table, keeping his hand upon it.

'There's ten guineas for you, Jack, but in return I want some information about those early days when you lived with your parents and sisters and brother at Ash-Pit End.'

'Oh, ah.' Jack swallowed a mouthful of neat spirit without turning a hair. His eyes narrowed. 'So 'ee be wedded to Sukey, then?'

'I have that happiness, Jack. And your poor mother died in the House of Industry this month.'

'Oh, ah? Oi thought her'd been gone long since. Sukey was a good'un, though. Her'd ha' runn'd off afore her did, only her stayed fur Polly. Ay, her was a reg'lar good'un.'

This praise of Susan should have been welcome to Edward, proving that even in his degraded state Jack retained some natural affection for his sister; yet Edward felt only a stifling sense of oppression, of evil creeping nearer with each minute. He was conscious of his heart pounding.

'What happened to your father, Jack?'

The boy's malevolently crossed eyes gleamed. 'Him ain't around no more.'

472

'D'you mean – is he dead?'

'Aye. Him was run in by the constables one night down by the rocks.' He gestured with his head towards the west.

'You mean the contraband trade, do you? Brandy?'

Jack tapped the side of his crooked nose with a grimy forefinger, and grinned. 'Hangman's rope ha' done fur a few on 'em, mister. Him picked up the wrong signals, if 'ee gets me meanin'. Hah!'

Another swig of rum disappeared, and Edward got the impression that wrong signals or not, some unscheduled plot of Jack's had gone according to plan. Better not to enquire further, but get on with the business in hand before Jack became drunk.

He leaned forward, keeping his hand on the money-bag. 'Tell me in truth, Jack, why did your sister Susan run away? And what did you mean about her staying for Polly?'

Jack squinted up at the smoke-darkened ceiling and refilled his glass from the bottle. The talk and gusts of laughter from the other drinkers in the Galleon washed all around them. Jack gaped at the purse and appeared to hesitate.

'Oi don't know what 'ee wants Oi to say, Pa'son Calthorpe.'

'Don't trifle with me, Lucket, but tell the truth, no matter how bad it is. I shall not blame you for the wickedness of other men, but I have to know—' He drew a quick breath and forced himself to utter the words, 'Was your sister ravished by some farm hand or more than one – in the open field or – or anywhere?'

Against every instinct Edward now prompted this degenerate to tell what he knew: he heard his own voice begging for the information he feared to hear.

473

The rum was taking effect, and Jack leered hideously. He was enjoying having this Parson Calthorpe trying to worm out what only he, Jack, could tell. He remembered the Calthorpes of Beversley who thought themselves so fine but never raised a hand to help the poor.

'So 'ee married Sukey, did 'ee, Pa'son?' The words were a jeer. 'And now 'ee wants to know who laid on her afore 'ee?'

Edward's features hardened to a rigid mask. He could have thrust his fist into the middle of Jack's face, but he kept one hand on the purse and the other clenched at his side.

'Just tell what you know about my wife. Your sister Su-Sukey.'

Jack gave a conspiratorial, gap-toothed grimace that passed for a smile, and, stretching across the table, he put his mouth close to Edward's right ear and began to tell.

As the words assailed him like a foul stench, Edward's world trembled and shook like a ship's timbers cracking up. Nothing was real any more, nothing was safe or secure.

'What?' he whispered hoarsely. '*What* did you say? *Who?*'

'Oi says, Oi reckon Sukey got too old fur Bartlemy to come on her. Her got too big fur un. Her kicked an' hollered an' wouldn' ha' no more on't. Oi see'd uns, Oi did.'

'What?' The word sounded faint and guttural. 'What did you see?'

'Many's the time, out in the fields, down in the ditch, bottom o' Bennett's home field, in the bracken 'side o' the woods – evenin's when none but Oi was

474

there to see uns – went on fur years, it did, till her got bigger an' wouldn' ha' no more on't.'

This was good sport to be paid gold for! Jack grinned scornfully at this ashen-faced fool who looked as if he'd been stabbed in the gut.

'Aye, him 'ud come up on her from behind an' grab hold on her. "Shut yer mouth, Sukey," him 'ud say, and down her'd go, and him 'ud be in *by the back port*. Oh, ah, Oi see'd uns 'cause Oi used to look out fur un, same as Oi looks out fur the boats comin' in!'

His excited hee-haw rose above the general babble, and then by degrees a silence fell on the company as Edward rose unsteadily to his feet. Necks craned to see what was going on behind the partition, and there were shouts as Edward grabbed the youth by the throat and began shaking him as a dog shakes a rat. Jack's face turned purple and his eyes and tongue protruded as the fingers pressed hard against his windpipe; his limbs jerked like a body hanging from a gibbet.

'Hey, lay off the boy, will ye?' shouted the landlord. 'Ye said ye wanted to give un gold, not choke un to death. Lay off un, let un go!'

Edward suddenly released Jack, who fell lifelessly across the table, knocking over the tankard and sending the bottle flying. The purse was grabbed by one of the men, who soon lost it to another, and in the ensuing fight the golden coins rolled in all directions, and men tumbled over each other for them.

Edward lurched blindly towards the door, his only thought now being to get out of this accursed tavern. And that was the moment when his stomach rebelled.

Heads ducked as the stream of sour, undigested food and ale spattered on tables and floor. At the

475

threshhold Edward leaned on the door frame and shuddered violently, sending another shower of yellowish-green vomit cascading down his frock coat, soiling his white linen bands. The onlookers broke into jeering applause and clapping.

'Tha's right, Pa'son, give another heave – spue it up! Yer flock be waitin' fur 'ee at the church!'

'Got yer sermon ready, pa'son? Fetch it all up!'

Heaving, retching, eyes streaming and with a shameful wet patch in his breeches, Edward staggered out of the Galleon, still dribbling bitter green fluid, which was all that remained of his stomach's contents. His new shovel hat fell off and blew towards the waste ground where it was eagerly seized by the children playing there. Swaying from one side of the unpaved road to the other, he crashed full tilt into a stall.

'Look at un, did y'ever see such a sight?' cried the woman selling fish. 'A man o' the cloth, drunk as any rat, spuein' all over hisself an' pissin' down un's legs – filthy swine!'

A passing housewife recoiled in horror. 'Ay, things ha' come to a pretty pass when a churchman ha' no shame. What times us lives in, missus!'

But Edward only heard Jack Lucket's demented braying over and over again: 'Oi see'd uns, Oi see'd uns!'

He thought it would echo in his head for ever.

Chapter 33

Susan faced Charles Parnham across his desk and heard him say what Sophia had said.

'Edward must be told, my child. He must know the reason why he is being offered his freedom, and allowed to make his own judgement. There is neither sense nor kindness in letting him think himself an object of your fear.'

'But 'tis not Edward I fear!' she cried, clasping her hands together and shaking them in her agitation. 'I ha' loved none other but he, as God sees and knows.'

'But how can you explain that to him without telling him the truth about yourself, Susan?' reasoned the doctor. 'Now be quiet, sit still and listen to me, I command you.'

It was difficult to be stern when he longed to comfort and console; but once again he had to repress his own feelings and consider the husband who also loved her.

'I will tell him, Susan. Send him to me when he returns from Oxford. I will put the facts before him, and if necessary will tell him how the marriage may be annulled.'

And if he's half worthy of you he'll knock me down, he added grimly to himself.

She stared back at him, uncertainty written in every feature.

'D'ye truly believe that any man could forgive such a thing, sir? If it had only happened the once, or maybe

477

a couple o' times, a man might overlook it, but I – it went on f'r four years, Dr Parnham – *four years*!'

To see this remarkable girl reduced to such degradation of spirit made Parnham long to get his hands on the throat of the guilty man and choke the life out of him. Yet he spoke quietly.

'You were an ill-used child, and could not help yourself nor escape from it until you were old enough. I will put all this to Edward and let him make of it what he may. It is my firm belief that he will share my view and absolve you of all blame. And then you too must put the past behind and let him show his love for you as a husband for a wife.'

'If only I could – if I but *could*!' she cried, and Charles Parnham had to ring for the maidservant to bring in the teapot, or else he might have taken her in his arms.

Susan wiped her eyes. 'Thank ye, Dr Parnham. Edward should ha' been told before the wedding, I know that now. But I loved him so much, and thought I could forget – what I so much hated. But knowing how I'd been defiled – oh, I could never tell him. But as soon as he's home again, I'll send him to ye, Dr Parnham.'

She poured the tea and handed him a cup.

'And, Dr Parnham . . .'

'Yes, Madam Trotula? What else?'

'If Edward wants to – if he chooses the way of annulment – how soon could it be done?'

Parnham's attorney in Winchester had had the drafts of the affidavits drawn up for many months, ready for names and signatures to be added, upon which he would apply for a court hearing. Parnham knew how tardy the processes of the law could be; he cleared his throat.

478

'In the unlikely event of such a decision, you would come straight to me, of course, to claim every help and assistance I could give while the case was ongoing. And I'd find you a place as midwife in another part of the country where nobody knew the circumstances. But come now, be resolute, put your faith in the future, Susan. I look forward to seeing you as wife of the rector of Great St Giles.'

When they had drunk their tea he took her arm to escort her out to the patiently waiting Brownie.

'I'll let you drive me down to the town square,' he said, climbing up beside her in the trap. 'My mare has sore eyes, and I must seek out the apothecary for some mercury ointment.'

When he took his farewell of her neither of them noticed the arrival of the Portsmouth stage at the Wheatsheaf Inn, to set down a solitary passenger.

The Widow Smart was anxiously looking out for Susan when she reached May Cottage.

'Young Mrs Spooner started her pains this afternoon, just after you left, Mrs Susan. My Lizzie's been there nigh on three hours,' she added with more than a touch of reproach.

Susan was at once alert and apologetic, stopping only to snatch up her straw bag.

'God forgive me f'r not being here,' she muttered; this was Mary's second child, thirteen months after the breech delivery on the day the *Royal George* had been lost.

Edward had chosen to ride on the open top of the stagecoach in spite of a stiff breeze. He was conscious of the unpleasant smell of his clothes, which he had not been able to change, though he had thrown away his soiled collar. In war and battle, and during his time as a prisoner, he had often worn dirty, ragged garments; but for an ordained priest of the Church to walk abroad in clothes smelling sourly of vomit and breeches rank with stale urine was an affront to his office. His stomach was empty and his head throbbed: of the money he had brought with him, not a penny remained.

This is a taste of the life of the poor, he thought: to have no facility for washing the body or the clothing, and to stink as a matter of course. He thought of the Ash-Pits, that malodorous huddle of one-roomed hovels where the lowest of Lower Beversley had lived – the drunkards, the feckless, the aged crone Goody Firkin, reduced to beggary.

And the children who grew up there. He had never faced it before, the squalor of his Susan's childhood in deep poverty where want and disease claimed the lives of half the infants and women were old at thirty. Himself a child of comfortable minor gentry, never lacking for food, warmth and shelter, he had not had the slightest knowledge of what his wife's life had really been like.

But now he felt he knew.

On arrival at the Wheatsheaf at Belhampton, he climbed stiffly down. The landlord stared at his creased and crumpled appearance, hatless and chilled by the journey; having no money, Edward refused a hot drink and asked for his box. He took out a grey jacket and a pair of buff breeches and changed into them, rolling up his black clerical garb.

'Is there a wash-house nearby where I may leave some garments to collect in a day or two?' he enquired.

'We send our linen out to a washerwoman a couple o' streets away,' replied the man, eyeing him curiously. 'If ye care to leave it here, sir, I'll send a boy over wi' it. And d'ye want to hire a gig, sir, fur yeself and the box?'

'No, a good walk will stretch my legs. I'll take this washing to the woman myself, and send for my belongings tomorrow, with payment for storage,' replied Edward, ashamed that anybody should see the state of his new clothes.

The washerwoman grimaced when she saw them.

'Them'll need careful hot pressin' after washin' out them kind o' stains,' she said, and demanded half payment on the spot. When he said he had no money on him she at first refused to accept the work, and only when he gave his address as Bever House did she reluctantly agree. Tired, cold and unrefreshed, he then set off to walk the five-mile distance, but before he was out of Belhampton a man's voice called his name.

'Good heavens! It *is* you, Parson Calthorpe – but this is providential, sir!'

Edward recognised the man-midwife, and felt at a disadvantage.

'Let us walk together, Calthorpe, for I have to speak with you on a matter of the utmost gravity,' went on the doctor quickly, seeing this meeting as a heaven-sent opportunity to save Susan the shame of sending her husband to him. 'I take it that you are just returned from Oxford?'

Edward bowed, not wanting to be delayed further, especially by this man whose partnership with Susan was something that he had never quite trusted. And *a matter of the utmost gravity* had echoes of what Sophia had said; he was put on his guard, and was reluctant to parley with the doctor, to whom he gave the slightest of nods.

In the fading afternoon light Parnham took in the

481

young man's wan appearance – almost as if he had been indulging in some kind of dissipation, the doctor thought. And surely the Oxford stage had arrived soon after midday: it was now past six. And why was the man on foot, with no luggage and nobody to meet him?

'You look cold from your journey, Calthorpe,' he said. 'There is a quiet little tavern over there, where we may talk.'

'You will excuse me, sir,' said Edward shortly. 'I am on my way home, and have already been delayed for long enough.'

'Stay, Edward, I crave but a little of your time. I promised Susan that I would speak with you, but I hardly dared hope for such an early opportunity to do so. For her sake, stay and hear me out, I beg of you.'

He laid a restraining hand on Edward's arm to guide him towards the open doorway of the tavern, but Edward sharply withdrew.

'Take your hand off me, damn you,' he snapped, his pale features flushing. 'And don't ever dare to speak of Mrs Calthorpe in that familiar way.'

Parnham recoiled before the glare of the icy blue eyes.

'My apologies, sir. I hold your wife in the highest esteem, and 'tis for that very reason I beg for this interview with you. She has honoured me with her confidence and given me leave to speak to you on her behalf.'

Edward stared back as the import of the words sunk in. Was it possible that this patronising middle-aged doctor knew of his Susan's dreadful secret? That she had actually confided in him? Edward's mouth hardened as he pictured them together, the man listening to her, comforting her and wiping away her tears. It was not to be borne!

482

'You and various other busybodies seem to have knowledge about my wife that was denied to me until I went in search of it. Why could she not confide in her husband?' he asked bitterly.

When Parnham saw that Edward knew already, he guessed that the shock had been recent.

'Because she was terrified of what you would think – what you would say to her,' he pleaded. 'For God's sake, Calthorpe, think of the shame and misery she has endured, the – her defilement—'

He stopped when he saw Edward's fist raised against him.

'Damn you to hell! I warn you, Parnham, I shall not hesitate to strike you here in the street for uttering such—'

But Parnham leaped forward and seized the upraised arm.

'One moment, sir. You may call me what you like – I care nothing for you – but don't ever let me hear anything but good of that virtuous woman, Mrs Edward Calthorpe. My God, I only hope you are half worthy of her love, Parson!'

And turning on his heel he strode away, leaving Edward in a confused state of anger and increasing regret, to continue on his way towards and across the common. He now admitted to himself that he had never got over his resentment of Parnham, though he had every reason to be grateful to the man; Susan's close attachment to her teacher and the time they spent together as fellow practitioners had always made him feel excluded and therefore jealous; but now he began to suspect that he had not only misjudged the man, but insulted him deeply.

Plodding his solitary way across the darkening heathland, his main concern now was for Susan: how he should approach her with his new knowledge, whether he should tell her where he had been and what he had heard. Parnham's words echoed in his head: *the shame and misery she has endured – her defilement.*

'Oh, Susan, Susan, my wife, my only love, what shall I say to thee?' he asked the empty sky: and knew he could never bear to see fear in those clear grey eyes again.

And as the ground began to fall away towards the valley, the answer came to him like a message from heaven. He almost groaned aloud with relief as he understood what he had to do, what he must tell her. His heart beat faster as he approached Beversley. Soon he would see her face again, and hear her sweet voice. He found himself longing for her, not with bodily desire, but rather with the deep and protective love of a parent for a child, or a brother for a dear sister. He increased his pace when he saw May Cottage: he was home. Home at last!

To be greeted by an astonished Widow Smart.

'Mercy on us, Mr Calthorpe, why didn't you let us know you were coming today? Mrs Susan and my Lizzie have been with a woman in travail these many hours. Mag! Go and boil water for the master, and bring a glass of ale!'

Mrs Mary Spooner had been delivered of a son, and Susan was in that exultant state known to all midwives when a child is safely born; to come home and find Edward waiting for her was further cause for rejoicing. She went to him without a word, and he held her close against his heart for a long minute.

'He's come only in what he stands up in, Susan. His box is still at Belhampton,' said Mrs Smart, bustling round them while Lizzie tactfully withdrew. 'I've put out a clean nightshirt on your bed, and Nathaniel's razor by the wash-stand.'

Edward slowly drew apart from his wife, checking the words of love on his lips. She looked anxiously up into his face.

'Edward, are ye not well? Ye look wearied and pale. What's happened? Why didn't ye send word o' y'r coming?'

He hesitated. 'The last few days have been difficult, Susan, and events have moved somewhat ahead of me. I find that I need time for reflection and to consider my new responsibilities as a man of the Church.'

'Ye mean as rector o' Great St Giles?' She looked worried.

'It seems that I must take charge of the parish while there is uncertainty over Dr Gravett's position – and whether I shall be appointed as his successor is a matter to be discussed before it is decided. Your wishes must be my guide.'

Mrs Smart set down a tray on the table, and Edward gestured to Susan to be seated.

'And in view of all this, and my own doubts about my fitness for such onerous duties, Susan, I have something that I must tell you. Thank you, Mrs Smart. Will you please close the door on your way out?'

They sat down together, and she looked into his face wonderingly; what was coming next? And how soon would she be able to speak of Dr Parnham, and send Edward to see him?

He took her hands gently between his, and spoke with the greatest tenderness.

'Dearest wife, I have taken a vow of chastity.'

She shook her head slightly, not understanding.

'Other priests of the Church have made this vow at various times, in order to devote themselves entirely to God's work and to hear His voice more clearly, Susan. I know that I have need of a deeper spiritual life, and so I have made this solemn promise.'

'Edward – why, Edward, I never expected to hear this,' she said in some bewilderment. 'How long'd it be for?'

'For as long as I know it to be God's will that I should continue in it, Susan. I trust that you understand and agree that we should live so?'

'Why, yes, o' course – 'tis my duty to obey ye, Edward. And I can obey ye in this,' she added, a smile lighting her eyes as she began to understand. 'D'ye mean that we shall live under this roof as – like brother and sister?'

He smiled and nodded. 'In a sense, my Susan, though closer if you are willing that we share the same bed as we have done. I am bound by my vow not to unite my body with yours, and shall not break it under any circumstances until such time as I know myself released from it.'

'And how'll ye know that, Edward?' she asked, her eyes searching his face.

'I think we shall both know when the time is right, Susan, and we would have to be in full agreement.'

'And if we're not, Edward, what then?'

'Then the vow will remain – for life, if necessary.'

'Oh, Edward.' She whispered his name, unable to believe that he truly meant to live in chastity with her. It was something she had never expected and could not possibly have hoped for. It was welcome news, of course, and yet there was something that struck her as strange in the very timeliness of it.

'Are ye truly sure o' this, Edward? Is it what ye honestly believe ye should do?'

486

'Entirely sure, my love. You need not doubt it.'

She felt that she had to persist, however. 'But if ye wanted to be free o' marriage, Edward, ye know we ha' never been truly man and wife – and without that, we're not lawfully married.'

He gave a gasp of shocked surprise. 'What are you saying, Susan? We took vows in a church before God, and that means we are truly married in my belief.'

'But not in law, Edward. Our marriage could be annulled in a court o' law if we were both to swear before a judge that we'd never been man and wife together.'

He gripped her wrist. 'You have been talking to somebody, Susan. Who has been telling you this?' he demanded. 'Was it my cousin Sophia?'

'No, Edward, no, 'tis o' no importance. I heard it somewhere, that's all.'

'Was it that man Parnham?'

She blushed and lowered her eyes. 'Dr Parnham meant well, Edward. He had your good in mind.'

So that was it. The cunning old fox had clearly had an eye to his own advantage, just as Edward had always suspected. Well, he had not succeeded.

Still holding her hand, he leaned forward and kissed her forehead.

'Let me say one thing and say it for ever, Susan. You are my wife, the only woman I have ever loved. I shall never seek for an annulment of the sacred bond between us, never as long as I live. Even if we never experience the bodily union. Do you understand that, Susan?'

And as if they were exchanging their marriage vows all over again, she nodded and replied solemnly, 'I do.'

Chapter 34

And so it was by mutual consent, unknown to the rest of the world, that when the bedroom door closed on Parson Calthorpe and his wife they slept together in peace and mutual understanding, lying side by side or with her curled up against his back. Warmed by their love, they were untroubled in their thoughts; she had no need to fear, and he, bound by the vow he had taken, experienced that total absence of carnal desire that many men discover when their wives are heavy with child or having their monthly flow or some other barrier to passion. Channelling his energies into parish duties, Parson Calthorpe's days were full of good works and his slumbers were sweet.

A new era began for the parish of Great St Giles. Holy Communion was no longer restricted to once a month but offered weekly at Divine Service. The musicians and choirmen were encouraged to try out new settings for the liturgy and Psalms, and the parson greeted each member of the congregation as they left. When there had been a birth or a death in a family, he visited the home, and on occasion would admonish a drunkard or a neglectful parent, though always holding out the promise of forgiveness to the penitent. It was said of him that he was as good as poor Parson Smart had been in Lower Beversley.

He made time to call at the rectory daily to sit and talk with Dr Gravett, who became more fearful and querulous as his strength ebbed. Miss Glover assisted Miss Gravett with his nursing care, which seemed to give him comfort, while the elder Miss Calthorpe took over more duties at the House of Industry, prevailing upon a Belhampton physician to visit the orphans and keep a check on their health; this led to reform of their diet and other improvements. Mrs Croker was replaced by a decent married couple who ran the institution in accordance with their strict Methodist principles, seeing each inmate as a potential soul to be saved and a body to be cared for.

Parson Calthorpe and his wife were regular visitors at Bever House, for Susan was welcomed and respected for what she had done for Mrs Osmond and baby Gertrude, both now making good progress; the baby's right arm was still weaker than the left, but was growing. There were even a few social exchanges between Susan and her brother-in-law, who complimented Edward on his good fortune.

'My God, she was a good friend to Rosa on that ghastly night, Ned. Mrs Ferris has curdled my blood with the hideous details, and God knows when Rosa will be ready to try for a boy – but your Susan worships the ground you walk on, you lucky devil.'

Their contentment was noted by Miss Glover, who gave fervent thanks for the outcome of her bold intervention. Although Edward never spoke directly to her of his secret visit to Portsmouth, his meaning looks and the firm clasp of his hand conveyed his gratitude well enough, while Susan's bright eyes and trustful smiles were sufficient proof of her happiness as a wife, and Sophia was convinced that all was known and understood between Mr and Mrs Edward Calthorpe.

Mr Roberts at the parsonage of Little St Giles was glad to have his duties eased and his stipend increased, while his wife grew heavier with their first child, due in December. She and Mrs Decker, who had grown up in the parsonage, became firm friends, and Susan promised to let her assistant deliver the baby if all went well.

'D'you think she'll give birth before Christmas, my love?' Edward asked his wife. 'Roberts is so taken up with her that he can hardly give his mind to his parishioners.'

Was there just a trace of envy in his voice? Susan was not sure as she replied. 'The child's head is well down, and she could be delivered by mid-December.'

But it was at ten in the morning on the twenty-fourth of December that the message came from the parsonage that Mrs Roberts' pains had begun.

'We'll go to find out her progress, Lizzie, and then you can stay with her while I come back to make pastry and glaze the apricot tart,' said Susan, busy with festive fare.

Jane Roberts was in early travail; the ring admitted barely two fingers.

'Is it likely to take long?' asked Mr Roberts anxiously. 'I hardly like to leave the parsonage while she suffers so.'

Susan assured him that he could safely attend to his morning duties, and told Lizzie she would return in the afternoon unless sent for earlier. As she left, Widow Gibson appeared on the back doorstep with a bottle of French brandy.

'Oi'll mix a few tablespoons wi' fruit cordial an' peel an apple in a pan wi' cloves an' sugar,' she told the curate. 'Best relief fur pain o' travail as Oi knows.'

Susan frowned and warned Mr Roberts not to give any of this concoction to his wife, though he might benefit from a little of it himself, taken in a glass of hot water. The delicious aroma of it filled the house, and when Susan returned just after three, she suspected that the whole household had tasted and approved the excellent punch, as the curate called it, though he wondered how the old woman had come by such coveted brandy.

Travail advanced slowly as the daylight faded, and Jane Roberts clung to Lizzie as the pains got stronger. When Susan went downstairs to check that there was water on the boil, she found the Widow Gibson in the kitchen, stirring her own heady mixture on the hob beside the open fire. Her face was flushed and her rheumy eyes gleamed when Susan entered.

'Ah, 'ee's a fine young parson's wife these days, Dame Trot! 'Ee's come a long way from the Ash-Pits, eh?'

She swayed slightly, and Susan saw that the young maidservant had also been tippling. She frowned and took the pan off the hob, putting a lid on it.

'We'll save that to celebrate the birth o' the baby,' she said firmly. 'I don't like folk drinking when a woman's in travail.'

Mrs Gibson felt her disapproval and eyed her thoughtfully.

'Tell 'ee what, Sukey Lucket – Oi hear'd as yer young parson got drunk as a rat when un went down to Portsmouth to seek out yer brother at the smugglers' inn. Spueing all over hisself, un was! Oi doubt as him'd mind us takin' a drop o' punch on Christmas Eve!'

Susan turned round slowly and faced her.

'What?'

491

'Oh, ah! Them two gold guineas Madam Glover gi' me burned a hole in me pocket 'til Oi hear'd as young parson 'ud got back safe an' sound! Oi didn't know as Oi'd done right tellin' her where him'd find young Jack, an' by what Oi hear'd, him got fightin' drunk an' nigh on done fur un!'

She gave a hiccuping laugh and raised her pewter mug to Susan, who stood stock-still in the middle of the kitchen, staring blankly back at her.

'Wh-when was this – when Parson Calthorpe went to Portsmouth?' she stammered, white to the lips.

'Go on, Sukey, 'ee knows well enough, 'twas just arter Dolly died, when him come back from gettin' hisself made a parson.'

She drained her mug to the last drop, grinning defiance at Susan, whose thoughts whirled round in her head like pieces of a broken picture gradually coming together.

She remembered Edward's unannounced return from Oxford, his box left at Belhampton; his pallor and tiredness as he told her of his sudden decision to take a vow of chastity. She had seen certain looks passed between him and Sophia; and there had been the odd matter of his newly bought clerical garb arriving wrapped in brown paper with a washer-woman's bill attached.

'And did ye say he saw my brother – Jack?' she whispered, sitting down beside the old woman and nodding to the maidservant to leave them alone. 'Tell me all about it, Mrs Gibson. What'd my husband hear from my brother?'

'Same as what Oi could ha' told un and many could ha' told un. Come on, Sukey, 'ee knows how it was wi' Bartlemy an' Doll an' 'eeself,' muttered the handywoman, drawing back a little from the

492

unblinking grey eyes. 'Nobody blamed 'ee, poor little thing, an' 'tis all past an' done now. No sense in lookin' back.'

'And ye say Miss Glover came to ye with – with money?'

'Oh, ah, fur what Oi could tell. Maybe Oi shouldn't ha' spoke, but her mind was made up, an' her made me tell.'

Susan found her voice, and held up a shaking hand. 'Enough ha' been said, Mrs Gibson. 'Tis well that I know.'

'And 'ee won't say nothin' o' the brandy trade to nobody?'

'Never a word, Mrs Gibson,' promised Susan, who knew nothing of the woman's connection with the smuggling ring.

At that moment the maidservant called down the stairs that Mrs Decker needed the midwife, and Susan rose at once.

It was after eight when Mrs Roberts was delivered by Lizzie Decker of her first-born, a son, to the joy of the curate waiting downstairs. The baby was named John after his father, and at the moment Lizzie put him into his mother's arms there came a sound of voices singing and a knock at the front door. It was the choirmen from Great St Giles carolling round the village and bidding all men to be merry. Widow Gibson's punch was liberally ladled out by the new father, and the refrain 'O tidings of comfort and joy' echoed as they departed, their breath visible in trailing clouds behind them.

'How wonderful it is, Susan, to see a new life safely brought into the world!' exclaimed Lizzie as they climbed into the trap to go home. Around them the fields lay dark and silent, but the arching sky was full of sparkling stars.

'Did you see Mr Roberts' face when he came into the room and saw Jane holding their sweet little son? How happy we are to be midwives, Susan, don't you think so?'

Susan was willing to let Lizzie chatter away in her exultation over the baby's arrival while she secretly pondered over what Widow Gibson had revealed.

Edward knew. He had known for the past three months. And like Dr Parnham he did not blame her: on the contrary, he had shown her nothing but love, denying himself for her sake. And as for whatever had happened at Portsmouth, her mind reeled away from imagining it.

Oh, Edward, my husband, now I can be honest with you at last, she thought gladly, for there is nothing to hide.

But when they reached May Cottage Edward was in sombre mood, having lately returned from the rectory with the news of Dr Gravett's death.

'Sophia was at his bedside when the waits arrived, and Miss Gravett said they might sing a hymn beneath his window, very quietly,' he told the household. 'And Sophy believes that was the time he drew his last breath. Poor old Gravett.' He sighed. 'We must be thankful that he is freed from his earthly prison, Susan, but the real tragedy is that there is nobody who truly mourns his passing. Yet I cannot remember a time when he was not rector of Beversley.'

Susan thought of Sophia Glover attending the dying man, giving him comfort and easing his fears. Edward also praised the help she had given Miss Gravett over the final months.

'It wasn't as if he ever appreciated all the good she did in his parish,' he remarked in a low tone, not wanting to be critical of the lately departed. 'How different her life would have been if Henry had not been lost to her.'

Susan was silent, remembering the rector's proposal of marriage. She supposed that Sophy had felt some kind of obligation towards the lonely old man at the end.

'It means we shall move into the rectory in the new year if you are willing, my love,' Edward went on, glancing at her anxiously.

She smiled. 'I wish only to be at y'r side, Edward, wherever ye feel called to serve,' she said with a loving look, and he put his arm around her.

'How John Roberts will be rejoicing this Christmas, my love! I hope he will remember to say prayers at Little St Giles tomorrow, for I am engaged to visit the House of Industry after Divine Service.'

'And we are all to dine at Bever House,' added Mrs Smart, delighted to be included in the invitation along with her daughter and Kitty. Parson Smart had never once dined at Bever House.

Edward picked up the candlestick. 'Come, Susan, you have had a long day, and another awaits tomorrow. 'Tis time you were abed.'

Up in their room they undressed quickly; Susan pulled her nightgown over her head, thrusting her arms into the sleeves while he divested himself of his breeches, shivering.

She said, 'Edward.'

'Yes, Susan? What is it?' he asked, pulling on his nightshirt.

'When were you last at Portsmouth?'

Silence. The question hung in the air between

495

them. She turned and looked him full in the face by the flickering candlelight. Their eyes met.

And he saw. And he knew.

'Ye spoke with my brother Jack, Edward.'

He nodded and lowered his eyes. 'Yes, my love. I did.'

'And the other . . .?'

'No, no, he has been dead for two years. Rest assured, Susan, you will never see him again.'

'Ah.' She nodded slowly. 'Widow Gibson told me today at the parsonage – the handywoman.'

'Ah, yes, I know – the contraband trade.'

'Come to bed, Edward. No, don't blow out the candle yet. Let it light us f'r a while longer.'

He got in beside her.

During the time that she had nursed him through the fever and in recent months when they had slept side by side, Susan had become well acquainted with her husband's body: the wholesome smell of his skin, the way he positioned his limbs in sleep, his cold feet that warmed with the bed; all was dear and familiar to her, and on a couple of occasions when he had been called to the bedside of a sick parishioner, she had not been able to sleep in his absence.

Now she turned and faced him, looking steadfastly into his eyes. She put her arms around his neck.

'Kiss me, Edward. Ah, kiss me, my husband.'

And so Parson Calthorpe was released from his vow. With her wide, trustful eyes fixed upon his throughout, she invited him to come to her. When he entered she uttered a low exclamation of surprise that it was so simple, so easy and natural that he should be within. When he began to thrust and pant she arched her back and gripped his shoulders, a drowning swimmer clinging to her rescuer. When his lifestream flowed she wept for joy at the cleansing power of love, driving out at last the fear and guilt that had darkened her life for so long.

She gave a long, long exhalation as the demons departed, never to return. She heard herself murmuring again the words: '*And I forgive you, too, Mother.*'

He heard and understood: there was no need for explanations between them as they kissed each other good night.

'Susan, dearest wife, sleep well.'

It was midnight. The chimes of Great St Giles rang out through the frosty air. The holy tide of Christmas had come in with a birth, a death and a healing of the years.

ENVOI

Susan opens her eyes. Sophia is still at her side, and gently presses a damp towel to her forehead.

'Will you take a sip of water, Susan? There, now.'

The slanting rays of late September sunshine have travelled round the room, marking the hours from first light to mid-afternoon. Hours of pain indescribable, pain unimaginable, tearing at nerves and muscles, causing her to scream out in agony every time her belly hardens. Time after time. Hour after hour.

Sophia asks: 'Is there any sign of progress, Mrs Decker?'

Lizzie shakes her head, gazing at the spongy circle about the size of a crown piece, which is all that she can see of the child's head at the height of a pain.

'The ring of the womb has been fully open for two hours, but there's been no advance in the last half-hour,' she replies.

A dismal howl is heard outside the bedroom door. 'Oi be feared! Oi be feared fur her what's bin so good to me – O Lor', O Lor'!'

'Stop your noise, Mag, for goodness' sake. Go away, do!'

Lizzie's irritation reflects her growing anxiety over this failure to progress after a promising start. Susan is a small-boned woman, and the child is large. Lizzie fears that the head may be arrested in its descent, and become stuck fast in the narrow outlet.

Susan knows that this is so. She also knows that she cannot push the head any further down, and that inertia will intervene, with lessening of pain but no progress. She wonders if Lizzie senses the presence of Death in the room, waiting to claim her and her child.

Sophia's face is a pale blur above her, exhorting her to put her trust in the Almighty. Somewhere Edward is demanding how much longer she must suffer, and what may be done to hasten the birth. There are whispers, consultations, and a decision is made; a messenger is sent.

'Can you bear down again, Susan?' asks Lizzie's distant voice.

Another futile straining of her muscles, another failure to move the object she can feel filling the narrow space deep down in her pelvis.

'Rest now, Susan,' says Sophia. 'Lie back and rest.'

But she is rising from the bed and drifting upwards, away from pain, away from the heaviness of her flesh. The voices grow fainter as she drifts out into the golden sunlight, and she can look down through the window at the swollen body upon the bed, the face congested and eyes bloodshot from pushing. Sophia is weeping.

'Susan, can you hear me? Oh, Susan, do not leave us. Oh, God, be merciful and save her!'

But Susan cannot answer. Below her in the rectory garden she sees Edward pacing the shrubbery with his father. He too is weeping as he speaks, but cannot see or hear her.

And now she is ascending in the clear blue air, lighter than thistledown as she moves upwards. She is above the rectory chimneys, and now she can look down and see the whole valley. Free as a bird she

499

soars up into the cloudless sky, and calls out to her sister who died with her babies unborn.

Polly!

She is drawing towards a great light beyond which lies eternity. And no return.

Suddenly from far down below a sound reaches her. It is a horse at full gallop.

Sweating and foaming, the animal stops at the rectory, and the rider dismounts with a clatter. He strides into the house, and his footsteps thunder on the stairs; he bursts into the bedchamber.

'How is she? Oh, my Trotula! Good God, why wasn't I sent for earlier, you stupid creature? How long has the cervical ring been fully dilated? How long has she been pushing? Where is the husband? Make haste, there is no time to be lost.'

In the confusion of voices Edward's rises above the others.

'Save her, Parnham, save her who is everything to me, I implore you! Destroy the child if need be, but save her. I cannot bear to lose her!'

'Hush, keep your voice down, man, think of Madam Glover. D'you think I would do otherwise than save her if I can? Listen, I will apply the Chamberlen forceps and make one attempt to deliver the child by their use. If I fail, I shall conclude the matter speedily.'

He does not mention the other instruments in his bag: the skull perforator and decapitation hook.

'Go over to your church, Calthorpe, and pray for her. For us all,' he adds in a softer tone, for he wants the frantic clergyman out of the way.

'Come, Madam Glover, Madam Decker, get me water, soap and clean towels. Now, then – move her to the side of the bed, so – bring her buttocks right to the edge, and each of you take a leg and hold it up, like this – higher and wider apart – that's right. Now, my Trotula, I hope your husband is praying. God give me the skill and right judgement.'

He takes the scissors and cuts a slit in the stretched flesh. There is a clink of metal as he grasps the forceps blades and pushes them into place around the child's head. There follows a fearsome pulling, a sustained dragging: Sophia turns her face away as she holds on to the upraised leg. Lizzie gives a cry and the doctor an oath as the head is drawn forth, an inert child out of an inert mother.

The child is born, but it seems that Death has won.

The women watch while Parnham wipes the blood and mucus from the child's mouth, blowing on its face and chest. He mutters under his breath.

'Are you staying with us, little one, or returning forthwith? Hah! It gives a gasp and has a heartbeat. Come on, come on, take a breath of air – and another – yes, it lives and breathes. Oh, my Trotula, you have a daughter, but at what a cost. Take it, Madam Decker. I must attend to her.'

Sophia helps him to lower the legs gently and place them together. The body lies upon the bed, pale and lifeless. Charles Parnham groans aloud.

But Susan is no longer ascending. She is falling from the sky, falling back through air to earth, down to the rectory and into the bedchamber. She re-enters her body with a moan of pain and discomfort: she is the mother of a daughter.

Sophia cries out: 'She's opening her eyes – she lives! Oh, praise God for His mercy, she lives!'

They all exclaim with joy, and Parnham utters his own silent thanksgiving with a prayer: God grant the child be not damaged by my handling: I shall have no peace until I see its progress.

He gives leave for the husband to be called, but Mag is already running down the stairs, out through the kitchen to the garden and the gate leading into the churchyard.

'Parson Calthorpe, Parson Calthorpe! 'Ee's to come up an' see uns! Her's had a little gal – it's a gal!'

In no time Edward is on his knees beside the bed, giving thanks for his wife's preservation. He rises and seizes Parnham in an embrace.

'I shall be for ever in your debt, sir.'

'You'd better baptise the child today, Calthorpe,' advises the doctor gruffly, for once again he has to hide his own feelings.

Susan whispers: 'Ha' ye seen her, Edward, our little daughter? Show her to him, Sophy – isn't she beautiful?'

Sophia's eyes are brimming as she holds out a white bundle of towelling in which a squashy little face can be seen. The head is elongated, and there is a livid red mark on the side of the face where the forceps blade bit into the tender flesh.

'Don't mind the shape o' her head, Edward,' says Susan. ''Tis like Sam Twydell's was at birth, and she's bigger'n he was. 'Twill be as round as a ball by tomorrow, ye'll see.'

'Sh-she's beautiful, my love,' Edward stammers. 'I will fetch water from the font of Great St Giles straight away. Is it still your wish that we name her Mary?'

'Yes, Edward, but I'd like to call her Polly, if ye don't mind,' answers Susan, thinking of the baby's aunt.

'Just as you please, my love. She shall be chistened

Mary and known as Polly,' says the father, his eyes fixed upon the wife and child he has so nearly lost.

The baptism takes place in the birth-chamber, with Parson Calthorpe conducting the short ceremony in the presence of his wife and his mother, who has just arrived from Bever House. Miss Glover takes her place as godmother, and Dr Parnham agrees to stand as godfather. (It will give him a reason to keep a check on the child's progress.) Mrs Decker is, of course, present as midwife, and Mrs Smart comes in holding little Kitty by the hand. Mag just manages to squeeze inside the door.

Edward gingerly puts out his forefinger to touch the baby's hand, and she instantly curls her little fingers around it. He gazes down at this child – his child – and his heart seems to melt within him: he knows that he loves her.

Susan sees, and clasps her hands together in rapture.

'Oh, isn't she sweet? Look at her, Edward – our pretty little Polly!'

AUTHOR'S NOTE

Trotula was an eleventh century Italian woman doctor. She lived in Salerno, which still has an old-established medical school. She was married to a doctor, Platearius, and their son Matteo also became a doctor.

Trotula specialised in obstetrics and gynaecology, and wrote several treatises on women's health, some of which were used for hundreds of years for their practicality. She was an early advocate of making an incisión into the perineum to facilitate delivery of the child's head, and stressed the necessity for repairing it by stitching. This procedure is now known as episiotomy.

It has been suggested that Trotula may have been the original for the character 'Dame Trot' in children's literature and pantomime, but I have found no substantial evidence for this.